The Expedition

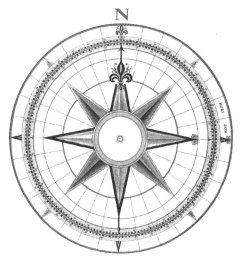

Clayton Bailey

GREAT PLAINS
PUBLICATIONS

Great Plains Publications
420 – 70 Arthur Street
Winnipeg, MB R3B 1G7
www.greatplains.mb.ca

Great Plains Publications gratefully acknowledges the financial support
provided for its publishing program by the Government of Canada
through the Book Publishing Industry Development Program (BPIDP);
the Canada Council for the Arts; as well as the Manitoba Department
of Culture, Heritage and Tourism; and the Manitoba Arts Council.

Design & Typography by Gallant Design Ltd.
Printed in Canada by Friesens

CANADIAN CATALOGUING IN PUBLICATION DATA

Main entry under title:

Bailey, Clayton, 1947 -
  The expedition / Clayton Bailey.

  ISBN 1-894283-40-6

  I. Title
PS8553.A36E96 2003   C813'.6   C2003-910811-2
PR9199.4.B34E96 2003

For Karen Handford of High Bluff,
Always watching over us

*H*e thrusts his features so brazen at the lens, and inverted on my ground glass they transpose sharp. Standing next to the empty chairs, he commands without having effected any act. The force is interior, and emanates from somewhere in his guts. Such vitality I cherish in a man. He does not remove his broad hat. Sets it square over brilliant eyes, thus shading and augmenting their dazzle. In them I see a disposition I covet. Internal fire. The me I've mislaid. How necessary the inferno that lights these eyes like two thorns. "All will yield to me," they cry. And how terrible their loathsome aspect. The despot.

So mighty is his presence, for the first few moments I overlooked that not a little of his overwhelming deportment owed to a stump of horny flesh protruding from his right sleeve. He does not costume this absent forearm, but exposes it for all to see, like a medal or prize and stands erect, looking straight towards my camera, it seems directly through the lens at me, as if the instrument was not there. There is an infinity of strength, a dauntless ardour in that glance. All and all, though the tyrant within him frightens, I am heartened by his vigour. It fills the studio with a kind of energy invisible and unmeasurable, a supernatural radiance that emanates from the persona itself.

I wait too, patient portraitist behind my apparatus. He turns to observe something outside the camera's frame line. Someone has arrived, but by his face, someone has not also. Enter his expected. Not three as I prepared for, but a misfit duo. One large and long, one small and round, as if cast for the parts of squire and jester to a knight in a classical play. The lanky one, by the elemental grace of his movement and every simplified gesture, was born on the frontier. The second is a man of the cities, his demeanour equally graceful yet because of its refined embellishments, his beauty emanates from his very lack of motion, like an Oriental meditator. The leader looks entirely over the short one's head to the tall one, and signals he be seated. Not a word has he spoken, nor have the other two said aught to him, yet they clearly demonstrate, by gesture and mien, an anxious knowledge of his subjugating gaze, and suddenly have the look of men under orders. A resignation, a slight bend in the spine.

I was informed the sitting would comprise four. A medium lens. I would like to shoot them as they are. Three makes a good composition in a portrait. Four is never right. Too balanced perhaps. Square. I've done my best with the placement of the chairs and backdrop. But where is the other person? Time grows short. I have the town council at nine. Where is my technician with the plates? I flip off the black cloth and stand erect. The leader's gaze, unmediated, is direct and hard. A man's assessing look, yet he cannot possibly know what is hidden beneath my smock and trousers. By feelings, I am female. At this very moment, under his stare, oddly the more so. Yet I am not at this moment a woman. I am a man to him and to the part of me that controls my appearance, my gestures, my voice. This is strangely true. I am outwardly a man even to myself right now. If I were a woman, I would never allow a man to look at me thus and I am certain no man of my previous acquaintance would do so.

Is this what technique is applied by an actor or actress? Become on the outside another? Or do they become completely another from the inside out? Does the actress become as she steps behind the unopened curtain the stage queen, and at the end of the play does she return home an actress, perhaps a wife and mother? Or does she stay a queen, sleep that night a queen, a queen even in her dreams?

Strange, me, the man. They put on amateur plays here. Bawdy and vulgar. Men, for lack of women, and by ancient theatrical tradition they are no doubt ignorant of, play the female roles. If I were to participate, and I have been invited to play a woman's part, I would go as a man, then dress up and act a woman. A woman acting a man who then as a man acts a woman.

Yet not entirely strange. I was very much the tomboy, and my mother had great difficulties getting me into a gown. I remember well my first dress ball. I'd been climbing in the trees all day. One of my knees was scabbed, and I had an unscrubable grass stain across my thigh, yet there I was at the ball that night, smiling and giggling. Accepting my first dance partners, I tilted my head back, blushed at a compliment and shouldered aside other girls in the dressing room to get at the mirror.

Such musings. I am here, in my studio, clients before the camera. Their leader inquires if we have the collodion process, thus possible duplicate prints, but I inform him we offer only tintypes. They want two images, full plate. The collodion process would seem to have many advantages. I would need make only one exposure. Two prints, or more, would follow. Each identical. From descriptions I have read it tempts me, but given our remoteness, my only opportunity to master it will be upon returning to an urban centre. And return with what? It was my vow only to return with a completed portfolio. The leader motions me over. I am to be introduced.

Captain Aaron Masse. An electric shock as I touch his remaining hand, for something tells me he lost the other only recently – the pain is in his eyes. The arm still exists in his mind. I face him. I am a complete physical specimen in every way but missing something too, something in my mind that would allow me to push on. I am missing the energy of obsession.

The tall one – Dunbar Bain. Stiff, reticent. Now, the short man – Carlo Guzman. Delicate soft fingers, like a violinist. He stimulates painful memories of my childhood sweetheart Wendel. Such a gentle boy. Where is he now? Still at home?

'The empty chair, Captain. You await a fourth person?'

'He is your equivalent, our photographer.'

'You have equipment?'

'The finest: collodion process, macro lens.'

'Why not use your own man?'

'He is my brother-in-law, my sister's very recent spouse. He is to be a subject of this portrait. I will send it as an assurance of his well-being. Our own apparatus is securely packed for the trail, we will begin to use it only at the Fort.'

'I have other clients, Captain.'

'Then attend to them now. I must go to the telegraph office. If there is no report of our missing compatriot, I have serious decisions to make. May we return later?'

'The light will hold until six, Captain.'

The newly elected Mayor, with his recently espoused bride, is here at ten, but before that, the also newly elected town council is to be photographed on Main Street. I have a minute to compose myself. In public I will act the role of highly trained engineer and scientist with artistic abilities...the consummate photographer. I usually bow slightly, one hand to the apparatus as I set the shutter. I peer at the lens as if checking for finger prints or dust, and continue my adjustments till the clients are suitably impressed. The exact moment to begin I determine by some nervousness on my subject's part: a cough, the rustle of a garment. Then I adjust my focus, try a composition.

That empty chair in the studio disturbs me. Its barrenness is a distress, heightened by the waiting men's anxious attitudes; the one trying to stare through our wall, compacting himself into a rod of tension, and his companion, elegant but seeming much more stouthearted, sitting ankles and wrists touching as if manacled. But whatever apprehension I feel, I ascribe it to this strange day, when my thoughts are so black. In truth, there was nothing unsettling about those men before me. Though utterly unalike, they were solid, hearty citizens, and their presence allayed the unease I feel. Before me on the ground glass, their capable energy, utterly without immobilising introspection, showed the force that won the frontier.

The strange and motley clients of the studio – vanquished tribal chiefs, arrested thieves, painted Jezebels and pretentious bureaucrats – usually stimulate me to gloomy musing. I believe my pessimism to originate in the singular savageness of living on the trailblazed edge of civilisation.

A vagabond mutt sniffs the mule sweat suffused in Captain Masse's boot, and decides to follow at his heel. The swing of this one leg makes a shallower arc than the other, balancing the absent arm opposite each step. He strides at speed, forcing the dog to trot, yet it keeps near, for the odours, some familiar, some strange, are enticing. The awesome perspiration of a grizzly bear, the mineral clarity of mountain springs, the steel of a stirrup, the hide of an acrid, nervous mule and the soft musk of a quarter-horse mare.

A steam whistle sounds in the distance. The dog halts, turning an ear towards it. Captain Masse stops as well, closing his eyes to listen. No further sound ensues and he sits on a basalt outcrop. The dog risks an approach, unable to resist the temptation of sniffing each delicious fragrance and when he nears the man, a hand pats him on the head, then sets a flat thing across the man's knees and takes a long round object from a pocket. The man pulls something off its top with his teeth. At this the dog shies, seeing the bared incisors, but the man does not bend and bite. Instead, manoeuvring his single arm, he opens a small journal pulled from a deep pocket along with a larger, leather bound one, and slips a forged iron clip between the pages to stand them open. With the other hook of the clip he fixes the journal to the board on his knee, and stooping over it, presses the long round object to it and there begins to move his hand in tiny ellipses.

[Entry: Captain Aaron Masse]
Day 1 – Grand Trunk Railway Survey and Mapping Party,
April 1st Year of our Lord 1858.

Having quit the trail, mark the need for a personal memorandum. My wife's coldness & certain remarks of my sister, in whose opinion I have full confidence, have lead me to consider that perhaps I must reflect more upon my deeds. The man of action is fine when situations require only that but there is more to life. Some part of me is well tuckered out. I wish to settle down after this expedition & having mastered one-handed penmanship tolerable well, will render into this diary what my faculties deliver towards that end.

Daylight the morn was awoke in my blankets by the echo of steam whissle from plains below, it being a clear day. How penetrating is a mechanical sound. Following river down into settlement, observed one osprey searching out fish. He sees but the water's dark surface. Looks for the shadow of a sucker in a backwater, flash of trout behind a rock, but fish do not lead their daily lives at flood, do not eat. Osprey will neither eat. Relations in nature are so direct, unlike the labyrinth relations of man. Have little read, my school being this life, yet I cannot avoid the potent sentiments rising in my breast. War put me up through the ranks on luck & natural ability. In contact with exceptional men & women, well lettered, I saw this grand plan for our nation a'drawing, not copied from some other, but a true & new design. We now struggle to accomplish the noble task God hath laid before us. & how will we be judged? Is the critical aspect of inspired character wisdom, toil, or practical dementia?

I add this latter from the experience of war, for certainly in the heat of battle, the madman far outstrips the clever man in accomplishment. Is triumph, or folly, the reliable measure of a man? Perhaps only the failed task – every ability exerted to the maximum & there proven inadequate – is the best yardstick? What strange ruminations, so unproductive. Be they are my last.

I now detach myself from recent duties & embark on this future one, vast & arduous & I mark commencement of expedition by beginning daily log. Our Cartographer and Navigator, Guzman, will keep the mapping log, with latitude, longitude, barometric pressure, altitude & geomorphy. Must see to my tooth.

>–‹–•›–O–‹•–›–‹

By an indolent push, a hawk abandons its branch and drops, wings tucked. At speed, blooming plumage, catching the air with a hiss, it lays a course over the ground, following two parallel ribbons of shimmering steel set on oak sleepers so fresh cut their hewn faces glow in the morning light. Any animal attempting a traverse of the black cinder rail bed, so sharply silhouetted, will pose an effortless target for the hunting raptor. It flies directly above the rails, wheeling through a turn, searching for prey, making distance westward on a slight following wind, then abruptly levitates, flight feathers aback, when the track, leaving the unobstructed plain, curves toward a row of false front clapboard buildings.

In front of the buildings, a waist height wooden tripod, bright varnished camera atop, is set directly between the rails. Rails of steel so new as to be without rust, newer even then the paintless buildings on the one-sided esplanade of taverns the rails run in front of. Each facade sports elemental identification – Whisky, Beer, Porter. Before the largest saloon a row of drab clothed men face the camera; bottles aplenty, and cigars indicate a celebration, but there is not a smiling face to be seen. Women watch expectantly from the upper floor windows, one waving a rose handkerchief.

The photographer Reid, lithe, pale, steps under the dark cloth, hand appearing to make an adjustment, then stands beside the camera bellows, gazing at the men assembled before the lens. One touches his forelock, another adjusts a celluloid collar as several button their coats and pull at trouser creases. At the photographer's raised arm, all movement halts. The shutter is tripped open. One man coughs. That man will be an unrecognisable smudge. The shutter clacks shut. Reid bows to the group, and as their joyless activities recommence, detaches the camera, collapses its bellows, folds the tripod, and departs, walking along the cinder rail bed, turning aside where the rails, following the ground's contour, descend to submerge in a flooding river. The hawk, still hungry, loses interest in the terminated railway, circles, feeling for a rising current of air where the sun has heated the ground, finds one, climbs, and disappears into a sinuous colonnade of trees along the river's far shore.

>⊶⊶O⊷⊷<

[Captain Aaron Masse] Day 2

Rail head. Wind nor'west in clear sky tipical such wind direction. Arrived here on day estimated after riding cheerful all the morn through pine scrub dropping in rock terraces to river. Consequent to recognisance whilst following eastern slope from Mountain House, I assess the interior terrain as passable and of moderate difficulty.

Judged well departure date. Spring in full force at this lower altitude. w no winter signs, though snow can be seen in mountains to West. Reckon snow line 1 wk. travel or less. By then, it will have risen & with luck we will follow thaw into the highest passes.

Rendezvous W Bain, Guzman but no Brother-in-law. Must have met some delay or misfortune. Bain assures me all equipment is here & in good order, especially the survey & photographic apparatus & chemistry, of the most recent manufacture but somewhat fragile.

Reckoned on greater publicity being given our departure, in spite of secrecy surrounding the progress of our labours, & expectations to be formed as to the result. Perplexed as to lack of advance preparations made for me by the Geographic Society. Irrespective, I consider myself duty bound not to retreat from this attempt as long a there is possibility of success. Inclusive control of what resources are directly available a must. They & circumstance can be bent to my will. Telegraph just installed here. Will wire Minister of the Interior who must have news.

>·+·◆·-·O·-·◆·+·<

*T*oday, I feel so absolutely alone, denied any intimate relation. I think it is because this place has changed, is of a sudden engorged with humanity and their most banal endeavours. The town council portrait brought this home to me. Those rough and ready men suddenly so formal and stolid. Like the camera's shutter, they have willed time to stop. They will make their stand here, raise families, celebrate anniversaries. I was a participant observing through my ground glass, and paid to be so, yet hiking back to the studio with my equipment, I became completely anonymous. Memories emerged to fill the void. Rising from the past, a thin and thwarted schoolgirl. Outraged by some adult ordinance, head pitched left, taut lips baring canines, strained fingers bent in clawed hooks, she demands to be shown the dreams that were once my expectation. Receiving no answer then, my solitude bloomed, now grown to a fiery and ingenuous fruit, nourished by my search for the philosopher's stone in ancient libraries of the Continent.

Cool and astute in contrast, this morning's impartial radiance permeates my studio. It is a pity the council would not fit in here. This is excellent light for photographic purposes. If it is clarity my subjects seek, a penetrating light, yet with the overcast today, dim.

Pale faces; miners, powdered ladies – ten seconds. Darker subjects; frontiersman, mulatto whores...must hold still a good half minute. My technician has sensitised two plates. Our recently elected and more recently married mayor has fixed an engagement for ten. By telegram no less. It will be the first time I have photographed our incumbent. But not her. Does he know of our secret session?

>–**·**·O·**·**–<

The dog inhales damp coal smoke of a locomotive and this acid stink clinging to the ground, seeking the lowest ravines, masks all the delicious fragrances of Captain Masse. The dog hears the click, space, long cliick of the telegraph. Dot dash, dot dash. A new kind of sound for the dog. Unlike nature's perpetual din; wind, water, bird cries, scurrying squirrels. Unlike machine noise; the steam locomotive, wagon wheels, whirring blower on the blacksmiths forge, this virgin sound has a piercing clarity that bewilders.

The Captain's aromatic boots disappear into a box-sized clapboard office. The dog stops. He's learnt the rules. A kick if he follows, a tossed bone if he hovers near long enough. He smells tobacco, tar, and a curious new scent, like the smell after a lightening storm. The odour of ozone. He sees the boots turn, watches them come back out and the one hand clenched into a fist. He prepares for a blow but the hand unclenches, and he follows the heels back into the settlement. The locomotive stench fades. The aromatic man sits again on the same rock outcrop.

>–**·**·O·**·**–<

[Captain Aaron Masse] Day 3

Station master informs me there was delay. Washed out tressel needed be bypassed. Perhaps brother-in-law was forced to wait for tracks laid around the wreck. Collapsed bridge typical of the dangers of mechanical transport. Loaded train, dozen cars of high grade ore, left here in a raging thunderstorm. Section man at river was in his railside shack. A boy ran in, wet to the skin – the tressle above had washed out. Section man ran up a stop signal but train's engineer, bent to some task, went by, gathering speed down slope. Engine, tender, & eight cars plunged into the ravine, killing all aboard.

I have no affection for these steam pot behemoths. How much more true a good mule, & how paradoxical it is for I, & said mules, that the sole purpose of our endeavour is to ascertain the path of least resistance for this new conveyance, child of iron father & fire mother. I've seen already the settlers from far away continents, desperate as stampeding horses. When the line is built they will increase. We walk the unkind path of destiny.

Renowned cartographer our penal system has provided me seems a rare bird. Better this brilliant man as companion than a dull & lawful citizen. Brother-in-law presents another dilemma, but only a family member, honour bound, can be trusted in certain affairs. The cartographer is bound to me also, by his own secrets. As for Bain, we are forever brothers in the fraternity of mud, blood & bullets, never to be separated.

Guzman & Bain unalike as oil & water, but am well content I secured Guzman, his criminal past by my reckoning more result of the strength of women's affection and weakness of husbands' jealousy than any unethical behavior on his part. Certainly his diversions pose no danger to us. I chuckled inwardly when I read the cockold's testimony. As I myself have no charm with women, I find Guzman's recorded ability in that realm a wonder.

Surveyors such as Guzman are of a singular ilk. More akin wizards than mortal souls. In the war, our advance regiment trekked behind such a land navigator for weeks across unmapped terrain. Cooked only at night, so no smoke would be seen, & then in hollows, to hide the flame. Great errors in reconnaissance can be made when seeking the most advantageous trail. Our Colonel gave over all control of our movements to the man & his mysterious ways. He could smell the path & weather with his instruments, guided us over the Western gap, & finally delivering us to exactly the rendezvous point. Each navigator has his own strange instruments, his journals, arithmetic tables & charts, full of magik learnt & stolen from others. Lucifer has touched their souls. Irritable & jealous, such types are to be handled with care. I am the Captain to be sure, but our lives will be in his hands muchly.

Tooth vexatious.

➤⟡⟡O⟡⟡⟨

Today's first image ripens over the vaporised mercury. Across the silver coated tinplate, traces sublime as the tones on a butterfly wing. A thing of beauty in itself yet I find, more and more, when I have a picture before me, it brings to mind my memory of the person in it, and I cannot reconcile what my eyes see with that recollection. What I see in the photograph, and what the person photographed wants to be seen are two entirely different things. There is such complete opposition between their desire and my result that I see not their projected illusion, but only its failure to convince.

These two for example, now completely modelled on the plate. Our new town's first mayor, elbow propped on a stub of fluted plaster column, one of hundreds copied from its ancient original in some back street factory. In his city suit, just arrived from his city wedding, his new shoes built up to increase his height, he turns his face to one side, hoping a profile will achieve the image of august public servant he aspires to project.

Yet, the artless column, every wrinkle of his garments and frozen visage speak only of his rough and ready ways, the brash vitality that gave his electorate confidence he could manage a frontier town of a dozen brothels, two dozen taverns, a tent church, a river boat landing and a rail terminus.

And his wife, in this studio for the second time, seen for years in harlot's finery, now done up as a matron and not near so forceful or attractive. How much more beautiful she was in the two illicit plates we took that Sunday. And how much more kind and open she was with me. Unlike now, when she puts on the airs of a bourgeois, treating me, her brief confident, like a servant. But she will never hide the past, never disguise the allure of her rough beauty as I photographed it so carefully that day.

I found her a sympathetic personage then. She insisted the pictures be made in confidence. I took them on a Sunday and did not call in the technician, prepared the plates myself. She confided she had a customer willing to pay the full fee plus an additional amount if he could have an "intimate" portrait. I delicately inquired as to the amount of money in question, and was hurt to find she could make more in one night than I in a week. She was nervous to be alone, undressed, with someone whom she thought was a man, although in her profession being alone undressed with a man must be a common thing. I chose a reclining posture, her head up and facing the viewer, much reminiscent of a great master's classic compositions, being reminded of one in particular, the model's bared body ivory white, a study of a duchess by an earthy painter reputed to have been her lover. My own subject's naked grace was credible, and for its sensuality, worthy of a study in oils. Alas, I had not the talent, time or propensity.

I felt such profound empathy with that woman. Both of us, she publicly, me privately, are pariahs. I wonder who is worse off. Although I do not envy her life I coveted her irrefutable identity however base. She had nothing to hide then. My social position as a man is secure, but the true creature living it is concealed. The constant masquerade wears me. The emotions, the desire for a woman's company shared as another woman perpetually suppressed. I enjoy the freedom my trousers give me, but I pay a price.

When we two were alone, enclosed in that delicate intimacy any portrait requires, I came so close to revealing my sex to her. I felt I could exchange secret for secret, and both of us, woman to woman, would be the better for it. But I did nothing.

And now she bends her face away, my fine lady, to conceal the scar made by a broken bottle in a bar room brawl. She contorts her voluptuous body and to hide the scar twists her neck into a line that says, in the composition of the photograph and her averted glance, that she is hiding something. This only encourages one to peer at it and discover just what that hidden thing might be. This ability to capture what much effort has been applied to conceal comes easily to the photographic art. I have seen such 'double entendre' done consciously by those who painted portraits of the old world's aristocracy, or so it was explained to me by those who knew the intimate details of old world portrait painting. Such works are rare, and their rendering was dangerous for the artist. With photography, it seems this kind of cleverness is commonplace, and all ignore or accept the deception of it.

To think how long I laboured to arrive here, the dangers, my many deceits, always dreaming of virgin landscapes, untouched vistas, only to find myself paralysed by this wall of pretending faces. I have forgotten my desire for poetry, for the ecstatic encounter with undiluted beauty.

Discontent builds in me, will soon boil and bubble over. I can feel that uncontrollable desire, learned from my father, to offend. I have well demonstrated this wretched talent over the years. My caustic tongue has upbraided servants, head mistresses and college rectors. But in all these incidents I had the recourse of my home's sanctuary. Here, I stand alone, and fear the day when I will burst out laughing, or spew a string of insults in the very face of a client as the technician hands he or she their finished portrait, and be expulsed from my employ. I cannot lose that. If I am to go into the mountains and photograph, as is my ambition, I must both rekindle said ambition, and retain this position. Access to the materials and apparatus is a necessity.

I proclaim my manifesto – *Pulchum en ominus*. Be it resolved, here and now, that I will devote all subsequent surplus energy to the quest for beauty. I'll photograph sunrise and sunset. I will go out once a week on a day trip.

I'll negotiate longer leaves from the studio, for I have taken no holiday since arriving, having spent my energies basking in the success of my disguise. I will make week-long expeditions into the wilds.

><del>·</del>+<>·<del>·</del>O·<del>·</del><>+<del>·</del>·<

[Captain Aaron Masse]

Sky continues clear. W. calm. Serious setback. Second train arrived. By all evidence, my brother-in-law has absconded. There are no reported deaths. Disappeared along a stretch of track that included two soon-to-be cities, several towns, & unsurveyed tracts of tree'd & barren wilderness. No finding him. Loss leaves us without photographer. Need the publicity value of the pictures as much as the topographic & scientific. The risk of waiting is too great. Take weeks to get another man, or months. Spring would advance to early summer. Setting off thence, we would never make the sea, & surely perish in the mountain passes.

Solution is to filch the photographer in the studio here. From under the nose of his avaricious patron. Am informed that the ferry, a flat bottomed scow, will recommence operations tomorrow. River has peaked. Must be first on the ferry. Guzman will thus have virgin trail to botanize and make geographic observations before it is trammelled by South West bound settlers.

Our portrait will be made as planned. If my first impression of his competence is confirmed, will make Reid a proposition on the spot. Leave the morrow & he can master the teknicalities of our newer apparatus, which he seems to know about but never have used, at trail end. We will be there more than a week. Plenty of time, & plenty for him to do. I intend to make full use of this new art's magik. God grant me luck in this endeavour.

><del>·</del>+<>·<del>·</del>O·<del>·</del><>+<del>·</del>·<

*T*hey have returned, and though still just three, will sit immediately. That is good, the light is high and manageable, and three a finer composition. I will truly do my best, if only to profit from the presence of Captain Masse, so that by osmosis I will absorb his energy and resolve...without approaching so near I am brought within the boundaries of his dictatorship. One father was enough. I must imbibe sufficient of his dangerous male elixir that I too may set off on my own expeditions.

The Captain seems distressed, and how he stares at me. Is that anger? Because the anticipated fourth man has not shown himself? This perturbs me not. I'll sit the Captain in front, and stand the short and tall man behind. Asymmetrical, yet dynamic and humorous for its contrast.

A good grouping. The classic triangle. So much more alive than a four-some. Only to dolly back the camera and choose a longer lens that will flatten my subjects. Light reflected from floor is making the backdrop pale at bottom and dark at the top. Perfect. All three faces stand out against it. The Captain's complexion is the darkest. He has just come off the trail. A reflector lightens the backdrop behind him to give separation. Now an angled mirror to push in eyelight for contrast. A bit of netting to block reflections on foreheads and the cartographer's round chin. I will not ask the Captain to smile, he is a serious man. The others I will ask. They say they have just eaten, and after meals people's teeth reflect much less. There. Perfect. But the Captain seems unsatisfied.

⊱┈◈┈◯┈◈┈⊰

'Captain. You don't like the composition?'

'No, the composition is fine, it wants another sitter. I command you to set a chair.'

'That only worsens the problem, it will symbolise absence.'

'That chair will want a photographer. It will be filled by you, Mr. Reid. I propose, rather I insist that you join our expedition, and make our journey with us. I can see you like me, I know that look, and I can see you work well. Please, sit beside me, here.'

'Am I not allowed a response? Am I to be given no time to reflect? Think of the preparations to be made.'

'Already made; contracted, boxed, crated, shipped. Lock, stock and barrel.'

'Have you thought of my employer? It is not I who made the investment in this apparatus and facility.'

'He will gain all subsequent Government contracts, more than compensation. A dozen survey parties in the next three years, plus all related work for the government offices.'

'And what of my present clients?'

'The technician can trip your shutter. Look at him, staring out his cubby hole. He covets your job and he shall have it. Today, all shall have what they dreamed of, I proclaim it. Cease your dithering.'

'I do not appreciate the term. Attend to my questions please. In what exactly to I implicate myself?'

'Envisage this, if you will. Not a decade hence, steel rails will unite our nation coast to coast. A transcontinental journey measured in days, not months. It is for us but to find the route.

'We are bound for glory Reid. This elite corps, you now included if you are the man I think you are, will survey and map the first and only route by which the rail line will proceed from here, through passes yet to be discovered, to the western seaboard. We have till freeze' up next autumn, our strictest limitation being to transit the Westernmost mountain range before first snowfall, by all reports copious, blocks its passes. We then have the option of return by land or by sea. In addition, the Geographic Society has funded a series of ethnographical pictures, to be exhibited in the capital upon our return. Your name in the history books Reid, there for your grandchildren to see. Ponder that.'

'I will be employed for how long, Captain?'

'We have signed one year contracts, as would you, and with option of a second year, for compiling the report, printing the images, and advising planners in the capital. And before you ask, the wages are a goodly amount, deposits on the central bank. Triple your earnings here, for I have already investigated that.'

➤┼◆➤─O─◄┼◄

My urge was to display myself to him – my sex, my womanhood. As boldly and simply as the mayor's prostitute wife did for me that Sunday. Let him make his choice then.

I looked at the technician, tidying up. How hopeful he was of my departure. I sat alone till the light had faded, my limbs heavy as lead, my eyes shut, my mind a torrent of memory.

My mother's sick room was a place for sharing secrets. Mine. She usually asked me to describe the world beyond her drawn curtains, a world whose brightness gave her only cruel headaches. I would begin my stories at a whisper, but oft times end by shouting.

Once, standing at the window where a rift in the brocade sealing her room dark as a cave allowed me to see outside, I was overcome with the emotion of my description. I yanked on the drawstring clutched in my hand. It entered the thick fabrics via a grommet, but had, with age, detached, and so pulled completely out. A perfectly circular hole, its perimeter the ring of brass, was opened like a tiny porthole in the side of a ship. Instantly, an inverted image of the sun outside appeared on the papered wall next to her bed. The clouds surrounding it glowed like a saintly halo. Unaware of the optical phenomena resulting in my creation of a camera obscura, but very aware of the image's allure, I stopped my monologue. We both watched the golden orb transit the wall, creeping silently towards a coppery sunset. Thence, making a haphazard appearance whenever the sun or, after a little adjustment by me, the moon angle lay right, the image transmitted by the grommet aperture rendered our intimate unions magical. The representation on the wall became a mute visitor that deeply pleased my mother. She named it Scamp. We kept this all a secret.

>———◇———○———◇———<

[Captain Aaron Masse]

Mid-day repast in the settlement's best Lodge, consuming one pike a good arms length long, steamed in spiced broth. This fish always best when taken from frigid ice-out waters. Boiled potatoes served also, small enough to eat whole, lightly buttered. A toothsome repast, & welcome after so many weeks of pungent, overcooked venison. Tooth again gave me trouble with the tougher vittels.

Resolved to rectify & this led to adventure & useful information. Our inn keeper, seeing me clutch my cheek, proudly informed me the settlement boasted a professional district & dental facilities were available there morning noon & night. Her directions sent me along the board walk to a box canyon of frame buildings. A pair of dentists offered their services at that hour. The first, sitting on the elevated sidewalk, feet on his native soil, had as equipment: a wooden chair, steel basin, iron pincers large & small, folded towel & a bottle of trade liquor. This last the worst & most potent, used only by unscrupulous merchants. Price a dollar for each extraction & twenty five cents a finger for the poteen, with the patient inebriating himself to the degree of choice.

Second establishment marked by carved set of dentures the shape & width of a span of elk horns, the gums red lead crimson, the teeth sun bleached wood. Within, I was informed the newest techniques were applied. Ether, a recently developed narcotic compound, when inhaled, renders the patient unconscious, the amount taken calculated on body weight. The operation accomplished on a hinged back chair with the patient prone & unconscious. The tooth or teeth are extracted, the patient in complete comfort, the extractor able to work in peace. Revival some half hour afterwards, on couch provided, & effects no more arduous to bear than those of a night of debauchery. Price, five dollars.

Availed myself of this solution. The compound was as effective as described. Purchased a small amount for use on the trail. A vial could help so much the setting of a broken limb or a surgery. Remember well my own gory amputation, though unconscious the most part, having swooned. Thanks to God for my life. Many did not survive similar battlefield efforts.

Returning to lodgings, slight headache from tooth extraction, I prayed, asking Heaven for guidance. He who hesitates is lost. Resolved to remain not another day, to take what I had & proceed. Replied to my letters, returning best thanks to friends who had expressed much kind interest on our behalf. Having finished these & verified the state of the stores with Bain, I contacted the ferry boat captain & gave orders to prepare before first light.

The party consisting at this time of: self, Bain, Guzman, newly acquired Reid if all goes well (a man of slight, but well proportioned stature, pale skin of the type that browns readily in wind and sun. Long fingered, adept hands. Careful of speech.), nine Quarter horses, two Bays and a Palomino mare, baggage being divided into sixteen heavy units for the pack animals and four light units to be carried by each of us.

Though I await Reid's decision, I have arranged for what trail gear my brother was to have brought – all the necessities – to be supplied to him. I informed him thus by note. Though he's still not replied to my request, I expected him to be along the ferry landing at dawn. He has the woebegone look of someone easy to lead. Time waits for no man.

I calculate this first push at maximum 3 weeks. Reid should not slow us down, he claims to be an able horseman. 6 pound of flour each weekly, with proportionate quantity of tea & sugar. Meat we will hunt. Guzman has supplied himself with coffee & the apparatus to make it. The horses have enjoyed oats & bran & are in good condition & strong, though according to Bain, they are of unconstant temperament. We could not commence a journey under more favourable circumstance. My final prayer for our safe passage, & the fruitful outcome of our labours.

><+>—O—<+>—<

Thus day's last shadows, of needled pine and spruce, point east across plain and river, growing long and sharp, as if cavalry pikes fixed to dissuade westbound travellers and set them away from the rise of young mountains yonder. Virgin contortions of the continental plate, their valley peaks secure a breastplate of alpine plateau with ribs arching to join a north-south spine. The continental divide. Breached in places, granting passage, its western slopes detach boulders to tumble disintegrating down valley sides, to crumble into rill gravel which frost or wind pulverise to sand and water finally mills to dormant dust. To mix with dead things becoming soil thickening the torrent of canyoned river veins that discharge in a far sea where rain wrung from maritime clouds ascending the coastal ridge irrigates fern plumed forests, fecund with growth and death.

><+>—O—<+>—<

I drifted off for some time, to awaken from such a dream as I have never dreamt. Was lying in bed, as I lay in bed while dreaming the dream. It was the bed in the room I have here, with a window above it from which I may observe the sky's transformation. I was looking at these black heavens, waiting for sunrise, yet rather than seeing, I was listening. Not with my ears, but with my skin, a taut, sensitive diaphragm. I heard my father, though he was not speaking. I sat up, putting my feet on the floor, and I could feel the sounds vibrate the tensed skin of my breast. I understood him to say, though he did not use words, that he was there.

Beams of overhead light fell in pools at my feet. Between them opaque shadow. I heard the scuttling sounds of a two-footed animal. I stood and moved towards it. As I crossed into a pool of light, I was struck so hard I fell forward. I turned, arm raised, instantly belligerent, and my first blow landed on empty air. Blind in the impenetrable shadow, following the sound, I punched and jabbed until, on one un-met punch, my arm flew off with the blow's force. I stopped, falling backward, and saw my adversary bolt cross a pool of light. Its back was covered with tiny round mirrors and they reflected the luminance in bright circles that fell within the space around me like an ephemeral galaxy. I almost comprehended where I was then the beast passed into shadow, and the illuminating comets faded. I awoke, curiously calm. Around me – I reached out and touched my trunk – my worldly goods. The wool blanket covering me is the property of my landlord.

A simple affair, departure. Dawn is far off. Will I go or will I stay? There is no complication to the logistic. The technician, with his pay rise, would take my rooms, I consulted my landlord on this. I would leave my trunk to be shipped…and here I use the word home. Am I someone who has left home and will go back? Go back to pick at the wound, so it will never heal.

That is my debate, the yes or no to Captain Masse is secondary, although the prospect of adventure entices. Do I send my possessions home and set out on a trip from which I will return, a great circle in effect? Or do I set out towards some new place, which could become the centre of my universe. A place that will then be the place I return to. A new place perhaps physical, perhaps in the mind. All that I have dreamed of I could possess if I go. A fine sum of money. The newest photographic method, collodion, applied to the vistas of entirely virgin territory. An exhibition in the national gallery thence. And after that, the world is my oyster. I would be at the top of my profession, and could return home victorious. My college too, would be proud. I have heard the other emancipated women are making their mark on the world. What fun it would be to expose my sex to that world at the very pinnacle of my success.

Have thought of nothing but change this last while, and here, with it before me, I balk. Why? It is the oppressive aspect of Captain Masse? That terrible power, fascinating when mediated by the camera lens, repulsive in actual contact. Truth be my fear is that I shall only descend into the maelstrom with a facsimile of my father. Not progression, but relapse.

I care little for religion, so can expect no aid from that quarter. A phrase in a book I chanced upon comes to mind. A collection of esoteric essays. According to one, every human must face the dangers within. The dragon. We must go deep into its lair and wrestle it. Not to defeat it, but to learn of its power. I surmise that this is what I face.

And reality, so obvious as to be comic, confronts me. My life amongst three men. By subterfuge, I was able to establish that there will be three separate tents – one for the Captain, also his office, one a darkroom and repository for my equipment where I may also sleep, and one for the other two, also to be the mapping room. Privacy at night is assured.

But how will I carry out the bodily functions on the trail? I know men's habits. I admit to watching them. Walking to work the morn, the alleys near the taverns and saloons reek of urine. Men consider this their right, a satisfying public piss, though in defecation they are as private as women. How will I accomplish satisfying my own necessities, daily and monthly, in secret and without distress, and how will I participate sufficiently in male rites to not be discovered? Thus far, my disguise has not only been for the privileges it has brought, but also for the mystique, the escape from ordinariness. Even the mundane experiences of the world have demanded cleverness and intrigue to survive, and I relish the danger of living on the edge of being exposed. Even as a girl I imagined being disguised as a boy with its self-imposed loneliness, an isolation much less disheartening than the loneliness I suffered amongst my peers. But months alone in party with several men. How will I accomplish it?

Two solutions present themselves. My observation is that only the more coarse men take pride in public display. I can assume the Captain will do no such thing. I will take my side with him, and affect a slightly diffident, private air. This will support a second theatrical device. Hereabouts, the greatest respect is reserved for the taciturn man, he who can answer "yep" and "nope", to any question, or as a response to any situation, with perhaps the occasional, almost effusive "maybe", reserved for exceptional situations.

I will become one of these uncommunicative men, much as it goes against my loquacious nature, repressed already so long. I will alter the vocabulary, since I am from the urban East, to "yes", "no" and "perhaps". I will also use a bit of theatre that has already proved useful when my faux masculinity could have been compromised. I will act out some male gesture with great gusto. I believe that expectoration would do nicely. I have a phlegmatic biology, and am often stuffed up upon rising. I have seen and heard enough men spitting that I should be able to execute a loud and repulsive version complete with snorts, coughs, and hawking. No one will challenge me there. I may also consider smoking. A pipe would be best.

To camouflage my menses, I will admit to bouts of indigestion, certainly a possibility with camp food, and dispose of my soiled linen secretly. In fact, all things pertaining to personal hygiene must be accomplished at night or early in the morning. Men greatly respect the early riser, so that will do nicely. For the rest, one of the male habits I most enjoy is getting truly filthy, and staying that way for days on end. I will never be able to swim, which is a tragedy. I see an idiosyncratic character a-building; taciturn, afraid of water and very private.

As for my bosom, it is thankfully of small stature. I will keep it bound as I have. There is little discomfort. Our clothing is rough, and men wear thick undergarments, and on the trail, seldom disrobe. Several examples, redolent with weeks or months of body odour, have set before me for their portrait.

This same bosom aches at a point just below my sternum, as if my heart cannot absorb its overcharge of sentiment. I put my hand to the spot and feel the life pulse, so strong, yet so vulnerable. I use an old trick to get my answer. I imagine myself here tomorrow night. How would I feel? Poorly – the coward. I imagine myself on the trail tomorrow night, camped under the stars. How would I feel? Thrilled.

➤─┤◆➤─○─◆┼─┤◆─┤

Day comes slowly. The sun, as the earth turns, emerges in increments above the eastern plain. A patient light. A sign to nocturnal animals of the forest cross the river that darkness has gone and they must cease to satisfy their cravings. The burrowing rodents and the creatures of the forest floor, then the large and small birds of the night, finally those tiny beasts who occupy the arboreal canopy fall silent.

Into this hushed world a thirsty doe approaches the turbulent river's edge on sharp black hoofs, glancing back at her milk-fed fawn hidden in forest shade. Satisfied, she bends to the water, but stops just before taking the defenceless blind position of drinking because she hears, then smells something from the river. She looks towards a tenor gurgle on the water, a thud of oak against cedar, a muffled utterance not animal. But she sees no movement other than the swift river sliding by – the curls of boiling current, the chunks of detached trees – and does not separate the image of the loaded jonboat ferry from this, as it slides past in and with the same speed as the stream, water lapping its gunwales.

She cannot process it as a separate element in her vision, as the source of the smells and sounds, until Guzman turns and points at her, his bleached sleeve and shirt front flaring in an aggressive human movement like the flashing white tail that is danger signal of her species.

It freezes her; lean ivory legs, tawny abdomen and head against the dun-pebbled strand. She then understands that what she sees is a beast somehow capable of floating upright on two legs, like a standing bear, and she's experienced no precedent that could inform her what danger that may imply.

She has some sensation too of her own kind, of four-legged creatures, and she focuses on the contents of the drifting jonboat behind the sitting cartographer. She hears the deep chirr of a breathing horse, recognises some-thing in it, sees the hindquarter of a roan mare twitch, there too recognises something in the taught curve of muscle, and sees another two-legged crea-ture, clothed in black, move with a slow motion as it strokes the mare's flank. The doe finally separates the various elements of what her eyes behold, for she herself floated on the river only a few days before, trapped on a spinning ice flow broken off behind her when she sought a drink. She was forced to swim ashore. She perceives, now, that floating in front of her on the stream, on something like a big tree trunk, are both two and four-legged animals.

Guzman sits at his oar beside the ferryman, waiting. Bain, upright, is calming with whispers and caresses that no human, male or female has ever enjoyed, four silent standing horses somehow coaxed into and persuaded to stand on the flat bottom of the jonboat ferry.

Horses pacified, Bain lights a cigar, its reek drifting to the doe, bringing her a faint memory of danger, a native hunting camp, an arrow goading her foreleg. The ferryman nods as the boat sweeps past a point. He and Guzman lift the long sweeps dripping from the water, and to the sound of the horse's nervous breathing, bend their backs over the oars, pulling hard towards shore, swinging the huge skiff into the point's back eddy, and with growled commands from the ferryman, they drive its square prow aground on a shin-gle spit, throwing the horses forward with the arrested inertia.

The deer sees the flash of Guzman's smile, and old threat instincts rise, again the danger signal of her species, the white flash of a tail. But from his mouth exits a sound she has never heard, laughter, and it holds no tone of malice. She watches the other two-legged creature, dark coated but never dropping on all fours like a bear would, step out along the shore and fix a rope to tree trunk, then lead the huge four-legged creatures from the boat, one by one over its prow, and attach them there too. Guzman laughs again when the final animal is safely ashore, and turns towards the doe, smiling his white toothed smile. The ferryman hands him a box. He takes it, swings it to Bain behind, and in rhythmic brigade, they discharge the ferry. Boxes, canvas sacks and oiled leather trunks. When it floats light, Guzman, extending his leg so as not to wet his pant cuff, pushes the jonboat off with his foot and the boat swings upriver in the back current, then the oars dip and angle it to return to the far shore. The doe hears a shout there, and sees more four legged beasts, two-legged ones standing amongst them.

The oddly paired men ashore watch the ferry return, backs to the forest rising steep behind. Their faces bear resemblance, not through any trace of common parents, but by the mark of some similar anxiety. This distressing force pulls Bain's protracted jaw down, and stiffens his long arms to lie flat aside his ribcage like planks nailed there. Introspective, as if he's deciphered a secret message at the place were the jonboat disappeared around a point, he turns, and extracts a folded sheet of paper from a trunk set atop another trunk. He smoothes the sheet flat upon its lid. He prepares a pen. Bending from the ankles, for he seems to relish his stiffness and not want to ruin its advantage, he writes, with cautious deliberation.

>⫯⫯•⟡•⫯⫯⟨

[log insert: Dunbar Bain esq. for Captain Aaron Masse] Day 3

Departure inventory as received, repacked with no additional purchases, sealed photographic apparatus not listed. Unused items waterproofed:

6 Work saddles, leather   8 army pack saddles

16 saddle blankets no 1 wool   10 coils jute rope

14 sets tack: reins, bridles, bits and thread and awl for repair

2 double barrel 12 bore

4 breech loading rifles .45 calibre

200 pin fire loads, bird shot   600 fulminate percussion caps

600 cylindro-ogival ball   600 rounds paper encased

4 square wall tents with fly, medium canvas, four man

1 square wall tent, two man. Darkroom, double weave black cotton

1 rectangular wall tent with fly, heavy canvas, eight man

1 tin tent stove, cooking   10 length tin stovepipe

2 tin tent stove, folding   4 shovels

1 mess kit 8 man   2 mess kit boxes 4 iron pots

6 lanterns with globes   6 globes packed in excelsior

1 roll cotton wicking   1 keg lantern oil

650 candles   6 sleeping robes

1 set iron fittings and nails for 6 man skiff packed in grease

2 sets iron fitting and nails for 4 man skiff packed in grease

8 axes medium weight   12 hatchets

12 bolts cotton trade cloth   12 barrel mirrors beads trinkets

3 barrels black powder   1 roll fuse cord

10 squares waxed cotton   10 coils sisal rope

10 waterproof boxes with attachment for regulation packsaddle

>⫯⫯•⟡•⫯⫯⟨

Tensions elongating the lean man Bain compress the stout Guzman, bulging his cheeks and sagging him forward, immobilising him, setting horizontal corrugations into his forehead that ripple in sympathy with his changing thoughts. To look at the tall man stooped over him like a heron, he only rolls up his eyes while still facing the boat's disappearing place. He cups his hands and brings them to each side of his nose and exhales gently, his fingertips gauging his internal state from the feel of his breath. His face is unlined, its even forehead breached by a peak of the hair he's pulled back into a single plait. Bain's long fingers pass him another sheet of paper and the pen. He takes them, pressing out the blank page with his hand's edge till it is flat across the top of an oilskin covered box. He examines the pen nib and cleans it with a preoccupied swipe on his thigh. Satisfied, he writes, his forearm pivoting from his elbow, his hand moving swiftly across the page.

[insert: Carlo Guzman, for Aaron Masse] Day 3

Departure inventory as received, all in good order:

1 plane table	1 tripod
1 double screw paper holder	1 sketch board
2 bundles sketch paper w waxed paper	
1 set drawing pen, pencils and straight edge	
1 telescopic Alidade	1 vertical angle alidade
1 full circle vernier protractor	1 three arm protractor
1 sextant	1 set trigonometric tables
1 brass chronometer	2 iron mount chronometer
1 prismatic compass	1 bell odometer
2 level rods	2 target rods
1 survey chain	1 theodolite
1 tripod	1 bubble level
1 aneroid barometer	1 pantograph
1 telescope	1 long base range finder

Captain Masse's shout echoes across the river, followed by a rattle of curses from the ferryman. A horse whinnies, something in the harsh tone indicating refusal. Hooves drum on the bottom planks of the jonboat, and there is a splash, another curse. Bain smiles, looking over at Guzman in the shadow of an overhanging branch.

He returns Bain's glance, but his face remains immobile. The animal cacophony from across the river builds, the difficulty the crew there suffer as they load the horses becomes painful to listen too yet Bain's smile grows, and when a second splash and curse are heard, he chuckles, at the same time reaching up to caress the flank of the horse beside him with a long, gentle stroke.

Satisfied the animal is content, he walks to the water's edge and looks up river towards the unseen but boisterous ferry landing. There is no sign of the ferry. He finds a flat rock, chair height. He sits, back to Guzman, and relighting his cigar, falls to contemplating a swirl of current down river.

Guzman has not taken his eyes from the place where the returning jonboat will appear around the point. The protesting clamour of human and beast crescendos. It is clear the boat has not even left the landing. Stepping from the shadow of the tree trunk, he blinks as if exposed to the light for the first time and repelled by it. He walks down towards Bain. Though elegant in a fitted coat, his stride seems that of a guarded prisoner, a short and hesitant gait. He tilts his pale face to the sky, considers the sun angle and sights it, his arms in front, placing his hands one atop the other to measure the distance from the horizon line to determine height and inclination, compares this to the slant of the tree's shadow across the shingle spit and the time on a large watch he withdraws from a pocket. He flips the watch cover shut with his thumb and strolls out, cautious, taking inventory of the flotsam on the beach, his gaze settling on the wreck of a wooden stage coach floating on its side, the horses lost or drowned, empty shafts poking into the air fluttering bits of broken leather harness that catch on a shoreline cottonwood and swing the carriage to jamb against a rock, crushing a delicately panelled door, splintering the varnished woodwork. Its long wheel spokes turn slowly in the current.

The two men's tense dissimilarity is inconsonant and unsettling as the presence of this wreck in the flooding river. They know they must talk, and overwhelmed, they inexpertly ease towards conversation, drawing their hands across their faces, looking down and scratching the backs of their necks, as if they will find something to say written in the black sand and glinting feldspar pebbles at their feet. They seek some means to keep the words from coming out, as if the amount of time they have will always be too long, too large, for what they have to, or know how to say.

Bain, so much taller, seems closest to risking a word, his greater height lending him the disposition to proclaim, like a lighthouse or a minaret. At birth he was named Dunbar by his mother, after her father, which name he keeps and uses. His own father, since the boy would automatically carry the family name Bain, expressed no opinion. Dunbar rubs the stubble on his chin, forcing a soft whirr. He looks again at his own watch, then elevates his head towards the risen sun. He clears his throat, the sound beginning its ascent at his thorax, finally issuing from his long windpipe in a spatter of coughs, as if lifting his head opened a leaky valve above his vocal cords. But he then says nothing.

His sound and gesture affirm he's not one who speaks easily. He bends and closes his watch, the valve in his throat closing too, cutting the last cough short, yet the noise hangs in the air between the men, alien as laughter in a church, contesting the silence.

The short man, Guzman, was bestowed the name Carlo Amour de Cosmos by his father at birth. His mother's opinion was not consulted, as she was a mulatto slave, soon to be traded off to prevent any contact with her son. Amour detested his name as a child, with its howled variations ranging from "lover boy" by the more imaginative to a slurred "Amos" by the indolent. Events in his adult life caused him to change it several times, out of prudent concern for his own safety. He always kept some part of the root in these mutations; Albert de Cosmos, Andy Cosby, Cosmo, Aristot Universe, finally Carlo Guzman which is how, in his last episode, he referred to himself, and the inside pocket of his closely cut waistcoat contains documents, under this name, attesting to his profession and experience as a master surveyor and cartographer. Inside those documents is folded a smaller, single leaf, a written and sealed letter, putting him, by ticket-of-leave, in the charge of one Captain Aaron Masse and granting him full pardon, by a district judge, of any culpability in the death of a touring opera diva's husband found, skull split, in an alley on the outskirts of a rough and tumble port city well accustomed to sudden disappearances of some of its citizens and sudden appearance of good fortune for others.

His fine fingers touch his slender nose then drop, exploring his clothing as they descend, their nerves sending back messages as to whether a seam is straight or not, whether a pleat needs tucking. They tug at his shirt to straighten its collar, caress his wool jacket as if the nerves see its houndstooth pattern, touch the tight cut trousers as if sensing the cloth's tension and stop, resting along a thin silk stripe. He continues to stare into some intermediate distance, also avoiding the idea of talk, but then, his grey eyes droop and he decides in favour of it. Guzman opens his mouth:

'And every voyage begins with the first step, this being what they say, so thus it could be said our voyage has begun, and immediately, one ponders an ancient enigma, a venerated mathematical conundrum involving the idea of the infinite. For if we travel, we do so to a destination, thus we move between two points, one the beginning, the other the end, alpha and omega if you will, the travelling itself being the middle, for one does not travel at the precise beginning and end of a voyage. One has not begun to move at the former, and has ceased to move at the latter. Yet we know not our destination, have never been there, thus, since our journey has no end place, it has no middle, it has only a beginning, and if it has only a beginning, a place where there is no movement, we will never leave. Do you get my drift, Bain.'

The syncopated rhythm of his speech, larger syllables exaggerated for the pleasure of how their sound decorates a word, creates a marbled paragraph like sweet and bitter fruit mixed in a cake. The honed skills of one who likes to talk. Yet, in Guzman's eyes, it can be seen his reaction to his own words as they resound off the forest wall and granite cliffs is fear. He looks around him for the sound's effect. It is not because he fears being heard. It is because making the sound places him where he is, and he does not want to be there.

This sentiment overcoming him, he grows passive as a statue, seeming to have mastered a perceptual trick of not being where he is. He avoids the further necessity of talking, since Bain does not respond, by appearing to neither hear or see. He raises his hand to his eyes, palm facing, scrutinises it for blisters caused by the jonboat's rough oar, and finding none, draws it over his face with a conjurer's swipe. When his palm slides from his chin, his acquiescent aspect has returned. He says nothing more.

>-+•>-0-<•+-<

[Captain Aaron Masse] Day 3

Weather steady. Reid's contract signed & sent to Capital with tintype and last document parcel. River traverse fraught with trials & horses not settled till near midnight. Some very wild but trust Bain they will prove apt. Own mount bolted into river up to its belly. Melt runoff, dense with sand. My legs, immersed only at the knee, numbed to useless stumps in a moment.

>-+•>-0-<•+-<

*M*y allotted mare a fine one for the trail. Fifteen hands. Round at the withers and comfortable. No beauty, short necked, with a big chest, she breaths deep and easy even on the hard climbs. I treat her as my solitary female companion.

Before we re-packed after the ferry traverse, Bain, making an inordinate fuss, dug the instruction manual for the photographic gear from one of his precious trunks. Though I share a tent with the oilskin wrapped apparatus itself, a curious black tent which will also serve as darkroom, I am not allowed to unseal it and take a look. That will come at trail end, where we are to spend a week or two preparing our advance towards the great divide.

The manual describes a fascinating process. Instead of coating an opaque metal plate with the light sensitive emulsion, the collodion technique requires that the photographer coat a transparent glass plate, then immediately set plate in camera and expose a negative. That is to say, bright areas of the subject become opaque areas on the plate. Immediately, before the emulsion has hardened, this plate is developed in the requisite chemical baths, then dried. As with a tintype. But this is not the final product. Sometime later, the glass plate is pressed against a sheet of paper likewise sensitised with emulsion, and a negative of the negative, thus a positive, is made. The tones being again reversed, what was bright on the subject becomes bright on the paper, the shadows too are replicated as dark tones, and a perfect reproduction is the result, with the added advantage that a multiplicity of duplicate prints can be made – any number in effect.

The glass plates are cumbersome and delicate. Thus Bain's due caution in packing them. For transport, the negative image, which is truly the original, may be stripped off the glass, rolled up, and stored like a drawing.

><+>-O-<+-<

[Captain Aaron Masse] Day 5

Wind Calm. Overcast. Heavy rain. Guzman packed his city duds first night. He begins & ends the day with a sun sight and various investigations with his instruments. His eye is well trained to estimate slopes & distances. I find that mine exaggerates the steepness because of the difficult travelling over broken stone, fallen timber, criks & swamps.

He demonstrated, swinging his theodolite, that in viewing the terrain with an eye for a possible rail road, a rugged mountain gorge with occasional precipitous narrows, such as the one we now set up camp in, separated by river flats, may appear much rougher than it is in fact. Construction of a line here would actually be less expensive than on rolling country which, although appearing flat to the eye, is full of elevations or depressions, which must be cut or filled at great expense. Railway reconnaissance, he says, should not be of a line, but an area of sufficient width on each side of an air line between the fixed points to include the least circuitous route, in horizontal and vertical planes, connecting these.

Have lead a survey crew using the old method; transit and chain, stadia & spirit level, with the map being made later at headquarters from the surveyor's notes. Guzman works with plane table, sextant & logarithmic tables, rapidly procuring his measurements & plotting them. The resulting map, drawn in the field with notes, is a much more accurate representation than one done in an office. Even rain today did not stop him, for he works under an immense oilskin umbrella, which we take turns holding.

Other than annoyance of finding a place for his trunk amongst our baggage, & his absolute insistence that he occupy the tent used to shelter his photographic apparatus, am well content with Reid. J. Reid, this is how he signed his contract.

>·―·◆>·•O·•<◆·―·<

This evening brought for me a revelation which I could never have anticipated. Such an undramatic moment. It rained the whole afternoon and when time came to set up camp it was decided instead of our separate tents, which has been the habit until now, that all of us excluding Captain Masse would bunk down in the one large tent, supplied with a stovepipe and stove, which we use as a kind of mess hall.

During the day we forded many streams and were constantly in contact with wet foliage. The first order of the camp was to set up a tin stove and get a fire going in our tent. By the time we'd supped and bedded down, its interior was tropical. Guzman, the first man to strip off his boots, and the only one who had not taken the Captain's advice to fix pant cuffs and sleeves with tight wound thongs, discovered several bloodsucking leeches on the softer parts of his lower anatomy. All modesty was immediately forgotten and the search was on. Of course, Guzman's first concern was to identify species and genus. For Bain, it was an obsessive inspection of the most intimate places.

I lay on my folding cot and watched the men strip off their clothes. Wet, steaming shirts and trousers were soon hanging from every part of the tent, dripping onto the hot stove, filling the air with a fog of human and equine sweat. It was immediately made into a game to throw the detached leeches onto the stove top, where they simmered and popped, giving of a stench of singed flesh. This added to stale tobacco smoke, unwashed bodies and feet, all pressing down upon me like the weight of an avalanche.

I have seen naked women – my more daring college classmates, the Mayor's wife – but I've never seen a naked man before. I watched the hunched figures with paralysed fascination as they scrutinised their most private places, describing their discoveries in language I have never heard. Prone on my bunk, eyes fixed on the damp slope of canvas above me, I felt shyness such as a young schoolgirl might. I've lived through fears of being exposed as a female, fears of rape too. I feel keenly the possibility of sexual vulnerability should I be recognised but with those men I do not think that threat exists. As I lay there, flushed with embarrassment, my one thought was how profoundly I am not a man. I now speak from experience. If one wishes to gaze upon it, the female body is a far superior sight to the male. Though I have donned, and long worn trousers, and profited thus, I cannot ever nor do I want to become a man physically.

I claimed excess fatigue, and strict adherence to Captain Masse's instructions, thus no fear of the little animals, even though I could clearly imagine them attached to my legs. I pretended to drop off to sleep.

An hour or so has passed. Only one remaining lamp lights the interior, burning low. I roll over and look at my comrades. The embarrassment of my own very different physique, my revulsion at theirs in the close quarters has evaporated. I smell myself, equally redolent of unwashed body parts and horse sweat. Calling quietly to my comrades, I confirm they are asleep. In the privacy of the half light, I attach my sleeping robe by its drawstring to the pole above my bed, thus forming a small tent, much like a portable darkroom. I slide my trousers, then my underwear down, and probe my own anatomy, searching in the most vulnerable places. I find my quarry there, the highest above my knee, and like the others, launch them to fry on the still hot stove.

In the morning, using the trick I keep in my back pocket for such times, I'll play the virile male to their more dormant masculinity. I'll harass them for their fear of the leeches, saying that I found none because I had fastened my leggings properly. I'll remind them of the slimy animal's medicinal use, and suggested a contest, with the host of the most blood bloated creature being the winner, this determined by weight. I'll have no takers sure, and no doubts as to my virility will arise.

[Captain Aaron Masse] Day 5

Low cloud. Wind S by SW. Weather holding. Heavy rain the morn. Sun shone brightly afternoon, charring air. Insect life immediately manifested itself. Those vulnerable were afflicted with numerous bites, especially Reid. I told him to desist from washing with soap every morning as the smell attracted them, & I am quite certain he blushed in response. He is a man of gentle breeding, & good family.

Downed a ten-point buck. I made first sight, but rifle jammed on packing grease & when I got it cleared, could only see a hip. Made two shots, second into empty air but Bain followed and dropped it a willow copse, where it lay.

>─┤◆>─◦─<◆├─<

*T*he deer have had a hard winter, for they are not shy, and desperately hungry. The buds and softer bark of many trees and shrubs are missing each morning, fresh scars in the new wood showing they were eaten during the night. This shows in the taste of the meat. When gutted and butchered, there is no fat on them. Flesh is rangy and tough, and tastes of willow bark.

>─┤◆>─◦─<◆├─<

[Captain Aaron Masse] Day 13

Sky inconstant, wind shifted from NE to NW at noon. Half way to last outpost by Guzman's sextant, which he claims is precise to one hour's walking distance. There we head Norwest, while all others head south . Bain did choose well our mounts, now all trail broke & strong & able. Horses are at times to their bellies in snow but making, with extensive mapping activity & botanizing, good distance each day. Camps comfortable, excepting one night after a full day of rain. Well worth trouble & expense of being the first group across the river. No single party of settlers has caught us up, though twice met descending dispatch riders, one military, one government, benefiting from still frozen ground.

Untrammled trail gives Cartographer\botanist Guzman & amateur geographer Bain much pleasure. Both happy to observe the virgin track right from the trail. From a difficult start, they have grown to respect each other. Often, when the way is distinct, I let Guzman ride ahead. If he escaped, where would he go?

Guzman's scientific & cartographic propensities much evident. Each sun shot made twice. We know precisely where we are. He is able to do his sight in a few minutes if clear, and his calculations in ten. This rapidity I have never seen. Bain is astounded, & learning the techniques & tables though with the dead reckoning compass & pacing (he has averaged the step of his mount, with compensation for rise or fall, & has a small machine which counts it), though he is can be equally accurate. Guzman's sketches are detailed, precise & of first rate artistic quality.

Guzman has introduced us all to coffee. A densely black liquid from a bean he grinds, then, pouring on boiling water, steeps an infusion twice daily using a small bag, the size of the end of a sock, on a hoop with wood handle. He maintains it can be taken with milk also, which is boiled & mixed in frothy. Its stimulant effect is instant, excellent upon rousing or when sore fatigued. I take it with him the morn, still preferring tea afternoon & evening time. The others do not like its bitterness. Another detriment, Guzman relates, is it stores poorly. Tea suffers not this, I have drunk it from decade-old packets. I also observe that though coffee stimulates the brain to clarity the morn, it lacks the capacity to take off a body chill which sweetened tea possesses.

Little game & that lean. Again short of meat.

Reid's roan mare picks her way through a rubble of frost cleft schist – thumb thick slabs of rock still in shadow, slick with a skin of dirty snow. The upslope grows more dubious as the gorge deepens. The horse pokes at an icy spot with her right forefoot, uncertain of the shoe she can feel loosening at its toe. A nail has fallen out. Too long ago the powerful hands of the blacksmith, his tart chewing tobacco, his rough grip on her shank, and the twisting rasp of his file. He pounded in the nails looking up at his next customer, the shoe still hot from the forge.

She tries the slippery patch, ripples the muscle along her side, a signal to her rider – who she can sense well balanced as since the first day – to prepare, allowing the mare equal weight on each leg. The mare extends herself, placing her weight forward to make a shallow jump over the ice. Her rider's legs close, her weight shifts, ready too, leaning forward, weight transferred slightly to her pressing knees and thighs, but still centred over the mare. The mare feels the whole of each of the rider's legs, from the top of the thighs to mid calf, press evenly around her belly.

She hops over the ice and into the sun. Sudden heat after the gorge. The mare recognises sensations of her youth, from yearling to three year old, in the southern desert. With the sensations of the dry, flat desert, some deeper recollection prods her, species memory, going back thousands of years to other deserts across the sea, emphasising how possibly dangerous her surroundings are. She smells and is aware of a waking bear in the bush nearby, knows it hears them, maybe watches them, knows it will do nothing. She senses that all the men around her are friends except for Captain Masse, who she senses as the enemy, who she perceives could kill.

>─┼─◆─○─◆─┼─◄

[Captain Aaron Masse] Day 14

Have the measure of my men. Not dead certain of Guzman, but I must rein in my fret here, men such as he being so different in temperament from men such as myself or Bain. It is his temperament that troubles me? For him the art is everything, he would risk all for the endeavour, give no quarter. Myself, & I know it, I will push to the limit, but if in the end the risk to the men has no merit, the odds are too high, loath stand fast, I will retreat. Guzman, at such a time, damming the odds, would advance, even in the face of certain destruction. Time will tell. Bain solid as a rock. My faith in him is total.

Of my brother-in-law I will say nothing, save to wish my dear sister well. My prayers this last night for her alone. Appears my mother is a more astute judge of character than myself. When she saw him waltzing ineptly at the Regiment New Years Ball, she told my sister "never marry a man who cannot dance, even your brother dances passable well, I assured myself of that" & remained dead set against him throughout the nuptials.

James, John, Jack, Jerome? What is Reid's first name? Have heard it not. We use family names in the camp as is military custom. Seems a quiet, studious man Reid, robust beyond what his smallish physique would belie. I have seen this type before. On many a long march, the large built, big fisted soldier is the first to fatigue. The more compact ones, all sinew & bone, ever more purposeful, are those that still hold their own at days end.

Something about him jogs my recollection. Again from the most intense interval of my regimental command. The desperate days, long marches when we were pressed to our limits in the border war, advancing one step, retreating two. Those days the government sent us battalion after battalion of green troops, clerks & schoolboys hardly competent to aim a rifle, unable to hold a line. A time of many desertions, harsh disciplines. What is it that I seek within my recollection? It will come to me, as such answers often do, during the night. Perhaps my ancestor will pay a visit with the key to my puzzlement.

>─┼─◆>─O─<◆┼─<

Through some tradition known to him and Bain, the Captain cooks breakfast. I, taking for myself the role of earliest riser, have already set a fire in the flat top tin cookstove, which is put outside in fine weather, under a canvas in rain or snow. His cooking technique is elemental. He sets a kettle, and small skillets from the mess kit, one per man, on the stove top. Into each he plops a spoon of lard, a sliced potato, and strips of what meat we have. The first days it was pork bacon. When the meat is cooked, he forks it onto plates, with the potatoes. The first days we had eggs also. He would break four into each pan and stir them up. These went beside the meat. When they ran out, they were replaced by hard tack biscuit boiled in the skillet. The kettle, now boiling, has tea thrown in it after Guzman takes his water for his coffee and the kettle is re-filled for hot wash water. We each scrub our own utensils. The captain also uses it to shave.

In rotation we others cook the evening meal from what stores we have, what we shoot, and what we gather. I have proven an indifferent cook, much like the captain. Guzman is an enthusiastic one, his suppers supplemented by wild plants and mushrooms he gathers and identifies. Bain obviously detests this obligation. He is painful to watch, working in careless haste, and his meals are difficult to get down, of which he seems to be proud.

>─┼─◆>─O─<◆┼─<

Just beneath the earth's meagre troposphere – infinite space beyond it – a mass of dry air pulsates. Thin clouds of ice fine as dust trace mutating tendrils. Drawn down by gravity and dragged east with the spinning planet, they beget long curlicues that look, to anyone on the ground glancing skyward, like the tail of an immense and raging mustang.

A gloomy squall of the lower atmosphere ascends to caress this thirsty air's belly, condensing water, releasing rain, snow, hail, releasing heat.

Expanding. And forced up by a wall of mountains, the same ridge the expedition climbs, this particular storm punches an escape hole. Boiling with thermal energy, racked by sheets of lightning, it ascends west over the peaks past the line of horses and men, leaving a ravenous vacuum in its wake. The dry air of the plains is sucked into this hungry maw. An immense flat spiral, swelling across the grassed prairie, it takes up their mid-day heat, and now an estival wind, surges over the foothills.

It evaporates snow still lying in shaded gullies, against the north face of crags. It warms the trunks of willows, pulling up their sap, and stirs the sleeping bears. Submerged larvae struggle towards its oxygen, and leaving their shucks in the surface film – translucent, slate torsoed – they dry their wings to flutter amongst the budding trees.

The expedition tramps over pools of slush, across rain-slick rock, through clinging snow, the horses only secure purchase patches of still frozen earth. Noon thaw reveals harsh mementoes of the land hungry settlers who passed a year previous. Whole ox skeletons, neat piles of hair cluttered around white ribs and vertebrae, the rest of the animal consumed by wolves, then vultures, picked clean by crows and finally rendered to fleshless bone and hide by seething hosts of pearly maggots. Tangled cart tracks, ruts still frozen and deep as graves, that fill with water so by the hottest time of the day the horses stagger nerve racked and desperate along an uncertain track, the expedition meandering in ragged single file, to follow a narrow strip of shade under conifers along the trail's southern rim.

Just above them, a torrent bursts from the mountains ahead and spreads out across an alpine meadow, its dense surge exploding over the ice and snow to form a glistening flood plain. On this flat, the rushing waters slow as they have every year, and loosing their power to suspend the heavy particles of mud and mineral eroded from the mountains, they relinquish a thick deposit of smooth grained sand suspended in a matrix of greasy blue clay.

This entire altoplain, proud to the sun, is a quagmire of parallel lesions cut by the huge two wheeled carts the advancing settlers favour. On these muddy flats, the trail grows wider and wider, bulging like a burled tumour on a slim tree trunk. It can be seen from the pattern of tracks that when one set of ruts grew so deep a cart's axle dragged, that trail was abandoned and another started alongside. In the middle of the plateau the road has enlarged indefinitely. The visible hoof prints, and the skeletons along the trail prove it could only just be conquered by most powerful oxen. The worst ruts are littered with effects cast off to lighten load – bureaux, woodwork already split after one winter of exposure, rusting stoves, wads of sodden clothing.

Discarded books, hair brushes and a broken vase mark the trail's impassable core. Centred in this clutter of jetsam, one ox cart is still hopelessly mired, sunk to the rims of its high wheels. The gouged ground in front of it, still frozen hard as rock, shows the tracks of three or four brace of oxen used in trying to extricate the cart. And on it, attached by ropes and blocked with wedges, the cargo sits, seemingly abandoned.

It is a religious icon, full human size, once in transport to the interior to be enshrined in a chapel, or establish a church. Perhaps ordered by an already established frontier congregation, perhaps laboriously transported by a group of pilgrims seeking religious refuge in the new lands. But the image is not altogether forsaken. Someone in the group, or someone who followed, if the original transporter gave up or perished, decided that the icon wanted to remain there, and dedicated a shrine on the spot. The image's head is draped with the stems and winter faded blossoms of spring and summer flowers. Of the varied persons who have passed the spot, many faithful have made a contribution; scattered coins, sodden plugs of incense, ashes of burnt tobacco and guttered candle stubs. Its back to the mountains, the carved wooden head, paint skin already peeling, stares down the trail towards those voyagers labouring up, its line of sight catching them just as they crest a dire slope of splintered glacial till. Here, for horse and human, each step requires individual effort to avoid instant catastrophe.

The sky lightens, but a coverlet of arboreal shadow from a tilted pine tree envelopes the ascending expedition. Bain's horse finds the sure path, gaining a few brief steps on the wider stretch of firm terrain, passing Reid, her mount balked on boggy ground. She eases her reins and lets Bain advance, and so it is Bain, as he crests the last rise to look across the bemired meadow, who first beholds the stark and solitary statue. He stops, and even Reid, just below on the narrow path, cannot see what he sees. Such a sudden halt would normally mean game has been sighted, but Bain makes no move for his rifle. Instead, he stares ahead, his mouth, his eyes slowly curving to a scowl of distaste. Digging a heel into his horse's flank, he crests the ridge, picking his way across what ground has least thawed. His mount sinks above its knees, but Bain forces his way straight to the icon as Reid follows his path onto the boggy meadow, then Guzman, the pack horses, and finally Captain Masse. The natural trail circumvents the rutted ground, and all the other horses take it instinctively, leaving Bain to struggle out alone, in a direct line contrary to the weaving ruts, to confront the wagon bound sculpture. There he stops his horse and sits, mounted, unmoving, eye to eye with it. The others circle the furrowed plain's perimeter. Above them, naked tree branches rattle and clack in the wind. The conifers long needles sing with it, the forest setting off a sighing chant, background to the soggy plod of the expedition's horse, the muted cries of the men as they slip and slog around the plateau.

Toward day's end, they negotiate the river that formed the delta. The icon disappears behind. The wind drops. The boughs cease to sing. A sharp, solitary report, clean as the noise of a snapped tree trunk echoes across the vale. A rifle shot.

>─┤─◆>──Ο──<◆─├─<

I still do not know what to make of this shocking incident. The wind shifted, I felt it, the very sound of it changed sometime last night, and perhaps it was a harbinger of ill fortune. The bizarrely decorated icon seemed to mimic the wind's warning. It was not the killing of my mare that disturbs me. I know the rules of the trail. Yet, even then, perhaps the broken shin could have been splinted, and the animal healed.

Again, some fear deep within me piqued by a look in the eyes of Captain Masse. A delight in the cruel and absolute decision, transforming my noble mount into material for the stew pot. In an instant, he beheld my beautiful and affectionate beast as no longer animal companion or transport, but simple flesh, and immediately applied the techniques of the butcher. Why he cut its throat first I do not know, but the bubbling clamour that issued from the dying animal's throat, its desperate thrashing over the ground, the river of frothing blood were too much for me. How can one think of a living animal as just its parts; the flesh as one thing...something to eat, the hide as another...a skin covering for one of our trunks, and the tail and mane as simple material for braiding ropes. I could not consume my supper, though, since it was my mount, I was given the best cut. The others noticed this. Did they remark also my ill-concealed rage?

>─┤─◆>──Ο──<◆─├─<

[Captain Aaron Masse] Day 15

Wind dry, SW. Sky clear. Temperature rising day cold nt. Ground fog at end of day as air temp drops. Lost one mount to broken shin. Gained one hide without worm holes & some good weight of fresh meat, which is welcome. The deer hereabouts are winter starved, thin as rails & what flesh they have bitter with the taste of willow bark. Last repast of jerked venison so much spoiled we et it thro necessity. Some error in our recipe. Loath to use too

much salt, for dislike of the taste, I was miserly with it. I believe
this brought on the rot, for the meat was smoked all night. We
cut off maggoty edges and boiled the pith. Expect the horse meat
will last till we gain the outpost, which saves us lost time hunting. Reid seemed squeamish about eating mare flesh. Every cavalry man knows it is not to be preferred to beef, but certainly
beats mule or donkey. When I noted his repugnance, he related
there are races who will not eat pork, and others who eat dog,
monkey & grasshoppers. His reasons were his own. Many preju-
dices are in the mind.

Animal dispatched with one ball, also an advantage. The
average deer hunt requires three shots, none of us being great
marksman. Must improve. We are entering bear country. They
will be out of their dens soon. A life can depend on one good shot
to a vital organ.

Odd request on the part of Bain to take a lit faggot from our
cooking fire & set an abandoned wagon, & its load alight. I told
him what he did was his business but, when out of simple curiosity, I inquired as to the nature of the wagon's load, thinking he
wanted to burn some pestilent vermin he'd found, & he informed
me it was the carved religious figure, I forbade it.

><+><+>—O—<+><+<

*S*hooting my mare set us up to make early camp. The butchering
occupied only the Captain and Mr. Guzman, who, for so sensitive and artistic a man, was indifferent to the gruesome nature of the task. I had forgotten
he was an amateur biologist. As he eviscerated the horse, he examined every
organ, squeezing it bloody in his hands, pronouncing on its state of health,
describing the animal's history. Bain, who seems tougher, much more the
woodsman, showed no interest and wandered off. I believe he had some
slight disagreement with the Captain. I saw him lean against the basalt face
of a ledge, pressing his leg muscles to the warmed stone, then sit at the top
of a gorge where the miniature river that formed this sand swamp tumbles
out of the cliffs. I went over. There was a depth to the view which struck me
with admiration. The panorama of the hills we've climbed these last days
spread out to the west, suffused in a golden haze. Stretching before us in
unbroken outline, they presented a singular and romantic appearance of a
soft and mythic land, glittering in the sun that was now descending. A rich

and gorgeous view for a painter. I never felt so much regret at my inability to sketch as I did at the moment.

Saying that I found it a spot worthy of a photograph, lyrical in its simple beauty, I drew beside Bain, bemoaning the elaborate logistic of my art that prevented me from beginning a picture in an instant. Bain did not look up. I indicated the tableau with a sweep of my hand but when I turned to him he was looking down instead, into the frothy water, his eyes following the swirls and eddies as he traced it upstream, past undercut banks, over rocks and around gravel bars till it disappeared into the pine forest.

⤞•⟡•◯•⟡•⤝

'What brings you here Bain, with such a magnificent vista just in front?'

'I am in a foul mood, and seek to calm myself.'

'We are unified in that, but why your perturbation?'

'That is between me and the Captain.'

'I saw you looking at that abandoned wagon, with the statue. Something to do with that?'

'I don't wish to speak of it.'

'Well, to open a subject you may wish to speak of, for I wish to talk…do you not think the sapphire-hued panorama before us is of great charm, and worthy a glance.'

'Charm it may have, Mr. Reid, for you the photographer. The light, the atmospheric effect. But those attractions are lost on me. I am prone to other enticements.'

'What could be more beautiful and unique than this broad sweep?'

'The crik right here holds far greater wonders.'

'How's that?'

'It's new to its course, no more than a few years. Has fought hard with the mountain for the right to flow here, and as a result, floats within its water that which allows human existence, the makings of the soil which provides our food, and food for the animals we eat. This young and virgin stream, fresh composed from the mountains yonder, is a miracle.'

'If I may say Mr Bain, though it is wonderful to hear you talk, I would never has expected such exalted language from you. I'd put you down as a dour man, of thrifty speech. Please continue, you have my every attention. What makes you see so much in a creek?'

'I have been to war, and known men who love war. Our leader is one. There are men who are lovers of women, Guzman is perhaps that, and I have heard there are men who are lovers of men, which idea repulses me. I am a lover of rivers.'

'And why is that?'

'As you remarked, you know me as a man of few words, and that is correct, but the reply to your query is a lengthy yarn, and, it may surprise you, I am proud to say I am well practised at it. The Captain knows it well. War is short periods of dread spaced by long times of dullness. In those times we yarn. Have you the patience to hear me out Reid?'

'Sadly, patience is at times my whole aspect.'

'I was taught a story must begin at the beginning. I was born in a village set on a floodplain, treeless North, South and East to the horizon. A poplar planted to honour me, the firstborn, grew a forearm length a year with our careful watering. Other than in buckets and barrels, I saw water only in puddles after a cloudburst, deep enough if I put my hand in its back would be covered. My tradesman father saw these puddles as a sign the ground had not been properly levelled, and would rake them full of gravel or earth. Collected water was the citizen's enemy. Drainage was the key to good agriculture, and our mercantile life depended on the farmers. Water meant mud. A messy porch for my mother. Standing water was mosquitoes, crops seeded late or flooded out and rotting on flattened stalks. We prayed for water from the clouds each Sunday but fought its physical presence on the earth each week.

'Last Sunday in April, before church, I came to the door of my mother's kitchen. It had been raining for three days. My one hand held a clear glass fruit jar in which swam the first living thing I'd managed to capture, a finger-long minnow with yellow stripes I'd found in the depth of a trench. The minnow fought gainst the glass. The few cups of ditch water I'd provided were not enough. It flipped its tail at the palm of my hand over the jar mouth. I waited for my mother to notice my presence. She spoke finally, but her voice came from the adult world.

' "A terrible thing has happened. The river has burst its bank," she said, her face blank, til she laughed, "But what have you got there? A fish. Do you know that all fishes are sad? God would not let them into the kingdom of heaven as animals like us because fish don't sleep. Their eyes are open all the time. They can't dream of quitting this life and going up there with the angels. If you don't dream of heaven, God is not interested, so fish cry all the time. And that's where rivers come from. Rivers are the tears of fish. I don't think your fish is crying enough to fill that jar. Let's give it some more water, though Lord knows, more water's the last thing we animals want today, but your fish needs it," she said, and went to the water bucket, and poured a dipper full of water down the side of my jar. "Like a lot of things, water's good in the right place and bad in the wrong place. Will those clouds never go away?" '

'They did. The sun shone and there in the heart of our great continent, the ice dams on choked criks collapsed, loosing their waters for the long journey to the sea. I had not seen it, but our own river then raged bursting. That night, I dreamed of a shiny snake that crept farther from the river bank each hour, coming closer, devouring the fields, growing fat with swallowed land. In the last dream the river was almost upon us. Water gurgled like thunder in my ears. Forced awake by this awful vision I ran out and in the dark climbed my tree, which had pushed above sapling height against winter cold and summer heat. I gained its highest yoke in as night faded into a day that revealed, there in the distance, the flood spread out in a silver sheet. Like a laid-down looking glass it took the colour of the dawn sky above it. First the grey end of night, then the rising sun's orange and last the blue of day. That would have been a photograph for you, Reid. Is our apparatus able to capture colour?'

'No, I know of none that can. Please continue your story.'

'I see that they have finished butchering your horse. Captain Masse is struggling with his journal. It is my turn to rustle up supper. Ride beside me the morrow.'

><•>•○•<•>•<

[Captain Aaron Masse]

Bain much chafed by my refusal to let him burn icon. I know nothing of idol worship myself, but the desecration of the symbol of any faith I will not allow. I have noted this illiberal tendency in my fellow frontiersmen. They are uncomplicated, democratic & God fearing, respectful of life's fundamentals & would describe themselves proudly as such. Yet, this avowed plainness carries within it a dormant intolerance that wakens when events or things unfamiliar are encountered. This I fear, for if the basis of the nation we are building – & our expedition will allow the laying of what is the last block in its solid foundation – if that basis is the elemental concept of equality very much represented by men & women such as Bain, then how to avoid this puritan desire to retain only the elemental that seems to accompany our grassroots democracy. How to stop its growing into brute fear of that different.

Bain went off wandering to cool his temper. Reid took charge of baggage horses & adjusted loads to suit. I observed him as he walked off. After a long day still competent & full of life. A vigorous young man with a light step, he participates fully in every task, but retains something of himself we are not allowed to see. He is not a natural soldier, like Bain or I.

Was brought to mind of the raw recruits so common in the war's latter day. Gawking farm boys, young sons of kind mothers – frail in ill cut uniforms, not without grace, but lacking the soldier's sure gate. We never spoke of it, the leaders of Brigades & Regiments, but offering so much young flesh to the Gods of war, watching them march off, lean & out of step, caused me a father's pain.

I feel some such sentiment of fondness towards Reid. An affection I could not accord a rough man of the frontier. It is the precision of his demeanour I reckon, & his book learning, for from his comments & Guzman's respectful glance, Reid is uncommonly well educated. It could be that men such as Bain & I represent the past, & the future citizen, more refined, will be like Guzman or Reid. Perhaps some day, when our mission is accomplished, I will have a talk with him. Though I do not know him, I trust him in his task, yet still, do not ken what it is about him that jogs my recollection. Often, when he is at a task, or mounting or dismounting his horse, my mind is within a hair's breadth of recalling something particular I want to recollect, but I do not grasp it.

>─┤◆├─◦─┤◆├─<

There is some sense in Bain's view of the world. Men as lovers, though there is something superficial about the word. A lover of war would seem an oxymoron, since war, although I have never experienced it, is to me based on hate. My own father, with all his pent wrath. Was it not having anyone to love that rendered him thus? Certainly my mother could be the object of no-one's affection. And myself? Who or what do I love? There is no answer to the question. And I have no answers to so many questions. I will bear in mind Bain's hypothesis. It seems to have served him well, for though tight strung, he has every aspect of a contented man. I will steer my queries by this lodestone until my own metaphysic emerges. How I detest Captain Masse. And he, with sublime cruelty, offered me a ride pillion behind himself. I replied that it was my decision to take the extra packhorse. I will be much more comfortable on a beast trained to carry boxes of equipment and follow another baggage horse at the end of the line, which will put me as far from the Captain as possible. A cold morning, my stirrups slippery with frost.

>–⊢◆>–O–◆⊣–<

[Captain Aaron Masse]

Reid in a long jag of talk with Bain. Our youngest participant, bending his head, the junior man taking sage counsel. Betimes an excess of bravado, betimes fractious, Reid rides harder, always makes the morning fire, carries more load to the horses, yet was absolutely shocked when forced to live in a tent with the others at night. I saw the reluctance to go in, even with the rain pouring down & I saw the drawn face the morning, evidence of a sleepless night. Also refused to eat the mare, just now refused to ride with me & showed too much sardonic gusto in bantering with the others. Untempered youth mayhap, yet I am certain there is something else there. Reid is hiding something & this not uncommon on the frontier. For some decades now our governments policy has been to pardon, or give paroled sentences to those who would come here. This is how I obtained such a highly trained man as Guzman. I deduce there is some chink in Reid's armour. The usual circumstance would be a petty crime such as theft or assault, though he does not seem capable of injuring another. Given his good manners & education, I surmise that he may have got some innocent maid, perhaps a servant, with child, & was banished by his father. I do not know, & cannot ask him, for that is the unwritten rule of the frontier; no questions about the past, so he continues to be a puzzle, our photographer.

More clement than most, like me he never urinates outside his tent & unlike me is gentle with the horses, yet he curses roundly in jest or in anger, & is the first to rise & the last to sleep each day. How he has come to engage my attention. I will get some answers when I see him do his work, for we will arrive at the fort hence, & I have much I want done by him.

>–⊢◆>–O–◆⊣–<

The sun rises, flashing the mountain peaks before it with fire. Ascends. Its quick rays slipping down each cragged face, lighting it crest to foot. They touch the boulder strewn plain, charge across it, pushing the shadows into retreat, and drench the expedition in golden lustre. Sun heat penetrates the rider's spines and shoulders, warms the horse's legs. They lengthen their stride to traverse the flat brow of an east-west ridge standing proud in the dawn.

Then a steep ascent. The light hardens to illuminate stepped notches in solid rock continually rising. The deep cut ends far to the West, where its fractured flanks curve up to meet and form a shimmering, snow capped bowl, a porcelain wall cracked by one dark fissure marking a pass. Captain Masse's eyes follow an invisible line from the pass to where he stands. The trail, already suffering landslides and washouts, presses against the mountain side until they drop into the stone-littered bed of a dry river, its waters switched by an avalanche to a new channel farther down.

The horses tread doubtfully across the round stones, pigeon egg to fist dimension, mobile as greased bearings under their hooves. A goat-sized rock clatters down the slope opposite. It splinters into fragments when it hits a sharp boulder. Guzman dismounts, and hobbling the packhorse near him, takes a hand compass and a rangefinder from its saddlebag. He makes a series of observations, rotating his body in a half circle as he levels the compass at the steep slopes opposite. He turns to Captain Masse, preoccupied with prising a stone from the hoof of his horse's forefoot.

>―‹›―O―‹›―‹

'Captain, I believe the railway engineers will be forced to cut a series of switchbacks here. An expensive proposition. The slope is too steep.'

Bain points across the valley at a ragged cut, the rivers new bed, a horizontal slash in the rock wall facing them, just above a haphazard jut of stone terrace that breaks the mountainside's even slope.

'You are wrong, Guzman. That is where the rails will run,' he shouts, pointing at a horizontal flaw in the slope. 'A river has a natural intelligence brought on by gravity. Far more astute than human survey, it seeks perfectly the effortless path. I can already hear the sound of exploding powder, the clatter of steel on stone. The way will be easily cut through in a summer. Plenty of timber for trestles.'

'What do you know of the technicalities of the endeavour.' retorts Guzman.

'Listen to him Guzman, he is a man of some experience.' the Captain cuts in, taking both Guzman and Bain in his glance.

Guzman makes no reply, and occupies himself with repacking his instruments. Bain rides ahead, his head high, the practical man having defeated the professional one. Reid goads her unresponsive packhorse horse past the Captain and Guzman, to ride alongside Bain.

'It seems a river figures in your every observation, Bain. Have you forgotten your story? Please continue it, as much for the tale as for the surprising pleasure of your eloquence.'

'My eloquence is the result of much practice. Flowery speech like Guzman's in day to day life was not a habit amongst my people, in fact mistrusted. But at school, precise oratory was a respected subject, and eloquent speech associated with clear thinking, not bombast. Each year there was a district oratory contest with prizes. I entered school two years late, due to the education charter not being passed till my eighth year, when a school was then built. I suffered difficulty with arithmatic and reading, but in my sixth and last year, gained a silver medal from the Council for the Promotion of the Sciences with my address on rivers. Where was I in the yarn?'

'You had just looked upon the flood.'

'I wanted to throw stones into that flood, to touch the mirror water surface. It seemed a desire I would never fulfil. I lived the day without hope then at the hour before sunset my father set our biggest draft horse in the traces of his produce wagon. He offered to take any child that wanted to go into the flood. Mothers piled us in the back like bags of potatoes, repeating strict injunctions not to jump off or poke sticks into the wheel spokes. With the oldest child in the seat of honour beside the driver, we drove towards the flood we had heard so much about. My father seemed to have thrown off his usual dour air, and we sensed this and were soon screaming and laughing. This youthful exuberance was drained off by our first actual sight of the waters. Our voices failed us as we came close. There, at a point we would soon reach, land ended and water began. After that only the road's built'up surface rose above the inundation, which spread undisturbed to the horizon. The wagon's high wheels flipped up clots of mud as they spun in the wet clay. The old draught horse breathed deep, and settled in for a long jag of a pull.

'We passed onto the floodplain in silence. First, stubbled fields to right and left, then the water's edge, then water all around us. It grew so deep only fencepost tops could be seen. The littler children clutched at each other's sleeves and waists. I felt for a handhold inside the wagon. But no disaster struck. We looked down into the water rushing past a broom-handle-length away. We looked at each other. My grip on the wagon eased. Regaining our gall, we bounced and whacked each other, cheered our driver on, begged him to go farther. A can with its lid cut off sat beside my father's foot. Each time he managed to lead us back to the safety of centre road, he would take his eyes from the trail for an instant to launch a shot of black tobacco juice into the can's bottom.

'The track climbed a ridge. Wild rosebush clumps pushed up along its shoulders. We crested the rise. The road dropped, ending in a word I did not know at the time, a peninsula. With a whoop, we slid to a halt. Before us stretched a grand sea, the likes of which we had never seen. With our own movement stopped, we saw that all around us the water moved. It was alive, pushing through breaches in the natural levee to course past our spit of land. We watched its edge, now retreating the width of a hand, now advancing towards us two strides, stopping, advancing again. In front, the sun cut through the clouds. With the water flowing past on both sides, we seemed to be a ship steaming directly towards the sun.

'We stared up at my father. Were we to fear this inundation? Or could we fly in fantasy out over the surface, play tag with our reflections, dive to look through the clear water at tadpoles, surface to swim on our backs like whales, live all the stories and poems of the sea we had read in school but knew nothing about? My father said nothing, gave no sign. A flight of migrating ducks passed overhead but I did not look up. Head down I watched them slide in formation past my boot toes and away to meet their sky born doubles at the horizon and disappear, dropping down the earth's curve.

'I was succumbing to love, but my love was not perfect. Her water's were in truth brown with mud. The silver sheen was just the sky reflected. Night came as we trundled back. The sky went purple. Venus took her place in the east. The air turned cold. The stars lit themselves above us.

'Now inspired, whilst preparing the essay for my oratory, I found out much. My teacher was enthusiastic, and ordered several books which came by the new postal service. Rivers. Rivulets joining criks joining streams. These forming branch tributaries to feed the main course. Tropical; their waters hot, full of man eating fish, deadly snakes and crocodiles. Temperate rivers; friends of the human race since early times. The first communities were built upon their fertile floodplains, as my father told me, the first commerce took their winding courses, the first money lenders set up shop along their banks. In the old world, the subject of myths, of painters and novelists.

'And arctic rivers; Frozen with blue ice much of the year. Frigid, holding the northern species, charr and salmon. Good sleigh tracks in winter, estuary's breeding ground for whales in the summer.

'But what I learned was that rivers, like people, slide from vitality to fatigue. A flat and meandering river is old. It washes the land down to its mouth, and seeks to become the level of the sea. This was the river of my youth, running black with soil. Later, in the war, I saw one such run red with blood.

'Rivers like the one we traversed at the ferry are middle-aged rivers. Each year they rip chunks off the valley sides and flush them out. They eat up as much land as they spit out. Lofty mountain rivers are the young rivers. They have not made their mark upon the earth, only tumble from pond to lake, seeking a crevasse, a valley, their water not burdened with sediment, clear as air.

'These are the rivers I have never seen, the rivers of my quest. I am still in love, but I seek a pure and unsullied object for my love. I want to watch a river's virgin birth. My reasons for accepting commander Masse's offer to make this trip were many, but above all, it was to be the first person to see a river in her pure and complete vitality; reckless, powerful, untamed.

'I wish to look down into those clear waters, be at the point where the fearsome power of a flood begins. I want to feel that primary vigour, take it within myself. For it is only by seeing the source of a power that we can fathom it. The great and awesome flood I saw as a child began with the accumulation of water in mere cupfuls, criks I could dip water from in my hand. I want to drink from such pristine waters, imbibe their purity and strength. Such forces are the true revelation of God's power and will, the immaculate and elemental vitality of nature. The representation of God is not made in graven images, nor worship of him correctly done by bowing before them. God can be inhaled on the wind of a storm, drunk from the high mountain stream, smelt in the reek of red hot iron.

'But I, bound lover of rivers, seek God's presence where I may ken it. High, close to heaven, on the undefiled mountainside, at the place where a river is begot. To drink of this pure newborn water, this elixir, will be my act of communion with God.

'Why are you so confident Bain, that when you find the river, you will be the first person to see it, drink from it? The more I see of the country, the more I see that it has been, or is everywhere occupied, and that others have explored before us. It seems everywhere we find trails, or traces of hunting parties, or lone wanderers.

'Where we are going, no man has been? Of this I am certain, they told me so in the Capital. And the savages, do they count? They cannot read or write, have no history, have no books such as I have read. Discovery is not in their vocabulary. They are part of the land, not countable, or accountable as citizens. In their unpious rites they defile the very landscape they are but part of like the beasts. And where we are going, they are not capable of going, for from what I have seen, their travels are greatly limited by their ignorance and sloth. No Reid, when we arrive, we will truly be the first one's there, as God is my witness.'

'But Bain, there may be people everywhere. Look at this track. Hundreds have taken it. And at the outpost, where we will arrive hence, the Captain says we will seek a guide or guides, for the passage from tribe to tribe through the interior will require great diplomatic efforts if we are to travel swiftly and surely. If this is so, and so well known, what say you? Perhaps it would be better to presume that you will encounter other river worshippers on your pilgrimage, in fact may be part of some universal brotherhood.'

'I cannot appreciate your conclusions, Reid. I have shared much with you, and you seek to demean it. My pilgrimage as you call it is unique and I alone pursue it. The Captain signals me. We will speak no more of this, you have lost my trust. I do not wish to resume the subject.'

>—!—◆>—O—<◆—!—<

The two sides of the valley's hollow end, which from a distance looked innocent and welcoming as the open arms of a snowman, become an ivory quagmire. The horses struggle. The sun, twice reflected in the concave white mirror, heats their hides to steaming. The lead is switched every hundred paces, one animal punching trail in the clammy, breast deep mass then retreating to the rear.

The sun passes behind the valley rim. A sudden chill – the soaked men and animals shivering as the heated air rises toward the stratosphere – leaves the valley silent, darkening from indigo to purple. No bird call, no moaning wolf or coyote yelp. No hiss of wind.

Stiffening with cold, deeper into shadow, the expedition staggers up the snowbound trail. Short of the pass, still in tree line, they dismount. Captain Masse takes a pointed shovel from his packhorse, then shuffles, waist deep in snow, to a niche in the dense mass of timber, poking through the snow with the shovel point. The ground feels flat. He indicates to Reid to set the horses along the tree line's lee. Bain and Guzman unpack flat mouthed shovels, and bent beside Captain Masse, dig three rectangles through to lichen-covered rock. The Captain begins a forth alone, and after some protest, the two other men help.

Bent at the waist, swinging axes held at the handle's end so the sharp heads pass as far from their toes as possible, they quickly fell resinous pines, ankle thick at the trunk. They lay them, stripped of branches, parallel, as floors for the sites already dug. Reid brings the first trunk of waterproofed baggage, beginning a stack on one platform as tents are set on the other three. The cut branches are thrown into the tents, an aromatic emerald carpet.

>—!—◆>—O—<◆—!—<

rutal conditions. After half my allotment breaking trail, fifty paces, I could feel my new mount's foreleg quake with the strain. How strange there at the head, the incandescent bowl of the valley confine rising before me, the pass a tempting black fracture. How will we ever make it? I heard the Captain and Guzman muttering. Bain, each turn trailbreaking, counted out loud, "ninety-eight, ninety-nine, one hundred," and pulled off to let the Captain lead, which he did well, always going ten extra paces. These I counted. Yet for all the effort we were forced to bivouac and I would like to know by what miracle Captain Masse divined my nervousness at sleeping with the others.

In spite of the difficulties of making camp, here I am in my own tent. Practically my own. I share it with four saddles, six rifles, and the delicate photographic apparatus. My sole luxury is the fragrant pine bows. But I am alone. What ecstasy. Tonight I saw the others exhibit skills I have not. But I must master the line cutter's axe. Guzman explained it is a tool of the surveyor's trade, meant for cutting sight lines through the bush. Its handle is long to keep the head away from feet and knees. This latter is light so it can be carried in a pack, and honed to razor sharpness by holding a file on the head, and dragging it back and forth in an arc across the blade. This makes a perfect cutting edge, more like a knife than an axe. Bain issued me one for my own, with a file, and I sat late on the branches by candle light, sharpening it.

One constant preoccupation is the simpler bodily functions. Defecation is approached in a private manner. I am able to accomplish it as the others, but as I expected, the men seem to consider open air urinating a demonstration of camaraderie. Typically, they walk off some dozen paces, choose a small gully, turn their back, then proceed to evacuate whilst talking, head turned towards the listener. If the day is hot the odour is quite marked. I do not think anyone notices I forego this recurrent rite. The long days, on the open trail, I creep out in the early darkness and perform my tasks, yet even then, by the afternoon, I fear my bladder will burst or my eyes pop from my head when my horse vaults. I have learned to avoid drinking tea or too much water. I am inspired to find a solution, and think that there is perhaps a disguise, a bit of judicious fakery that would allow me to replicate the male anatomy and attendant ability. All I need is a piece of well worked, waterproof hide and a private hour with a needle and thread, ancient tools of the women's trade.

The sultry wind again finds its earth. It circles the expedition's quickly erected camp, growing pungent with cut conifer sap smell. Rolling into the bush, it softens snow in hollow and ravine, and expels chilly air collected in the entrance of a shallow cave. Another transient's abode. A hibernating bear. The bear's nerve ends, those spread across that patch of its thick hide facing the cave mouth, are fanned by the soft breeze and replying to what warmth is in it, send signals to the bear's brain of spring.

The bear has been aware, from the vibrations, of the activity nearby, the camp being set up, but these tiny tremors have stimulated no reaction. Its chilled body makes no demands, its comatose stomach feels no hunger...and danger? In its long life the bear has as not yet perceived a circumstance worthy of being interpreted as danger. Still, in the small part of its mind that has been assigned to winter-long watchfulness, the signals of warmth accumulate, and messages are sent out. First to the olfactory venation. It begins to smell. Odours of the sleeping camp; the horses, fresh-riven tamaracks, a damped-down fire, and one man, Guzman, for he had spilled ink upon himself, and scrubbed his shirt with soap to remove it.

More messages have gone out from the watchful core of the bear's brain, and now listening too, it laboriously cants its head so one ear faces the cave mouth.

The bear cannot see Guzman stick his head out the tent flap, nor, under starlight illumination, look upon the full thatch of his unplaited black hair, same colour as the bear's, or the reflected light glittering in his eyes. The bear hears Guzman blow a puffy cloud of condensing breath, then inhale, pressing his tongue to the roof of his mouth to constrict his larynx and cough, deep and hard, to clear his mucous-filled throat. It remains blocked. The bear recognises some labour in Guzman's breathing, and casually decides that he could be prey, but still feels no need to eat, thus, in this case to kill, though his stomach reacts and the bear farts, noiseless but rank, a half-season's accumulated digestion.

And in the same way Guzman cannot know, for he has no experience, that the rancid stink teasing his expert nostrils is a bear's. He thinks only of his unwashed comrades. So in this manner, the bear and the man are both ignorant of and have knowledge of each other, and, on this silent night, represent opposing predilections of all motile animals. The bear wants only to stay. The man wants only to flee.

Yet, finally, though it is the one with the simplest want, it is the bear that displays curiosity, listening with interest as Guzman again breathes deep, hawking to pull the flem up his bronchial tubes then exhale, unblocking his nose. A few quick snorts mould the night's slimy accumulations into a wad, and forming his lips into cylinder, like the barrel of a short gun, he spits a luxurious, thick gob of mucous and saliva. It splats several paces off, near the cave mouth, where stone meets snow, and he contemplates the distance achieved with satisfaction. Nostrils held between thumb and forefinger, he empties his lungs with a blast of air, blowing his nose clear. He flicks what snot has clung to his fingers into the snow, but it falls far short of his first gob.

The bear feels Guzman take a few steps in the direction of the cave, and his awareness quickens. Again, insensible muscle replying slowly, he turns his head full face to the entrance. He catches the acidic odour as, facing south, Guzman urinates, a shiver wracking his torso. The hot liquid steams, trickling towards low ground. The bear now knows this animal not far from his lair is male, and listens, and smells with greater care, ready to respond if the other beast approaches.

The mountains are a jagged silhouette against the pulsing firmament. Wind chatters in the tallest trees. The chill always companion to night's deepest hour settles over camp and cave. The bear waits, near making a decision. The pressure in his bladder relieved, Guzman turns, and crawls back into his blankets. His last thought, as he slips downslope towards sleep, is of the outpost they will soon reach and the possibility that some of its officers are billeted with their wives, he then drops into slumber deep as a trance. The bear too, its outer nerves no longer stimulated, its nose finding no new smells, its ears catching no sound, yields to its body's desire and regains the seductive void of hibernation.

Not half day's climb from the expedition tents, the temperate wind escapes this cooling earth. Free of terrestrial encumbrance, it ruffles a gale frayed shirt hung to dry in the pass the summer previous and forgotten. Pulled by lower atmospheric pressure in the next valley, where the day-warmed soil still retains some heat, the wind glides away from the camp, westward along the unbroken trail. Below the snow line, it thaws the fresh track to mud. Descending, it mingles with a huge bubble of temperate, smoky air caught in the cupped valley bottom and slows where the trail passes a scatter of mortarless fieldstone houses terraced into the slope, walls blue in the stellar light.

The wind eddies, rolling down rough paths between the houses, to pool around the tall, hexagon palisade of a fort. Its warm touch causes a young sentry at rigid attention over the palisade gate to drift asleep, but when his chin drops on his chest, his head jerks up, his eyes start open, and he looks up the trail between the houses, for though his eyes were closed, his ears have registered a sound.

Which originates from the structure farthest away from him along the trail, the first house the descending wind passed. Plumb walled, this building is elaborate for the location, with roof beams of squared poles, and a roof not sod, but sheets of tin, each sheet carried up from the rail head ten walking days below the pass. A glass window, a door with metal hinges, and a walled terrace with a table fashioned from a slate slab face the trail. A goat is tethered to the table leg with a fuzzy strand of jute. A hole has been heel-dug in the hard packed yard for children to roll pebbles. The wind penetrates an unmortared wall.

Inside, a low kitchen. A servant girl squats stiff and silent at the fire and drinks her tea. Holding her back from the cold stone wall, she sways towards the weak flame. Her body shape is indistinct and the robust clarity of her face in the firelight makes it seem too large for her frame. She skims a second round of the dark tea into her cup, and sips, one hand on each side of it. On these mornings, when it is her turn to light the fire, and the old woman is still asleep, she lets her hate for her mistress fill the room. It usually gives her a thrill of pleasure to feel so much fury, but today her pleasures are more concrete. Her man sleeps in the next room. Just another lodger as far as the landlady is concerned, but great things have been planned. The servant girl has her savings wrapped in a kerchief tied around her middle. Her man has two horses tied in the hostel's manger. And the high pass is open. An express rider has gone up through it and not come back, and an army scout reported that a party of West-bound travellers have been seen heading towards the fort. This will be the week she will escape. The only problem is the two children her man found. She must solve that today.

The sky above the smoke hole lightens. She snuffs her lantern. The goat bleats. She steps outside, into pale light. She wears three dresses with long skirts, arranged in layers, the lightest against her skin, the darkest and most grease stained on the outside. A thick bladed cutlass is tucked into her woven sash. Her sleeves are rolled to her elbows exposing brown, muscled forearms that bulge rhythmically as she pitches a forkful of hay to the goat.

The goat munches, its stance defensive, as if another animal might steal its morning meal. The goat is not alone on the levelled plot of land that surrounds the house on three sides. There is niche in the back wall. There, a prone shape stirs, moaning, startling the goat again. With a little more light, the shape's outline shows two figures, vaguely but possibly human.

Bending to the goat, the girl pulls her dark hair back and ties it with a red cord, tightening the skin around her eyes, emphasising their slightly downward cant above bevelled cheeks. She pulls the eating goat's teats, sending an ivory stream ringing into an enamel pot. When it is near filled, she goes behind the dwelling, and sets it beside the still prone, still slumbering, but now clearly human forms in the back wall's niche.

She looks up at the place in the east where the sky is lightest, tinted orange, where the side of the mountain pass facing her is deeply shadowed, vague and almost invisible, like the two shapes on her terrace. It is an assessing look, the look of a whaler scanning the sea, a prostitute a darkened street. It says, simply 'let there be movement there,' and with this thought, the girl returns to the fire, closing the brightly painted door behind.

In the outside wall's niche, one of the sleeping shapes moves, and the thick shadows allow the features of a head to be only just defined. It is a boy's head, and it seems that he is trying to confirm that the woman is no longer outside. This done, his head falls back on his straw pillow, and he adjusts the worn and ragged horse blanket covering him and the form beside him.

The person who still sleeps is his sister. The pair of them, ragged girl and boy, lie curled like two nested question marks at the spot along the stone wall the sun lit last, and heated most. Now the stones have given forth all their warmth and grown clammy with night cold. They emit discomfort into the boy's spine. He pulls away from the wall, and nestles his sister in a tighter curve against his stomach, breathing lightly in her ear, saying, within in his mind, projecting the thought with such force his toes curl, 'Sister, sister, wake. I will put my finger tips upon your eyes. If you love me blink once. If you are able to run blink twice.'

In the congealed light, more setting moon blue than rising sun red, a blue the shade of a vein just under the skin or the edge of a bruise three days after a wounding, he massages her large shoulders, and long arms, working her spine straight. Her hands, elbows and knees are thickly callused. As she sleeps, she pants, and frequently bares her teeth. She groans, writhing inside a loose, animal hide doublet covering her from calf to throat.

Her brother, taller, older by several years and less callused except his feet, also wears an animal hide. He reaches past her, pulls fistfuls of scattered straw over them both, straw littered with chicken faeces, reeking of goat urine. He builds the insulating quilt high. The heat within accumulates but does not ease him. He opens his eyes, stares at the low fading moon, his expression seeming to wish it away, as if its light was the source of his discomfiture, an irritant.

He convulses with the distraught fervour of an insomniac, rubbing his fists into his eyes, drawing his hands across his nose, sniffling, coughing. He stretches his limbs, thrashes, yet the warming contact of his stomach against his sister's back remains constant.

It is difficult to read the boy's face. It is at the same time blank – no recognisable expression comes across it – and extremely active, for the boy appears to have no conscious control over the twitches and ticks that torment his brow, cheek and lips. Yet, the whole effect of his expression is to convey a sort of distraught terror. He seems to be remembering, or trying to remember something, there is enough decipherable in his expression to imagine that, and the incompetence of his effort is what frightens.

The pain of the boy's double expression, simultaneously empty and full, could arise from a powerful sensation that his memories have a life of their own, and they do not allow him access. He looks as if he can only feel them, far away on some cognitive horizon, like a lost homeland across a river to which the bridge has been destroyed. In his most desperate moments, when his face is a battleground of conflicting aspects, it could be imagined he would like to return somewhere, or knows there is a place to return to, but knows little else, least of all the way to it.

Yet, aside from this profound internal confusion, the boy appears in intimate and secure contact with the world around him. His head moves to catch every sound, and he digests the information confidently, the wild animal and bird sounds, the goat, and the domestic noises now coming from the other side of the wall.

He may have lived both lives, the animal and the human. And this may be his desperate distress – the certainty of his own humanity, which he is conscious of, and his uncertainty his sister's, of which she herself is not aware. He touches her rigid limbs, feels the animal in them. He smells her foetid breath, the reek of beast upon it. He hears her groans and grunts, absolutely unmodified by speech, and is wounded by the wildness in them.

And through the wall at his back, in contradiction, as if a metaphor for his own mental state, he hears the meticulous human sounds of the innkeeper's servant girl stirring something over the fire. Thus, the external world reflects his internal one, one side bestial, one side human. He understands what the girl is doing from the tiniest sonic hints. He hears her blow on the coals to bring the flame, hears her rip a sheet of bark and cast it on the fire and hears the popping as its oily sheaves catch flame, then deeper detonations after she throws on a pine knot.

Household affairs inside the dwelling occupy all morning and the front door is not opened till well past noon. Again it is the servant girl who does this, to fling some scraps to the goat, and to again look up towards the pass, which is now sunlit mountainside. So she is the first person to see the expedition arrive. A straggled row of mounted men and pack horses struggling down the mud-covered trail. One of them, apart and ahead of the group, turns to look up at the pass.

In the hour it takes the expedition to complete its journey down from the pass, the servant girl looks at it twice. She counts the number of riders, the number of pack animals, and sees that no horses limp. The possibility of her escaping the very next day, or the one after, becomes more concrete. In that same hour the trail, the lanes and paths that extend it towards the fort, the front and backyards of the houses and the drill field outside the fort, all are set into the last stage of thaw by the sun. The runoff water, the water frozen in the soil and the remaining snow, pool and soak into the clay, rendering it a knee deep, at times waist deep mire too liquid to walk or ride upon, too thick to row a boat or paddle a canoe across. And from its heated surface, wherever water moves, rises a silent insect vapour, the first black flies. And from any standing or stagnant water rises, with falsetto shrieks, a graphite vapour of mosquitoes.

Upon the fort's palisade, a lieutenant with a telescope observes the expedition navigate the last section of the trail. A young man raised along the shore and familiar with boats, he has the distinct impression of watching a line of primitive and clumsy watercraft forge upstream against a heavy current. The struggling horses' hooves mire in the mud at every step. They row with their forelegs so their bellies can slide over the greasy goo. Two men dismount, to ease the animals, and find they cannot walk. They stumble, ungainly, like mariners who have jumped from a dory too far from shore and are foundering in the surf.

Above each labour-heated living thing, man and beast, floats a wavering, opaque column of flies. The men beat their hands in front of their faces. The horses twitch their flanks, and their tails are in constant sweeping movement.

The sun grazes its apogee, strong in a clear sky. The ground grows hot for the first time in a half a year. Rank mud, old mud, within it bubbles of suspended methane gas expanding. The cool smell of newly wet, slippery clay – the smell a sculptor knows. The reek of winter's accumulated offal, in outhouse, stable and field; horse a light bouquet, pleasing to the nostril, mule more insistent, turning the head. Donkey, elemental faecal matter – nose wrinkling. Cow odiferous, vegetal, rotted to a high state, inoffensive in shade, oppressive in sunlight, non-existent where desiccated. Pig putrid, sour, searing the nose's lining and scratching the throat. Chicken, acrid but weightless, drifting up on the air and away.

Human faeces variable. The alcoholic priest, metallic. The feverish baby's mustard sharp; bingeing prospector beer mash ripe, a full and stagnant strata supplemented by the sour bite of uric acid; carnivorous hunter potent, a severe odour heavy with protein lying close on the ground; dysentery racked prostitute runny, mucous rimmed and caustic; opium addicted porter odourless and hard as a lump of coal.

The cacophony of rubbish heaps; chatter of rancid coffee grounds, hum of moulding bread. The sigh of coagulated bacon fat and shriek of spittoon jetsam. The groan of filthy washing cloths and blood-and-pus-soaked bandages. The soft murmur of potatoes, beans and carrots. The yelp of onions and bark of garlic from the smoke hole of the woman's house.

Her kitchen growing so hot she must open the door, the girl looks up the trail a third time, standing under its red-trimmed lintel, flipping her hand in front of her face at the insects. She's tied string tight around her wrists, and thankful she has not washed with soap, the odour which would bring them to her in clouds, she drops her two outer layers of skirts to her ankles. She sees the erect riding posture of the lead horse's rider, the military pack saddles, and is wondering if she will be made to cook a meal when the Captain stops a few paces before the door of her building, not having to rein in his horse, just relaxing his grip so the animal can stop. Smoke seeps from the chimney hole. He smells hot fat.

'Do you think she has tea on?' asks Reid, 'or perhaps soup, a bit of meat?'

'You have seemed so reluctant to eat meat these last days Reid. Why the sudden interest,' replies the Captain.

'Let us stop, take a mid day meal, the journey is done.'

'It is not done till we reach the army post.'

'Are we a military expedition, Captain?'

'We are whatever I say we are, and we have no monies to pay this harpy the outrageous price she will charge.'

'I will pay, Captain.'

'Why not, Captain,' chides Guzman. 'We are here, the bugs will be as extant anywhere, in fact, judging by her primitive lack of chimney, I would say the interior of this place will be quite comfortable.'

'We are travelling in a semi-official capacity, Guzman. The first contact must be with the Commander of the fort.'

'By all means, make that contact, Captain.'

Guzman dismounts and wades through the mud to the patio where the girl stands. With a few words, he determines that she is a servant. Ducking his head to miss the thick lintel, he steps inside, to return, the heavy set, grey-haired land lady in tow.

'She'll have the cook prepare tea, then a meal. They have chickens they are going to kill.'

The old woman shouts. A side door opens. A girl, much younger even than the early riser, pokes her head out. By her face, she could be daughter, or niece to the proprietress. She sets a metal pan on the flagstone. The servant girl grabs at one of the chickens pecking where the earth is drained and dry. She catches it by the neck, her palm covering its eyes, her thumb pressing hard at the base of its head and with a twist of her wrist, whirls the animal's body once around in a wide arc, snapping its neck at the same time she pinches its head off where the vertebrae have separated. She throws the body to the younger girl who, urged on by the proprietress, has come out of the painted door balancing plates of beans. She rolls her sleeves down. The girl picks up the blood drooling headless body and plucks its feathers, stuffing them in a jute sack. When four birds are ready, she disappears inside. The servant girl picks up the severed heads and tucks them into her outer skirt.

>─┼─◇─◯─◇─┼─◁

*T*he Captain is in a rage and it is I who have prodded him. We are not an army unit under his command. We are paid professionals. In any event, he has ridden off to the fort in a sulk sparked by our inconsequential rebellion. The rest of us have stayed, Bain after asking the Captain's permission. I could not go another step in this mud. And the bugs. They are much less here, now that the wind is up. What a delightful idea it is to think of

someone else preparing us a meal. The tender, white flesh of a chicken.
Beans, simmered for hours in a pot.

A motley low roofed hamlet spreads itself before us, mired in muck. The
fort seems from another time, with its palisade of pointed vertical logs, flagpole and cannons. As does this extraordinary mixed-blood woman, with her
servant girls, of bloodlines even more diverse. She reckons a canny wench.
This house, or inn, is well placed. Every hungry or thirsty traveller entering
the locality must pass it. The smell of her cooking pot alone was overpowering. She must get steady customers all the summer months. And from her
looks at the men, I assume she offers other delights of the evening, for I see
the unmistakable outline of a distillation apparatus in her back yard, and her
girls, if I can assume that a certain type of glance retains its meaning everywhere, have talents beyond those of assistant cook.

[Captain Aaron Masse] Day 17

Wind SW, calm but rising, clear. Arrival at Fort. An important
time to observe men, the release of tension after a difficult passage can be telling. Some defiance manifested in unruly behav-
iour by Reid (not surprising given his youth) & Guzman (not
surprising given his artistic character) but I judge neither muti-
nous. The secret of command is never to give a man an order he
will disobey. They remain, with our pack animals, at a trailside
hostel on the outskirts of this community.

I proceeded to the Fort to pay my respects to the
Commander & seek some permanent lodging place that will
allow us comfortable stay. I sit outside his office at this moment.
Faces around show varied racial origins. About the settlement a
number of handbills & broadsides pertaining to our recent
nationhood. Those tacked to the fort gate indicate a vital, yet
divisive population, Some examples, the first not immodest:

"...a young empire of the mind, and power, and wealth, and
free institutions, rushing up to a giant manhood with a rapidity
and power never before witnessed under the sun. And she will
carry with her the elements of her preservation, the experiment
will be glorious – the joy of a nation – and the joy of the whole
earth, as she rises in the majesty of her intelligence and benevolence, and enterprise, for the emancipation of the world..."

"...I stress the urgency and advisability of building a
transcontinental railway across the continent as the only means

by which troops might be moved quickly to any threatened area. These must function in connection with trans-oceanic steamship lines. Many commercial advantages will accrue from these arrangements, but the stress must be made on defense..."

"...what percentage of the local inhabitants would be effective as of Cavalry and what of infantry? I recommend those of mixed blood. They are adept horsemen, the only persons mounted capable of function when the thaw or rains have reduced the plain to an endless sea of muck. Quite remarkable for their activity on foot, and from their constant use of the snowshoe in winter, could during that season when the employment of horses would be impracticable on account of the depth of snow, perform journeys on foot which the whites are not capable of. All this, and in addition is the familiarity with river navigation by canoe large and small as well as flatboat. There is no doubt in my mind of the loyalty of the mixed blood population..."

I wonder about this last statement. Inside the Fort, only soldiers, strangers to this place. Two types: raw recruits from urban areas, utterly naive as to the life here, or men drawn from the frontier – an often brutal place. Either way, I sense no respect for the dominant population, the mixed bloods. They are allowed into the Fort reluctantly & treated as second class citizens thence. I cannot see how this would inspire loyalty. But I will await my meeting with the commander before forming opinions.

Reid will soon have his job of work set out. Bain is happy. He anticipates being in the company of soldiers. Guzman too, takes pleasure in this shabby place, I know not why. We will do well here.

>-⬦-O-⬦-<

What joy to consume a meal cooked by another, in the smoky but insect free confines of the little inn, and pay for it at the end. As we await the word of Captain Masse, who seems to be in the fort negotiating, we check our baggage, it being impossible to keep still in the bug dense air.

One strange thought lingers. I am quite certain that I heard additional human sounds, and saw human shapes without the dim confines of our eating place. An extra presence, human, yet feral. The sounds and faint images

play upon my thoughts. I cannot dismiss them, like one cannot dismiss a sound heard in the forest outside the tent on a moonless night. Such impressions effect us more for what they could have been than perhaps for what they were.

<hr />

[Captain Aaron Masse] Day 18

Wind calm.. At this time no suitable guides. We have longer stay than anticipated, perhaps two weeks, even three. The Commander of the Fort relates that migration pattern of the natives in the interior has changed dramatically. The tribes we should be put in contact with, that are peaceful yet far ranging enough & polyglot, have not appeared, whereas they usually have by this time. The Commander attributes this to caprice.

I know better, having seen the migration patterns of the food species, the birds & animals, change with the flux of plant growth as well as their own interactions. A high population of coyotes brings about a low population of deer. A low population of coyotes allows a high population of deer but these eat all the soft parts of the plants early in the season & must migrate. Guzman concurs. Anyone killing said species for food must migrate also. These are probably the factors underlying the tribes' "impulsive" actions.

Issued the men lengths of fine gauze to protect them from the bugs. I counted, upon my own body, seven kinds: mosquitoes, tiny biting black flies, a smaller hard-bodied insect referred to as no-see-um, one wood tick from my walk on a dry grassed ridge, blood suckers (leeches) as they are called here which live in the mud and two types of biting, soft winged fly; the horse fly & the deer fly.

Of interest are their bites. This I learned from a doctor tending our troops when many succumbed to malaria. The mosquito inserts a probe. The small flies nip through the skin. The larger flies seem to rasp away the skin & create a kind of drinking place for blood. The tick digs in, guzzling to fill its abdomen. The leech seems to render the skin transparent, the blood then passing through it.

<hr />

The Captain has issued clever nets to protect us from the insects. This has stopped everyone spitting, the one aspect of my disguise that has been a failure, and caused me to respect a male habit which I thought required no skill. Expectoration. Guzman is by far the best. He deposits his spittle, from his horse, a good five paces away at the place of his choosing and is a proud marksman. Fortuitously, I made my first attempts while off by myself. A terrific mess dribbling down my chin and onto my coat. I tried several times, alternating techniques, but to no avail, so I have been watching the men surreptitiously. Each has a different routine. The captain is very discreet. He leans his head to one side, and forming a small opening at the lower corner of his mouth, spits out a compact gob, using air pressure alone. Bain, who has a brief gap between his upper incisors, uses this to advantage, forcing a stream of spit through it at high velocity using air pressure and his tongue. Guzman begins with an intake of breath through his nose, thus delivering all mucous in it to his throat. He then collects this at the back of his mouth with a sharp snort, which brings any stray matter up from his throat. Thus collected, with a snap of his diaphragm, he launches his slimy projectile through lips formed into a tight barrel. An elaborate, but effective procedure. I vow to practise.

Suddenly came to mind my thoughts as a young girl, early imaginings of disguising myself as a boy, this from watching a bunch of them play games on the empty field next to our house. Never a girl amongst them they caught balls, dug in the mud with sticks, pitched stones at birds and squirrels, punched and kicked each other, tore the knees of their trousers and elbows of their shirts, and went home for supper, ragged, filthy, exhausted, and I was certain, utterly joyous. I imagined myself becoming one of them, stealing the clothes of the cook's young son which she would wash with our own. I practised. What defeated me was launching a stone in a flat trajectory with a hard over arm throw. I could not master it, and I felt the same way some days ago when I was trying to teach myself to spit. When and where do the males of the species learn these esoteric talents? Oh that I would have had a brother.

We are to be stationed here a time. There is no permanent lodging available. Our field tents, erected on platforms with board floors, shall house us. If I have divined the Captain's intentions correctly, he wishes me to unpack and begin practising with my gear. How tantalizing, though in this mud-covered sprawling place, there is little to inspire the aesthetic sensibility. Why did we, as a race, cross a wide ocean to come...here?

I had conceived a world of landscape...but everywhere there are people of all races and sizes. Why did I think that somewhere the earth was unoccupied, that it was waiting to be "discovered"? There are all around native peoples. Tall and short, well dressed and shoddy, angry and pacific. Some scrounge around the edge of this sodden place, looking for scraps, appearing, disappearing. Others ride proudly into the centre, demanding respect, radiating a warlike confidence, inspiring fear. These are the people Bain dismissed as below the bottom line of the human scale. I would debate him on that now, but he no longer talks to me. Why did they, already here, allow us occupancy?

Most intriguing of all are those whose faces show mixed blood. They, the new race, seem proof of the will to live instilled in us. They are the adaptive ones, like our lady inn keeper, our first contact here – aware of the foreigner's, and the native ways in equal amount. So much cleverness and vitality.

I feel casualty to this idea of landscape, the idea of pure, unsullied wilderness. Such ideas not only deny what I see before me, the occupation of these lands by those who live here, but the beauty of all that we the human race have accomplished. The veritable trace of our existence. If perfection is that which is untouched, even if there is some place untouched, what of the day when we have touched all. Are we then forever imperfect? Bain's philosophy comes to mind. And my own question to myself. I am a lover of what? I do not know, but this mad, mud buoyed place stirs something within my breast.

An unromantic desire to comprehend. A deep desire to master my new apparatus and render what I see on the sensitive plate. Tomorrow, I will unpack the expedition equipment assigned to me. The bill of lading informs there is both a stationary and a portable darkroom.

➤—◀◆▸—◯—◂◆▸—◄

[insert, for Captain Masse by J. Reid, expedition photographer]

The following apparatus unpacked, found to be entirely undamaged, and checked against the bill of lading. No discrepancies.

1 full trough Nitrate Bath
1/2 pint additional Nitrate Bath
15 measures Plain Collodion
5 measures Iodizing Solution
5 measures Cadmium Collodion
Collapsible canvas bucket
1 measure bromide iodizer
2 measures Ether and Alcohol
3 measures absolute Alcohol
3 measures spirits of wine

Various size stoppered bottles
3 Developing glass 12 drachms
1 Minum Measure
Scales and Weights
Gutta Percha Funnel
Full plate Gutta Percha tray
Half plate Gutta Percha tray
Spare dipper for nitrate bath
Broad Camel's hair brush
Pneumatic Plate Holder

1/2 measure Pyrogallic Acid

4 measures Glacial Acetic Acid

1/2 measure Citric Acid

1 measure Sulphite of Iron

8 measures Hyposulphite of Soda

Bottle saturated Hyposulphite

Bottle Varnish

1 drachm Carbonate of Soda

Bottle Pyrogallic

Dropper bottle Nitrate Bath

100 flatted glass full plates

200 flatted glass half plates

Sliding Box Folding Camera

Bellows camera half plate

1/2 Quire Blotting Paper

Linen cloth and chamois

2 cotton hand cloths

1 bundle yellow calico

1 bundle black calico

1 sponge

lump Marine Glue

Ball of string

Paper of pins

2 stoppered bottles

Grooved box to accommodate

Grooved box to accommodate

Focusing glass to fit

Focusing glass to fit

Single Landscape (30 degree, F15) achromatized lens

Doublet (21 degree, F3.5) portrait lens

Universal lens (F7) in brass tube Aperture stops F4 to F56

Brass bound ash tripod

Half plate portable darkroom

Full plate transportable darkroom

Camera base and set screws

Pack frame

Framing poles, pegs, floor

[Captain Aaron Masse] Day 20

Sky clear. Hot. The land dry as suddenly as it grew wet, and the flies somewhat abated, allowing preparations to continue in comfort. Above entry confirms all photographic apparatus in good condition. Have arranged for a floored tent to be erected, there being a stand of tamarack nearby will suit this purpose if stripped and laid stump to tip. Pump water & a stone sink are available in the officer's mess of the Fort.

The boy lays his head back on his straw pillow. The flies hover over him and his sister but few alight. Unlike everyone else this day, he makes no move to repulse them, does not seem to notice them as he listens to the sounds coming from within the house. The wall is warm now, and to hear more clearly, he shifts his head, to set his ear at a gap in the mortar. The servant has placed a tray of food scraps and the four severed chicken heads near him. He takes a bone stripped of flesh, snaps it, and sucks its marrow out.

With the coming of daylight his mind has calmed, and his memories are no longer inextricably mingled with nightmare. One recollection comes clear, the connections to it still intact. A memory from before, which is how the boy has divided the things he feels in his head..."before" and "after." The sounds coming from within the woman's kitchen are from before. Sounds made by women. The person who is making the sounds he calls "woman"...not the woman. He knows that during these sounds, the air within the walls becomes heated by a bright thing, the fire, that he has no specific word for but more a category that includes the sun, and that it is not necessary to huddle for warmth if you are inside. He also knows that the product of what the fire is also light, the same as from the sun. Things can be seen inside even at night, somewhat like in the day.

The boy knows too that some time after the heat and light, food will come. Warm food that only has to be chewed a little bit. A kind of food he can sometimes like. The soft interior of a bone, the round hot shape of a potato, the stringy mass of a piece of meat. His sister will not eat this food. She would always rather climb a tree for bird's eggs or pick nuts off the ground or root for tubers.

His nostrils dilate as he smells the fire. Its pine and birch and poplar smoke is drifting low in the wet air of a windless early morning. He smells also the human odour of someone he calls "the man." Not a general category of "men" but a specific one. "The man." This is a dim memory, without defined edges but deep and inescapable that covers the periods before and after. "The man" is inside the room. He hears him now. He knows his morning sounds – is able to attach images to the sounds of the days when he and his sister were inside with him. The boy presses his ear to the gap in the mortar. Inside, the servant girl speaks in a low, pleading tones with a man.

'I got to do something about them younguns,' says the man. 'Found'em, but I don't want'em. What could a trapper do with two half animals? I tell ya, they was live'n with wolves. The filly, she don't hardly know how to walk on her hind quarters.'

'Are you going to keep your promise and take me. Working here is nothing but drudgery. She's got me up before sunrise and I'm not abed till long after it sets.'

'I'll keep my promise. Three days most before we head down the trail. The buyers will be at the fort soon. I want to get these furs in first. I got ermine, mink, fox. I'll get big money and we'll set out a land claim and build a house. I haven't thought of anything but you all, don't worry yourself. I'm bound to you as you're bound to me...body and soul.'

'Can't leave them to die. The old woman, she'd let them wander into the bush. They act like animals, but they're people.'

'I know. They need some kind of doctor. They ain't stupid, specially the lad. They got to get all the learning they missed I figure. Too complicated for me all that. I want my own tykes. Raise 'em good, not leave 'em to the wolves like them poor beggars.'

'Me too, I want my own.'

The boy feels his sister convulse and loses interest in the conversation inside the hut. Her eyes under her eyelids roll to some amorphous dream or nightmare. Her lips pull back from her gums like a grazing horse's and she inhales, a staccato burst of snorts. The boy rolls to face her. Her eyes burst open, as she's emerged from a horrific depth. She shakes, flailing her limbs and trying to get on all fours. The boy restrains her, squeezing her to him until she ceases to thrash. When she has calmed, he picks a small boiled potato from the plate near him and holds it to her mouth. She twists her head away, refusing it. He takes a bite himself, and offers the potato again but she refuses. He picks up one of the chicken heads. She snaps it from his fingers, sucks what little blood and raw flesh can be taken from it, and begins a stuttering moan of complaint. The boy slips his hand across her mouth to muffle her, for the voices on the other side of the wall have risen sharply. He knows this means conflict, and conflict can mean danger, which would be bad, or an opportunity to escape, which would be good.

He knows the sounds communicate. He does not understand these particular sounds, but in another of the clear spots in his brain are sounds that are his own, that he learned when he too lived inside with people, sounds that still wait there, like a dark house at the end of an unlit street, to be reopened and used, so he leans his ear towards the chink in the mortar, still retraining his sister. He listens with care, and hears rhythms in the exchange, rising inflections that mean questions, falling ones that mean answers. He does not know he and his sister are the subject of the discussion. He has picked out "the filly", "the lad", from the man's vocabulary and memorised them. He hears anger or concern, but no love in the intonations. He does not feel fear at this, but knows that it means no one will help him, that it is all up to him to save himself and his sister, to find what he needs to cross back over the murky gap in his mind and get to the place of memories of a warm fire, a soft voice, cooked food, the language he could still understand.

He looks at his sister's face so close to his. He is troubled by her. He can imagine himself learning the habits of the beings on the other side of the stone wall. He knows how to move and wait in ways that do not scare them or make them angry. He prefers to walk straight. His sister knows not of these things. She feels fear, and she causes fear. She will only eat what she has learned to eat in the bush. She will not stand straight, will not go out in the sunlight or sleep covered in a bed. She pulls potatoes straight from the fire and eats them hot. She takes fright at horses and lays down with any sleeping dog she sees for the warmth. The boy does not know what to do with her, and knows that the people inside the hut do not know either. From within the hut, the man slips into a long monologue.

'It's been two years I seen'm round the winter cabin. Seen their footprints and had'em steal food. That valley's a hot valley. Got desert parts with cactus. Never did find where they stayed, but normal winter I don't think life would be too hard. Lots of fish in the rivers and wild apples and plums.

'Always had the funny feeling someone visited them every once in a while or something. The filly she acts like an animal. She's spent time with coyotes or wolves sure. Maybe that's where they wintered, in a den, for the warmth.

'Lad's different. He's the one sought me out this winter. Hard winter. Hardest I've seen. They were about dead. They'd come around but wouldn't come near me. I had to trap the filly with a noose, and she got away twice. The lad would run off but he'd come back on his own. He understands talk in a way. If I say lad he turns his head. And I think I heard him mumbling some kind of gibberish to the filly one night when she wouldn't settle down. A full moon. Almost sounded like a lullaby. He knows about cooking too, knows what the fire and pots are for.'

'I'm not having him in here,' the woman snorts, 'if that's what you mean. I don't care if he was pageboy to the King. He may be a lad now, but he'll be a buck soon. You can imagine the trouble that will bring. And they stink those two. The lass will wreck things.'

'I'm just saying there's something there, human like.'

'There or not there, let's be sensible. When do you start down?'

'In a week or less, and you're coming with me, sure.'

'Then I've got to find somethin' quick. I'm not having them with me, but I'm not having them on my conscience either. They should go back to whoever left'm. Who do you think that was?'

'The way they look, flat forehead, one of the interior tribes. Maybe all their people were killed, or died from starvation. That happens. Don't know...but I'd put my money on the interior.'

'Well then, I've got to find a way to start them back.'

*M*y first professional exchange with the Captain. He requested a meeting in his tent and I went with some trepidation, sure he was going to upbraid me for my impertinence when we arrived at the post's outskirts, but no, he had serious issues to communicate.

I am to master my apparatus as quickly and economically as I am able, then set up, with as much precision as possible, a portrait studio like the one I have just left. I will be given two soldiers to help me for two days. I have at my disposal also a well with clear running water and a small room in a well heated, well insulated officer's quarters.

The Captain explained several things to me I would never have guessed at. For one, part of our funding is from the nascent National Geographic Society. Their wishes are part of the reason Captain Masse pressed me into service. Well aware of the changes wrought by the advancing frontier and the rapid dissolution of many of its local people's, they have supplied a grant for a type of "ethnographic" survey. A large series of portraits.

Here I see an opportunity. The work will be displayed in the national capital. My reservations, and recent musings about the veracity of photography, its actual potential, must have shown in my tone of voice or on my face, for when I told the Captain that it seemed the local people had already disappeared, or were corrupted, he understood. No rebuke was forthcoming.

He perturbs me. Brutal one moment, sensitive the next. A cliche perhaps...but there I was, again ready to chide him, thinking automatically that he would be imperious and unyielding yet in fact his thinking was far advanced from mine. He told me he had observed the changes of the past ten years in great detail. It was not the pristine simplicity of the native tribes that he thought should be captured. What should be documented was the strange blending of race and cultures that is the reality surrounding us. He informed me that this was not exactly what the society wanted, but he was willing to defend me. Although the work might prove less popular with the naive and the romantic, in the long run, a factual document would prove most valuable, and also more reflect the Society's mandate, which, if I understand, is to pursue the fact of culture, not the illusion.

Hearing this gave me great relief as a person, and exited me professionally. For a brief moment we were co-conspirators, plotting our revolutionary act. He counselled me to take care to make flattering, quarter-plate portraits of all the officers as well as a large group portrait of the enlisted men. In addition, I should take several landscape studies and look around for some "primitive" subjects so that a few images may be sent back to the capital to assuage any doubting minds in the Society.

⊱─┤◆├─○─┤◆├─⊰

Captain Masse, standing in the doorway of a solid timber shed set at the nucleus of the fort, salutes towards the building's interior. The rising movement of his arm is effortless, the final cock of his elbow economic, and the parallel fingers of his good hand just touch his eyebrow, steady an instant, then drop to his side. He turns on his heel, and a blue-sleeved arm closes the door from within. The back to back L shaped ridges that have hung above his eyes since the expedition left the railhead are gone. He looks around the interior of the fort with, although it is too understated to be called a smile, a look of consummation. He sees an inner courtyard of packed earth large enough for a hundred men on horseback to muster, a flagpole, three storeys high, of barked, perfectly straight pine, its base surrounded by melon-round rocks, and the inside of the stockade wall, resinous, barked spruce logs twice his height. Below its top edge, set so the soldiers standing on it can peer over the edge, yet with an easy movement duck behind the wall, is a horizontal balcony running the whole perimeter of the interior and serviced by a number of stout, steep ladders with sapling handrails. At each corner, the distance between them farther than a strong arm could throw a stone, a taller bastion supports a brass cannon. Their muzzles cover every approach. The bore of each barrel would just accommodate an adult head.

Crossing the yard, the Captain mounts a ladder near the two braced doors securing the palisade's only opening. He salutes the soldiers standing above each doorpost. This salute is slower, softer, and his body does not tense. He clatters along the catwalk to a point where the inward swing doors meet to close. Here, the palisade has been built up, on both sides, higher than the top of his head. Exactly where the doors meet, at the Captain's eye level, a hole large enough for a fist to has been augered through the waist-thick centre log. Through it, a wide angle view of the stone bordered entrance to the fort, the outpost's main concourse which directs all traffic into it, a well drained flat area below where a number of tents, both domed and peaked, have been set up, and the mountains beyond is given anyone who presses their eye to the circular aperture.

Captain Masse does just this, spreading his legs to a comfortable stance and bracing the stub of his handless arm in a notch between two logs. Satisfied with his commanding panorama, he turns. From the catwalk, he is also able to survey the complete interior of the fort; the Captain's hut, the two storey officer's quarters, the enlisted men's long, low barracks, the gabled horse barn, its attached stockade, the mud-mortared stone godowns, a large building attached to them, and both the entrance door and interior when it is opened of the fort's administrative office, the only structure which seems to have a floor worth keeping clean, for it is the only door with a boot scraper and a stoop.

Captain Masse turns to the guard at his left.

'Where are the horses, I hear no sounds from the barn.'

'We picket the pack animals behind the fort, sir. The riding horses are turned out in the hills. We bring them back to the fort and put them in the horse stockade every night, with an armed guard. There's still danger from horse thieves, but I think your animals will be safe out for a few nights. They need feed after your trip.'

'The administrative building's bigger than the Captain's office?'

'We have the largest staff of any post. We're the supply depot for the Northern station. A lot of men work here, and we buy meat from the natives as well as from the mixed-bloods who hunt and fish on contract.'

'What's that building beside administration, where the civilian is opening a door?'

'That's for the exclusive use of the native trade sir. Look, here they come, the second tribe out of the hills this spring. They have to stand in front of the gate till we grant them admittance. Those two are envoys. The band'll come in later. The situation is tense because their enemies are camped down on the flat. See those round-topped tents. If the trader gives out tobacco, that means he wants to deal. Those two will take it back to the tribe and they'll smoke it, then come in. Part of the arrangement will be that they cannot make war while in sight of the fort. We will train two cannons on them, and two cannons on the other tribe. Any trouble, and the greater part of the killing will be done by us, from a safe distance.'

The other soldier approaches along the catwalk. Under his arm he clasps what appears to be a bundle of three sticks. He touches Captain Masse on his shoulder.

'Captain. Commander sent message you will be here all day. Take this sir, we're not allowed to sit but you may. Lunch and tiffen will be brought up to you sir, compliments of the Commander also.'

Captain Masse unfolds the bundled sticks, which become the three legs of a canvas camp stool. He sets it on the catwalk, but does not take his eye from the observation hole. The two envoys enter the fort, both passing under the catwalk, their heads an arm's length from his boot soles. The hair has been shaved from the sides of their skulls, leaving a bristled central strip that runs from forehead to nape, where the hair has been allowed to grow long, and is braided into a single thick plait decorated with bead and feather. As they enter the trade warehouse, another pair of envoys, long haired, walk up from the encampment, but are refused entrance.

>─┼─◆─•─O─•─◆─┼─<

[Captain Aaron Masse] Day 22

Sky clear. Wind light NW. Most fruitful meeting with Commander of this post. His company fought alongside us during the last six months of the war, albeit in another battalion. Old times aside, he conferred good council. Our efforts are not without precedent, so many factors that seemed unknown can be predicted. However, no-one has completed the trek through the Northwest angle, all the way to the sea, & this is were we are ordered to go. What will come to pass there is a matter of conjecture. I place us in God's hands. The river courses are by all reports ferocious, but the good Commander agrees with me that they shall inevitably yield the best passage through the mountains for a railway.

The Commander postulates that our true contest will not be geographic, but tribal. He has been little in the deep interior, but even the most ingenious traders have difficult times there. Each valley has a separate language and custom. There is little travel between them. Their peoples seem more similar by the altitude at which they live, the temperature, the plants they eat and the animals they hunt, than by their attachment to a specific location.

Must explain this to Guzman. He, like myself, imagined our mapping problem to be one of horizontal planes. From what the Commander says, some of the maps, of minerals, fauna, and especially the "ethnographic" maps desired by the Society, may also have to have a component that indicates the vertical plane, for the placing of the aforesaid rocks, plants and peoples is much more related to their elevation, than to longitude and latitude as viewed from above, as it would be indicated on an ordinary map. It is an appealing idea, a form of citizenship based on altitude rather than proximity.

With language, we may have some luck. There is a man in his thirties, who has traded around these parts for years, and who seems to have many wives in many places, who is supposed to be at the Fort today, having been engaged to translate for the factor of the trading post during the week of spring trading, when all the best furs are taken. He is a mixed blood & his name is Charles Caan, though he is referred to every place, by the soldiers, by the native & mixed bloods, as Charles Many Tongues. It is my constant observation that it is those of mixed blood who show signs of genius. The Commander has never met him but he is said to be capable of speaking twenty languages, many of the interior. Even if this is overstated twice, & he is capable of ten, I believe that we must engage him. His reputation is that he constantly seeks escapade & travel & is coming to the Fort hoping to find some adventure.

Reid will photograph the officers & company this afternoon, I have sent a messenger informing the Fort Commander, as well as the chief of what is said to be the largest & most warlike tribe of the area we are about to traverse.

>—+—‹›—•—‹›—+—‹

Captain Masse returns to his stool on the catwalk suspended around the interior of the fort's palisade wall. He sits directly at the entrance portal, above its one now open door. To his left and right, uniformed corporals, rifles at ready, survey the interior of the fort. The military precision of movements within the fort, the saluting and standing at attention, has softened, and many civilians go about their business. A stout woman pulls washing from a tub and hangs it on a clothes line strung just above her head. A boy peels potatoes. Three hunters unload the skinned and gutted carcass of an elk from a two-wheeled cart.

A tall, red-haired man astride a roan mare passes under the lintel of the double doors, an almost equally tall, dark-haired woman, her horse a flagrant piebald, beside and a half step behind him. The Captain's eye is attracted to the man's crimson waistcoat, but it is the duo's demeanour that creates the desire for a second glance. Both man and woman carry themselves, and guide their mounts, with an effortless exactness that is neither precise, like the military men around them, nor diligent, like the hard-working civilians. It is, rather, the easy motion of a confident predator. The pair come to a stop just within the entrance. They face the Commander's office, backs to Captain Masse.

'That is him Captain, the man our Commander told you about. Charles Many Tongues.'

'How do you know, corporal?'

'His red waistcoat. A dozen such like were shipped out from the east. He bought up every one. Red hair. The Commander told us to watch out for such a man.'

'He is not alone.'

'He travels with his favourite wife. She is a princess or something, I don't know the story.'

'They both sit very erect in the saddle. Look at their bridles, only two loose knots of rope around the muzzle.'

'With only that, I have seen men...and women, bring a galloping horse to a stop in its length. The mounted tribes are fearsome in attack. I have endured one. Thank God for repeating rifles.'

'Why have they come?'

'They are here to translate sir. Look outside the fort, just at the edge of the settlement, a big party is coming in. There will be some serious trading today. That is why we're rifles at ready.'

'Have you had problems?'

'I've never been called upon to shoot anyone. Usually a couple of shots fired into the air settles things down.'

'Good. Would you summon a messenger, I must send for my photographer, Reid.'

⊱━┥◆┝━O━┥◆┝━⊰

*T*oo soon, but this is often the way, Captain Masse pressed me into service. Even as I was laying out my apparatus and stock, a messenger came from the fort bidding me prepare for a portrait. I made the soldier stay, and loaded him with my chemicals and portable darkroom. I took the lens and camera box.

I arrived just as the big band appeared, and was summoned up to stand beside Captain Masse. When I expressed worry for my equipment, the soldier told me to leave it with him, for he seemed set to obey my every whim. The band leaders came in sight strung out along the deep ravine that sweeps into and becomes the outpost's thoroughfare. They were followed by a long line of dogs and people of lesser status carrying huge packs suspended from a leather trap strung across their foreheads. They kept to the ravine until opposite the fort, then crossed onto the flattened road. A number of men armed with long muskets appeared over the last ridge of the hills, taking positions were they could see from horizon to horizon. I assume they were there to protect the rear.

By this time I had mounted the bastion and, at his command, stood beside Captain Masse. Several of the porters at the front of the band were summoned forward. With a guard at each side, they approached the fort, close enough that we could plainly see they carried all kinds of furs and tanned hides. I could not ascertain exactly from what animals, but a commercial agent near us assumed the bundles contained the finer pelts taken in winter trapping, rather than the large hides from summer hunting. Such furs would all be shipped east, and commanded the very highest prices.

An erect and elegantly decorated man strolled out from the main troop. He was followed by bodyguards with muskets raised and a corps of female singers whose voices, in an eerie, minor key, rose into the silence produced by the band's arrival. As the whole assemblage eased towards the fort, they continued to chant in this strange but melodious style to the rhythm of their slow footsteps. At some command I did not see, they stopped. The chief and his bodyguard discharged their muskets to the heavens. I must admit I jumped. The Captain chuckled, and pointed to a hillock not far away where Guzman and Bain had found spectator seats. The fort's cannon replied to the muskets with a volley. A soldier near us said this discharge was to prove all arms were now impotent. The native muskets, being flintlocks and the cannon muzzle loaders, would make any attempt to re-arm on either side obvious.

The gate was swung open. We all turned. The commercial agent had already descended, and stood at one side to welcome his visitors. The bodyguard and the singers passed within, as did the chief, who then stood opposite the agent, and so close to me I could see the flower and animal designs worked into his tunic as well as the deep-etched wrinkles at his eye. He motioned with his head to the porters and, in company, they walked past the agent, who fixed his exacting gaze on every bundle. He motioned again for the porters to move towards the trading house, where several dark-suited clerks waited. At another signal from the agent, a clerk opened the door and each porter ducked in, unshouldering their bundles. When all were inside, the agent and the chief followed, walking side by side, leaving the bodyguard, the singers, and all the rest of us transfixed in the hushed courtyard.

A monumental visual spectacle. Yet my most potent recollection is of the smells. Even when they stood outside the gate, a powerful aroma of rancid fat permeated the whole throng, and drifted towards us. I was told that they use the fat as a dressing for their hair, and as a waterproofing agent for their clothing. This intense fragrance was by no means displeasing, it being so pervasive that it became the very atmosphere. Then, with their entrance came more intimate and refined odours, for up close, the women were permeated with the scent of wood smoke, I imagine from their cooking fires. I recognised hickory and plum, for this is what my father used to smoke the deer he shot on hunting trips. The men smelled of gunpowder from the discharge of their flintlock rifles, a sharp tang of sulphur and saltpetre I recognised from school chemistry.

I felt the deep mind-fatigue a child knows after a visceral entertainment, and was trying to recover from it when the Captain Masse spoke sharply to me to follow a soldier who had tugged my elbow. I looked at him, seeking a reason, but his eyes were following the one movement within the palisade, the slow passage from the outer perimeter of the fort's parade ground towards the trading shed, upon unsaddled horses, of a man in a red waistcoat and a woman dressed in well-tanned hides that hung, supple, around her.

Ushered through the trading house, but overcome with curiosity, I took advantage of my special status and forced the soldier to let me watch the proceedings. I stood beside one of the riflemen stationed at each corner. The trading house is a special building, very long, with a hearth and chimney at each end. The door giving entrance to the porters is fastened with a heavy bar similar in construction to the outer gate and also opening inwards. From were I stood, I surveyed the whole room, which was divided in such a manner that any trade goods handed out from the warehouse half would pass through a small opening above waist height. A ledge allowed their display. Too large a display at one time excited the customers, the soldier explained, and added to the potential for danger. The most powerful smells were now of the furs themselves. Bundled by species, the dark bales had been warmed in the sunshine as the porters waited. The soft perfume of fox, the acrid reek of racoon, the fatty rankness of beaver and the overpowering stench of bear permeated the room.

Suddenly so close, with time to observe, I realised I was not prepared for the beauty of these children of nature. Their colour is magnificent, a complete spectrum of earth tones from near black of the richest soil to fine and glossy copper luminescent as a new penny. On these radiant tints, and the jet blackness of their hair, they capitalise hugely. The men often pull their hair up off the head, emphasising the arch beauty of their angular visage, rendering it fierce...almost cruel. Others let theirs tumble long and thick, and decorate it with trinkets. To this they add barred designs, horizontal and vertical, on cheek and forehead with all the cleverness of the finest theatrical makeup, a masculine vanity our own timid culture would shun.

The women are more subtle. Their long hair inevitably frames the face with two dark plaits. Beneath this wonderful design, they wear blouses of the most delicately tanned skins, from sand to bronze in hue, and for decoration, worked stones of turquoise which raise flames on their cheeks and throat, and deepen the brilliant abyss of their black eyes. The way they live adds a rare complement to these accessories. The life in tents, the constant presence of the cooking fire, sets upon the skin a smoky patina that could not be duplicated with the most artfully applied cosmetics, a kind of delicate varnish like one sees on finely worked mahogany.

And over this, nature's great hand burnishes their aspect. It is in sun, and wind, and rain that they must spend their lives. This constant assault they use to some effect, for they all seem to glow with the heat of the sun and cold of the snow. How different the pale ladies I know at home, with their parasols, and shady bonnets, though they are not without charm too.

>─┼─◆>─◯─<◆>─┼─<

Bain squats upon a rock, knees folded near his chin, and his elbows set upon them to brace a telescope he has trained on the multitude gathered below. He twists its inner tube to focus, panning along the column as it waits, silent except for sporadic coughs, gusts of wind and the neigh of a staked out horse. Guzman kneels on a folded piece of oilcloth, his gaze wandering from the members of the band passing through the opened gates on foot to the mounted couple – the red-vested man and deerskin-robed woman. They've ranged on a hillock opposite Guzman and Bain, at about the same height, and like them, watch the ragged assemblage as the pre-business formalities terminate. Guzman looks back at Bain, and with a swift yank, makes the telescope his own.

'I should have it, then both of us will have something to do, Bain.'

'Why is that?'

'You say nothing as you observe. I cannot share in it. With me at the spyglass, and talking, you may share in what I see. A privilege you deny to me. Look across there, at our height, the mounted pair standing apart. Yon filly is an excellent specimen. She holds herself like a queen. This is no common squaw. Squeeze her into a corset and gown her, she would be the match of any woman for beauty. Mind how the wind presses her raiment to her. Finely made. Well-bosomed, thin of waist and long calved. This is quality stuff.'

'You sound like a cattle buyer, Guzman. Would the poor woman could hear. And I think she does, she's turned towards you.'

'Impossible at this distance. What a specimen. Her man has chosen well...and he looks to be white, or half so. Yes, a Métis. Perhaps our time at the Fort will not be so fruitless.'

'I'm convinced she hears you man. Why have you put the glass down? You wanted it so.'

'She. It is not possible. That she heard me. But...she drew a knife from her girdle as she faced me, and raising it...do not forget, I had the glass to my eye, for me she was as close as across a dining table. She brought the knife up, blade flat, horizontal, point towards me, and, of this I am certain, when she knew my gaze was fixed upon it, she thrust the knife forward, a movement that, if we had been sitting at a table, would have driven the blade into my throat.'

⋊⊷⬥⊷⬦⊷⬥⊶⋉

A clerk appeared from behind the store room's wicket and passed through the window a suit of jacket and trousers, black cloth with silver buttons, a tall felt hat decorated with a red silk. The chief nodded, for it seems he had spoken for this very item, and it was handed out in exchange for a knee-high bundle of fox fur, glowing red in the dusty light.

Next, a tightly rolled bundle of tobacco was set out, the size of a haversack. This brought grunts of satisfaction from most of the assembled men. Again the chief nodded. This time, a bundle of racoon pelts seemed the exchange and was slid forward but the chief spoke this time, through the translator. The porter kept his hand on the bundle. A half hogshead of spirits was slid out, probably rum. The chief spoke again, the translator nodded, and this deal was accepted.

Next, a single lead musket ball was placed on the shelf. The factor's subaltern described what value it was to be given to the translator. In effect, it was to be the basic monetary unit. The chief spoke, the factor himself spoke, some of the porters stood, voices rose in the room, to a palpable level of tension, then the factor nodded. A value had been decided upon.

Thence, all exchanges were by barter. A bundle of furs would be set forward for evaluation by the clerks. A pile of bullets would be counted out and pushed toward the porter. I estimate their value at about twenty-five pennies. From there, he would bargain to agreement, and the sale then completed. The bullets would be taken, or a measure of shot or gunpowder weighed on a set of scales the clerk produced from under his counter, or some knives or hatchet heads. There would be short verbal exchanges, then the bundle would be pulled into the godown and the package taken by the porter.

What was remarkable was the similarity of the two social orders. Only important issues caused the chief or the factor to speak. All other exchanges were carried on by subalterns, who, in the case of both us and native, maintained constant eye contact with their superior. It was evident from the tension in the room that the elaborate ceremony was the result of long practice on both sides, and assuaged their different, but mutual vulnerabilities.

When only a few fur bundles remained, and each porter had a package of powder and shot, or knives or hatchet heads, the chief called out. A woman, elaborately dressed in well-tanned doeskin decorated with beads of industrial manufacture and furs which she must have worked herself, entered the trading hall. She took a position beside the chief. Again the factor nodded and this time various items of clothing were displayed in the window, many, being of garish calico, were not to my taste, and to hers neither from what I could see, for she refused all.

The clerk grew exasperated, but my queenly dame was methodical as she picked out items she liked. The chief never wavered during this, standing tall and respectful beside her as she bargained. Via the woman translator interestingly enough. Finally an exquisite blue dress, very close to a turquoise, was put in the window. A kind of soft cotton, almost a velour. Her eyes glittered, and I had no trouble imagining how it would flatter her high colour, and the red beads she had around her neck. She accepted this and the penultimate fur bundle was taken. For the last bundle, the negotiations centred around a half dozen or so iron pots. In this, like with the clothing, she bargained sharply through her translator, with much more intensity than the men.

As I watched, what struck me was an inferior aspect of our own society. Here we all were in this outpost, which was natural home to none of us, and the mixed-blood translator and the natives seemed to have a much healthier social circumstance. By this I mean the simultaneous presence of men and women. I looked around me at my own race; clerks, factors, officers and men, and realised that no women lived with them or socialised with them. How perverse I thought. Why do we do things in such a way?

The chief gave an oration, which when translated, showed of his appreciation of the generosity of the factor and his promise of fraternity for him and his people with the agents.

The agent returned the speech, translated back, indicating his high regard for the chief and his wife, and his admiration for the fine braves accompanying him. On behalf of the company, he hoped the they would continue their trade in good fellowship and friendliness, and expressed his personal opinion the chief's people were the finest people in the land.

The chief spoke a few words of appreciation. Then, seemingly by magic, the singers who had been waiting outside the door were summoned in by the most fiercely costumed of the chief's guards. They filed in to pick up the packages of clothing and one iron pot each. The chief walked towards the door, his guards in step astern. When he was outside, the singers departed two abreast. As they passed under the lintel they again began to sing, their voices blending together with a thrilling penetration that made the hair on my arms and back of my neck stand straight up. I could not stop tears from coming to my eyes because of the emotions the strange tones and rhythm seemed to trigger – a mixture of loneliness and dread. My thought was that if this is their music to signal the happy end of trading, I wanted never to hear a funeral dirge.

>─┤◆>─○─<◆┤─<

[Captain Aaron Masse]

My new man's companion, by local custom his wife, is the most charming woman. Her eyes bright with cleverness & a warmth we seldom see in our own more prim & proper female. We are twice blessed this day. I admire this duo's every aspect. During the excruciating afternoon of trade, where many a time past a mis-understood word has led to massacre, they never wavered, back & forth between languages, maintaining the nuance of each exchange. Their work is perfection & equally it is plain they have much local experience & are both hardened to the rigours of the trail. I watched them ride in, master horsemen. Their kit, though compact, had been sufficient for travelling some two weeks.

It is the man Charles Caan who has the reputation here, but from what I saw, his qualifications consist equally in having this clever young woman for a wife. It is she who possess the greater wit. It seems that she was captured by a party of braves that raid-ed the northern interior & brought back with others as a slave. Her mother tongue is from that region. Caan, who has traded round these parts a decade, & to give him credit speaks tolerable well the local dialect, took a liking to her, procured her, & made her his wife, in addition to others which he already kept at vari-ous locations. When she discovered his additional spouses, she put up a great stink, claiming her royal blood, forced him to leave the others, & thus they are on the trail together, he seeming well satisfied.

Our photography begun. This very moment Reid prepares the first plates. The tripod is set up & the camera placed upon it, though not yet adjusted. The tribe, having had the procedure &

its results explained to them, are gathering in the courtyard. The soldiers, many familiar with the daguerreotype, are enthusiastic, too. They will go first. I await this spectacle with the greatest personal & professional interest. As Reid went into the warehouse to prepare his plates, I swear he walked on tiptoe, so excited he was. A much more complex personage than I assumed.

⤐ ⤜ ⬥ ⭘ ⬥ ⤛ ⤜

Lady luck with me today. Two pictures. My first attempts. I consider them experimental, their faults can only be corrected by experience. Of composition, I feel I am a master. The intricacies of my equipment another affair. Upon being shown into a clean storage room, I saw that a soldier had already set up my darkroom and laid out my chemicals and a supply of water. I thanked him, for he had well divined the nature and intent of my activity. As I was pressed, having spent too much time in the trading hall, I requested he apply his ingenuity to setting up my camera outside.

I first cleaned two plates, rubbing them with polishing powder, spirits of wine and a little ammonia. I then rinsed and polished them with my silk handkerchief. I mixed my prepared plain collodion into a solution of alcohol and ether and potassium iodide until I had a straw-coloured solution, as recommended (this latter the best for bright light). Grasping the plate by its corners, I poured the syrupy mixture onto it, expanding the puddle until a circular pool extended almost to the edges. I tipped this into the corners and returned the excess to the bottle via the right hand corner nearest me, then rocked the plate to make the flow lines coalesce.

Placing, with great care, the drying plates into my darkroom, I closed its double door flaps and stuck my arms in the sleeves. I filled my bath trough to finger depth with the silver nitrate solution I had mixed that morning and stored in a black bottle. At that moment the soldier rapped on the door and shouted that the Captain was impatient. I replied I could not care less, they were about to witness a miracle, and such phenomenon happen when they will.

I immersed each plate a full minute, as the manual specified for bright days, then drained it onto a felt blotter. I set each face down in a plate holder and inserted the dark slide. Almost ready. Arriving at the camera site, I found it well set up. The soldier received my warmest smile, I hope not too feminine. I checked the bellows for dust, cobwebs and insects, then mounted the lens. Removing the lens cap, I threw the focusing cloth over my shoulders. Before me, the blurred outline of several tiers of faces. I focused. Three entire platoons in three tiers; sitting, kneeling, standing. Their own Captain with his sword, sergeant with double pistols, soldiers with rifles, one with a bugle, two with snare drums. I panned to my left and silently complimented them on their gift for composition. I inserted a plate, smiled again, this time with more authority, pulled the slide, requested immobility, took off the lens cap, counting 'one hippopotamus, two...' until I reached eighty.

The tribe came next. Quite a different sight. Men, women, even some children filled the ground glass. As I worked, I understood why Captain Masse, usually an exigent perfectionist, did not seem worried if my first attempt at image making was a failure. The act itself was sufficient to impress the chiefs, princesses and braves assembled for their portrait. With silent fascination, they watched me prepare and as my movements became more precise and dedicated to the task, I sensed I became one with them, no longer a stranger. Analysing this feeling, I think what occurred was that my movements – careful, delicate – were universal movements. The same as theirs when stalking an animal or bird. They understand such skills and state of mind – the hunter's dance for want of a better description – and it united me with them.

Finally, all were immobile. Off came the lens cap to my chanted hippopotomi. As I set the slide across the second exposed plate and withdrew it from the camera, I heard a single pair of hands begin to clap, and was embarrassed, then tumultuous applause burst forth from the regiment, as at the end of an aria in an opera house. The men and women from the tribe took but a moment to understand what the soldiers were doing, and they joined in, laughing. I could do little else but bow, indicate, with a burlesque stage gesture to the soldier who had set up the camera to take it down, put my plates under my arm and stroll – offstage if you will.

>—◆◇—◦—◇◆—◦

[Captain Aaron Masse] Day 24

Reid indeed the showman. What an entertainment. I have assessed well the hypnotic potential of this new art & science of image making. The whole Fort, Native & White, was at our bidding, & they have yet to see the images. Reid dramatic, every movement calculated to mesmerise the subject into obeying his lens's demand. The polished gestures of a stage actor, ruling this most rowdy crowd.

Who is this man Reid? I commanded he come with us, & he obeyed. I was confident of his weak nature. Now I am less sure. He is a man of strange powers, graceful as a cat when he is in front of a crowd with his camera, clever & charming with the soldier assisting & the Fort's captain, yet utterly content to live alone in his tent with his apparatus & still rise before dawn each day by the sentry's account.

>⸺◆⸺O⸺◆⸺<

Back in the room assigned me, I saw that the window and door had been blocked with black cloth, allowing development to take place in the open. The clever soldier no doubt. I laid out my things and was about to develop the plates with Pyro-Gallic acid, and had poured it out into a beaker when a knuckle tapped on the dark room door. I recognised the rap of my amiable corporal. I replied I could not be disturbed, but he insisted, saying I had a guest – to be shown the process on the direct order of Captain Masse. With a silent curse, I came close to refusing, but took a breath and opened the door. To face a tall woman, facial features and bearing similar to the striking woman who had been bargained so sharply during the fur trade, the only flaw in her beauty a scatter of pock marks across exquisite cheekbones. A personage eminent and unstoppable as a monarch. Behind her, a veritable lady in waiting, stood the woman who had translated so long and well. Both pairs of eyes glittered with excitement and knavery. The corporal explained that the lady before me, sister of the chief's wife, would be shown how the pictures were made. Not could she be, she would be. The second lady would translate my explanations.

To be truthful, my anger at being disturbed had utterly evaporated. I was in an instant glad of the female company, and while I smiled to myself at my good fortune, I kept my facial expression that of the moderately vexed man disturbed during his work – something between schoolmaster and safecracker. My expression was perhaps stronger than I had intended, which sometimes happens. I tend to exaggerate my masculine force when anxious.

In that instant, as if to overcome my resistance, the queenly woman slid an object from within her deerskin wrap and held it in front of my face. It was an image. A leather framed octo ferrotype the size of her palm. I took its frame between thumb and forefinger, and without removing it from her grasp, I tilted it so it could be seen by the light of the window at the end of the corridor. The image was of a society lady in all her finery. I was aware that people collected not only records of outings, mementoes of friendships, and portraits of their family and loved ones, but also images of the exotic and historic. The multi-lensed camera allows multiple images, and after processing, the grid of pictures on the plate is cut into single ones with tin snips. These were sold to collectors. And this woman had obtained one, and more important, she had deduced that what I was doing was connected to the image she had obtained and kept with her for however long. I chuckled openly.

I showed them in and before closing the door behind me to cut off the light, explained that the plate holders lying on the counter held the images I had exposed, and the beaker contained chemicals which I would pour over them that would reveal the image. I used the word reveal instead of develop. This was duly translated. I closed the door.

In the darkness, to my rapt, unseeing audience, I recounted that I was pouring the pyro evenly from the beaker over a plate. I counted my sixty hippopotomi, which caused much giggling. I realised suddenly it sounded like a magician's incantation. The chemical reek rose to my nose like so much spilt wine gone to vinegar. I stepped to the window and let in a crack of light. An image was appearing on the floating plate. My companions lapsed into silence. The regal woman bent avidly towards the plate, then stopped herself and looked at me, asking permission with her eyes. I nodded. She put her face almost against it, lost in contemplation. There seemed to be the right spectrum of tones, from opaque black to clear on the glass. I washed it, then opened the window. How wonderful to get my head into fresh air. We three stared at the plate, equally amazed, if for different reasons.

What a marvellous thing, the negative. Floating at the proper angle in the black rubber tray, with just a slit of sidelight, it would transmute to positive tones, as if predicting the final print in secret, just for me. In the daylight, all is reversed. The regiment's dark skinned groom is white, the pallid accountant black as pitch. The soldier's uniforms are bleached and pristine as busboy's in a fine restaurant. I fixed it in Hypo and washed again. On to the other plate.

The woman, an aristocrat to be sure, spoke at length to the translator. There was some discussion, of which I was the subject, I could tell. At last the translator spoke to me. She gave me her name, Water Music, and revealed that her husband had been asked to travel on our expedition, and she would go too. She explained that the woman with us was a very highborn woman who had not married but was a...here she looked for words, but from what I understood her to mean...this woman was a kind of nun, a sorceress, a medicine woman.

The queenly woman talked for a long time, a virtual monologue. Water Music further translated that the woman's people, and my people, the strangers, were enemies. The woman's people would endeavour to oust us all. At that point I wondered if she knew how many we were. The translator continued, saying the woman perceived that I was also a sorcerer, that my magic was light. She said that she had put a curse on our expedition, because it was going into the sacred mountains of her tribe intent on defiling them. She said that all the expedition would die horrible deaths, caused by the God's of the angry mountains and their demon assistants, the rivers, but if I remained pure of heart, I would be spared, saved by my light magic.

I had no idea how to reply, but since she had addressed me as one professional to another, I gave a tolerant nod, and shook her hand in what I trusted she would interpret as a collegial manner. They left. I continued. While the plates dried, I repacked my camera, which the soldier had brought in, stored my chemicals and rolled up the darkroom. The whole operation had taken four hours.

I printed the images the next morning, the Captain having obtained for me several sheets of fine paper sized with the same gelatine I used for my negatives which I then sensitised with silver nitrate. I exposed the paper, with the glass negative over it, fifteen minutes measured by the cook's hour glass in bright morning sun. Back into the developing tent, another soldier arrived, inviting me to dine with the Captain, his lieutenants, and Captain Masse, and bring my prints.

I was not satisfied entirely. The sun being more intense than I had anticipated at this altitude, the prints were a trifle overexposed. But they certainly fascinated the others. Over a succulent steak, I remarked on the difference between the two images, that in the first there were no women, and on the tendency generally of our society to populate its outposts, and of course its ocean girdling ships, with only men, a policy the natives did not seem to adhere to. Our Captain Masse remained oddly silent, but the fort's Captain replied, to wit, that our women are much too sensitive either to want to or be able to survive such conditions as those in the fort or on a ship. I stuck my face in my plate, and laughed the deepest laugh I could without emitting a sound. I am positive Captain Masse read my mind, though he gave no indication as such.

>─┤ ◆>─O─<◆ ┤─<

[Captain Aaron Masse] Day 26

Being amongst soldiers again brings formidable recollections. In an idle moment, cooling my heels as I waited to speak to the

Commander about enlisting Caan & his wife Water Music, I watched some green recruits at drill, one of them particularly inept, clumsy as a girl.

Was reminded of a letter from my friend Colonel Jackson, who was then holding front line with two much battered regiments. Men had been sent to forage. Some discovered concealed distillation apparatus & several bottles full. Upon getting quite drunk, two fell in a spring river, still with ice, & near drowned. They had a peculiar way about them but this was ascribed to the drink & they were taken to the surgeon. He resuscitated them with hot bricks wrapped in blankets but discovered both were in effect girls, or young women uniformed, hair cut short, & plainly known to be thus to their fellow infantrymen. In contrast to their accepting fellow soldiers, Jackson was deeply disturbed by the discovery. He wrote it troubled him so that he dismissed the women, & had them transported to a nunnery, & put in care of the sisters.

It makes me wonder about the clumsy lad here on the parade ground. It is easy to imagine him, with his long fingered hands & slight build, a girl in disguise. What perplexity that would create. A good joke for me, an ordeal for the young Commander of the Fort here.

⤐ ⊷ ◦ ⊶ ⤐

The fort's interior is dark and its silence interrupted only by the murmur of horses settling to sleep, the slosh of soapy water in the cook shack. Of human activity there is no more than a lone sentry in his watch tower high on the palisade catwalk. His ears are set to catch the sounds beyond it, thus his world is suffused by a rhythmic, torpid chant coming from not far off, a low flat where many cooking fires gutter and flare. The sentry buttons his coat and moves out of the wind. He commands a view of the concave field, where tall lodge poles and smoke columns of a impromptu tent city are bleached by the light of an errant moon peeking and ducking through the cloud.

The log wall at his back and gleaming cannon barrel against his thigh comfort him. He puts his hand upon its barrel, the embossed lettering of the maker's nameplate pressing into his palm, and feeling thus more secure, lets the minor key chant floating up from the camp grounds invade his mind. This is what he enlisted for, adventure. The unknown. But tonight, alone with the truth of it, he feels his limits, and leans away from the eerie sound, towards the clink of tack and rattling pot lids within the garrison. A door slams, then a soldier slips out the gate, carrying what looks like a dead goat, body under his arm, death stiffened legs in the air. The sentry nods, complicit.

The pulsing chant floats up to his ears, swelling. Sounds or words he cannot tell. A cyclical bass refrain – three syllables repeated, one beat silent, again the three – undercut by a minor dirge that weaves in and out of the invariable bass note, teasing it, irritating it, pushing it to greater and greater volume, the bruising solidity of a climax, then retreating.

As the theme subsides, the sentry detects within it some familiar note. A high drone, also in a minor key, that blends with the chant yet holds its individual, more precise, identity. He leans forward to catch it, twisting his head, left, right, to localise the separate sound and when it is equal in both his ears, he is looking at the closest cooking fire, a stone's throw distant. Within the fire's ring of yellow radiance, a few people squat, faces lit, and others stand back, mere outlines, and in the deeper dark, dim forms of new arrivals ruffle undulating shadow.

The drone persists. Without seeming to have a source, it plants itself within the ebbing chant, and is heard, and the distant chanting quiets more to accommodate it. The sentry counts one-two-three-four squatting forms round the fire, male and female, ten-eleven-twelve standing shadowed, impossible to identify. Further removed, dun upon dusk, the farthest forms coagulate, no single one identifiable.

Then, clear, unique, but still within the idiom of the chant, a language of wind, human pain, and animal cries, the wavering drone is abruptly relieved by melody. A theme on a five-note scale, a variation, the theme repeated. The sentry sees two hands move in the flame's penumbra, fingers laid flat across a narrow black horn with a bell mouth, their precise motion of exposing or covering the pipe's holes preceding by an instant the actual note that reaches him. The player steps forward. Colours and forms detach from the darkness. It is the man who ducked out the gate, his distended face a blood smudge, his instrument a silhouette, its long drone shafts vertical upon his shoulder issuing from three legs of a distended goat's body, furry hide puffed to balloon roundness through a breathing tube he clamps in his teeth. Keeping the bladder tense with alternating squeezes of his elbow and pumping breaths into the fourth leg, both hands laid flat upon a bell mouthed flute set in the animal's mouth, fingers rising and falling on its sound holes, he formulates a lingering melody.

Which comes to dominate the nocturnal amphitheatre, gathering force as the chant recedes, respecting it, complimenting it, and finally replacing it, while a bottle glints in the hands of those around the fire, passed back and forth, finally brought delicately to Guzman's welcoming mouth to be sipped with eyes closed. The sentry regrets his post, his uniform. The pipe player sways, shuffling forward, his cheeks blushing ruby as his melancholy air too subsides, pianissimo, with a cluster of quarter notes, the crowd now pressing to him, near the fire bodies so compressed, raised bottles must be passed, glittering, hand to hand overhead.

Guzman places his bottle on the ground, and laughing, shouts something the sentry cannot hear. Water Music smiles. Guzman's head swivels to assess the effect of his exclamation upon her. An appreciative, and provocative look. In answer, she touches the handle of the dirk tucked in her belt. Guzman smiles, his forehead smooth, eyes content she responded, as the player pumps his instrument, squawking the drones with a jerk of his elbow. Reaching above his head, Guzman slaps palms together in a brisk meter. The piper's foot taps in sympathy, and leaning forward as if against a gale, he flips his fingers to unleash a hornpipe's opening notes which surge into the crowd, enveloping it, heels and toes, full flat feet pounding the same time before the tune's second bar arrives and departs. Guzman up the instant, and pirouettes to the far side of the fire, feet persuaded to a blur by the bouncing tune.

Yet his upper body moves not, his hands hanging loose at his side only swaying slightly as he floats, left, right, forwards, then spinning once, on his tapping, jigging feet. His dexterity moves the piper to greater feats of finger work. A rattle of grace notes, double time, sixteen to the bar, brings his enthusiastic air to a fever pitch. And Guzman is the match for it. His feet accelerate, raising dust and cinders. He levitates to the pipes mad harangue, dancing in and out of the light, the others around the fire now beating time on thighs and hands, and from the native tents drifts a crowd, drawn to watch the madly gyrating Guzman, who each time he emerges from the shadow like an actor in the wings from behind a curtain, has managed to bend his body into another maniac shape, now a dervish, now a spinning top, now the wind itself.

Neither the piper nor Guzman being modest, the growing observance feeds their energies, the piper breaths his all into the bag, pumps it, and when Guzman reaches his hands out to Water Music, she accepts, another person leaps up until all near the fire are on their feet dancing; primitive reels, elegant heel toe's, demented jigs, or simply movements that imitate these, anything to participate.

And the sentry waves his arm to someone within the fort, motioning him towards the rousing sounds. The gate again opens a crack, and several soldiers slip through, one with a fiddle, another an accordion, this carried on a neck strap, its master squeezing its bellows as he runs towards the fire, already cording a syncopated rhythm by the time he reaches it, only to nod to the fiddler, playing out a G insistently till the fiddle is tuned and joins the fray, climbing fast up the scale, supported by the pulsing accordion, then united with it, all three instruments taking turn about chorus and verse, wailing and wheezing into a frantic hornpipe contrived entirely of eighth notes.

The crowd grown too large to be illuminated by the fire it seems to have no limits, and become a pulsing extension of both the fire at its centre and shadows of night at its edge. Sweaty reek of human and beast, damp leather and wool, oiled hair, tobacco, rum, spit, gunpowder, blood, animal fat, wood smoke, spruce gum, pine sap, rancid milk, black tea, and breath sweet with digesting flesh. Crushed together, thudding feet, convulsing as one so the ground reverberates, a dust cloud rising, the pipes drone and rant exhorting epileptic spasms, madness. A roaring and ravelling snarl that churns and boils. Exhausted dancers careen away to fall quaking upon the earth, or clutching torsos vomit, or one hand bracing them against a tree urinate shuddering, or simply stagger off, mumbling, twitching, slavering and it's here that Guzman gropes for Water Music's waist and she eludes him, whirling back into the throng eyes exultant, while he collapses into the dark outer boundary beyond the fire, rolling on his white shirt front, soiling it, exiting the maelstrom, rolling down slope to bang his head against a knotted root with such force his teeth click. Surviving this, he lurches almost upright to tilt, the sounds drumming his back, towards the dark's deeper stillness.

>—◆>—○—◆—◆—<

[Captain Aaron Masse] Day 28

Clear morning. High cloud in mare's tails. Wind NW. Negotiations with Caan who informed me he is a skilled tracker as well as proficient hunter. That should serve us well. No-one in the present party has proved to be a crack shot. He also comes with his own travel kit. He made one request other than the customary one for shot, powder, flour, sugar & some small amount of salt. He demanded an example of the new breech loading rifles. Having only three, I hesitated, but seeing our bargain would turn upon the issue, I acceded. At this moment in our discussion, his mate broke in, never looking at me. I was quickly informed that he would not part from her nor she from him. Any discussion implied I would engage the twosome. Having long decided to take the two, but wanting to gain bargaining advantage, I expressed regret at this, claiming the difficulty of the trail.

The woman is plainly clever & high born, I can see it in her carriage, & more important, she was captured from the interior, speaks three of its languages. This alone makes her worth double any encumbrance of her presence. Just as I was contemplating the culinary advantages of having a woman in camp, Caan made haste to tell me that his wife would not act as camp cook, as is usually expected of a woman. She would do her part only, in rotation with the men if that was the system, & dress any game killed by Caan. Point blank.

My intention was to negotiate his services to the great divide, perhaps slightly beyond, planning to build skiffs & thence descend the rivers, surveying, from the first navigable headwaters encountered, leaving him to make his way back. I was surprised to find him interested in the seaward voyage. When questioned as to why, he replied that it was not he, but his wife, Water Music, who wanted to see the ocean. When questioned as to how he would return from the seacoast, he replied...or in effect she replied, for I suspect what he said was a literal translation of what she was saying to him...that the people inland, far to the Norwest, had long made trade with the people of the coast & the trails & seasons of safe travel were well known.

Caan & Water Music will accompany us to the coast, there being no complication on my part, for I had planned to engage two oarsmen & will now only need one, or perhaps none if she is willing, for the downstream trip.

These things being settled our mutual satisfaction, I left their camp, intent on satisfying our final need for a half dozen mules or large donkeys to act as pack animals. This negotiation must be made with the army, they being the sole possessors of such beasts. I have, to my advantage, the fact of which Caan informed me that bartering rate stands at present as two donkeys per horse, which should set us just about right.

Mother Nature co-operating, I estimate our time here at two weeks, with Bain husbanding our animals & repacking, Guzman setting out a baseline & adjusting his instruments as well as drawing up the charts of the voyage we have already made so I can courier them back to the Capital & Reid photographing. Of this latter activity, the importance cannot be underestimated. I have emphasised the importance of the photographic work, yet I think Reid already understood this. I will command the resources he needs & with the co-operation of the Captain here, who has a certain sense of humour about his surroundings, dedicate as much time as needbe to assuring Reid a constant flow of notable subjects. To this end I have had drawn up a notice advertising that we will give a small cash award to those specimens we deem unique.

Reid affirms photographic apparatus and chemical compounds tested. All in good order and uncontaminated by travel.

⪼⋅┼⋅◈⋅┼⋅◯⋅┼⋅◈⋅┼⋅⪻

*H*aving terminated my turn as an entertainer, Captain Masse now wishes that I begin my photographic enterprise in earnest. I am to make portraits, a kind of cross section or archive, of the various human types around us. I saw such attempts in the large art galleries of the continent when I made the 'de rigour' continental tour every young lady of my crowd made after finishing and coming out. I remember one painter in particular, a brilliant portrayer of royalty, violence, and daily life. His final work, to which he dedicated the last decade of his life, was an awe inspiring series, hundreds of sketches in lead and charcoal, of all the citizens, high and low, duchess to peasant, from a small town. I believe this is what the Captain, in his uneducated but astute manner, wishes I aspire to.

Again thwarted. My dream of pristine landscapes is no nearer. Alas, I must content myself with the same dull round of intimidated bumpkins. But at the very least, I shall use these wasted hours to learn my apparatus, so that when the important times come, when the moody daybreaks and spectacular sunsets, the craggy, snow swept peaks and breathtaking valleys are before me, I will be instantly ready, full master of my technique.

⪼⋅┼⋅◈⋅┼⋅◯⋅┼⋅◈⋅┼⋅⪻

[Captain Aaron Masse] Day 30

The stub of my arm has developed a monstrous itch, I think due to the poor quality of wool in my shirt, which sleeve is doubled over it every morning. Paid a private visit to Caan, for the purpose of negotiating his service as guide. Their camp a scene of recent debauch, something I recognize from soldier's camps. Broken liquor bottles, firewood scattered hither & yon, bits of clothing, a moccasin, a hat, and a shirtsleeve which I recognise as Guzman's. How I envy their free & easy pleasures.

Tapped lightly on the tent's lodge pole, then stood away. A

female voice enquired in a language I could not comprehend. I gave no answer, but coughed & moved back from the tent flap. After some minutes, Caan stuck his woolly head out, exclaiming "Thought it must be a white man," then, "Start the fire," to someone inside, before he disappeared, only to reappear, after some amount of giggling from within, fully dressed.

Caan recalcitrant, head sore from too much drink, but he brightened some after a breakfast prepared by his woman, her head bent modestly, never once looking at me in the tradition of this locality. But I know that every detail of my actions would be considered by her before a deal is struck & her every sense was focused on divining my intention. I did my best to interact with her as correctly as I would with a maiden aunt, knowing Caan's acceptance could be based on her judgement of my character. He expressed interest carefully, a man well used to frontier barter, his enamel cup of hot tea pressed against his forehead to relieve its ache.

I am struck, not for the first time, by the vanity of my own race. Our every exploration is couched in the language of discovery. A boot-shod foot is placed on the land & it has been 'found'. Here I am, making the 'first' penetration of the Northwest interior to the sea & a charming, modest woman is telling me her own people consider my planned route to be as familiar as a turnpike. There are some things I can communicate to our sponsors in the East, but this is not one of them. I am certain that, if we are not the 'first' to find the route, they will feel sore deprived.

The types that surround us, White, Native and Mixed Blood, are here living in a way that has persisted for almost a century. As a group, they represent a unique people, a new, adaptive species. And they will die a-borning. Within ten years they will be no more than a vaporous trace. I saw it happen in the South. The copper telegraph wire & iron rails will sink barbs deep into their bowels & bring them down quickly as a hunted animal speared in the heat of the chase.

>─┼─◄♦►─○─◄♦►─┼─◄

My work has commenced, this now the third day. I repeat all my well practised courtesies, indicating please be seated, soliciting a smile, an upright posture, a telling gesture. My apparatus is mechanically different, my processes chemically different, but the essence of the act remains indistinguishable though the faster shutter speed is a great help. My studio is a tent, my floor well packed grass, my assistant a young private, but the light, coming through the canvas from above and to the side, equals in intensity a skylight, and in effect has a pleasing diffuse quality that reveals without harshness.

I ask myself, has anything changed? My answer. Yes, something. What is it? That is the truly difficult question. The something is my subjects. Few have heard of a photograph, almost none have seen one. They are universally uneducated, thus have seen neither painting or drawings as we make them either. The know not of their own part in the theatre of portraiture, its conventions so to speak. There is no smile, no casual leaning of the elbow on a support, the turning of the head to show a profile. And I for one can do nothing to solicit such contributions as they know not of what I speak when I ask for them. My rogues' gallery.

I have concluded that I must assume an attitude somewhere between that of a scientist collecting strange fauna and a circus ringmaster preparing his menagerie. The results are mixed. With the improved shutter speed, I have few problems with blur even in morning, evening or cloudy light. To swarthy skin and beards I am accustomed, and this new process renders such details, after printing, in tones that could never even be imagined with the older process. In terms of subtlety of tone however, I believe the well done tinplate unequalled.

My greatest problem the people themselves. They stand before me like lumps of stone, many not even looking at the camera lens, because they do not know that is the mechanism through which their image will pass. Some seem to have come on their own free will, and others have been brought or persuaded by others. The private gives them their silver coin at the termination of the session and most seem quite happy. Many have smallpox lesions, more than in our eastern cities, where such disfigurement is rare and found only amongst the lower orders. On the continent, I remarked that such scars were to be seen in every class. None of my subjects have asked to see the results of our sessions.

>─┤◆>─O─<◆├─<

In the same way that the daguerreotype studio could, on a busy morning, become the social locus of the riverside settlement where Reid worked for over a year, her tent studio at the outpost has become a destination for many of its transient and permanent inhabitants. At this moment it seems to be the objective of a peculiar foursome. A pair of adults, a crude-dressed man and the servant girl from the inn, who drive – there is not better word – before them the two reluctant children so long hidden in the niche along the inn's wall. The challenge of these drovers task is immediately apparent, as much a result of their own deportment as because of their charge's hesitation. The man, rough-hewn, by clothing and carriage one whose vocation takes him into the bush. The servant girl shows herself, by posture and poorly restrained anger, as one always forced to obey. Both, in their lives, have suffered much rough treatment, and have experienced no other manner of social interaction.

Thus, the two of them are prodding, herding, or trying to herd the ragged boy and girl from their sleeping pallet against the stone wall down a rough and muck strewn alley at the end of which lies the door of Reid's tent studio. Their actions and shouts are more suitable to herding animals than the humans they are actually dealing with; the two fatigued and filthy children. The boy in early adolescence walking more or less upright and pulling his compatriot, perhaps his sister, much younger, not only ragged but wild because she tends more to scramble on all fours than to walk.

The children, covered with grimy callous and scab, resist being moved from their nest along the stone wall of the inn, resist being shoved into the light, resist entering the alley way. The boy balks, and stands with his face to a wall, back to the sun. The girls scrabbles on all fours to bury her own face in the dark angle of the wall and the ground.

The man, seeing the woman's screams and blows are useless, understanding that the children cannot abide the light, rummages in his pockets and finds a dark cloth sac he's used to carry ore samples. He slips it over the smaller child's head, thus providing portable darkness. The child fights him with the ferocity of a snared badger but she is quickly subdued when the man winds a wrapping of twine around her thumbs, binding them painfully together, the string's standing part in his hand, when tugged, becoming an effective lead.

He takes off his own broad brimmed hat, and tugs it down on the boy's head, pulls the brim low over his eyes, and seeing that the boy will be obedient to protect the girl, he opens the gate of the courtyard and the little band files down the meandering garbage fouled lane; a man dragging a child with a sac over its head that insists on running on all fours followed by an upright but hunched boy, head down, hat low on his head, staying in shadow, followed by the servant girl, still swinging her cudgel, a rear guard.

They pass two stout horses, loaded, saddled and ready for the trail, reins staked to the ground behind the inn, and the man strokes the head of the larger horse with an affection he has not demonstrated for the children, patting the animal's flank as if to say, "I'll be back."

>──◆◇──○──◇◆──<

[Captain Aaron Masse] Day 31

Clear, wind SW, warm and dry. Plans advance most excellent. Will set off presently. Almost all our needs are met, Bain being a matchless forager & sharp trader. Guzman has set all his instruments, including his gravitometer, this being very delicate, & my plan of using Reid's photography is having most admirable results. A photographic of the locals is almost complete. We have captured every type, which enterprise, I must admit, is driven by my own caprice. Have also given a few printed images to the Chief of an interior tribe. I am presuming that they will precede us as they return home & our fame will be carried with them in advance of us. I know the human mind & am certain that every chief will want like images & be ready to do anything to obtain them. This may, more than anything, insure our safe & rapid climb to the great divide.

>──◆◇──○──◇◆──<

I have been photographing with my eyes closed. The camera oculus has done my seeing. Since arriving at the end of the line to work in the daguerreotype studio, I have not looked, not seen the subject before the camera. Is it necessary for a photographer to look? Or is it sufficient that he or she simply place the apparatus in an advantageous place, adjust it, trip the shutter at a fruitful moment, then perform the necessary chemical ablutions.

This day I looked, and sheer fright compelled me to recognise what I beheld. Can the human degenerate so far...or to put it another way, have we advanced such a long way from our animal origins that we've forgotten the truth of our ancestry? I am not ignorant of evolutionary theory, in fact am partial to it, in spite of its much debated deviation from the scriptures, a debate which to me means nothing. Our college was proud of its avant-guard reputation. Saturday night suppers had brilliant speakers, and we were taught the most up to date biological and physical chemical theory.

Who, or what then, do I see before me? Monsters, faces hidden by tangled hair, one perched on all fours? A stone age boy and girl, brought from some place where they have been isolated from the evolutionary process? Can I expect to encounter this phenomenon often in the interior? Whole tribes, living in ways closer to the apes than to us?

The girl, though she is hardly recognisable as female, I would estimate to be seven years of age. Her tongue hangs out through thick red lips and she pants, and bares her teeth. She gets about on her knees and elbows here in the tent studio. When they brought her in, she'd seemed to run on her hands and feet. Her spine appears to be permanently bent, and her knees also.

The boy, looking to be on the cusp of adolescence, stands about thirteen hands. He has large shoulders, long arms, and his spine is quite straight. I showed him his reflection in a mirror I keep to aide those who would primp themselves, and he looked behind it for the person he saw, certain someone was hiding there. His skin is delicate, though from the way the woman – his keeper for want of a better word – pinched him, he is insensitive to pain.

I have had before my camera much evidence of human brutality. Murderers in leg irons, one accused of cannibal acts – this particular subject held at gunpoint by a sheriff the whole time of his portrait. A mother who had methodically suffocated her four children and thrown their bodies in a well. She was transported before me arms chained to legs, all held by a turnip-sized padlock that was undone for the picture. One wild occupant of the forest above the fort – a trapper – brought a captured bear, which he keep obedient with the most cruel harness of barbs and neck yoke.

Yet I was shocked at what manner of technique used upon these children. The younger was brought in first, as she appears to draw the older with her, he being perhaps her brother, and protector. She was still hooded, and while she was held by her tied thumbs, the man holding them drove a ringed stake into the ground before her, attached a tether to it, then slipped it around her neck and tightened. This done, he pulled her head cover off with a circus ringmaster's flourish, and she immediately pressed her hands over her eyes. I wanted to cry out, but the horrible event could not be stopped, and I must admit to my own perverse fascination.

The boy was much more docile, glancing all the while in a piteous way at his cruelly treated companion. He was made to stand beside her, facing me, though he did not know why, and his gaze wandered all about, constantly going back to her, who he would try to touch, to always be prevented by my soldier assistant by a prod with his rifle barrel.

Their woman keeper demanded her payment before the photograph, and was emphatic, a veritable strumpet, in insisting that since she had brought two specimens, she be paid two coins, which we finally did, she stepping out of the tent immediately upon their touching her outstretched palm.

I felt the challenge was to have them look at me. In this I succeeded with the boy. His glance would hold steady some seconds, long enough for an exposure. There was nothing to be done with the girl. Her sensitivity to light was so great I could not get her to look at me, though it was possible to get her head up, and facing my direction by making certain loud noises. This I did, and I believe I have two exposures that will be the most realistic possible, and reasonable pieces of work given the conventions of my art. Which are? That it concentrates the eye upon the superficial. As for deeper things, I leave these to the philosophers.

[Captain Aaron Masse] Day 32

A corporal conveyed to me the news of two most odd subjects being photographed in Reid's tent. I made my way there immediately, encountering Caan & Water Music on the way. A condition of their accepting employment as guides was two printed copies of their portrait, a copy to be kept by Water Music, another copy to be sent to the man Caan claims as his father, now residing in the East.

We arrived at the photographic tent simultaneously, but I begged them to wait, my authority giving me precedence. Upon stepping inside, I confronted two of the most extremely degraded examples of our species I have set eyes upon, bar one or two prisoners we discovered when liberating the Kingsport dungeon. What rendered these two more pathetic was their youth, the girl being no more than seven, the boy at most thirteen.

I immediately demanded to speak with their parents, or guardians. This caused great confusion, for the woman who brought them could not be found. A runner was sent to search for her, as she was known in the town, having somewhat of a reputation, a doxy belle.

I waited. Before me, staked out, like captured beasts of the forest, cowered two children, some combination of wolf, bear & man, the larger boy acting more the human, the smaller, the girl, tending more towards the animal. She arched her back when approached & shook her head to & fro like the most wary cur. The skin on her hands knees & elbows is heavily calloused & her knee ligaments seem to be so locked in the bent position she is unable to walk upright. His knee ligaments appear normal & his visage reflects greater activity of the brain. His face twitched nervously. He rubbed his eyes a great deal & gnashed his teeth & jumped up & down when the girl was harassed.

><-•+>-•-O-•-<+•-><

Reid responded to the pair of urchins in a very delicate & refined way, his voice at once soothing & restrained. This in contrast to the other onlookers, for a crowd of soldiers & residents had gathered. He had the presence of mind to offer the wild things food, going through a selection – he was impressively scientific- until some boiled potatoes & chunks of raw meat were accepted. I should admit that even I had forgotten this universal attribute of living things – hunger – & how useful it can be, whether training a wild horse or comforting a wild infant.

The photography being accomplished, the two were lead out with some difficulty by a young private, the woman who had brought them still unaccounted for. Their appearance outside brought on something of a human explosion. An outpouring of emotion from the sober Water Music. She fingered the fringe of the boy's frayed & rotted doublet, & in an instant was babbling to him in a tongue of which I could not understand one word. Madness followed. Upon seeing the children's state & getting no replies from them other then grunts & snarls, she became quite frantic. There followed a long exchange with Caan.

At this same moment, the runner sent to find the children's guardians returned to tell us they seemed to have absconded. The young woman's belongings had been taken from her room & two horses known to belong to a trapper who frequented her company had been seen leaving the settlement each with a rider, the pair heading towards the eastern pass at a canter. Upon hearing this, Water Music interposed herself as the children's keeper, Caan's resistance aside. When I reminded them, in a polite way, that in a few days they would leave with us on expedition, Water Music stated flatly that the children were to brought with us & I replied, equally absolute, that this was impossible. A stalemate.

After some investigating, speaking with Caan & several people in the settlement, it appears these two children (they are brother & sister) were captured by the same raiding party that took Water Music. Some twenty or thirty souls in total. The raiders, upon returning to these parts from the interior, had stopped to hunt & fish in a valley noted for its temperate climate & fertility. This valley is also hallowed ground for the local people, the birthplace of an important spirit. Here they met with a platoon of soldiers & many were killed. The children, already far from their parents, were abandoned. Because the raiding party had hunted in a sacred place, it was felt they were being punished, so no rescue attempt was made. The children have lived the last four years in the forest, seemingly in the company of wolves. This I find hard to believe, but the physical aspect of the younger child confirms this. They were captured by, or at least came into contact with, a frontiersman & trapper, who is the person responsible for their presence in the settlement. It is my assumption that he & his woman friend who brought them here have forsaken the children.

The boy, standing beside Caan's tent, happily inhaling the smells of Water Music, letting the sound of her voice, the possibility of understanding her rapid words permeate him, watches his sister as she snaps the short twine tether hobbling her and runs, zig-zag on hands and toes, breaking for a nearby bluff. Caan bolts from his tent, running after her. She sprints low in the tall grass, and the boy can follow her only by the trace she leaves on its waving stems. He watches, undisturbed by her departure, having seen such activity many times before. His gaze slides towards the larger trees of the bluff where it finds bird's nest in the higher branches, and rests there.

The girl is into the bluff, trotting through the low scrub easily. This thorny wall of vegetation obstructs Caan, and he runs along its edge until he sees the girl mount one of the trees. She climbs slowly, whistling the soft call of the nesting birds with perfect fidelity of tone and volume. The birds fly close to her, attracted, and she grabs one, ripping off its feathers, tearing the minuscule bits of flesh from the bones with her teeth, and finally drinking the blood, then climbing higher, towards the nests. Caan finds several stones, rounded moraine granite the sized of apples, and hurls them at the girl. His aim is good, and the third one thuds against her breastbone, sounding loudly.

At this, the boy also bolts, running directly towards his sister's tree, and keeping her always in his sight, scales its trunk, putting his body between her and Caan, who is looking for more stones. The girl slithers higher, towards the nest, exposing herself to reach up into it. She finds eggs, and biting off an end, sucks at them. Another of Caan's stones finds its mark, slashing a cut above her eye. Her brother reaches up, and yanks her down towards the shelter of his body but she kicks him and he tumbles backward, his hand fast around her ankle. It is then she who falls, hands slippery with egg, grasping at the trunk, and her brother watches her drop past him, the momentum of her fall already such that she pulls from his grip and crashes through first branches, then spiked shrubbery, to the ground.

>─┼─◆>─●─<◆─┼─<

[Captain Aaron Masse] Day 33

Stiff breeze from SW. Cool, ground fog the morn. A tragedy, but in my favour. The wild children adopted by Water Music yesterday met with a misadventure. The older one, by my observation the much the more tractable, seems to have killed the younger one quite by accident. While I could not imagine us setting off with the two children, I can accept travelling with the oldest. He is mobile, social in his way & probably capable of improvement. He might even prove useful, his ability to find edible nuts & fruits is reported to be astounding. I said as much to Caan, who relayed my words to Water Music, who although deeply affected by the tragedy, agreed.

Rumours of smallpox amongst one of the tribes coming in to trade. Regiment physician investigating. Quarantine here amounts to banishment, the fact that the disease is spread by contact now proven. It is seldom seen in the east these days, the last serious outbreaks occurring in the previous century.

>─┼─◆>─●─<◆─┼─<

The old man raises his head, a huge effort, and looks around the camp. So small, not like when he was young, when there would be a dozen families. Only three conical wikiups of patched deerhide with no decoration, worn and torn where they abrade against the sapling poles. Three children sit on the bare ground of a knoll. Two have stained cotton shirts, the third a rabbit skin doublet.

Several adults move around the camp. One holds the skewered body of a prairie dog over a dung fire. Two mend garments. Another cleans an ancient flintlock musket. Three more human forms rest prone beside the old man, on crusty blankets spread over the ground. There is no shade. Their faces teem with filling and bursting pustules. One woman, her skin pimpled raw red, shakes with fever, and she sips water handed down in a willow bark cup. One man has his chest exposed. The eruptions on it are less, and some have scabbed.

The old man smells horse. With his remaining strength, he rolls himself over to face the scent. A cavalry squad approaches, in military dress save for one – a scout in long fringed rawhide. Mounts at a walk, they circle till directly to windward. Each soldier's, and the scout's, face is wrapped in ivory gauze, a topless turban, the thickest wrapping around nose and mouth. One man, body also encased in ivory, a long double breasted smock, the only soldier without a rifle, raises his hand and the squad stops. He rides closer to the forlorn camp. Its occupants turn to watch. Two men stand. One rams a charge down his musket barrel but he does not cock or level his weapon. The squad's horses munch the short, thick stemmed grass.

The lone soldier remains mounted, scrutinising each face in the camp. He motions the scout to come beside him.

'Tell them that they cannot come to the fort. They must stay away from all the others. They must go back alone.'

This is translated by the scout. After long deliberation, the old man replies.

'We cannot move the ones on the ground, and two others are so sick they cannot walk. We want food and water. We have not eaten for three days,' the scout retranslates.

'Tell them they must go. The ones on the ground will die, the sick ones will die. Leave them. I will set food and water at the top of that hill there. They may take all of it but must not come back.'

The reply is translated by the scout and relayed to the soldier.

'What they say is thank you for the food. They will take it. But they want to come back for their brothers and sisters.'

The white-frocked soldier orders one of the squad to load up with food and a water barrel. This done, the man starts at a trot towards the rise. The frocked soldier throws his full water canteen towards the camp.

'See. I keep my promise. Tell them all is theirs if they move.'

'They thank you again. They will go, but they will return for their brothers and sisters.'

'If they return, they will be shot. We will take care of their brothers and sisters.'

>─┤◇─○─◇┤─<

[Captain Aaron Masse] Day 34

Physician confirms existence of smallpox. I have every confidence in measures taken, but we will set off as soon as Reid packs his equipment. The developed plates we will leave here, soldered in a tin box & they will be transported to the capital when the trail is secure. Our expedition now consists of myself, Reid, Guzman, Bain, Caan, Water Music, the boy, seven riding horses (one spare), eleven pack mules (an extra one being negotiated at the last minute for the boy, which will be set at the head of the train, tethered to whatever horse is last) & Caan's dog, a hunter.

Bain to be out of camp till the morrow having volunteered to accompany a cavalry detail lead by a physician assigned to enforcing the smallpox quarantine. He has spent all his spare time in the army camp, & has made many friends there. I encourage this, as the soldiers are those most familiar with conditions here about.

⊱—+◆⟩—○—⟨◆+—⊰

Nearing the camp, Bain rides ahead of the physician. He can see by the moonlight all three wikiups are down and gone. A fire smoulders. He reins his horse to a walk. Two figures still lie on blankets and two more near them, an old man and a boy, lie on the bare ground. The physician hands Bain a long swatch of gauze then dismounts, hitching his bridle rope to a shrub. Indicating Bain should follow his example, he wraps and tightens his length of gauze into turban, and unties a small wooden keg labelled kerosene set behind Bain's saddle, putting it on the grass.

As Bain watches him walk to the camp, the only sounds are the laboured breathing of its occupants, and the low, delirious, chanting of the old man on the ground. He knocks the bung from the barrel, and tipping it, trickles a constricting spiral of the liquid across the still forms. The old man's eyes follow his every action. He raises a withered arm, then drops it.

The doctor sloshes kerosene till the ground, cloths and blankets are well soaked. He walks back to his horse, dribbling a liquid trail. Halfway, he sets the barrel down. He unwraps a flint and powder, dusting a small pile onto the barrel top. He strikes the flint and its spark lights his face, sets brief embers in his eyes. The powder flashes, the liquid in the barrel blazes, and the flames snake towards the camp, reaching it, rushing into it as the hot air ascends to finally engulf it in thundering orange light.

The doctor remounts and turns away, goading his horse to a trot. Bain remains, hands crossed on his pummel, face lit bronze by the blaze. One supine body, burned muscles contracting, jolts suddenly to sitting position, spraying fragments of flaming cloth, hide, and skin. It blazes, upright, skin blistering, body fat bubbling, hair aflame, seared lips seeming to shriek its death dirge, before crumpling to the ground across the corpses beside it, seeking, even after death, community.

⊱—+◆⟩—○—⟨◆+—⊰

*I*t is that time at night's end when every bird is silent. I cannot put the two wild children out of my mind. Their demeanour a great shock to the sensibilities, yet the appearance of specimens such as these in civilized society is not without historical precedent. Ancient history abounds with animal human myths; two brothers suckled by wolves, a Queen raised by swans, a boy living to adulthood amongst goats. Bear teachers, nursing monkeys, the list is long.

The world of science too has chronicled their manifestation. They are referred to in historical accounts dating from the middle ages. The children I have just seen illustrate the two extremes. The younger one was almost completely animal in aspect, a 'true feral child'. The older one is utterly human, but distracted, without any trace of social influences. They are probably congenital idiots. Seeing that most of the possibilities of human inter-breeding have been explored by the desperate and lonely inhabitants of this place, it does not surprise me to encounter nature's plan gone awry. The savage temper of our surroundings certainly provides for circumstances that would not improve, but rather sustain their present condition.

I think of my mother alone in her huge bed this night. My father one floor below in his smaller berth. Aunty in hers. The servants in theirs. The sky lightens. The sun will soon rise.

>─┼─◆─┼─O─┼─◆─┼─<

The boy regards only the rump of the horse in front of him, and the back of its rider, Water Music. This is enough for him, as his mind closes to the loss of his sister. Balancing on the mule's back, though possible, is terrifying. The hard things they tried to tie on his feet are repugnant. It takes little attention to maintain his place behind the horse, but all his willpower to suppress his fear of the huge animal; of its jerky movement, the equine sweat reek, the position he's in on the narrow path, with many large animals behind him, many large animals and other humans in front of him. He has a fearful memory of travelling in similar fashion, trapped, but in the opposite direction, into the sun, not away from it. This memory tugs at other memories. A nebulous notion of being removed from life's succour its comforting sounds, smells and tastes. The fact that he is journeying in the opposite direction of his removal is somehow good. It calms him.

>─┼─◆─┼─O─┼─◆─┼─<

Clayton Bailey

[Captain Aaron Masse] Day 35

I have suffered a blow, in the form of a dispatch delivered to me but an hour before we left the outpost. I was informed, most respectfully by my sister, that my wife has moved out of our house suddenly, to live in the company of her own sister, where she has been staying off & on for some time now. She has applied for divorce, pertinent documents to follow. Condolences, but few details were provided. My daughter also informed, but no communication from her.

The exit of my good wife brings musings of her, my now departed spouse. Although her move separates our houses, we have been separated in body since I returned home with my arm amputated. She found it of such ugliness she lost all interest in the marital relation & our life settled into a pattern of segregated beds & rooms. I cannot be so dishonest to pretend this was easy for me. I yearned for the comfort & pleasure of her body every night. I had always tried to be attentive in loving her & I missed her more then, when she was near me, than now, knowing she resides forever in another city, with another family.

The wild boy we have brought has sunk into depression. He too has suffered a loved one's death. His gloom, my own & the tedium of slow trail riding causes me many memories. Some in particular perhaps, because they bring me to mind of the boy's physic, but also for the resemblance, when times are tedious, of their affect on me. I tend to recollect those things that were a shock to my thinking.

We were advancing at a rapid rate towards the rebel stronghold, fatigued but victorious. Upon breaking down the doors of the lowest level of Kingsport prison, we came upon a man, one of our own, arrested as a spy, who had been isolated the whole of the war to that time. Some three years. When we brought him to the light, he was absolutely befuddled. His huge eyes slid sleepily over people & things. He did not speak. He had quite forgotten how. We showed him things; a horse, a gun. He did not know their names.

Many captives were taken that day. All were stripped of their uniforms in the dispensary, a policy at the time to prevent lice. Among them were several women, which did not surprise us, having already encountered several uniformed female rebels. None above the rank of corporal. They seemed to share the discomforts & camaraderie of war equally with their mates. When asked by one of our nurses how they enlisted, they replied that joining up with the rebels was simply a matter of appearing in uniform.

Remain convinced more women disguised themselves & enlisted in our army than is given credence. Shocking anecdotes circulated throughout the war, accusations these females were worse than the lowest camp follower, mere Doxy Belles seeking greater access to the soldiers. Extravagant as the stories remained, I am sure many had foundation in actual fact, & I do not doubt that those women who disguised themselves did so for patriotic impulsions as honest as their male compatriots.

& here, thinking as I write, wonder if the quandary of Reid's bearing could be that he is a woman in disguise. Certainly I have been seeking an answer to the question of his peculiar qualities for weeks now. Would this affect the expedition greatly. No, not if the others were ignorant of it.

Much reason to the conjecture. His desire to sleep alone, the difficult night in the tent with the others, his rising early each morn, & even, for Reid is clever, the over-acted bravado at times. Will watch him closely.

Temperature increases each toward days end. Guzman making two main sights a day, sunrise & sunset & intermediate measurements from any advantageous prominence. Bain husbands our mounts, finding pasture every night & cajoles the Mule train along paths a goat would shun. He also assists Guzman & at times Reid, who working in rhythm with Guzman, using the smaller, portable apparatus, takes an image, remains behind to develop the plate, then catches up. On occasion he finds that the absolute beauty of the environ must be recorded.

Caan a crack shot, we sup on mountain sheep, grouse, the former prepared in an ingenious way. The hoofs are cut off while the killed animal retains its heat & a length of hollow bone is inserted into the leg between skin & muscle. A mighty puff of air & the hide separates from the body, being stripped off by slitting the belly. The gutted animal then rubbed with tumeric, of which we have plenty. A fire being made, rocks are heated, ones picked by Water Music that will not crack. The sheep is then filled with hot rocks, & buried upon the fire. Quickly, the most savory roast is ready.

The boy, despite his depression, leads us to bushes of excellent nuts, which the squirrels do not seem to be able to detach. He has also once smelt a bear, communicating this with urgent gestures to Water Music. We retreated & waited till the dangerous beast lumbered off the trail. I know them well. Only a well placed shot can stop one. Discretion is the better part of valour, or as my grandmother would say, 'tis a poor set of legs will see a body hurt'.

Water Music tends the boy, who rejects the cooked meat, but will take boiled dumplings. She sings to him evenings, which moderates his wildness & then she strokes his tense limbs. He does not speak, but I see trust abuilding. With all this, we make 7 or 8 mile a day & I am well satisfied with our upward progress.

This country unimpressive. Steep ravines with small cricks, flowing fresh. There are no men to be seen, & little wildlife. We have developed a taste for the mountain sheep, larger than a goat, smaller than a wapiti. Caan brings them down with a single shot at a hundred paces. His well placed ball invariably bursts the heart. His new rifle delights him. We see bears, but at a distance. Caan killed one, three balls, two in the brain. Unable to weight the critter, estimate a quarter ton, but not such a menace as had been represented to us. Provided good meat & an excellent sort of cooking fat.

>—+◆>—○—◆+—<

*T*he Captain indulges my landscape work, if it is able to combine beauty with the function of topographic description. This I do, and though the wet plate process has proved to me its excellence of detail, it is difficult to surpass the sumptuous renderings of Guzman, thus I try, with the dispassionate exposure of each photographic plate, to compliment his fervid illustration. He places a camera lucida for his initial sketch, giving him single point perspective from the exact position of his plane table, but the minutia are rendered exquisitely by his own hand. A strange, and talented man, as they all are here, each in their way. He works in a trance, jolting himself awake with his coffee before sunrise, then proceeding in rushes, fits and starts, as the stolid Bain goads the mules steadily on, and helps us with our tripods and set ups when able. Guzman is the last to sleep at night, his shadow bent over his folding table, lamp above his head making his tent, lit from within, seem the levitating cabin of a ghostly ship as I pass it seeking some private spot to perform my evening toilette. On this matter I carefully watch Water Music to see how she accomplishes her own affairs in masculine company but she gives no hint, appearing to be a woman utterly without unseeming bodily functions. Another mystery.

These mountains never silent. Even nights they have their own life. Rocks tumble incessantly, at times ricocheting very close. Days, I train my apparatus on their craggy corpus, gliding clouds the only movement. Each image is burnt into my mind by the long minuets of composition and focus, and so, to my eye, they are so devoid of human life I seem to be photographing the surface of a unoccupied planet. Yet, the boy, who demonstrates strangely consistent, if not quite human sensitivities, and Water Music, react to certain turns in the trail, the heights of distinct ridges, with watchful suspicion. Perhaps we are not alone, for the horses too, my mare especially, swing their heads to unseen odours. And Caan's dog must be restrained, by the man's shouts and thrown stones, thrice a day.

>—‹•›—O—‹•›—‹

[Captain Aaron Masse] Day 43

Contact with first high plains tribe. Live as yet without horse. Some women & several dogs. We tried to make signs of friendship. Bain held out a handful of beads. Water Music shouted a word meaning "Peace" but to no avail. As they ran off, I advanced towards them & rolled up my sleeve, thinking to show them we were not coloured as them, since our faces are now all tanned the deepest brown, but they did not look back.

>—‹•›—O—‹•›—‹

The scout selects a rock with a notch in it about the size of his head and pulls his hair tight back, knotting it with a thong so it will not blow in the wind. He checks the angle of the sun. Its shadow falls across the notch, and is slightly behind him. He smears dirt across his forehead, rendering it the same colour as the dull sandstone outcrop he crouches behind. Belly to its smooth base, he eases himself into the notch till his eyes can see down into the canyon.

He considers the expedition's ragged line of pack animals led by Captain Masse, and the separate dots of Guzman, Bain and Reid in the hills beyond. What he sees has been described to him that morning by a woman and a girl in from berry picking, and over many winters by men who have ventured farther to the east than he, to the edge of the mountains. The scout is well content to finally behold members of this much talked about foriegn tribe.

'Six on horse,' he counts, 'one walking, ten pack mules, two behind without loads. They have many guns but they do not look like warriors, except for the one-armed man, who must be the chief. He sits on his horse like he is angry about losing his arm in a fight, and has killed many men to revenge it. Two of the others are hunters, they set up their three legged stands like animal or bird traps, very carefully, always finding a piece of flat ground. The tribe passing through told us about this. They put small tools on the stands, things made in a very beautiful way, of a golden metal and a red wood. These tools have an eye of smooth stone clear as water at the front of them. One of the tools, the one like a box, is a trap. The hunter, who must also be a medicine man, opens the front, the eye of clear stone, whatever is in front goes inside, then he closes the eye. Some time later, he goes into his magic tent and lets what is inside the box out onto a very flat, very thin piece of stone. When you look at it, it is what was in front of the medicine man before. Small people, or trees and clouds, but they have no colours, and do not move. The tribe passing through had one of these small flat stone pictures. The wife of our chief would like one.

'The other tool is there because it is well known that these people are forgetful and get lost very easily. Many people have observed this about their forgetfulness. Their memories are so bad that they must mark everything down, because they forget it, even the next day. The other hunter marks down where they are, that this rock has this shape, that this tree grows in such a way, that there is good water to drink in this place, so that he can find the way back, because he will forget it the next day, and they will become lost, and perish. The tribe passing through told us these people are on a long journey, over the mountains to the sea. For such a long journey it is necessary to have a very good memory. I cannot see how they will make it.'

'Their leader has one of the clear stone eyes also, in a tube. It is because his own eyes are very weak. He puts the tube to his weak eyes, and he can see distant things, like an eagle. This must be his totem animal. I was told that if he puts it to his eye, to hide, for he will see, and make trouble.

'Today, they had a small supper. I think they are running out of meat. There are no animals in this canyon, all the way to the ridge. It is too dry. We will wait one or two more days, until they have a supper with no meat, then we will talk with them, if they make the sign of peace, and make some trades, and get one of the flat stone pictures for the chief's wife.'

The Expedition

>—⊹—◇—⊹—<

[Captain Aaron Masse] Day 49

Wind following mountain pattern of afternoon williwas. Last of
meat eaten. No sign of game. We follow the trail & hope for the
best. Topped the ridge at the tail of this canyon & found another
stream flowing down the mountain, but to the west. Bain pas-
tured mounts. Beyond what seems to be an immense interior
plateau, several ranges of mountains. Now one lunar month since
vernal equinox. Guzman took a long series of measurements &
triangulated base line.

[Carlo Guzman]
Approached the height of land AM. Barometric altimeter reading
recorded and adjusted with triangulated sights. No great error.
Turned down PM and encountering first stream flowing consistent westerly direction took altitude sights West and deduced we
have attained height of land. This distinguished by a bare igneous
cordillera running NNW by SSE. Altitude by triangulation and
barometric altimeter again concur. We have transected the
Continental Divide.

>—⊹—◇—⊹—<

In irregular line abreast, about fifty men, medium to tall, advance slowly up
a grass ridge facing the expedition's camp. All of them carry a quiver of
arrows and a strung bow half the tallest man's height. Their thighs and arms
are bare, well muscled, and the moccasins on their feet are short, tied at the
ankle. Some wear leather chest armour, some have calve thick clubs slung
from their waists, and a few have metal bladed knives or hatchets. A handful
clutch long, muzzle loading muskets and powder horns. Their black hair is
pulled tight behind their heads. The low sun lies directly behind them, as do
several mountain ranges, those farthest the tallest and snow covered. In the
rear, below, a clutch of silent women in brown and tan deerskin robes wait
in a bluff of long leaf willows. One woman wears a full length bearskin cloak.

    Nearing the long promontory's crown, the men break ranks, each plac-
ing a boulder or hummock between him and the people and animals just
below, now a stone's throw distant. When the men are positioned, their
leader lets out a long whoop, and stands up, stepping over the height of the
ridge and placing himself, legs apart, arms akimbo, on the slope facing the
survey party. Bain swings his rifle towards the exposed man, but Captain

Masse, still mounted, throws his down, ordering the others to drop whatever arms they have. He advances towards the standing man, one slow step at a time, holding his hand palm up. Water Music calls out, repeating a soft, three syllable word many times but this has no affect. When the Captain is closer to the exposed man than the expedition, all the men who have been concealed behind the ridge stand and step forward. Water Music breaks away and runs towards Captain Masse but Caan calls her back. Bain again raises his rifle, and the ragged line of warriors surges forward, but Caan strikes the rifle barrel, knocking it to the ground.

Captain Masse dismounts. He calls to Caan, who fumbles in the baggage till he finds a long, wood stemmed pipe and a twist of tobacco. He brings it up, and is commanded to light it. After several puffs, the Captain takes it, and puffs on it, the smoke floating downslope in the light wind. The Captain again steps forward, until he is able to hand the lit pipe to the man who first exposed himself. The pipe is taken, the man tries to smoke it, taking a few pulls, but soon removes the pipe from his mouth and taps the bowl. Caan throws him the tobacco pouch.

The man sits, and motions to the others, and Captain Masse and Caan to do the same. When the pipe is recharged, he points its bowl to the four cardinal points, and smokes it again as the survey party, empty-handed, moves slowly closer.

> ⤳⊶⟐⟐⊷⤆

[Captain Aaron Masse] Day 51

Little wind. Warm. We presented ourselves this morning at an encampment of some several hundred souls, after a anxious night during which I posted guard, two hours each.

These people seem not to be transient, for they live in domed, branch roofed huts with a ring of stones around the base, but they assure me that late summers they venture onto the plains in hide tents like the others, travelling for months.

> ⤳⊶⟐⟐⊷⤆

In this stupefied state, how am I to photograph. Tobacco is a most powerful substance when inhaled. I wonder how it compares to laudanum, or paregoric. A mirage is what I could be in, the disguised Joanna Reid, bent over her brass and mahogany apparatus, surrounded by dark and square jawed faces, a village of the most softly rounded huts, and a line of forbidding mountains in the distance that await my footfall.

How did it occur that I am here, feet upon the moccasin trampled sod? Me, the observer, my every action now observed, more intently watched for the meaning of my movements than the most rehearsed ballerina. This is what I have discovered. I am not a stranger here. The human body comprehends much. A hunter is a hunter. A conjurer a conjurer no matter where. The act is identical, universal. I now understand why I was so affected by photographing the tribe of traders within the outpost's fort. Those men and women, children too, as do these before me now, all in their deer hide robes, saw in me actions they recognised, the mindful attentions of anyone intent on practising any directed art or craft.

Do they see in me the delicate movements of a stalking hunter as a I set in a wetted plate? Do they identify the precision of the marksman as I adjust focus? Does some local sorcerer recognise, as I set the diaphragm and shutter, the delicate preparations of a fellow trickster?

All along I thought it was waiting for the photo that caught these untamed beings notice and rendered them so quiescent, but it's not that at all. It is the language my slowly moving body speaks, my concentration, the discreet action of my hands. They comprehend truly the predacious, its pleasure and disciplines, the difficult odds against capturing a delicate prey, be it beast, fish or foul. And so also did I, the photographer, come to understand this, the necessity of imitating, becoming one's prey, through word or gesture, if only for an instant, before tripping the shutter. I had never thought of that, that there was an art to portraiture and I had learned it. But I have. What a revelation.

>—I—<>—O—<>—I—<

The boy, always in the vicinity of Water Music, shifts about the expedition camp with untroubled ease, even sitting down, sitting still in the light. His posture now plumb, he drinks water from a cup – small gulps. His face has smoothed, and no longer quakes, disobedient, but reveals the activity of his brain, bending into a smile when he hears Water Music sing inside her tent, pressing his eyes into a squint when he looks at the faraway mountains, and flattening his cheeks into vertical plates as he watches the tall man Bain load a long barrelled pistol.

The boy knows now what guns can do, has seen Caan bring down a mountain sheep from far away. Has clambered close, ahead of Caan, touched the bullet's entry hole, small enough his finger could plug it, and rolling the sheep over, off the blood spattered grey granite, seen the conic cavern of the shattered ball's exit, so big his head would fit inside, the torn guts, gory shards of bone, the bits of fur smeared across the stone.

Travelling with this pack of people, many of whom point things – Guzman his sextant, Reid his camera, Caan his gun – the boy has established the basic facts of what the objects do. He knows now that when Guzman points his object, he will touch a piece of paper many times, and at the end of the day there are many squiggles on the paper that everyone looks at. When Reid points his, later, there will be a small flat picture, in only black and white, of whatever Reid stood in front of. Everyone will also look at this object, though it is much smaller than Guzman's. With Caan's gun, the boy has established that the gun the marksman holds in his hand is not important as an object. It does no harm. The power lies in something that lands wherever the gun is pointed, near or far. Brutal destruction occurs there, much worse than the boy could do hitting with his own hands, and whatever animal hit thus loses warmth, and never moves again, like his sister after she fell from the tree, and like the rotting corpses they would sometimes find in the bush, attended by vultures.

Bain calls to the boy, and levels the pistol barrel between his eyes. The boy imagines the destructive power entering him, making a small hole in his forehead, and a huge crater at the base of his neck, where everything inside his head will pour out.

Bain motions him to the far edge of the camp, where some trunks are stacked. The boy goes there. Bain motions for him to sit, and turn away. The boy does this, now imagining the entry hole in the back of his head, and his face torn off, again his memories pouring out with his blood. This idea is so powerful they boy puts himself in a rigid trance, hoping that total mute immobility will please Bain. He looks at the faraway mountains. He hears Water Music's voice express surprise. He wants to turn. He turns. Bain, his hand on the tent flap, points the pistol directly at the boy, who turns back, vowing to stay that way until someone forces him to move. Not wanting to have his memories removed by the power of the pistol, not wanting to enter the motionless state called death, which will prevent him from reaching his home fires, he does not turn again, until he hears Water Music scream, when he hears the sounds of an intense close fight, Bain's harsh murmur, Water Music sobbing, and finally, a wail from Bain, clear and sharp, like the cry of a migrating swan.

>─┼─◆>─○─<◆─┼─<

[Captain Aaron Masse]

We were shown to a domicile larger than the others, its floor pounded hard & smoothed. Our party consisted of myself, Caan, who speaks a bit of the language, Guzman, who could not be restrained for his lively curiosity, & Reid, as the request communicated to us, after an initial entreaty for steel blades, was for a photograph, this tribe having already heard of our work at the outpost from a group returning to the interior. Caan translated the idea of photograph as 'careful picture on square flat stone.' I left Bain guarding camp, well armed, though I would be dismayed if he is forced to shoot. Also Water Music, who found herself ill this morning & wanted to take care of the boy.

We sat in a circle, four of us & four of them. This time pipe passed with great formality. They explained their desire for trade goods & their fear of our rifles, which they seem to know are accurate at great distances & their relief that we are not enemies. We in turn requested food & safe passage. Much counting by sign language. They dress in tanned hides, often leaving the fur on & sport little decoration, though a greatly requested item was red glass beads, these to be put in the hair of both men & women. I presented the chief, who is old, but with a young wife, with a red wool cape. He indicated to me that he wished to be photographed with all his wives his generals & his medicine man. Received a hundredweight of smoked meat & near a hogshead of a kind of pudding I understand is a pounded root, berries & tallow. When the sun was high, with drumming & dancing already started, attention turned to Reid, who'd made ready to photograph.

➤─┤◆➤─◉─◄◆├─◄

In the blustery dark, Caan, Reid and the Captain return to camp and tether their horses. No-one speaks as they seek their tents. Caan staggers to his, but its flap is tied from inside. He slaps the taut canvas with the flat of his hand. Water Music's voice inside is angry, rejecting him. He sits, back against the tent's canvas wall, banging the flat of his palm against it now and then. Finally, a strong push from inside throws him, face down, onto the turf. He stumbles to his saddle bags and fumbling, finds a blanket. He blunders away, into the dark beyond the perimeter of the camp. His snore soon stutters through the vale, then blows clear and mournfully deep.

➤─┤◆➤─◉─◄◆├─◄

[Captain Aaron Masse] Day 66
Wind switching from NW to SW. Temp rising. First successful meeting with a tribe unknown to us. Caan did yeoman work, also

Reid, the photographic ritual & quarter plate image causing much amazement. Secured food for one week, loaded on spare mule. Will proceed NW across plateau. Estimate first mountain range ten days ride.

Doubtful if boy will survive the trip. Found him in a catatonic state upon our return. Would not move until Caan struck him. Will no longer submit to Water Music's affection.

Left the native camp long past sunset, fatigued. They were dancing wildly, having begun their presentation for us, then continued of their own volition. Animal & times lewd gyrations & I wonder if such things are the Devil's work for certainly feel his presence in camp tonight. We all in a strange temperament. I attribute this to the rising temperature & our first contact with total strangers. We are alone here, straddling the great divide. The journey now a long descent. This bleak night, I say my prayers, as my grandmother bid me always do, & place us all, men, women and the child, in God's hands.

Caan's dog killed by wolves.

⊷⊶⊶◦⊶⊷⊶

A recently published book, an 'oeuvre' of the category I would call "tales written for youth," made its way around the settlement immediately before I left. In spite of its juvenile intentions, it was popular with the adult citizens, and I must admit, the author exhibited a sparkling style. The story concerned a party of explorers, who, by means of some rocket projectile, voyaged to another planet in our solar system.

They landed on a boulder-strewn, arid plain, utterly alone. Their problems became not understanding the pristine environment, but reconciling diverse nationalities and goals. And this is how our camp feels tonight. We sit upon the ridge of the great divide, an endless plateau below us, towering mountains in the distance. No-one spoke during our supper of dried meat stew and boiled berries. We are like those solitary fictional explorers; we feel not only the effect of our strange isolation, but the tensions of our odd social combination. We are all utterly foreign to this place and to each other, all aliens. And, perhaps we are, between us, rendered even more strangers by secrets we do not share. I have mine, and as I lie alone in my tent, surrounded by my stack of exposed and developed plates, my cold and mechanical photographic apparatus, which occupy me but give me no soul's comfort, I wonder what secrets the others guard, what hidden passions, what terrible crimes, what unknown desires, for this is how our little camp felt when I returned tonight, bathed in a grotesque atmosphere of unrevealed mystery. Bain, Water Music, neither would speak. Guzman stayed at the tribal dance, drunk. Caan returned home, also drunk, but he does not join his wife. Captain Masse went directly to his tent, and what did I see, getting a dipper of water to drink, but the great man on his knees, and that is not the first time. Imagine, our fate is in the hands of a leader who calls to God each night, like a child saying its bedtime prayers.

The positive feeling of reaching the great divide, our voyage now a simple descent, has somersaulted to negative. I am a woman disguised as a man. Could it be that every person and event, the world itself, has at its source an antithesis, like the positive print has as its source the negative? Are we closer to that other world tonight, being so high, and secluded? What reveals the heart's, the world's secrets, like pyro reveals the latent image on the photographic plate?

>─┤◀▶─○─◀▶├─<

[Captain Aaron Masse] Day 66

After many days covert observation, I set down the most unanticipated deduction, declaring that Reid may well be a woman in disguise. When I thought of this midst a long day on horse back & looked back at him with marked intensity, Reid almost jumped from his saddle. Did I see a bound young bosom pressing against a light cotton over shirt? Why am I so suddenly convinced? So many things; Reid's mysterious combination of modesty & bravado, the constant need for privacy. Finally, the affinity with Water Music & conduct with the child. While not matronly, it has a suppleness a man could never equal. I debate whether thence I will refer to Reid as him or as her. What to make of the situation? Cannot reveal it, if it is true, for so many reasons. Is it that important? Cannot see, if no-one detects Reid's true sex, how the expedition will in any way suffer. In the scriptures, there is no commandment ordering a man to not resemble a woman or vice versa. I believe God has no interest in such things & sought the council of my revered ancestor on this very private revelation. He appeared to me as he often does, just as I drifted off to sleep, this time costumed as the most ancient of soldiers of my family line, a helmeted charioteer, his bronze helmet under his arm. Of women he did not speak. Instead, he reminded me I have grand plans, & am part of a grander plan, the building of a nation, for which I have already given much of my life & my entire forelimb. Our need is for her competence as a photographer? That has been well tested. Her photographic work must secure us safe passage & the Nation's praise upon return. Little else matters. The die is long cast. His or her sex is but a simple twist of fate, yet I am hungry with the urge to know.

Rash, too inquisitive, did something I have never done. Whilst Reid, Guzman and Bain were far from camp mapping, stole into Reid's tent, having seen her scribbling away on a sheet of paper, a letter I assumed. Jealous to find the recipient, I slipped my fingers through the effects strewn about, & found it. A polite note to a mother, with some clever descriptions of the landscape but the letter unfinished, thus unsigned. No answers there, & I felt of a sudden contrite. Upon Reid's return, spend a long while in observation, myself unobserved, while our photographer went about photographing today. Great confidence has been gained & every movement, graceful & precise, demonstrates talent & a fondness for the task. We were even graced with a smile, something I have never seen, though it was not at me, but at a child. For me are reserved the deepest scowls.

I still do not know what to think? The most difficult segment of the expedition lies before us. The weather is good. I will set my tent a little ways from the others, & far from the horses. This will allow me to arise before Reid. I do not relish spying, but I must answer my now long standing question as to Reid's gender.

Depleted, Caan sinks to the ground. He looks to his tent. The flap is still tied tight from inside. He rolls in the thick grass, clutching at the long stems, till he is cocooned by it and his head finds a rock for a pillow. He lays his pipes out an arms length away, and pulls his coat over his stomach and chest, and turning his face to the point of sunrise, falls straightaway asleep.

[Captain Aaron Masse] Day 87

Wind NW, steady, day & nt excepting rain squalls. Anticipated crossing alpine plateau 3 days, we are now 1 wk & just reaching base of 2nd mountain range, this caused by worrying sickness of Water Music who cannot move from her tent till noon & remains ill disposed to travel the day.

Bain working as Guzman's assistant, the animals & trail requiring little time to manage hereabout. This much increases our speed of passage when we can move.

>─┤◆├─◯─┤◆├─<

*N*ow every day improving, the boy. Switching his affections, he cultivates the amity of myself and Guzman. Mayhap Water Music mothers him over much, her love too rich for one accustomed to none for he seems apathetic towards her, or perchance his desire to be with us stems from his wildness, and dislike of Camp life, since on these plains Guzman and I go forth each day with our instruments. The boy desires simply to wander with us, as was his previous habit.

We take him on our survey rounds, leaving in the morning, returning evenings, and, growing tired of his dragging behind on foot, we even persuaded him to mount, on the saddle behind me, with much cajoling from Guzman. He held on for dear life, his cheek pressed to my back, and I kept my mare at a walk until I felt his head lift, and turn. I remember well the magic of my own first ride on horseback. The lofty perspective, the magic of being propelled over the ground with no effort.

He now puts up our tripods, which he does well, scrambling through bramble and grass, and setting the legs solid. He does not understand yet the function of the levelling ball, but I expect he will within a few days. He has become our companion and assistant. Though his hands as yet do not possess sufficient exactness to handle the instruments or the camera, he's grasped immediately the nature of my photographs, which are much less puzzling to him than a mirror. I gave him a quarter plate print I made in the field, and holding it, he walked back to exactly the place it had been taken, and held the image in front of him, as if testing it for authenticity.

I have become closer to Guzman, sharing our workaday rhythm. For all his caprice when there is time to squander, he is a demon in the field. Early to rise, last to sleep, finalizing the details of his maps by lamplight. We shared a moment of repose, under a thick bluff of poplars as a rain shower passed. Still having in mind the long dissertation of Bain's on his love of rivers, and still aware within myself of the questions it stimulated, and my need for answers, I asked Guzman what he loved. To my surprise, given he is such an emotional man, he received my question with the cool logic of a scientist, turned it over in his mind the while, and looking up at the sky, which had cleared, since the rain had passed, said he would reply when nature provided us another recess.

One constant wonder, which understanding reveals my own naive illusions. I accepted this daunting task for many reasons, but if my memory serves me, the deciding point was the possibility of compiling a portfolio of landscape photographs, the first set of images from virgin, unoccupied territory. I saw myself as the direct descendent of the great explorers and navigators, my own footfall being the first upon undefiled rock and soil.

This is absolutely not true. There are people, or signs of people everywhere. We cross well travelled trails continually, each day we stumble upon an old campsite, or a group of women gathering berries, or hunters stalking game. Our good luck that these peoples are not warlike, yet, still, each contact has its particular diplomatic complexity and potential for inconvenience. Often we are forced to seek the aid of Caan or Water Music, which adds to our difficulty, for she is ill, and we must return to camp for negotiations. I feel at times as constrained as I did travelling about the old continent a decade ago by train, across its tiny countries, with constant border checks, and presentation of passports and visas.

>-+◆>-O-<◆+-<

[Captain Aaron Masse] Day 88

Crept out early morn, before Reid awoke, as was my plan, we being camped aside a wide creek, & waited above its nearest pool. My judgement correct & Reid appeared, the sky still black, & disrobed to bath. & truly she is a woman in disguise. A lithe & most exquisitely formed young lady of some twenty odd years. I waited & watched, truth be known, much longer than the instant needed to confirm my suspicion.

Perhaps my discovery has left me overwrought. Lost my patience with Water Music, cause of another delay this morning & unable to help break camp. Spoke to Caan, being in a very ill temper. Informed me & if this fact hidden from me since outset I consider him irresponsible, to wit his wife is with child, being in the 3rd month.

Reckon myself a man acquainted with overcoming the inconstants of any venture. I, Aaron Masse 2nd, set out in good faith some three months ago with my hand picked corps of four men, stout & true, aiming to gain perhaps one more, of equal talents. This day, our venture truly beginning, the party in fact comprises a ragtag squad including one ever more rigid & mute cohort for a hostler, one dipsomaniac madman as navigator, one melancholy half caste as guide, a pregnant woman as translator, another woman disguised as a man for a photographer & a idiot young one to round out the whole affair.

Knowing we would be in camp the day, & having risen in the middle of the night, I dozed. My mentor appeared, unbidden, his visitation lengthy as often happens when I nap from fatigue during the day. His uniform was from a recent time, my dead father's generation. I could smell the gunpowder on him. He spoke not, but wrapped me in his steely glaze. Stand fast his eye's unswerving posture said. Council well received. Stand fast it will be. The morn, I will awake early & take particular care with my kit & exit from my tent somewhat more the officer than I have been of late, to impress on all my resolution. I say my prayers for all of us this night, & on the morrow, with God's grace, we proceed.

▷━┼━◇▸━○━◂◇━┼━◁

Mules and horses nose to tail, the expedition ascends a rising plain, a tilted shield of sediment accumulated during Palaeozoic times, the floor of a once great sea thrust skyward by crashing continental plates, now exposed to frost, gale and torrent. Traversing deposits as deep as their distance travelled in a day, the animals tread humus stratum alive with worms. Under this, moles and marmots burrow into clays blue, ochre and black. One mule snaps a shin in such a hole, is shot, and eaten. A deep draw is located, and a shaft dug there for water, exposing the earlier glacial till. Petrified trees and ferns. Skeletons of the primal life forms, mollusca and trilobite. Below this, unseen, lies the pure antediluvian precipitate of volcanic eruption, adulterated only by the mineral spawn of fallen meteorites.

The men and women of the expedition, transiting this tableland via a slight trough, a fold in the ancient crust, think of the granite and basalt geography as absolutely immovable, the very embodiment of the solid earth's permanence, but this vital earth lives by a different time frame, millionfold longer in its rhythms than the animals' successive day and night, the woman's cycle of a month, the plant's annual winter and summer.

For the earth, these ridges the expedition treads remain fluid. The plain they climb still rises, the last affect of a swell of mountain making energy that rolled inland from the western ocean eons past with the same rolling energy as one of the ocean's waves only travelling at the earth time pace, imperceptible to late coming beasts and humans, perceptible only to the planet and its satellites if a gravitational field shifted, perhaps to other planets in some cosmic dance of near infinite duration.

⊱—⊹—O—⊹—⊰

The boy evolves, day by day becoming more able as my assistant. This since the onset of some tension pervading Water Music. The boy's feelings for her have changed. Something has passed between them, though he still loves her, I can see from his sidelong glances. His perspective has shifted. Could it be that he knows I am a woman too, or senses it, within the peculiar edifice of his unschooled mind and that is why he seems to have sought me out.

Or perhaps there is something else afoot with him – he is discovering, or rediscovering, human society. His first attachment was primal...to the mother. Now, that done, he has realised, is seeing, that we are a team, a society in miniature, we are united in purpose, yet have our disparate tasks, and earn our keep. This is a relationship less given than child and mother, something forged through negotiation and earned respect. He may want to leave the confines of family relations and join society, our Lilliputian one. How well I understand this urge – it has brought me here. Perhaps the boy, like I, seeks his task, wants to earn his keep and belong.

So he, still speechless, watches what I do, then, step by step duplicates it. He is neither a bad and nor a good student. He would have been a bad student at my college, but I am aware that many skills, from all those of the carpenter to some of the doctor, are not, "taught." They are, instead, learned by serving apprenticeship, by following the work of the master. In this way, the boy is an excellent student, he never – because he is speechless – asks a question, even in gesture. He watches, helps, tries the first part of a task till he has it right, then tries the second part, the third and so on.

The way I learned things, he would be terrible at – the student being taught then studying, the mind prepared for the tasks with books and lectures, until it must then make the jump to actually accomplishing a task. This kind of learning definitely affects the mind, now that I ponder it, for the person embarking on the task, actually uneducated in a practical way, is of course nervous in face of material fact.

This seems to be the way of our world nevertheless. Thinking upon it now, I realise many things are done in such fashion, the mind being predisposed for a task by study. A response of my mother's comes to mind. When I asked her how it came about she had the courage to leave her comfortable home in the old world and embark on the strenuous task of marrying, then following my father to set up home in the new world, a task which seems to have broken her spirit, she replied simply..."novels."

She had spent her young womanhood absorbed in romantic novels describing the exotic life and locales of the new world. When she was asked to journey and take up residence in it, she felt no fear, felt she already knew it, through the adventure tales she'd read.

I did not think to ask the logical next question – what was the real new world like in comparison to its literary representation – but I would assume, given her broken health and spirit, given indeed that she never went to the actual frontier, but settled in a comfortable zone behind it, that her encounter was a shock. Is it conceivable she regretted her decision, or that she dreamt of returning? Does my mother sway me more than I think? Was there more to her than I knew? Had the fire been put out, or did it continue to smoulder? Am I living a fiction she could not, a conquest over the new world wilderness?

On the practical side, I am exceedingly proud of my gutta purcha fabrication. Rolling the pliant sheet into a tube was not difficult, and I sewed it thus with a long strand of gut. At the top, I attached a triangle, corresponding to the triangle of my pubis. I put it on in my tent. It fitted well, the triangle tight against me, the rolled tube extending out my trousers, with a droop exactly corresponding to a man's penis. I am quite sure it will work in practice. I will make my first test at a distance, just in case of some miscalculation. Field excursions with Guzman should give me an opportunity.

The boy perceives he can control his hands. Setting the tripod is the most familiar act. The legs are tapered shafts of wood, like perfect, barkless tree branches. He spreads the three legs and slides his hands down their smoothness. He presses his foot on the tiny step above the metal tips, digging their points into the earth. He slides the leg joints till the top is at the height the thin man likes, then rolls the locking knobs tight. The knobs just fit in the curve of his palm, and he has learned the amount of rolling force needed, about the same as that needed to snap the neck of a rabbit. The next step is still a mystery to him, and miraculous when accomplished. He sets the tripod head on the base, and screws it loosely, about the same force as the leg locks. Then he stands on tip toe, and looking down at the round glass of the level, large as a deer's eye, he jiggles the head until the level's bubble, floating, small as a bird eye, centres in a tiny circle. This takes monumental concentration. His first movements are too abrupt, and the bubble moves contrary to any logic the boy has known, so he must forget all he understands about the physical world, and make his hand move in the opposite direction of his instincts. Which exhausts him, so when the bubble is centred or nearly so and the head is level, he invariably collapses onto the grassy, rock rubbled earth, thus signalling Reid that the camera may be brought out. When the boys sees Reid open the camera case, he gets up, and screws the head's lock screw tight as he is able.

He still has not learned the touch of the camera, but he calms enough, and the shadows and phantoms flitting through his head become memories, actual events past. He begins to remember that he long ago was taught, and learned to learn. He knows to follow the example of the teacher, to watch with his eyes what their hands do, put his own hands on top of theirs to follow movements, sense pressures.

Reid sets the box square camera on the tripod head, centring the female brass screw in its bottom over the hole in the tripod base. The boy reaches under, jiggling the screw, trying to enter it till overcome with frustration, his facial skin compressed into furrows of tension, his lips twitching, a long slobber of saliva tracing a shiny arc below the lowest corner of his mouth.

Reid laughs, an evanescent outrush of breath, and takes the male brass screw. She holds it in front of the boys eye, and rotates it between thumb and forefinger in a clockwise direction, then gives it back to the boy. He tries again, whole body now trembling with anxiety. He has lost control of his hands. The screw clacks against the hole, misses, scrapes across the head, and he drops it. His face and body are one massive tremor. Reid lays her hand lightly on his head. Slowly, the tremors cease. He picks up the screw, glinting amongst the blades of dusty grass, and hands it to her. She pushes his head down, then points for him to look up at the bottom of the head...where, before his eyes, she turns the screw in and tightens it.

Reid turns a knob on the side of the camera and it grows longer, the lens board snaking out on the bellows. Then Reid does the most magical thing the boy has observed. She removes a large black cloth from a draw stringed bag, throws it over the other, fat end of the camera, and climbs underneath it, her hand still on the knob.

The boy knows from her attentive posture that this is the essence of whatever she does. Like the final, delicate movements of the hand in the water before catching a fish, or the balanced posture of the arm and head before throwing a stone to hit a bird. Reid becomes so unsociable at these moments, that the boy has learned to retreat, and wait, but this time, just as he is stepping back, she reaches for his hand, and puts in on the knob. She pulls him gently under the black cloth, into the darkness of its shadow, and turns his head forward, slipping out from under the cloth herself.

He sees, just in front of his nose, a sheet of glass, smooth and rectangular, like those he saw in the windows at the fort. There is something on the other side of the glass, but he cannot see it. The glass is not truly transparent. It has a granular texture, like the finest river sand. It gives off light, a blue and diffuse luminance like the sky on a bright but cloudy day, or the eastern horizon on a foggy morning. Something about this light makes him feel he's looking at distant things.

Reid moves her hand, which is on the focusing rail adjuster. A miniature world appears out of the fog, upside down, like the way the world looked when he was forced to hang from a tree branch to scoop eggs from a bird's nest in the trunk. The world shimmers, like the world on the surface of a pond. It is difficult to look at, because parts are sharp and parts are obscure, and moving his head or shifting the focus of his eyes does not seem to change this.

Reid moves her hand again. Now accustomed to the upside down world, the boy understands it is the same world he was looking at before he went under the cloth. He realises that the round thing like an eye Reid always attaches to the front of the box is in truth an eye. It sees what is in front of it just like his own. He also comprehends that as Reid's hand moves, and the front of the box slides back and forth, the part of the miniature world the eye sees goes in and out of focus. Reid takes his hand and puts it under hers, then slides the lens board away from him. Things that are close become sharp. She pushes his hand the other way. Things that are far, until the horizon is a taut line, become sharp. Reid takes her hand off his. She pokes his elbow. He slides the lens board on the focusing rail himself. Again, the place where the world is sharp moves, this time from distant to close.

He feels Reid do something at the front of the camera. The image on the glass dims, but when his eyes adjust, he sees that it is now all sharp, like the world he sees himself. He has forgotten that the world before him is inverted. He watches a hawk rise in the flawless air. He watches Guzman, small, near the horizon, point the long tube of one of his own instruments towards

the sky, hold it steady, then lay it down, and make marks on a piece of paper he has flattened onto a board.

[Captain Aaron Masse] Day 92

Reid, she hath the air of a maid. I see there is a beauty about her, confined as she is to man's raiment & tasks, that would perhaps wane if she was allowed to be full the woman & indulge in their over wrought adornment. Her masculine attire eliminates any chance of this folly & reveals, without pretence, the essence of her loveliness. Her shoulders lay straight, well muscled down into her forearms, narrowing to a fine waist, much smaller than a man's would be, but only if one takes notice. Below the waist, she has little of the curve a woman has, certainly she has born no children, her hips being slimmer even than Water Music, & Caan informs me she too has yet to deliver a child. Her bosom is little in evidence, though she must confine it, thus why we have never seen her leave her tent except fully clothed. Yet today, as we broke camp & she loaded her equipment, I imagined I saw its delicate curves, the same smooth skin of her throat & back of her neck I saw flash at the pool, for she is the palest of all of us, having shaded to only a wane ginger, where the swarthy ones, such as Caan & I, are now almost black. Her hair, close cropped, is fine stuff, honey & wheat straw, growing back off her forehead. It is easy to imagine it long, falling to her neck without affectation. Her countenance is at once delicate & robust. A strong jaw, close to square & her head held always upright on a neck lacking but an inch to make it graceful as a swan's. Her lips are wide & full, at times compressed in concentration, more often slightly parted in amazement, which may be her natural state. Her brow is even, unmarked, showing a steadfast constitution, & her eyes, grey, shaded with the lightest blue, are large & wide apart, proclaiming a vulnerability she disguises with a brazen parody of maleness.

Guzman and Reid sit facing each other on basalt outcrops the height of kitchen chairs. Between them, a broken gallette of pan-scorched bannock, a marbled piece of dried meat and a water bottle sit on a square of canvas. The mountains rise behind Guzman, the plateau stretches behind Reid, where, not far off, two tripods support camera and transit. The boy scoots through the grass, zig-zag, chasing field mice.

'That strikes me as peculiar Mr. Reid, that Bain is a lover of rivers, for water is a such quiet stuff, and I sense in Bain an unexpressed violence I do not associate with it. Perhaps he seeks his opposite, the water soothing or quenching the fire raging in him, or perhaps it is the violence a river run gives water, the thrashing rapids and tumbling falls.'

'He did not say he loved ponds, Guzman. But you avoid my query: what is your love?'

'That question has not been answered already, Reid. I assumed my reputation preceded me, Captain Masse was certainly cognisant. I am known far and wide as a lover of women.'

'That in itself means little to me. What is it in them that you love?'

'You are still a lad, Reid, downy cheeked. A combination of youthfulness and bluster. Women like that in a man at times. Have you been intimate with a woman yet? And I mean intimate. You do not look like the type to frequent a brothel, and there is nothing intimate in that. I mean, have you been a woman's lover, with all that entails?'

'No, I have not, but why do you ask?'

'Because if you have, I will proceed directly to answer you. If you have not, I must introduce my subject before I respond to the question.'

'Introduce the subject then.'

'I will then use water as a starting point, and continue it as metaphor. Water is a substance of infinite qualities and form, as are women. I could attempt to describe the many qualities and forms I have experienced or observed, but this would just be a discourse on the separate aspects of these women, the parts. And a whole woman is infinitely greater of course than the sum of her parts, in effect there is no dividing her into her parts. She is indivisible and always whole, perhaps more than a man.

'A man's relation to women also affects the explanation. I'm sure if you asked Captain Masse about women, he would have two categories; wives and daughters. You could probably adjust mothers to this, giving three, then sisters, giving four. Try it with him.

'I mean not to discuss women falling within these four divisions, or in terms of their relationship to men, or to a man – that man being me. The women I'll consider were and are without doubt sometimes mothers or wives, certainly always daughters, and perhaps sisters, but this was not the category of relation into which my interaction with them fell.

'One could also create categories; the ugly and the beautiful, and within beautiful; the fair, the dark, the petite, the grand, the delicate, the robust. Or we could consider character, more interesting; the passionate, the timid, the truthful or the faithless. Or colour; White, Black, Red and Fair, Tawny.

'But my starting point would be to say that what I seek to describe would be the way in which they included me in their being, this magnificent whole so much greater than its parts. More than anything this quality of being, when you are embraced in it, is a cosmos, an immense mental geography, a physical and spiritual one, emotional too, an all encompassing set of sounds and sights and feelings. This is what I pursue. And I have reserved for myself the right, like any connoisseur, to pursue only the finest specimens.'

'And what is your goal, the culmination of your pursuit, Guzman?'

'Men pursue women for many reasons, seeking wives, mates, fortunes, healthy offspring, beauty, reputation. We live in a world that treats love itself so carelessly. My goal is extravagant love, for I am no beginner. Pure physical intrigue. I've got to burn with that mysterious fever.'

'And what of those women not affected by or interested in your sentiments?'

'A good question. Let us take an extreme case. You are no doubt aware that the holy books forbid a man to lie with a man.'

'Yes.'

'Yet you probably know that men indeed do lie with other men, clandestinely in many places, openly in others.'

'I have heard this.'

'Women, Reid, show the same inclinations. I have met some, in fact am a great friend of one. These women have no interest in me, nor I in them.'

'Why not?'

'My interest in a woman is sparked by her attraction to me, always. I do not want to feed the fire if the woman can't take the heat. But to continue, these women of whom I speak, women's women, for me they are still women, but not ones to be sought for the conspiracies of love. In the same way that...let us say, Captain Masse...when he will seek a wife, for his own has left or divorced him, he spoke about it one night in a fit of melancholy, in the same way he would not see the women I pursue as women, since these women are not candidates for marriage.

'And, conversely, they would not see you as a man because you are not a possible husband. But we digress, tell me about your love, not your politics. What are women like?'

'That is a fascinating topic. You must have gathered by now that though I am looking for more than modest diversion, I am not a hedonist. Smooth talk and pretty faces, all skin deep, do not interest me. In a ballroom full of belles, I am likely to go after the one with crooked teeth. I want a woman that cares more for me than her mirror.'

'But what do you feel, what is it like? Are they all the same? Or is a dark woman different from a pale one, a tall woman from a short one, a poor one from a rich one, a cold one from a passionate one?'

'What women are for me changes with who I am, yet there is one sameness. No, that word is unjust. There is profound consistency, which, perhaps, lies within me. The rest is differences, but you seem to want categories, no doubt because you are an artisan with a scientific bent. I cannot give you categories.'

'All right, what is it about them that is the same?'

'There is a similar potency, all pervading, like the force of gravity, but always in motion, like – still within the water metaphor – Bain's rivers. Necessary, and always there unchanging. And like the force of gravity, though it affects all, from the wheeling and diving bird to the immovable mountain, its source is in the centre of the earth. This is the constant.'

'That is very high-minded, Guzman, but for me unintelligible. Please go into the differences then, with specifics. Pick two women you have known, opposites, a tall, poor dark woman from the south and a short, rich pale woman from the north. How do they contrast?'

'I do not deny that women can be categorised, like men could be, or plants, or stars. I am just saying that there are other systems of definition. Take for instance these maps I am making. One look at them and you or I have a picture of the land around us, and what direction to go in to get home. Fine. But show a map to one of the hunters we have been meeting hereabouts, and for he it will have no meaning, yet he knows the territory and is equally able to get us home. How? He sees the land in a different way.

'A map is horizontal, but it is possible to think of a kind of vertical map also. For instance, and I know this because have I asked the native men who lead the hunting parties – the navigators in effect, practising the same profession as I. Think of our camp, without thinking of Bain, as lying in a river of vegetation flowing along at a certain altitude with a certain orientation to the sun. This kind of grass grows there, that kind of tree, in a certain state of health.

'Now, imagine we are miles from our camp and we wish to return. We have only to walk up or down a hill until we encounter the same flora as our camp, then walk along this river or channel of like plants towards our camp, and we will arrive. This system has many advantages. It works in the fog, and requires no instruments.'

'Fine, Guzman, but again, you avoid my question.'

'I do not. You want me to draw a map of women. I cannot. It is not how I see them, and if you will, not how I find them when I seek them. I have other methods.'

'Please.'

'You are putting me in a corner with your categories Reid, but all right. For rich or poor, the differences lie only in taste and manners – the surface. As for the differences twixt dark and light, they are only for the eye. The meaningful differences of the skin are with its textures. The most wonderful skin has a delicate nap, not unlike a finely woven cloth, silk of course. This is more manifest to the touch than to the vision. There is also temperature, a slight coolness that is exquisite and with this a fragrance which exhibits itself to the nose. I am not talking of perfume, or the more enticing and pungent odours that excite and provocate, no, more a smell inherent in the very fabric of the skin. This varies greatly from woman to woman, and is essential to her being. Think of it for yourself, you the photographer who works with light. The woman from the South, dark or pale, has been raised in sunshine. It has soaked into her all her youth, through the skin and into the muscles. Thence, it is always there, and when you touch her, you touch the history of the accumulated light, a divine immobility. When she takes you in her arms, all the flowers of the tropics embrace you, her skin their petals.

'When you touch a woman from the north, there is less sunshine, but the wonderful variations of the seasons are there. Not only heat, but also cold, and wind. There is restless movement underneath such skin. In her embrace, the seasons pulse. You might feel heat, or an invigorating chill. You might experience a soft summer breeze, or a the raging storm, and as you know, you who love this outdoor life as much as I, all these stimulate the soul.

'These qualities may even be transmitted through generations, for I have been with a woman, indolent and supple as a tropical morn, yet it was her mother who had been raised in southern climes, not her. One can also feel other men in that first touch. The imprint is always there, at times so strong you feel you've met him.'

'All right. Stop. The sun is fading and I have work to do. So do you. I appreciate now that you love women. The why I do not comprehend, it was not explained, nor the how. But I am tired of listening. The boy is crazy with inactivity. Let's get going. I will pack up the lunch kit.'

>─┥◆>─O─<◆┝─<

I no more understand women, or this woman herself, than before he began his discourse. I do feel though that I understand him more. He would be accused of licentiousness by most of my compatriots or my family, yet, I feel safe with the man, and I think that would apply if I was outwardly woman too. I wonder who the Captain would say he loves, or what? Perhaps some day I will have opportunity to ask him. I do not think, if I was in the guise of a woman, I would feel safe with the Captain, in some large way. I would not feel safe in what he expected of me. With Bain, the fear is sharper, more immediate. Some deeper animal fear.

And here I am, at this minute, very much acting the woman, for it was I who set out the lunch, and I who am packing it up. The reason I feel confident in slacking my male charade is the success of my prosthesis. I stood some paces from Guzman, my back just slightly to him, and slipped its place along my thigh, and pulled it out of my trousers. With everything in place, and my bladder full, I let go. Sure enough, a rivulet of urine gushed out. Seeing it worked, I turned to expose my profile to Guzman, as the hot liquid streamed to the ground. He made nothing of my accomplishment. What man would.

Getting it back into my trousers was accomplished with slightly less elan, and a small amount dribbled down one leg. I will perfect my technique. I am most satisfied with this final addition to my masculine costume.

Captain Masse warns us there will be horse thieves about now. We will let our animals roam to feed only in the day. My mare has wandered far. I trust she's sated her hunger in that draw.

><!·◆>·⊙·<◆·!·<

The boy has begun to understand something. That he is perceived as dim-witted. The disadvantage is the low regard he is held in, the advantage is in its disguise, he sees and hears many things he would not be allowed to if people thought he understood. He is using the disguise now, pretending to be simplemindedly chasing mice through the grass, but with each swerve, he has manoeuvred himself closer to the camera apparatus, untended on its tripod. He sees that Reid has finished packing up the mid-day meal, and has dropped into the gulley to bridal her mare. Her back is to him.

Hunched, he scrambles to the camera. His hands glide over the apparatus, leaving a finger print on the front lens element. He touches the mahogany frame, the fittings of the swings and tilts, the brass hinges and screws. His hands move slowly, carefully, deft when skill is needed, powerful when strength is required to swing it in the direction of the mountains. He quickly has it pivoted, but realises his body is not now well placed. Unable to take his eyes from the glowing ground glass, both hands on the focusing rail, he steps around the tripod leg but it is set on a wet spot and the slight pressure causes it to sink. The boy feels the tripod tilt, and with all his strength throws it upright, but he is staring at the inverted image on the ground glass, and pushes the wrong way. The off-balance camera tilts even farther from the vertical and he heaves again, again the wrong way until, its centre of gravity passing the point of no return, the camera pitches forward, the lens on a direct, arcing course towards a slab of gleaming schist.

[Captain Aaron Masse] Day 96

Wind from SW. Low, dense cloud. An unfortunate calamity. Reid's main camera irreparably damaged. The young one toppled it, though he cannot be blamed, in point of fact he was doing well as Reid's assistant, having of late transferred his affections from Water Music to Reid. Reid informs that the outer convex element of the lens is split in two, though the inner elements are not damaged. He has now only the smaller camera, which he calls a half plate. The one advantage in the whole catastrophe is that, since he can cut the full plates in two, we have effectively increased the number of possible images that can be taken, though they will be of lower size and resolution.

Water Music's health much improved, she no longer incapacitated mornings. Her nature seems more resolved, & she advises us that she recognises land forms, a mountain top shaped like a fish's tail, a tall rock in the form of a bear. Of the latter we have seen two. One ran off, the other towards us. At thirty paces, took three balls to dispatch it. One from Bain's rifle, a second from mine, both landing in the throat, causing much bleeding & a final shot from my pistol which entered its ear and tore out the brain. The new rifles, not requiring that the shooter stand them barrel up to ram down the charge, are a boon. I was ready for a second shot even as Bain searched for his powder. Conditioned to his muzzle loader, which he will not part with, he had not thought of a second shot. Bear's flesh I found to be stringy, & pungent, though Caan cooked & et certain morsels from the gut with great gusto. He remains our marksman, invariably downing his kill with one ball, often at two hundred paces.

We endeavour to reach the head waters of a navigable river. This central plateau is by and large level. An unnatural flatness, not the tilting plates of the true prairies. This the result, so say the naturalists, of it being long ago a lake bottom & born out by the test holes ordered by Guzman & dug by Bain along a gentle ridge. Once penetrating the topsoil & clays, he encountered what could only be described as shoreline, with sand, gravel & several kinds of clamshells. This gravel such a perfect mix of fine, medium & coarse aggregate that it could be directly applied to a rail road bed. We have been instructed to seek out, test & note such deposits. I estimate this one to encompass the whole ridge, which curves away as far as the eye can see & can be imagined as a pleasant strand. We have named it, on a whimsy, "Expedition Beach." I cannot estimate the number of wagon loads of useful gravel it contains – in the millions. Guzman predicts it is worthy of having a spur line built to it & could supply road bed for rails twenty miles each way.

As well, on the plateau, Bain dug & set a charge of powder, an activity he relishes, & set it off, exposing the subsurface. From this he pulled samples of medium quality coal. Bituminous according to Guzman. Anthracite is the hardest, highest grade & preferred for steam boilers, but bituminous, though it burns with a smoky flame, will do, thus the railway company will find itself not only with construction materials right here under the earth, but also the energy source for locomotion. Nature's bounty.

Thus far, Guzman estimates the route we have surveyed as buildable. I believe that crossing this plateau will be of no great difficulty. What distresses me is the absence of a river. I should have thought we would have found the head waters by now. If not the main branch, a tributary to the river egressing at the sea coast, where fortifications & a small settlement have been already established. Our destination.

My judgement is that we must find a river at the end of this plateau. Such a river will be running at the base of yon mountains parallel the seacoast. We have only to follow it, for at some point it must turn & descend to the sea.

The plateau, though to the eye fertile, is strangely uninhabited. Water Music tells us that it is a summer hunting ground & will be well populated within the month. I am sure she is correct, for we traverse constantly wide & narrow paths & pass piles of bones, one thrice the height of a man. For the pot, we shoot a kind of Elk, though somewhat more full in the hind quarters, source of the bones scattered about. We have seen this animal in herds of some twenty, but Water Music assures us they can mass hundreds.

Today we pass off the edge the incomplete map an explorer made twenty years previous while passing perpendicular to our direction of travel.

➤─┤◆├─⟶─O─⟵┤◆├─◄

Night comes. The cook tent and, in turn, the four dormitory tents fall quiet and dark, excepting that of Captain Masse. Its north face shimmers translucent with a candle's light, his shadow traced in black upon it.

And within the deeper blackness of the plain, a crouching horse thief creeps. Balanced on deer hide soles gnawed soft by his mother-in-law, he cants his body forward, toes taking his weight, one hand, two fingers extended, touching the earth for reference. Another step. The horses are windward the night breeze, their sweat perfume strong.

The horses know the man sneaks near. Quick breaths flutter their nostrils. They do not know he is a horse thief. Theft they know not. He is a man to them only, his movements delicate, a man as yet with little smell, being leeward and, since a man, representing no great danger, nothing terrible as the pulverising crush of a bear, or a puma's fleet slash.

The thief drops carefully to the grass, wary of getting his black woollen doublet, obtained from a trader, pride of himself and his wife, stained with dirt. Supine and comfortable, he counts the silhouetted heads and realises he cannot take all the horses. He knows too well the consequences of leaving even one for pursuit, has a lead ball entry wound in his thigh and its exit scar high in the fat of the haunch above it and a finger-size strip of hair missing where a waning bullet grazed his skull when a furious cavalry sergeant riding bareback clad only in long johns almost chased him down.

He must have help. In the night, four horses per man would be the maximum. He thinks of his brother-in-law, first recipient of his obligations to the clan he married into. His brother-in-law is a poor horsemen. He would rather his wife help him, or her cousin. For this he must seek permission of his mother-in-law. This will take time. A handful of sunsets. By then these people will be near the river. The moon will be giving light, but near the river is a good place for a raid. If we swim the horses downstream, no one will find the tracks.

>-+-<>-+-⊙-+-<>-+-<

[Captain Aaron Masse] Day 100

We are, the day, so close. She rides in front of me. We sit across the fire. We almost touch during a discussion of mapping strategy. I follow her limpid glance, from the others to me. She has several small gestures. When in doubt, a finger extended along the cheek. If angry, compressed lips & brow. Happy, her chin rises, she glances to the side, eyes large.

She handles the camera with wondrous agility, tightening its tiniest screws, shouldering its square bulk, & the boy, even after his calamity, she treats with the greatest tenderness, reserving a certain familiarity of relation for only him. I would describe it as untroubled, & I can understand it, for only with he, a dolt, has she nothing to hide. With the rest, including me, there must be the imperative tension of her disguise, & when I look sincerely at my own feelings, I realise I am jealous of the boy, what he can share with her that I cannot. If she only knew how deeply I desire to spend the day with her on one of her field trips, sharing a bottle of water, the little trials & successes of making each image, the hunter's sense of accomplishment at the end of the day, returning home with a good bag.

For, as I have reserved alternating pages of this journal to set down my most private thoughts, with the proviso they should be the truth only, I am developing sentiments towards Reid that go beyond respect & esteem. I desire her, as a man desires a woman. I yearn to touch her, & today, noon being quite hot, we had all opened our waistcoats & shirt buttons. I could see colour on the triangle of smooth flesh she exposed like the rest of us, &, only because I know of it perhaps, I think I saw the constrained form of her tender bosom there. I have lain awake these last nights thinking these thoughts, & they increase within in me. My only fear is they will cloud my judgement one day.

Bain is a fretful riddle. He seems not the man I knew, every day swaying more extreme twixt melancholy & wrathful obstinacy. When we shot the bear, I had the sudden sensation that he would have continued to discharge his gun into it, from unadulterated rage. I have seen this in soldiers, & it is a dangerous thing. With all the violence of war, those who take pleasure from it are the least to be trusted.

Clayton Bailey

[Reid for Captain Masse] Day 103

Photographic materials remaining and undamaged;

1 full trough Nitrate Bath
1/2 pint additional Nitrate Bath
10 measures Plain Collodion
3 measures Iodizing Solution
3 measures Cadmium Collodion
Collapsible canvas bucket
1\2 measure bromide iodizer
1 measures Ether and Alcohol
2 measures absolute Alcohol
2 measures spirits of wine
1/4 measure Pyrogallic Acid
2 measures Glacial Acetic Acid
1/2 measure Citric Acid
1\2 measure Sulphite of Iron
5 measures Hyposulphite of Soda
1\2 Bottle saturated Hyposulphite
Bottle Varnish
1\3 drachm Carbonate of Soda
1\2 Bottle Pyrogallic
Dropper bottle Nitrate Bath
43 flatted glass full plates
180 flatted glass half plates
Bellows camera half plate
Doublet (21 degree, F3.5) portrait lens
Compound (12 deg F7) in brass tube
Sliding Box Folding Camera
Brass bound ash tripod
Half plate portable darkroom
Full plate transportable darkroom

Various size stoppered bottles
3 Developing glass 12 drachms
1 Minum Measure
Scales and Weights
Gutta Percha Funnel
Full plate Gutta Percha tray
Half plate Gutta Percha tray
Spare dipper for nitrate bath
Broad Camel's hair brush
Pneumatic Plate Holder
1/2 Quire Blotting Paper
Linen cloth and chamois
2 cotton hand cloths
1 bundle yellow calico
1 bundle black calico
1 sponge
lump Marine Glue
Small ball of string
Paper of pins
2 stoppered bottles
Grooved box to accommodate
Grooved box to accommodate
Focusing glass to fit

Aperture stops F4 to F56
Camera base and set screws
Pack frame
Framing poles, pegs, floor

Early morning. Sun not yet risen, the sky pellucid sapphire. One prairie dog pokes its head from a burrow mound, fur fluffed against the rude chill. Light frost has dusted a glittering veil across the plain. Nearby, the expedition's five tents slouch in a open arch around a cold and smokeless fire, the larger cook tent's stovepipe also cold and smokeless. The staked out horses mutter, breath quiescent billows. The prairie dog hazards a short trip upon the grass but senses movement and settles on its haunches, nose to the air to watch a man cross from a small tent into the bigger cook tent. His entrance there is followed by metallic rattles, a silence long enough for one thought, and a soft whoosh, like the sound of a plummeting hawk. The prairie dog dives into its hole, turning to look when safe. The tent expands, as if inflated by a gentle giant's puffed breath. Its flat sides bulge outward until it approaches a balloon shape and when it seems this orb will burst, the travel stained canvas chars light brown, and quickly dark, then black, and ruptures, peeling open, allowing pale flames egress at the same moment a bent figure, the same who entered the tent, jumps, soundless, through the blazing door flap and sprints across the ground, jerking, slapping its burning cloths, then rolling on the earth until quiet, emitting only rasping breath and tendrils of ashen smoke. The horses turn their heads, as dully interested in men's diverse affairs, in their equine way, as the prairie dog.

>─┤◆>─○─<◆├─<

[Captain Aaron Masse] Day 119

A further misfortune, subsequent to the loss of Reid's camera. Neglect the cause. Bain, whose turn it was to cook breakfast, engaged in the forbidden practice of using lamp paraffin to light a fire. We had many terrible burns due to this the winter campaign of forty-five, & Bain knew of them. But, the morn being frosty, he persisted in using the inflammable liquid rather than expend a few moments splitting an arm load of fine kindling, there being no cedar, & the oak hereabouts very fibrous.

He stacked the stove hastily & cast in a lampful of the paraffin. In his hurry, he had not put his hand on the stove & taken note that it was still warm. Error number two. There were coals still smouldering from the late supper fire, the knots of oak being more like coal than wood. Their heat vaporised the liquid & before he even lit his match, having just lifted the lid, the air rushed in, a coal flamed & all the vapour, in the stove & the stovepipe, exploded.

Thus we are less a tent & Bain less eyebrows & forelock. His burns are not serious. The damage to his dignity is. We lost little else, not even foodstuffs or the lamp, as canvas tent flames are brief & have no intensity. The worst burns recorded by the regiment physician, being fatal, were when a soldier used a canning jar to bring his paraffin to the already burning fire, hoping to get green wood to ignite. The jar tapped a rock & burst, soaking him & spraying the fire. His Sergeant informed me the man ran past towards the creek they had camped beside, a screaming torch, but collapsed before reaching it.

Our second disaster. They usually come in threes. I await the final one with dread.

Bain is not the man I knew, the man with whom I shared every confidence, both in victory & defeat. The tent fire was caused, if the truth were known, by his absolute refusal to participate willingly in his domestic duties like the rest of us. He was adamant from the start that Water Music be camp cook, & has held a grudge against all of us, & especially me, for not either forcing her to do this work, or refusing to travel with her & Caan. There remains much bad blood between those two, for Water Music, when she thinks she is unobserved, addresses Bain with a hateful regard.

The other men, including the other woman, Reid, accepted the system of each taking a day of the week, & drawing straws for Sunday, leaving out the boy, who, of late I must admit makes himself quite useful around the (former) cook tent, due to his preference for the company of Reid & Water Music.

Bain fairly boiled each time our rotation brought his cooking assignment. His brow would be black with fury the evening preceding, & he would not speak at all his work day, save for cursing as he smashed the pots about. His food was just edible, & I can well imagine him awaking the day of the fire, which was his day to cook, loathing the task ahead, & doing his best from the outset to perform his duties with distaste, starting by lighting his fire in the most stupid way possible.

On top of this he is much angered by being forced into the work of Guzman's rod man, a much needed job, for Reid cannot do it, occupied with photography, & the others have no talent.

Bain's refusal to embrace his responsibilities is grave, we are such a small squad. His bitterness effects us all, not only the strain of the day he cooks, but also the other days, when he grumbles about Guzman, & slurs the name of any man who has, with some enthusiasm, concocted a tasty dish, as if that man was a traitor...or more to the point, a woman. Guzman is the most enthusiastic cook, though tending to great success or dismal failure. Water Music has a delicate hand with wild game. Caan is competent. Reid claimed she'd never cooked, & I loaned her, having kept it with me, a cook's manual from the Army, with the condition that she use receipts other than those I planned to use. Her efforts, like mine, are indifferent & monotonous, though no-one complains.

I did my best to speak with Bain about his opposition to his domestic duties & the fact that this in a roundabout way caused the fire. His response to me was insolent, but this is not a military circumstance, & though I have the role of leader, I cannot order him, or punish him. I do not want to. My original agreement with Bain was of equal association. This has proved not possible, & in fact, I will break off my friendship with him also. I cannot tell if he was affected in some way by the violence of war, & this had made him wrathful, or this was always his character, & like some men, war agreed with him, & brought out the best in his nature. If the latter, we are at peril, for no man adapts to civilian life more poorly than the ardent soldier.

>─┤◆>─◦─O─◦─<◆─├<

*T*hat was too close for comfort, Bain's misfortune aside. I am so accustomed to being entirely alone that first hour of the morning, before light has come. I had not realised that during this private interval I allowed myself to subside into femaleness. Doing my toilet abetted this relapse, as it is the most inescapably female of activities. Having washed my hair, and dried it largely by the stream on a thick rag I use mornings, I was walking into the camp, lost in thought, of I know not what. Those days when it is not my obligation to cook inspire a sense of freedom at that hour.

Somewhat in disarray, for I had not completely reapplied my physical male disguise, and certainly not at all my mental one, I heard the clink and clack of Bain messing about in the kitchen. His sounds are unique, for he detests this task, makes no bones about it, and prepares our meals, invariably tasteless, in a fury of ill temper. Then came the whoosh of the fire exploding, a sort of great inhaling, followed by its exhale, the tent blown up like a child's balloon, all the while changing colour from dirty white to near black. Then came Bain, at the run, madly pummelling those spots on his clothing already alight, and tumbling to the grass, rolling himself till every flame was extinguished.

My shirt was open near to my waist, and the instant I knew I was not alone and there lay the possibility of being noticed, I realised the feminine quality of my posture, my head to one side, my arm briskly ruffling my hair with the cloth to dry it, a general womanliness to the way I walked. And worst of all, I took such a fright, with the exploded tent and Bain, ablaze, running before me, that I cried out in my natural voice, somewhere on the alto soprano register. Closer to a shriek than a scream, then I realised what I had done, and how I looked, and stepped behind a shrub, hoping I had not been seen or heard. And I had not. The Captain was the first on the scene, shirtless, his trousers just buttoned, efficient as he always is, and very light on his feet during the emergency, no sign of his usual, somewhat ponderous bearing. His disgust with Bain was thinly disguised. The moment it was apparent there was no life in danger, and no serious injury, I saw the comedy of the situation, the two men, and me hidden, all of us caught unawares by the catastrophe of the fire, reduced to near buffoonery.

>–I–◆>–◯–◆<–I–◅

[Captain Aaron Masse] Day 120

Wind NE. Fire day previous. Loss of one tent & one sleeping robe. No serious injuries. Followed by steady, soaking rain. Second day in oilskins. Passed the first sign of hunting activity. Skeletons of many hundred butchered carcasses strewn along the base of a limestone precipice, blood & offal still clinging to the bones, maggots setting in. I estimate the kill at four days past. We scattered wolves as we approached but vultures remain on the carcasses, giving us only a shiftless glance.

Water Music explained the hunter's method & we could see evidence of it in two lines of stone piles that converged on the cliff's high side. Trees are stuck in these stone piles, making a sort of hedgerow & these face a spot where the animals are known to herd for the night. Early morning, young men & older boys sneak up on their other side & at a signal, stampede them towards the hedgerows. Other men are stationed there, with capes and flags, to ensure the drove continues to the narrowing end. Animals that fall over the crag are killed or sufficiently injured so the women waiting there can butcher them. Those beasts that balk are speared by the drovers as it closes, line abreast, ever tighter, upon them.

A good tactical use of geography. This technique applied once in antiquity by an army of foot soldiers twice vanquished by mounted swordsmen. They realised their only hope was to ignore the horsemen & frighten the horses, which they did with fire, driving the whole of the cavalry over a cliff, at the base of which they slaughtered the injured riders at their ease, sparing not one.

Water Music warned us that this tribe whose labours we've just seen, are ferocious, the female equal to the man & have equipped themselves through theft with some horses & through trade with axes & knives of steel. Each married woman sports a dirk & is to be as feared as her husband. Beyond their hunting grounds, we will enter the territory of Water Music's tribe. We have found the river. It is belly deep & bovine, but rising with the rain. We will ford it early the morn, before sunrise. I do not want to have to swim the horses, that would mean unpacking & packing, much time lost building rafts, & only two weeks to the vernal solstice. Water Music tells me the river closes to a fatal gorge below our station & thence not navigable all the way to her people's domain. Will there construct our boats. No practicality to risking them while we may still travel well on horse. As important, I seek a peaceable tribe to overwinter our animals. Leaving them with these plains horse thieves seems much like leaving the fox in the chicken house.

Of the last weeks' trail, the Company will get a good report. A straight & easy-to-build roadbed. Of the next section, I estimate it too will not be difficult & Guzman concurs. By Bain's opinion, the river is old, & we will find the raised plateau of its ancient bed on each side of the present channel. Easy riding for the horses, & easy building for the rail road engineers, much gravel, & both softwood & hardwood in abundance, & of good size.

>━┼◄►━O━◄►┼━◄

Three nights of delicate negotiation, gifts of fresh elk tongue, and promise of a mare, thus the horse thief has persuaded his mother-in-law to allow her daughter to come with him on the raid. Her son would wait, hidden in a gully or a bluff, to help ride the horses back.

They found the stranger's camp, but its occupants went to sleep late, and the light in one tent is still burning. The rain makes it uncomfortable, but they can wait. Dawn is far off. These people have many guns. Everyone in the camp must be asleep.

His grease-smeared cape, pulled into a cone, sheds water like a small wikiup. One toe is exposed. Water dribbles in through a hole in his moccasin made by his crooked toenail. He has always had this problem of wearing a hole in his moccasin. The cold trickle runs along his instep and pools at his heel.

>—+◆>—O—<◆+—<

[Captain Aaron Masse] Day 125

For love of her I cannot sleep, if I am to declare truly the sentiments bursting from my heart. Searching through my effects for some reading to divert these ardent thoughts, my hand came to the Good Book, wrapped in oil cloth, given to me at age twelve or so to mark the end childhood's religious schooling, now veteran of many travels in trunk and saddlebag, & a war.

Seeking council, for my problem with Bain distresses equally the dilemma of my unachievable affections for Reid, I leafed through the pages, wisdom on every one. In the eyes of God, I am sure I am free to love another, for my own wife has left me, by word & action, though in the eyes of the law, & these count less, I am still not divorced. Even now, so much time past & her so far away, my mind refuses to think of it, for shame. My marital relation an utter failure. On my return, opening the door of my own home, I'll find the rooms spick-&-span, yet emptied of her presence, my books in their shelves, dusted, my clothes on their hangers, fresh washed and pressed.

Reid is not so young as she could be my daughter. Though the difference in our age must be a score, there is no immorality there. As for the nature of my sentiment, each day it becomes more physical. I can see, looking off into the dark beyond the tent flap, the fine down that frames her upper lip, the fair radiance of her cheeks and luminous depth of her grey eyes. By discreet observation, I have divined the female in her form, which shows itself mounting the horse, washing her face in a creek, once soaked wet with sudden rain.

I yearn as much to convey this yearning to her, for what good is love unreturned. She does not know who dreams of her at night, who longs to hold her tight. Perhaps there lies the moral question. Is it right for me to live with so much unexpressed sentiment? Can it be in any way called love if it is not shared? The Good Book is clear on the subject. The man must go to the woman with his question. If she spurns him, he must seek another.

I cannot go to her with my question. I cannot even let her know I know of her femaleness. I cannot ask or know what she thinks of me. I must endeavour to divine it. This should be possible through careful subterfuge, or perhaps direct question. I will try the latter first. I am a soldier. I've never learnt the art of making love, though my heart aches for it. As a suitor to my wife, I was afraid & shy. I let society's cannon carry me along.

The need for secrets is causing so much misery, for her & I in such different ways. I feel my chance will go by, a chance that she might love me too. Within the actual circumstance of our expedition, I will do my best to share what I am able with Reid, & expose the good side of my character to her, hoping that when it is over, something can be done. Here is a verse from the Book to guide me, my finger fell upon it by divine providence,

Darkness falls, I am still a believer
If I hear a call, from out of nowhere
and everywhere, will I answer
If I see the light, will I follow
or feel a touch, will I hold on
And make joy reside, where there is sorrow

This inclement night, I will say prayers for myself, seeking God's guidance & service.

<hr />

A gust flays the ground with a final jag of drizzle. The horse thief shivers. He looks at his wife, and she is silent, resting, asleep but ready. His brother-in-law is probably crouched in the gully, sheltered under a horse, maybe chewing on a piece of dried meat.

The birds are silent. Dawn is not far off. The light is still on in the white man's tent and soon the sky will lighten. His foot is cold and wet. They must go now or creep back empty handed to endure the insults of his mother-in-law. He touches his dagger, and pokes his wife with a willow switch he cut while creeping to this spot. Her eyes snap open like black sparks. They will take three horses each, riding one, leading two, then drop two in the gulley for his brother-in-law. They must cut the staking lines at the stake, so they have enough rope. She touches her dirk. They both fold their rain capes, and tie them round their waists.

Bent low, he rises on his toes, humming a dirge that sounds like the wind but which the horses can hear, and be calmed by it. He touches the first animal, stroking lightly its flank as he passes, going to the lead horse, cutting the stake line behind the fourth animal, leaving three for his wife, and hearing a sharp sound, a box closing, he turns but cannot see what it is, the horses body blocking his view of the tents. His wife hisses. The horse shifts, and he cannot see her either. More metallic clatter from the nearest tent. The cloud scud thins. The eastern sky casts a pallid flush.

Reid pushes her tent flap open with the camera box, looking for a spot of higher ground to set it. She looks towards her mare, her morning habit, and sees within four animal legs two human ones. She does what she has been told to do. Horse theft is not tolerated. Without the animals, they are finished. Dropping the box, she reaches for her rifle, propped against the tent pole. She yells, "thieves," brings the gun up, cocking it, swinging it towards the body she assumes will appear from behind the horse, but her sights, the V notch close to her on the breech, the bead at the end of the barrel centred within the notch, settle on the horse.

She hears Caan curse, wonders what Captain Masse is doing as she realises now that when she stuck her head out the tent flap a candle burned in his tent. She hears the breech bolt snap on one…two rifles, and knows that it must be Caan and Captain Masse. Bain has his muzzle loader, and Water Music is unarmed.

Three horses move in unison to Reid's left. Below her gunsight, a hand reaches to the stake, and cuts the line. A figure pushes onto the horse, crouched for flight even as it leaps to the horse's back, digging a foot into its flank. Reid aims where the torso will appear, but horse rears, the hand loses grip on the sopping mane, the wet toes slip. The body tumbles, emerging under the horse's belly. She lowers her rifle barrel, hears a brutal crack, like a thick branch snapped, and sees a man's startled face in her sights.

And sees an upright form in the peripheral vision of her left eye, and keeping her rifle aimed, looks there. The wet, sky-lit form of a woman flips the halter rope of one horse around a stake and leaps to the man. Captain Masse shouts and she draws a bright bladed dirk from her belt to confront the voice, brow furrowed with rage. A gun discharges, her body snaps back with the ball's impact, and she falls. Reid turns. Captain Masse still points his rifle at where she's dropped, its barrel fuming wan breath as he levers in a second cartridge.

The male thief cries, one penetrating sound repeated. A horse and rider burst from the gulley, pulling a second horse. The thief stands, unbalanced, keeping the staked animals before him as a shield. Caan levels his barrel, sighting. The standing man lifts the woman's body to the rider's second horse, then, awkward, flips onto it himself. They bolt towards the waxing dawn. Caan takes careful aim, pulls the trigger. The thief, with the woman's body, topples. Another rifle fires, its discharge a deeper thud. Bain's muzzle loader. He's missed. The lead rider disappears behind a rise.

The smoke pall of Bain's rifle floats through the camp...past Captain Masse, who has turned to walk with Caan towards the fallen riders, away from Bain, now beginning to re-tie the horse's stake line, towards Guzman and Water Music in their tent doorways, and the boy, who has shut his eyes and covered his ears with his hands.

➤—I—◆➤—O—◄➤—I—◄

[Captain Aaron Masse] Day 133

Wind calm. Air dry and warm. Night offensive by a trio of horse thieves. Repelled through Reid's quick action.

Just before dawn, two crept to our stake line, I having ordered the feeding of horses in daylight & tethering them near camp the night as a precaution.

From the evidence, their scheme was to seize three animals each, & rejoin a third man remaining in a draw beyond our camp. The third man with two horses. The must have come doubled up on one mount.

Reid saw the first man while preparing equipment for our early morning ford of the river. Sounded alarm. I was still writing journal entries, & Caan was awake the instant. Reid drew a bead on the man but he fell in the wet and the horse trampled him, fracturing his femur, which sound we all heard, as loud as a pistol shot. The second thief, a woman, came to his aid. She drew a knife, & I dispatched her with a ball that took her brains out, not a bad shot for a man with one arm. The man made off, carrying her, dead or dying on a mount fetched up by the third thief but Caan, with a marvellous shot on a galloping rider in dim light, dropped him. Bain entirely missed the other rider with his blunderbuss.

Buried dead & rounded up their horse, a piebald mare. Dug proper graves for the two, depth a man's height & was assisted in this by Bain, who also joined me to say a few words over the dead. The others suffering shock from the incident, the two killed, & reluctant to assist with the remains except for Water Music, who asked to examine the female corpse, for reasons she did not explain & I did not ask but am certain she removed some artifact & tucked it in her bodkin. This act I put down to some rituals within her race. I implored our God to make a place for their souls in their heaven if not in ours, & to forgive us the necessity of taking their lives.

Gain, by virtue of the skirmish, one healthy mount not broken to saddle. Forded the river thence, going along the middle of it on the bottom to leave no track, almost losing two mules doing so but gaining the far shore intact some distance down river we pressed on. I wish to put as much delay as possible between us & the revenging war party that will undoubtable follow.

Will travel hard the week. Game appears plentiful & Water Music more & more knows the lay of the land. Guzman's survey uncomplicated as the river shore rises & falls, giving ideal observation points. Reid making plates of pertinent geography. Post sentry dusk till dawn. Regret we have not a boisterous camp dog or two.

>—<•>—O—<•>—<

A week has elapsed, seven days interlude to digest the events of as many minutes and still I cannot comprehend. Captain Masse had no reason to kill the women, and after his senseless act, he looked at me. What hubris, the marksman's elementary pleasure of a good hit, as when my father downed a high flying goose without wasting a second shot from his double barrel – on his face a vain smile, but eyes still seeking my admiration.

I will be unable to respect Captain Masse henceforth. The contempt I feel for his cold-blooded act is not naive. I know well the rules of the trail, and would have, could have pulled the trigger myself, was an instant from it. But still, that man was someone's brother, son, husband. The woman someone's sister, daughter, wife. The theft had been stopped already, by me. The horses were not in danger, no lines were cut. The man and women were no danger to us, armed with but daggers.

What outrages me is carrying the whole affair to its most irrevocable end, through the instant justice of gunpowder and lead. Could he have done it with a sword, the woman directly in his face? Yes. History tells us that. It is his idea of citizenship. I am certain he would see himself as doing his duty. He is a father. The same hand once stroked a child's cheek.

I must compose my thoughts. They are confused I now see. What if I had pulled my own trigger and the young brave had been my victim? Would that make me unfit to mother a child? I think not. Looking at it all, my revulsion is for the extreme measure, their instant and heedless application. Yet, on consideration, could we expect obliging conduct from that man and woman's vengeful people? I think not. So what am I asking for? A just world? Perhaps that was my presumption. Wishful thinking. I have seen too much to maintain such a sophomoric outlook.

No, what I desire, in my heart of hearts, was for Captain Masse to be different. A more honourable and virtuous man. Not so multifarious. More magnificent, more than merely competent. He is our leader. I want to admire him, in some large and complete way, that I can never now achieve. Perhaps, me, the sham man, wants all men to be different. A fact which I can neither achieve.

>–⊶–O–⊷–⦁

[Captain Aaron Masse] Day 146

Winds varied. SW & wet, then NW, cold, all in a matter of hours. Thunderstorms, occasional fine hail.

Reached the navigable portion of the river, our way on horseback blocked by ground more suited to goats. Thence, we will survey from the boats, landing shore parties. As Water Music predicted, we encountered a friendly & peaceable tribe, nomadic, coming together once a year to trap fish in willow weirs along the river bank, hunting spring & fall, & retreating to live in family groups for the winters. After exchanges of gifts & much smoking & talk arranged for our horses to be left here one season to be picked up on the return journey if we return overland or by some other party they having some knowledge of husbandry & many young bucks curious to learn about the animals they have heard much about & occasionally seen on trading journeys to the plains. Having been shown a long expanse of meadow, sufficient winter pasture, I feel much more confident leaving our horses here than with a mounted tribe who might be tempted to appropriate them. Full instructions as to care have been related by Water Music, who is now well along in her pregnancy & the object of pleased comment by the womenfolk. Caan himself evidently proud.

Bain set about splitting planks of local cedar & assembling the skiffs with the others helping & very happy to be in charge. Water Music also happy, making social calls & finding a cousin here with much attendant weeping & wailing. Of her tribe no news. By this season they have commonly passed through on the way to summer hunting ground on the plains we just left but no sign of them. Much discussion as to why but no answers, & no runners in from her tribe to indicate calamity. Of runners, note that this tribe's fastest, a man much revered & presented to us by the chief, adorned with smallpox scars about the face.

Cannot comprehend why Reid has wasted her female nature to masquerade as a man. She would make any active man a fine companion. She has the strength of character to endure a man's company. My own wife did not. I am certain she loved me most in my absence, & forthwith grew weary of me after the initial socialising the intervals I was home on leave. Upon reflection, it is no mystery that she left me when it became evident I might obtain a permanent post in the Capital, something I had worked for judiciously, in order to be more with her & my daughter. I knew her not, & never in any way as I know Reid, who, if the hours were totalled, I have now spent more time with than my own spouse, & whom, if the heart's opinion were also accounted, I now love more than I ever loved my good wife.

My ancestor granted me a long visitation during the deepest part of the night. He was dressed in the regalia of a desert campaign, & spoke of the duties of a soldier in foreign wars. We must ever respect our enemy he emphasised. For two reasons. First, if a soldier finds himself on the enemy's territory entirely, that soldier must pay great attention to the enemy's habits. How and what do they eat? When do they move and how do they disguise those movements on the terrain? What are their communication practices? All these things must be studied, and whatever seems germane, used to modify one's own tactics. At the same time, if their laws are very different, these must be respected if possible, especially concerning prisoners, death, & the proposals for treaties after the enemy is vanquished.

What I ponder is our own situation here. In creating this nation, we've never waged a foreign war. We've suffered our conflicts on our own territory, uprisings against two mother countries, a virtual civil war, & the longest campaign, our sporadic, but now decades old fight against the native peoples who have refused to vacate territory that could be settled. We cannot treat them as a nation, for they know not the meaning of the word, yet they occupy a nation & if rebellious must be put down to the last man. Are we the first to attempt this? In olden days, were the realms we now look upon as the solid, settled mother countries as untamed & savage as these mountain bands? My ancestor replied to none of these questions, for they speak of situations he knows not. He saluted me & bid farewell. I thanked him for his wise words.

＞－＋＞・○・＜＋－＜

C ruising upon the river has brought a theological side of my fellow travellers nature. Much religious discussion, little appreciated by me. Faith in God I do not understand. From where emanates this craving? It has no logical foundation. Science proved centuries ago the earth is but a dot in the cosmos and our ancestors sprung from the apes. Good men live well without God. Guzman in point. Others hold to it harshly. Bain. And others, feeble in the face of life's predicaments such as Captain Masse, construct a world with it such as a person would construct a house, then dwell within it.

I could never endure the company of a man such as he. The great warrior, when confronted with the demands of the spirit, thence reduced to inept romantic. How tiring a husband he must be. Imagine his wife, across from him at the breakfast table, drooping in the shadow of his lugubrious brow as it sheds its nocturnal accretion. Pitiable woman, and he never speaks of her, not once, not to me or the others. I will never allow myself to become such a person. With all the vicissitudes I suffer, I've made the right decision. This life is full of freedoms still untapped.

Not to say the Captain is without masculine presence. I have become so habituated to the other men, and they to me, that all thought of the body's sexual capacity has evaporated. Yet I can imagine Captain Masse in the marital relation. He is not without sensitivity. I see his hand upon his horse, ever mindful, and his courtly treatment of Water Music. In spite of his blustery nature, he would seem capable of intimacy, but without caprice, something I could not abide. A fickle fellow, such as Guzman, is of no interest to me, though I like him muchly. And what am I doing entertaining such thoughts?

Perhaps this is the river's effect upon me, for I find myself contemplating the erotic. These ruminations open a gaping portal on the problem of my disguise. What am I to do to satisfy the heart and body's needs. I am yet a maid, but now a woman too, I can feel the yearnings within. To be with another woman interests me not, though I've heard the brothel inmate's take this course. I am certain marriage is out of the question, whether I revert to the female costume or not. There is the possibility of a clandestine relation, but with whom, another woman's husband? Here too I am not capable. There are the gratification's of Onan, but only the body reaps the benefit. The heart is left to wither.

I have decisions to make. Not today, or on the morrow, but soon. Could I, upon my return, which I desire will be triumphant, terminating in a exposition of our work and future contracts, could I reveal my true identity, perhaps to some advantage? There is always the danger of scandal, but there is too the possibility I could strike the public's fantasy. All this I must give due consideration.

>─┼─◆─○─◆─┼─◄

A crow lands beside the body. The crow knows this supine creature's shape. It is potentially dangerous, but it has not moved all morning. It still does not move. He hops on to it, the toes of the moccasin, same size as a tree branch and easy to grip. He pecks the deer hide, the thick skin around the ankle. Nothing to eat there. He hops onto the shin, pulls at a few hairs with his beak as he struts up the thigh. Nothing. At the waist is a pouch. He twists his head inside. Strips of tough dry meat. He pulls one out and worries a few scraps from its edge. The sun shifts from behind a high tree branch, flipping a yellow flash he cannot resist. He taps it with his beak, dink dink. A knife blade. Same dink on each bright tooth of the fever-gaped mouth. Tap, the nostrils hold nothing. Pustules on the cheeks soft, but holding no edible morsel under their yellow dome. Then the glistening eye. Poke. His beak penetrates it. A viscous nugget. He tears away the cornea, gobbles the socket's succulent filling, pulls tendons from within, perches on the nose, pivots, does the same with the other eye.

>─┼─◆─○─◆─┼─◄

The Expedition

[Captain Aaron Masse] Day 154

Wind steady S. Clear sky.

At oars. Skiffs took water the first day resulting in some bailing. Planks tightened second day, a compliment to both Bain's talent as a shipwright & straight grained cedar cut for us by Caan. We make a morning survey with latitude & longitude sights from the campsite, land Guzman & at times Reid when geography dictates, taking rough sights, & make another survey the evening including samples of rock & river bottom.

By Guzman's assay, we now pass what will be the most costly section. His survey already indicates one tunnel & a high trestle.

In the week we set with the tribe, by their own name they are the "Flat nose" people, Reid took several portraits at behest of chief's wife. I reckon they were what we would call the royal family. Not a comely lot.

Reid also requested permission, this granted, the limit being six, to take some landscape pictures but this did not seem to satisfy her. She returned to camp, & used the last three plates on subjects I would not have chosen, portraits of women about the place, occupied with children & other ordinary tasks. These duly printed & given, they caused not so much delight in the subjects as excitement, being passed around & commented on all the rest of the day & finally put in the oddest places, set on a roof pole, hung around the neck & one given to a child as a plaything which without doubt will result in its being smashed. This frittering away of resource not without benefit as it seemed to consolidate us with the ordinary people who will thus in faith await our return.

Landed evening on shingle spit. River dropping. Caan, in pursuit of meat for the pot, remarked hunting trails, which would now be those of Water Music's tribe, appear unused, overgrown with spring flora.

Wind shifting. Chance we will make sail the morn. Test of our rig & a respite from the oars, one of which the boy has mastered & he cannot be taken from it though his palms wear raw.

>─┼─◆─○─◆─┼─<

Caan has seen moccasin tracks on the hunting path. First sign of use. Now, before his own foot, a nearly fresh print. Skim of dew in the bottom. No pock

196

marks from the rain two nights ago. Day and a half old at most. A man. Walking flat-footed, as if tired, and downhill, towards a creek. Here he sat and rested. Must have been tired, for he needed to pull himself up again – the bark is skinned from the small tree by his grip. Walked again, slowly, footprints close together. Perhaps he was injured, but no blood. Caan too rests.

And slips into a fatigued trance, eyes half-closed. Hears a metallic clatter opposing the forest breath, cricket chirr, rodent scurry. Tap, clink. A sound that should not be there, cannot be made by a wind blown branch or flapping wing. More like a pebble upon a knife blade. A signal. It is from ahead on the path, but he is certain there are no people about, the forest sounds have come back since he stopped moving. He does not pick up his gun or his pack.

He moves forward on the path, his own moccasins beside the fresh prints. One step, two, three, not breathing, making less noise than a scuttling beetle, keeping in the deepest shadow. Four steps, five. The trail rounds a rotting pine thick as a fat man's belly. Caan sees the moccasined foot, heel on the path, toes up, a coin-sized aperture worn through the sole. He moves only his torso forward. Sees the body, off the path. The short leggings, loincloth, one hand. He hears the tap. Clear, louder. This is the source but the hand does not move, the body is undeniably dead. He puts one hand against the tree, leans farther. Sees the crow's black, bobbing head, pecking at sunglint on the knife blade. Leans further. Sees the pustule ravaged cheeks, the emptied eye sockets fringed with threads of ragged tendon.

The crow cleans its beak against a gleaming wing feather. There is no more food here. It pushes up, flaps one wing to turn, then both, and ascends between two poplars. Caan knows what the pock-marked cheeks mean, the tiny haemorrhages at the neck, like flea bites. He knows he is looking not at a dead man but a source of death itself. He thinks of villages he's seen, where few escaped, where no stranger would go till the wigwams were burned. He sees the bark torn from the saplings behind the body, imagines the man seeking water for his fever, finally, knowing he was dying, trying to pull himself off the trail to lie in a quiet spot to chant his death chant, loosing his grip on the slippery bark and giving up, lying back.

Caan's urge is to bury the man, give him some dignity in death. He may be a cousin of Water Music, a brother, his own brother-in-law. The tattoos on his neck are her tribe, her clan, she has explained all this to him, even asked him to be tattooed so he could be a proper husband. He knows what this man's death ceremony should have been. All the clan gathered in one small shelter around the dying. Staying there, day and night, chanting, not eating, breathing their own breaths into the dying's mouth to give life, lying beside the dying one's body to give warmth, or take heat if there was a fever. This man he sees had none of this, was struck by the fever maybe while hunting, maybe while travelling or scouting. His soul is unattached, to his God's and to his clan.

Caan has seen the worst cases of smallpox strike in three days, the first pimples innocent, like a child's disease, the first fever invigorating, imparting a frenzied exuberance. Then suddenly the body has no energy. Muscles stiffen. This man might have left his camp already sick. He was travelling upstream, towards the tribe they just left. Perhaps he was a messenger?

Caan pulls saplings, groping under a heavy branched tree for ones that have struggled towards the light, that have put all the roots and leaves sustenance into stem growth, that are long and thin. He cuts the longest, thick as his wrist, and strips its branches save one at the base, and cuts this off at finger length. Returning to the body, he wraps his neck cloth around his mouth and nose, and extending his sapling crook, hooks it into the man's armpit, and eases him off the path into a depression. He pulls ferns and grasses over the body with the crook, then cuts leafed branches and throws them onto the body until it cannot be seen, all the while never getting within five paces of it. He throws the crook away and stands on the trail. He does not want to say the white man's prayers he learned at mission school. He knows this man's language but not his prayers. He takes off his red waistcoat, for which he bartered hard, by which he has been recognised for years. He slips it around a tree bent downhill towards the man, and fastens the buttons as he would fasten them down his own chest.

>—⊷—◦—⊶—⊰

[Captain Aaron Masse] Day 166

Wind quiet, unable to set sails.

Worrisome tidings from Caan returned evening from hunting. Discovered lone victim, undeniably of smallpox – for he is an astute & informed observer in whom I have full confidence. He has seen the disease in its terrible progress, having served as a helper to a missionary doctor when a young man. By his estimate, man found on trail died of high fever associated with most virulent form of malady, the proof of this being marks resembling severe insect bits on the exposed portion of body's throat.

There is no specific treatment I know of though was once told by a Physician in the Capital, a man well travelled, that ancient eastern societies had a preventive technique whereby the disease was artificially introduced under supervision, and immunity followed. Caan's precautions with the body impressive & I learned something from him here. Distressing is his belief & again his tracking abilities are wondrous, that the man was travelling up river, & away from Water Music's tribe. If they are infected, we cannot make any contact & I do not know how she will receive the news. She has told us that since they have not moved onto the plains for the summer hunt, they must still be in winter camp, at a place where the river widens, across from an island. It is at this place there is in constant supply small animals in the bush & river fish all the winter, obtained by fishing through the ice, which offers no risk, the river being so wide it freezes thick enough to support a man early in the season.

It is my conjecture, putting all the pieces together – the dead man, the trails unused this season, the lack of traditional spring contact with the neighbouring tribe – that her people may be victims of an epidemic & we should be prepared for the worst. It has been explained to me that on account of their habits during sickness, many tribes are severely stricken. I will present this openly to everyone before we break this camp and travel further.

>–I–+>–O–+–I–<

I realise I have not, or I had not, the faculty of self criticism. The unsullied natural world I seek, virgin vistas for my lens, the not finding of which has constantly left me disappointed – this world does not exist. Never did mayhap and I have driven myself to passionate choler searching in a void. It is time to turn my rational lens inward.

This new awareness by result of shock. Captain Masse told us, all gathered round the evening fire, that there is a good chance Water Music's tribe has been infected, perhaps ravaged by smallpox.

An old world contagion, one of the mythical plagues, the wasted cities of the continent, the quarantine ships, the jammed sick wards, carts of corpses dragging through congested ghettos. Images from another time, another place here before us. And I have been looking for pure wilderness.

Water Music's anguish I cannot attempt to describe. Both Caan and Captain Masse terribly emphatic about the disease, its potential fatality, and its manner of spread, which is straightforward. Each fresh case of smallpox ensues from contact, direct or indirect, with a preceding case. We must, by virtue of our river transport, pass directly the place where her tribe will most likely be. We must attempt to discern the state of their health at a distance, and if there is any sign of epidemic, we will pass by, since to make contact is to risk infection, and there is no cure or medicine that can stop the disease or ease its victim's suffering.

Water Music understood this, but I think she and Caan will discuss the matter far into the night, for she does not seem to suffer the fright of the disease we others, excepting the boy, do. Caan's love for her was most evident at this moment, and I could see he would spare no energy convincing her to not risk infection.

Captain Masse's plan is this. We will sail the boats as near as possible to the tribal camp. Since they make no use of water craft of any sort, and do not swim, we will either fix our skiffs with anchor, or use an island of which there are supposed to be many in the river. From this vantage point, Captain Masse will scan the winter camp, a sort of village, for evidence of the disease. If such should exist, we will reembark, and continue with our work. He has given us the night to reflect, and will only proceed with it if we all agree. He told Water Music she has a choice, and she too must reflect. If he feels the disease has taken hold, she may still request to be set ashore. That is between her and Caan. But if she goes ashore, she will not be allowed back in the boats.

Caan made some harsh sounding remarks to her at this juncture, picking up a coil of rope. She reacted with a flare of temper. There must be great passion between these two. I realise how much I have grown to love them both. Speaking for the boy, he is happily unaware, and happy too in the boat. He loves his oar, and one night, when Guzman laid it beside him as he turned into his blankets, he pulled it in with him, and slept the night curled to it. This began many simple minded jokes of which he is the brunt yet in the end it has also made him an appreciated member of the crew, and I think he knows this. He certainly has overcome his shame at breaking the large camera, for he is now such an adept assistant I am thinking of trying him on developing a plate. He continues to avoid Bain.

What is photography in all this, my dreams shattered. The very earth, which I thought secluded and pristine, befouled with the most urban of pestilence. My answer is that photography is an art and a technique for rendering what the photographer chooses to address with the lens in exquisite and permanent detail. My mistake has been to seek pictures already foreseen. This is wrong. The photographer may seek, must seek, to the exhaustion of all resource. But then, the camera set, the image framed, the photographer must embrace whatever is recorded, consequently admit its veracity, as the viewers who follow must also acknowledge.

And what now? I have lenses, plates, chemicals, cameras. What will my subject be? Do I invent a cause? No, I must have confidence in myself. I have learned well my trade, my other education has been good, I am not insensitive. I must simply wait. Some force will draw me out, show me the way. I learned this from talking to Guzman, who has been lost many times. He says that the path out never appears when we rely on the devices such as compass, maps, measurements, which we employ to tell us where we are. These things only disappoint us with their impotence.

The way out is only found at the moment of utter fatigue, every resource expended. That is the moment when we cast aside all preconception and actually perceive the world around us, are capable of detecting those subtle hints, the bent blade of grass, the bit of trodden earth that let us find the trail, and thence our deliverance.

>—+◆>—O—<◆+—<

A silky, golden dawn, the river wide now, its plane surface disturbed only by small eddies around submerged tree trunks and shoreline rocks. Its banks sloping out, both sides, with the slightest incline, to a rich floodplain, now thick with early summer mushrooms, ferns, berries, birds of the bushes, soaring birds of prey, and small and large timberland creatures.

The cook-fire's plume rises white and straight as a flagpole to the height of the valley sides where the breeze fluffs it, then bends it south. The clamour of breaking camp; commands given softly, mumbled replies, thumping sacks, trunk lid thuds and slipping rope, merge with river babble and forest din. The wind descends, fluttering the highest leaves, as the skiffs are slid down the pebbled shore and loaded, this finale a progression of thuds and muffled cries. A gust breaths its cat's paw across the waters, and Captain Masse stays the setting of the oars, smiling, for it is he who conceived of the sailing rig and forced the expedition to lug it so far. Passing Guzman the steering oar, he directs Reid to erect the mast in his own skiff, and orders Caan to set the other mast and sail in the boat commanded by a stiff, upright Bain.

Water Music helps her husband, but never looks at what her hands accomplish, every moment keeping her eyes downstream. The boy gives up his oar with difficulty, and is only taken from his black mood by the fascinating presence of the mast and its huge white sail. The two vessels, hand hewn, but the bend of their thwarts appealing, not out of place on the placid water, heel delicately and together as the light breeze waxes. Guzman leans his hip to his gunwale, his eyes drooping with pleasure, his grip on the sheet to trim the sail firm, the pressure on his steering oar steady.

Bain, in the stern of his own skiff, presses his lips to a flat grimace, loses his balance as the boat heels, trying to keep his body vertical. He has fixed his sheet to a cleat, and when a gust hits, the boat tips. Water Music presses her palms against the hull. Bain yanks the steering oar, and they come upright.

>—◆>—○—<◆—<

[Captain Aaron Masse] Day 172

Wind light. Temperature typical of summer's end.

With breeze astern, but not too strong to cause a capsize on our shakedown cruise, we have set sails. I much anticipated this. My most engaging term as an officer cadet was at the Naval Academy. I greatly enjoyed learning what I could of their craft & jargon, but due to his experience in the Southern latitudes, & my difficulty of keeping balance with my only hand on the bar, I have trusted command to Guzman, who captains excellently at this very moment, myself set comfortably in our sloop's bow. The other vessel under the command of Bain, its constructor, who would let no other man have the honour. From my vantage point, he finds his task passable hard.

Guzman estimates that the slightly sloped shores of this part of the river are underpinned by igneous rock, & would present no challenge to builders. Certainly the timber hereabouts is excellent for cross ties.

The irony of this quiet morning is not lost on me, nor the crew, who speak little. Around one of these bends, we know not which, there is a good chance we will come upon a scene of great human suffering. Caan has described the effect of smallpox on a native village to me privately. He must also have discussed it at length with Water Music, for she is in a state of great nervousness. I have no idea what her thoughts are, but it is easy to see Caan is greatly afraid, probably of losing her, & I sympathise, for she is a fine woman.

Reid particularly dour, lost in thought. Most times, when we pass through such spectacular country, she glances all about, a dreamy look on her face, & requests a stop to make one of her "artistic" images, which I tolerate, as it seems so important to her. But today she shows none of this curiosity. It must be that she, being a woman, like Water Music is more struck by the thought of what we may soon encounter.

Side by side the two skiffs drift. Infinitely slowly, for the current is imperceptible here. Hard scrutinised by the mute inhabitants of the settlement, the
boat crews too sit voiceless, until a groan from Water Music ascends quickly
to an undulating wail, and she thrashes in her boat, tearing at her cloths.
Caan he restrains her, but winning her struggle she breaks away, stands on
the gunwale, laden belly evident for the first time, the skiff broaching to with
her weight, water slopping into its bilge, and jumps. And rises, splashing,
inept but making progress towards the shore of her people, still wailing, spitting water, followed by Caan, who plunges, stripped to the waist, and floun-
dering with a useless stroke, grabs her legs and pulls her under, she struggling atop him, submersing his head till he ceases to fight, then, seeing she
could drown him, brings him up, both now swung by an eddy close to the
island, and she touches bottom, and drags him towards the inclined shore,
closer than the skiffs, which have slid downstream.

By the time she has him in shallow water, and upright, he is again conscious. Seeing this, that he is out of danger, she abandons him and starts back
across the river, and again they fight, but this time she is more dextrous, and
pulls away to stand in neck deep water, facing her people, first talking to
Caan in her own language, telling him to leave her be, then screaming across
the water. To be answered by dust-streaked bodies that labour nearer the
water's edge to speak with her as the skiffs set oars and come about to grind
their keels on the island's shingle beach.

And so, the forenoon passes, all the members of the expedition silent,
sitting in places they found immediately as they left the boats, on rocks or
felled tree trunks, as Water Music, up to her neck in water, cries, call and
response, her greetings, and love and pain to her people, and they reply. Reid
sits for a time like the others but as Water Music's rant reaches a climax she
moves towards her skiff and, making no noise, her hands moving carefully
as loving parent's over a child, slides the oilcloth from her camera cases. And
she is joined by the boy, the two working so much from habit she hands the
camera frame and bellows to him without looking.

Water Music continues, the apogee of her rant attained with some point
being settled between her and them. Forgiveness perhaps, or benediction.
The terrible nervousness leaves her body and she turns and walks up onto
the island to sit alone, but unrestrained, as the others light a cooking fire and
Reid, bent to her ground glass, facing the scene Water Music now regards
mutely, pulls the dark cloth over her head.

>·‹•›·O·‹•›·‹

Clayton Bailey

The boy, I must stop calling him that, for he merits now a name, when he tipped the large camera some time back, shattered the normal lens and lens board but there still remained the long lens for it, which I never used due to its extreme telescopy, a field of view about fifteen degrees, 3x power.

I fitted this to the small camera, half plate, and it gave me 7x, an extreme magnification. Set above the island shoreline, the forsaken winter camp at most a hundred paces opposite, I was able to expose several compositions of individual family groups, the clustered funeral biers, and the general disorder wrought by the disease.

I did this coldly and with great prudence, as one must in photography, but my heart was tuned to Water Music's wail all the time. This event has marked me. I see now that the human circumstance is not symbolised only by its aesthetic summits, but by those rending moments of extreme love, or hate, or pain. I have just lived the last, pain. I understand now that Bain and Captain Masse have lived extreme hate...war. I believe I also saw love, when Caan, unable to swim, threw himself, possibly to his death, into the river after Water Music, but I do not think I've yet lived it.

During the whole time I worked, the others moved not, even the Captain, who seemed stunned, and if my observation is correct, it was not by the horror of what we saw, but my action of recording it. At the end, as I fixed the plates, it was only Water Music who came to have a look, the first time she has ever expressed any interest in what I do. I will make a print for her.

[Captain Aaron Masse]

Reid's photographing such piteous humanity I found despicable. Such a cruel act for a woman to commit. Yet I did nothing to stop her, & I know not what repulsed me. I think it was a knowledge of my own limitations, a knowing that though she did something I could not conceive of, that fact did not render it inconceivable. I have heard that back in the old world, the society is much less advanced with regards to women's activities. The mere idea of women riding astride instead of side saddle was resisted & commented upon for a quarter century yet now, after so much resistance, is somewhat accepted there. Myself, I've never seen a woman mount but astride, & cannot imagine otherwise. Social decree change with time.

We build a new Republic here, this railroad to be the belt that binds its middle, a nation much preoccupied with the human condition, the rights of man. Man, a Godly creation, & the activity of his mind the highest expression of these divine origins. It seems no matter how slight a change may be, society's nature is to at first condemn it, then accept it. Perhaps I have been condemning Reid for naught. I should be thankful, what better thing than to have our old ideas broken, so that we may create something new from the shards.

Without change, adventure, we would all sink, like an overladen skiff, into the sea of our own stale thoughts & the source of change is the abnormal individual. I saw this in the war, in fact we devised a test for it. We would be sent officer recruits, fresh from the military academy, in groups of six. Of these, we could generally occupy two at the command post & three behind the lines, but often one would have to be sent immediately to the front, to lead a squad.

We would choose this man by giving the six some impossible assignment, a night patrol in rain or snow, with many rules typical of the military constraining the task, which we were careful to assure could not be accomplished by following said rules. Invariably, most of the green officers would follow these rules, & finish the night in utter frustration. These we would keep behind the lines. Oft times, one young man, crazed with frustration, would break the rules, thinking straight through to the task, & accomplish it, often to the loud disapproval of his fellows. If this was done without endangering the others, that young man would be promoted to captain & sent to the front, which is what they all desired.

Mayhap Reid is such a type. If she were in conventional society, I am sure she would be the focus of mockery & censure, for though we allow women many liberties other societies do not, there is one area were the constraints are dire – war & travel. I have seen the results in war, woman disguised as man doing as good a job of work as anyone, & I am now seeing the results on this exploratory voyage. Reid would never have been allowed to come if it was known she was a woman. I must admit that I would have been the first to disallow her participation. Why? It is not excessive to say that most women's place lies in the home, & most women of my acquaintance would not refute this. My own wife an example, who left the house little & hated even a long carriage ride. My sister too, utterly preoccupied by the domestic. I hope she liked the dining suite, but then, if her husband has abandoned not only us but her, I doubt that her thoughts will be of such trivial things. Poor woman, & my mother so astute.

Like men, women have their character, there are the curious & the incurious, the mobile & the immobile. Reid is of the former cut, & for her, & others like her, the denial of the right to adventure is unfair, with no base in reason, & certainly no support from God, who implores not that women only set home by the hearth.

Reid is, in her away, as much exploring new terrain, of a social sort, as this expedition explores the nation's geography. And for this I love her all the more. We have nothing to fear from women such as her. There is no more chance that mothers will desert their children to follow her example than men will desert their jobs to traverse the earth in gas inflated airships, such adventures I've heard have been accomplished, over longer distances in a day than we travel in a month.

I was afeared, upon agreeing to this commission, of the terrible transformations a railroad through the mountains would bring about. The end of the frontier, where I was born, raised, & spent my adult life in the company of other rough hewn souls, men & women like Bain, their blood & characters much mixed but all with a single, simple pioneering enterprise at hand.

In truth, the change was upon us before our expedition set out. Look at the dying village opposite. What will follow us, the arrival of the physical machinery of our grand national expansion, is the result of long standing political intent. The railway is this politic's aftermath, not a new thing in itself. The die is long cast. What has caused those miserable beings yonder so much suffering has its origins in our legislature, in the Banks of the continent?

Life springs from the rot of death. Witness the farmer's field, the forest floor. It is true I am abetting the death of those I now look upon, & of the frontier of which I am an element, heart & soul. But there is more to it, which I never, until this day, considered. I also stand mid-wife at a birth. Not so much of a nation, but of the possibility of new freedoms. Look at us here, working together, tolerant. Would this have been possible in the old world, in times past, with the constraints of religion & clan & rank. I think not. For some time now my soul has been chilled by a winter of despair for what is lost. But I was blind, for in those winter depths lay an steadfast summer, & by the grace of God it will warm me.

>─┼─◆──○──◆─┼─<

So far away from home am I. No familiar face around me, no familiar thought in my mind or familiar dream in my nights. I am a stranger, in the company of strangers. How clear is the mind when unattached, how inescapable one's character.

>─┼─◆──○──◆─┼─<

[Captain Aaron Masse] Day 183

High winds, rotating through the quadrant from SE to NW. Sudden warmth.

Disaster. Bain, whom it was quickly evident had no talent as a watermen, has capsized the larger skiff. No injuries, but much wetted food, gunpowder & supplies, & vital parts of Reid's apparatus lost. The breeze turned gusty mid-morn, requiring the sail's sheet be eased to spill each puff, & the helm shifted to windward. Guzman accomplished this on instinct but Bain, ignoring his example, left his sheet fast & surging ahead, was alarmed to distraction when struck by an exceptional blast. Skiff broached to, shipping water. Occupants & cargo slid to lee side, worsening the situation, & water poured in. All clung to the boat & we pulled them aboard. Many items floated – the sealed & caulked boxes of Reid's unexposed & exposed plates, the trunks – but the weighty guns, axes & such sank. Skiff undamaged. I am considerable vexed by the event, but give thanks to God we suffered no loss of life.

>─┼─◆──○──◆─┼─<

Cursed my luck. I am, by the forces of ill luck, being forced backwards in time. From commencing this expedition with the most up-to-date apparatus procurable, I have been reduced, by accidents no fault of my own, to a store of implements more primitive than those supplied for my use by Benson, and close resembling the earliest photographers paraphernalia. At least my negatives are unwetted.

The last three days leaving no time to consider the state of my affairs. The obligations of manoeuvring the skiffs exhaust us, at all times we are occupied with the oars and pike poles to fend off from rocks, the river, from one turn to the next, suddenly upon us, plunging now, I presume, towards the sea, each day growing more eager, each night more clamorous, pounding in our ears as we lie in our tents on the ever narrower and more precarious strand. Though our skills increase by the hour, so too does the river's force, and it seems each day we are not quite up to its demands, we have a close call which gives us a fright, so that each night we make camp exhausted, cowering a bit from the primal force we are now sequestered with, the canyon sides rising higher and higher, adding to the feeling of brutal entrapment. I wonder if Bain feels his love for rivers now. Bain, who is beginning to perturb me for some reason I do not yet understand, not just that he was responsible for the loss of so much of my equipment.

>―‹•›―O―‹•›―‹

[Captain Aaron Masse] Day 190

Wind not apparent, this last week in deep gorges. Temperature cool, constant, influenced by lack of sun & proximity of canyon walls.

Navigation difficult, neigh impossible at times. Cannot imagine this place in spring flood. Certain death. Skiffs holding up. Repairs each night with melted pine pitch, oakum & cotton caulk as needed. Several split oars, two broken. Guzman's survey reveals drop to have increased from 1 in 200 to 1 in 40, the steepest he has measured on a river used for navigation.

Guzman seriously injured towards days end. It being increasingly difficult to scale the steep valley sides to make a sextant sight, he resorted to primitive mountaineering methods, driving piton into the limestone to support his ascent. Climbing with his apparatus, he fell backwards, & took the fall on his arm, fracturing the left. In much pain & we would have had a difficult time if not for the ether I procured. Using the measure written out, I applied it soaked in a rag to his mouth & nose. He quickly swooned & I set the limb, the smaller bone snapped clean in two, & splinted it with a broken oar blade. He revived, & was in good spirits after a cup of the dark coffee he so enjoys. He will ride as invalid passenger in the bow tomorrow, & I will take the skiff's helm. He is able still to sketch with his right.

Tributaries feed main branch here, waters gaining strength. Immense canyon, a cut through impassable mountains. Stood on outermost accessible point & looked down at the ferocious river, an unending series of cataracts as far as can be seen.

Will press on. Boats to be loaded, weight in centre, with eye to extreme manoeuvres. I am partial to letting Caan helm second skiff but will discuss. As pre-arranged with our observation post on the western ocean, we have cut sixty logs exactly a man's height & nailed a copper medallion to the butt end. These we will set into the river, twenty at a time, every half day over the next day. This our signal we embark towards the coast & also a simple manner to assure them there that in effect this river does discharge in the ocean.

>─◇─O─◇─<

Descent into the maelstrom. Captain Masse had pre-arranged a most ingenious signal to our coastal compatriots. Sixty logs of identical size, each with a dated medallion attached, were set into the river twenty at a time every twelve hours. These will float together to the ocean, where several men have been commissioned to observe the two rivers that empty into the sea. A substantial remuneration awaits the finder of the first marked log. By noting the place and time of the logs' arrival, they will know where to expect us and when.

By luck, skill and strength we've make it down several miles of river until a huge surge cast us conclusively upon a steep shingle shelf. Ahead lie countless cataracts. The canyon rim is high above, and I feel I sit in a cathedral, its inner walls decorated by a frieze of striated, multi-hued stone cliffs unscalable, inaccessible as the sky dome their ragged edges frame. There is no possibility of turning back. Guzman estimates our position, he bravely taking measurements with his right hand, as five hundred miles from the coast.

Clayton Bailey

Captain Masse seems to have lost courage and we've camped on a rocky point, burning the remains of our broken oars for firewood. The evening meal passed and he made no decision. It rained and the river, rising, will soon flood the camp. For the first time, I smelt the putrid odour of mutiny. Late, around the tiny fire, he divulged his plan. He will go in the first boat, loaded heavily, with Guzman propped at the steering sweep and he and Caan at the oars. Every person is to strap an empty, inflated water skein about their shoulders, to act as a float should a skiff overturn. There were protests, especially Caan who wants to stay with his pregnant wife but the Captain explained we of the second skiff were to observe his passage, and use this knowledge to better navigate the river ourselves, it being implicit that Water Music should be given the highest chance of survival of us all. Bain will be at our helm. Water Music avoided his eyes when he glanced around for reassurance.

Guzman's complaint was that we had no wood to boil coffee for the morning start. Such a light heart in the face of oppressive adversity. We went to our sleeping places, each thinking the thoughts one must think when death is possible. For myself, I reviewed my life, and was not unsatisfied. The Captain gave me such a regard, after sternly ordering Caan to be in his own boat. I see our physical forces against the river as equally divided. Two one-armed men and a two-armed man in one boat. In the other a man and a boy and two women (one a man), and I have no trouble admitting that the ultimate capacity of our muscles is less. A just division. The worst danger lies with the first boat's run. There is no way of knowing if it is better to take the right or left hand passage, the fall is obscured from our sight. Captain Masse declares he is tempted by the left-hand passage.

Bain climbs a rock pillar giving him a sight down river. The first skiff is launched, pushed off by Reid. It skims the foremost rapids, well navigated until it reaches a high overfall and whirlpool. Caan and Captain Masse struggle against the current, striving for the left-hand passage. Trying to escape the vortex, Guzman leans to his sweep, but they are slowly overcome. The boat rolls, spilling out its crew, and tumbles under the stained lather of a vertical crest. Heads bob. Hands reach out, fingers splayed.

Those remaining stand in silence. The boy's face contorts with waves of muscle spasm. Water Music blinks but once, as if to erase the vision of Caan's desperate thrashing. She turns to the boy. With hand signs, she imitates the boat crew fighting against the current, and mimes their headlong struggle.

Then, she turns about face, and mimes paddling with the current, being flung to the edge of the whirlpool, out, and down the rapids. He nods in understanding, as does Reid. Bain descends, his face immobile. Reid asks for time to explain their plan but he looks away, ordering the immediate launch of the second skiff with he at the helm, the others at oars. They protest, but are not heard, and to emphasise his words, Bain shoves the second skiff sufficiently into the water that he could launch it with one more push as if to say, "get in now, or I'm gone."

They tumble in, and take their oars. Bain pushes off. They slip into the stream. When the current flings them into the whirlpool, the oarsman do not struggle, instead let the boat spin, and ghosting with its momentum, whirl in faster and faster circles towards the effervescence outer rim.

The walls of the canyon blur, the skiff seems ready to fly...and Bain panics. He grabs an oar, heaving on it to fight the current, digging in his blade. Water Music screams at him, yet he sets all his force against the current, standing up and bracing himself against the thwart. The skiff rolls, taking buckets of water. When it seems Bain will destroy them, Reid cracks his oar with the firewood hatchet, its shaft snaps and Bain near tumbles in. They fly to the edge of the whirlpool, crest the overfall, and are swept down river, slowly regaining control of the vessel. By mid-morning, the current is checked as the river flattens out. Soaked wet and exhausted, they float down its middle, drying themselves in the high midday sun.

>⊷⊶⊙⊷⊶⊰

*H*e is dead. I saw him, we saw them all caught briefly in a backwater down river. His ravelled hair a fringe around his head. His brow bumping against the dark middle striation of a pink, water sculpted boulder. His body suspended by his still inflated water skeins, he rose up, looked around, then lay back peacefully, prone in a lathered eddy, one boot nudged into a fissure parallel to the water line, a splintered stump of oar blade bobbing alongside his sunken shoulder. The current tugged at him. The skein soaking full, his body rolled. His boot toe disengaged from its cliff crack mooring. A submerged arm swung into the current and, with a half roll, he was sucked from his vagabond grave. The turbid water coursed over a sunken boulder, swelling to a standing wave. He ascended, eyes now closed. At its bubbling lip, the hand swung up, seemed to wave. He was gone.

Unreachable by any human ability or effort however miraculous. Yet I wanted to embrace him, bring him back, give him life. Futile. We'd lost our leader. The king is dead, long live the king. Now dead as the stone around him, the over fall impossible to survive. Is he forever now his last intention – to avoid an insurmountable wave, a sucking whirlpool, right the tipping skiff? Straining muscles, the smell of filthy foam, the irreversible slackness of a shattered oar shaft.

And his last memory? The smell of cinnamon as a child? His wife's body, a silky and astonishing territory, and the first time he touched her or the last time or the times between. Did they whisper confidences late at night? Did she cry out? Did he? Did he listen to his daughter's piano practise; day by day, page by page, the notes, the intonations, the rhythm pianissimo, fortissimo, finally the whole piece – the composer's account – with perhaps some evidence of her own personal force. Did he place his hand on her shoulder, to encourage but not interfere. Sandwiched between his memories of life, were there memories of death? The war, the nightmare our species commits, like a livid black strata in the layered composition of his existence. Its violence made of harder stuff, dark and convex like the sullen layer of stone his head bumped against.

So thus I watched him die. And saw in abstraction my own father die, and realised, at last was able to separate myself from him, his acts, to see our interaction as a morality play, a classic theme, with each in their role, but variations on the theme possible, necessary, and in my case yet to be played out. I see who he was and who he was not and who I was and who I was not. Only one who has suffered the loving of an oppressor can understand my sentiments. One who has not suffered such miseries could never understand such absolute power. They cover the sky such ones, black out the sun, and the only access to light is by running away from them, for they cannot be fought to a victory.

I also see the purposes of my disguise. Part of it was some desire to possess my father's power. That part has just died. But part is the very real safety and mobility that trousers gave me. That last is probably still the greatest benefit.

We can only assume the others have suffered the same fate. Dear Water Music. Here, I lament the passing of Caan, someone with whom I had only the most faint connection. There she sits, alone in the canoe, painfully far from her decimated people, her husband just this day deceased, and she makes no sound, nor looks at us. Watching the horizon seems to satisfy her, and the only sign of her immense loss and grief is her lethargy, for to this moment I have never seen her stilled. Yet now, it has been half the day, and she has not moved, only slumps, bosom pressed to the skiff's gunwale as if to keep her overburdened heart from exploding itself within her, and tearing open her breast.

And now she turns and looks at the boy, at Bain, finally at me, her face a mask, and I cannot comprehend why she does not cry out to me and this must have shown on my face, for she directs towards me an ancient regard that says, and what a shock for me to receive it, a look that says "what do you know of woman's grief" and I realise, though I have been thinking of her all this forenoon, thinking woman's thoughts, that what she sees when she looks at me is a man.

And she is right. What woman shares the grief of the death of a husband with other men? Not one. It cannot be. The death of a child one shares with one's husband, the death of a mother or a father with one's sisters and brothers, the death of a friend with their friends. But the illness or death of a mate. Some quality of it must be retained within the community of one's own sex. As my father kept his grief over my mother to himself, or to his community of male companions, however stoic.

I'm enraged at my situation and inadequacy. What horror to be a man today. So much denied me by the wearing of these trousers. What profound impotence. I will make the camp tonight, and cook the evening meal. The boy may help me as he is able, though he seems to be strongly affected by circumstances, and especially Water Music's dour mood.

Clayton Bailey

[Captain Aaron Masse]

As often happens in the case of my extreme fatigue, the spectre of my ancient soldier upbraided me during a night of fitful sleep. My poor thinking, combined with mischance, has cast a pall of shame upon my ancestor's & his. I did what a warrior must never do, I chose the wrong path. It was to the right the river flowed clear, dropping faster, but without overfall or rocks. It is still rising, & dark as pitch with rainfall from far upstream. I am sore of body, & exhausted. At the last moment, when I tipped over the falls, I gave myself to God. Always a fighter, I released myself from the earthly battle, & made ready for my soul to enter into heaven. All became black, there was no pain, & when I opened my eyes, I expected to see angels, not the smashed face of Guzman bobbing next to me. I owe my life, such as it is at this moment, to the still inflated water skein.

The corpses of Caan & Guzman, I have attached to the wall with rope that floated in. There are also some splintered bits of plank and much of the contents of the skiff, water skeins, sacks of food, and in their oilcloth pouch, my journal and personal effects including my trail-worn prayer book, a gift of my sister, all completely dry, rendered up by this same back water.

I saw the other skiff skim by, a good three arm lengths below this curious eddy, a water floor piled up by the river's terrible hydraulic force. Their eyes were downcast, all upon the river, & no one observed me though I raised my hand. Reid's wonderful head was the last thing I saw, her eyes shining, bent to her oar, as intrepid as a warrior. The wind pressed her wet doublet to her body, & it gives me great happiness that my last vision of her was as purely a woman.

They will come back to look for us when they are able, but looking at these canyon walls I doubt it will be any easy task. I may have to wait a day or two. The river could rise during the night. If it is too great an increase I will be washed away from here, & would never survive the cataract. This niche is large enough to sleep in. I will set what material I have along its ledge, a long notch, which formation Guzman explained to me. Hereabouts, the canyon walls are made of granite. Rock once greatly heated and liquid, now cooled and hard. But throughout it, in near horizontal layers, there are thick strata of sedimentary rock, a soft limestone. This was formed in another manner, it being the gradual accumulation of sand mud and debris on an ocean floor. Where the river runs swift, and comes in contact with it, the waters erode the softer stone, cutting deep into it and leaving the hard granite above and below. I am in such a formation. An indent high as I am tall, and near just as deep, it slopes gradually, twenty paces both up and down, until it is at the place where the water cannot eat at it, and it becomes flush with the cliffs, regretfully disallowing exit.

One duty to perform. The burial of Caan & Guzman. There are rocks about, curiously round, for they have been spun in conical holes in the river bed for millennium. I will fill these good mens' shirt & trouser pockets, so they will sink.

⊱┈⊰•⊹⊙⊹•⊱┈⊰

[Captain Aaron Masse]

My prayer book served well my compatriots yesterday. I tipped them, weighted, into the current & read over the sinking bodies of these my two comrades the prayer for sailors buried at sea. Not the complete maritime ceremony, but what was appropriate I feel. My understanding of the sailor philosophy is that if the sea takes you, you must be rendered back to her. It was the river that took them, so I gave them back to it. God bless & keep their souls.

As to myself, am comfortable in this niche, waiting to be found, or for the river to drop so I may walk out. Have hard biscuit & plenty of water. The night was damp, but not cold. Oilcloth wrapped around two trunks I use as a cover. Body should recover from its battering in a few days. Will then consider my resources & method of escape. Several options seem evident. I will be found by my compatriots. I could scale the cliff above me, easily possible for a mountaineer having climbing equipment & two arms. I obtain neither. I could dive into the whirlpool in front of me, & shoot the cataracts. Certain death on the violent flood surge, the sand heavy water more oppressive than when clear & this side of the river impossible.

Must wait awhile for my body to regain its strength & reckon that a few days hence the river will have quieted. At a lower level, it may expose ledges wide enough to serve me in making my way past this deadly overfall to a launching place for I have collected all the bits of broken skiff & the two wooden boxes which should serve me as a float to descend until I reach walkable ground. It cannot be far down current. We have already come a good distance. No canyon can last forever.

><-!-<>-•-O-<>-!-><

would have thought only a machine could produce such steady, horrible pounding. With each descent, my head thumps the bottom of the boat. The canyon rim rushes by. At times I see a tree, once an eagle. We have covered more distance today than in the previous week. I cannot look at my comrades from fear of shifting weight and upsetting us. But for Water Music, we would surely be casualties. She understood we could do nothing to help ourselves on the steep river run we saw before us, there being no shore, only cliffs left and right, but neither were there rocks, just an endless, straight stretch, a huge stone trough, the deadly force of the descending water undulating the river's surface into steep, brutal swells. The first pitched us down into the bilges. Bain struggled up twice. We others lay there, less enthusiastic. The boy out of fear, me because I could think of nothing better and Water Music through intelligent and rapid appraisal of the phenomena. Realising the benefit of our low placement, though Bain resisted until I screamed at him to get down, she forced us all into the centre of the boat, and here we lie. The boy is beside me and his muscles have relaxed. At first, his limbs were tense as iron bars. Bits of foam slop over the gunwales the boat slews wildly left and right, but comes back to a true course on its own, no doubt because we are dragging several ropes that came undone. We hold a course down the river's centre, for here the water has the greatest velocity I believe, and by the laws of physics, is a slight depression, within which we glide.

If it were not for the rough bouncing, there is a pleasure to the journey's swiftness, for we gain miles with no effort. This brought on a terrible realisation which we all shared but never spoke a word of. There remains no chance to ascend and look for our comrades, if one or more of them survived, which we all doubt. Bain is now in name the leader, and he spent a good long time in the stern of the skiff, gazing back upstream, yet gave no command that would stop our descent. I detect no diminution of the arc described by our plunging bows, meaning that we will not soon exit this gorge. When we do perhaps we will leave the mountains also.

I have never indulged the question till now, since we are so pained with what calamity lies behind, but...I wonder what lies ahead? It is the absence of Captain Masse that lets me think this manner of thought. Previous, I let him think such for me, a not unenjoyable mental state for it allowed me to concentrate on my pictures. Now that I think the thoughts myself, my position as photographer changes. Is it possible that the conceit of the photographer is bound up in some symbiotic way to larger events and that the photographer can only serve a cause, but never be one autonomous?

>─┤─‹♦›─O─‹♦›─┤─<

Night approaching, weariness conquers the skiff's prone occupants and they do not remark a gradual cessation of the river's tumult as they settle to sleep. Save the boy, who wakes later in the dark. Overcome by the wide miracle of the river, such a thing as he has never seen, making no sound he pulls himself eye level with the gunwale, his sole desire to enjoy alone the pleasure of floating on the level mass of water.

And the river rises to the occasion of having this enraptured audience of one, like a virtuoso would rise to the occasion of performing in private audience before a king or queen, and calls forth a seductive veil of haze as its overture. Across this translucent backdrop, it sets a theme of nocturnal fish and foul. The boy's eyes, long used to night hunting, perceive the unlit spectacle as apparent as in day. Fish surface to gobble hatching insects in such profusion the intersecting rings of their rises create a moire pattern that obliterates the continuous surface of the water and the boat seems to levitate. The only remaining bond with the earth are the ripple rings made by ducks along the shore, hens out with their cortege of ducklings, all upending themselves, tails in the air, to scoop whatever nourishment they seek from the shallow bottom near the riverbank.

The river allows this theme to pulse and build, and the boy succumbs to its hushed cadence, happy in the security of the skiff, happy in the company of his slumbering boat mates and happy to be alone, gazing across the vibrant water at the ducks, black shapes bobbing against the vertical filigree of reeds and long stemmed rushes. He is beginning to think that his terrible struggles to survive with his sister are over and that nature is a benign and motherly force protective like the mother ducks yonder with their young, when the river closes it performance, a tail fin swirls the water within the reeds, a pike's flat jaw breaks the surface and a duckling, inhaled, disappears just as the worn bottom of the skiff bumps across several rocks then thuds solidly to bind itself against a wide sand spit, its movement stopped, the river moving past it no longer silent, but gurgling, and human noises beginning too, as the others in the boat awake.

>─┤─‹♦›─O─‹♦›─┤─<

[Captain Aaron Masse]

Second grave mischance but no visit from my forefather to rebuke me. Due to the same peculiarity of hydraulics that cast us upon the rocks, the whirlpool below me drained suddenly in the night. I now see how. It was fed by an overfall much higher up & drained through a hole bored into the soft limestone river bed by centuries of spinning granite stones. It is through this exit, much like a sink drain in a kitchen, the bodies of Caan and Guzman passed out.

Once the river dropped below a certain level, the waterfall that fed this basin of a sudden dried, & the pool drained, like an unplugged bathtub. I now look straight down five or six heights of a man into a smooth rock bowl, with the drain hole its lowest point. If I were to jump I'd break my legs. I see no foot holds or crevasse large enough for a hand grip. Yesterday read several extracts from the prayer book, such guidance as I need, & with my spirit uplifted slept well.

The boy sets himself apart from the adults, and they ignore him as they make camp. He watches their faces, the gestures their hands make, the emphasis of their movements, and the distances they keep between themselves. He sees that Reid and Water Music always seem to be close together as they move from the boat to setting up the tent to collecting driftwood along the strand and starting a fire. They look over at Bain often, though never directly, and their movements are more subdued than when Captain Masse was there. Bain in some way has become the centre of attention, though he says little. They boy does not think Water Music and Reid are afraid. But the boy is afraid. He knows that Reid is a woman, accepts that she wears a man's clothing, which he attributes to some caprice on her part. Something will happen between the two women and the man he thinks. They are not friends.

Bain walks to the extreme down current end of the long sandbar, where the next curve in the smooth and level river can be seen. Several heron poke awkwardly in a shallow. One spears a fish and flips it up. Water Music watches Bain, concealing that she does so by peering between the thick plaits of her hair as she walks, bent, seeming to look for firewood, in the other direction. Her hands reach down to inspect objects near her feet but it is not the weathered pieces of branch and root she sorts through. She is inspecting stones, picking up, then discarding any that show a flat face. She sees a grey and mottled one, plane as if cleaved, large as her foot, and snatching it up, dips it in the river. She turns her back to the camp and Bain, though she remarks that the boy watches her. Crouching, she settles the stone in her lap and slips a wide bladed dagger from within a fold of her clothing, the knife she removed from the slain horse thief's blouse. She lays its blade to the wetted stone and strokes it in an oblique arc, drawing the steel out from the blade to a fine burr, then turns it over, again stroking to draw the burr off, laps it till its edge gleams, a slight and pleasant curve, menacing as a card sharp's smile.

>→·┤·◆>··O··<◆··├·←<

*A*woke this morning, we being arranged for the night Water Music and the boy in the last and smallest tent, Bain and myself under the upturned skiff, to find Bain not there. I heard him rise at sometime in the night, but assumed it was to relieve himself, a man's habit I have long become accustomed to. He is nowhere on the sand spit. His footprints go to the far side of the bar, it being heaped high as a horses rump by the spring runoff, and they end at the shore, with no other sign, the sand around the spot we found to be without detail and smooth as a ballroom floor. It is as if he disappeared straight into the river. I know not what to think. He seemed to be a man of dark moods, but of such a rigid moral fabric I cannot conceive he would take the option of suicide. Water Music makes little of it, and for the first time in a long while, the boy is again friendly with her. I must say, for myself, that the recent disasters and deaths have so benumbed me I find myself perfectly exhausted in spirit, and also little affected by this concluding loss for in truth Bain was the one of my companions I liked the least.

>→·┤·◆>··O··<◆··├·←<

J. Reid, materials remaining:

1 Developing glass 12 drachms	1 measure Plain Collodion
Half plate Gutta Percha tray	2 measures Hyposulphite Soda
1/2 Bottle saturated Hyposulphite	Small ball of string
13 flatted glass half plates	Grooved box to accommodate
88 exposed plates in oilcloth	2 measures Pyro (diluted)
Bellows camera half plate	Focusing glass to fit

Compound (12 deg F7) in brass tube Aperture stops F4 to F56

>→·┤·◆>··O··<◆··├·←<

O ur first night with just we three, selected an island for its isolation from large predatory beasts. Our skiff swung in a natural curling of the current towards a flat gravel beach, and its prow grounded upon several splintered planks. There we found our the prow of our comrade's shattered boat, first evidence of their fate. I dread to find the bodies.

The island somewhat wooded along its centre spine, where the spring flood could not inundate the tree roots, nor its ice pack sever their trunks and the far side offered a shore entirely private from our bivouac. Water Music having finished her contribution to the camp's domestic affairs, she set off behind this dune to bathe...her first opportunity in near a week.

I follow her. We are hidden from the boy. She looks back twice to be sure of my intention to follow, and turns, at the defence, gleaming dirk in hand. It realise she thinks I am a man, perhaps bent on mischief, and without thinking, pull up my blouse to reveal my breasts, and seeing that is not enough to convince her, I down my trousers. What satisfaction to expose myself, a pleasure near ecstasy. What delight to see the look on her face. As her eyes focus on the triangle of my pubis, I feel very much the teasing harlot, and within me uncurls the wish to strip and show the beauty of my form to a man of my choosing. No chance of that here, perhaps why I indulge the musing as I stand near naked.

My first thought rising like an elated shout – I may now relieve myself when and where I choose, no more passing the day with distended bladder, waiting for night's veil to mask my toilet. No more limiting my cups of tea, or drinks of water so as not to fill that same bladder at an inopportune time. My body sags with relief, and I laugh, for the joy of this simple thing.

To find Water Music is a woman with a sense of humour. She laughs too, uproariously, at my caper and then embraces me, her bulging belly pressing against my naked one. Our first conversation, she speaks tolerable well, continued in this jocose vein. My first question to her I had literally been bursting to ask – how did she accomplish the amazing physical feat of never appearing to need a toilet place the whole day? She told me that in her tribe it was considered ill luck, worse than that, a hex, for a woman to be seen at any bodily function. Thus, from girlhood they were trained to go out in the dark of morning and the dark of evening only. For a woman with child this caused great agonies, which they accepted.

>–+◆>–O–‹◆+‹<

[Captain Aaron Masse] Day 204

The river continues to drop. No chance now of a spate raising it to fill the pool. And then what would I do. Swim. No, I have miscalculated and had bad luck. Water I have aplenty. The vapour in the air from the rapids is of such wetness that it trickles down the rocks early each morning. I have only to lay my canteen under it before sleep. I awake to it half full of the most sweet water. Food I estimate at one month, dried beans and peas, and one packet of dried meat.

Soldiers think of death seldom. Perhaps once when we are young, and leave our mothers to go to war. My own told me to return upon my shield, if I could not return victorious and carrying it. Perhaps again when we see our first dead, usually overrun enemy, or some poor unfortunate in front of us. We think of it for the last time when we see a killing, a ball tearing into the breast of a man beside us, or a sabre decapitating a cavalrymen.

Death becomes a fact which we share. What is seldom spoken of is the difficulty of killing. I was kind to my men as a young captain on the front line, and never shot a deserter or a man who balked as many of my fellow officers did, but I can say that fully half of the young soldiers in my command could not pull the trigger the first time their sights were set on an actual man they could see, be he behind a trench wall or charging them. I would prod them with my sabre point, or discharge my pistol at the same target, or pull their trigger myself. They seemed stunned.

The worst case was a freshly promoted sergeant I had ordered to shoot several prisoners we could not keep with us while advancing. Near a half dozen. I told him to go over the brow of a hill where he could no be seen and get on with it. Cannon shot was landing all around us. He returned, and told me he could not do it. I replied he could be shot for insubordination and drew my pistol though it was a ruse. This was a man who had been fighting hard the same enemy for nigh two years. He faced me without fear, ready to be killed. All I could bring myself to do was rip his new-earned stripes from his shoulders, setting him back to private. We left the prisoners tied up in a house, with documents explaining our actions for any rear guard should arrive.

During a lull in the advance, he was allotted night watch, and we were alone along the temporary clay ramparts. I questioned him as to what his thoughts were. He replied that he had never looked directly at the enemy. Face to face with the manacled prisoners, he saw each as a man; one probably had a family, another would have one some day, a third was someone's brother, the fourth a son.

>-+-•-O-•-+-<

*T*wo dry weeks now, the river waning, yet ever wider.

>-+-•-O-•-+-<

[Captain Aaron Masse] Day 206

A remarkable discovery. One portion of my notch's inner wall evinces, within the soft stone, the exact patterns of many kinds of sea shell. Of course Guzman explained that this limestone, now much compressed, was once sea floor. But think of the time it would take to accumulate a layer tall as I. Guzman spoke of geological ages lasting uncountable years yet I did not listen. It was part of his professional vernacular.

The implications are enormous, now that I ponder it. Has the earth been here so long? We were told the earth and all those alive upon it, man and beast, arose from a brief display of God's creative power. This came to pass some score centuries ago, no more. What I see before me, if what Guzman said has credence, casts doubt on my learning.

>-+-•-O-•-+-<

Pulling the skiff's bow upstream to set it in a creek mouth, the water at her thighs, Reid sees first the sole of Bain's foot. The current's caprice has slid a tapered tree root poking from the bank up his trouser leg to his crotch, and the dropping water level has left him suspended on it. One hand dangles on the water's surface, the corpse, face up, beginning to desiccate though stream side rodents and birds have plagued it.

The bootless foot summons her. Five toes curled tight as claws, a rim of cracked callous along the heel, the instep a white and puckered crescent. She has a presentiment that he died happily, something in her peripheral vision. Looking at his face to confirm it, she sees why. It sports an immense grin, from ear to ear, for his throat is cut cleanly thus, a magnificent leer making his actual mouth, lips rolled back against his teeth, insignificant.

She understands his mode of death quickly. She does not look back at Water Music, though Reid knows she too sees as does the boy. The skiff, tugged by a back eddy, slides her into deeper water, away from the wrinkled foot. She is forced to clamber over the bow, tipping the boat till its gunnel submerges. Several bundles tumble into the water, but she manages to pull herself aboard. To face the boy and Water Music, who look at her, expressions devoid of comment, as she shivers in the fresh breeze of day's end, having wetted herself above her waist. The boat, full of water to their ankles, spins, deep set and sluggish, down current.

>—◆—O—◆—<

[Captain Aaron Masse] Day 207

A startling event. Damselfly hatch in the river filled the canyon with fluttering blue insect life. Their lives were brief. They hatched, male & female, flitting off the water's surface whilst shucking their skins, took to the air & dried themselves clinging to the cliff sides, alighting even on me. They made their mating dance, the males expiring straightaway, the females staying alive till depositing their eggs in the river then too subsiding. All this passing in a day & a night.

I could not discern the males from the females, only by their order of death. They are identical to my eye, unlike the higher forms of life, so different male & female. The human the most dissimilar, yet capable of disguise, like Reid. There was once a theatre troop in the Capital, the very latest thing from the old country. My sister dragged me to the entertainment, which I found frivolous, though I am fond of the classics. The attraction of this troupe, full of bluster and affectation, was that it was composed entirely of men, though the plays enacted had the full complement of female characters. This practice dates from ancient times, when women were barred from acting.

I must admit that the men portraying women did so successfully, with only at times a hint of parody & I could not make an honest judgement of their sex. I did not preoccupy myself with trying to detect the disguise of their manliness, instead accepted the callow vigour of the performance, though there was little warmth to it. In some ways, the character in a play has no

sex. We are interested in the drama of their life, their character &
dilemmas. Males & females suffer these equally.

Men actors disguised as women, Reid disguised as a man,
both doing so for what opportunities this offers, choosing to do
so perhaps by the nature of their own constitution. Even stranger
things occur, one incident never discussed by the men of my
acquaintance but recounted by my sister, an unrepentant pur-
veyor of gossip, & like many a wholesome country girl, obsessed
with the debased aspects of urban life. The source of her most
treasured yarn was the indiscreet wife of a prominent medical
practitioner who let circulate, in certain circles, the story of a high
ranking army officer who, suffering an attack & losing consciousness in his office, was found by the same physician to be
attired, beneath his uniform, in women's undergarments, which
fact was discreetly forgotten by his staff at the request of the doctor. The delicate clothing was the property of his foreign wife,
who knew of his pretence.

⇒┥◆┝━◯━┥◆┝⇐

Reid bent over a stew on the small driftwood fire, beside Water Music who
agitates a pan bannock. The boy has chosen to sit across from them. Night in
back of him, the trembling firelight underscores sudden vibrations of his
physique which tense his shoulders up and inward, and smear his features
from chin to forehead. Reid watches the boy, judging his distance from the
fire sufficient he cannot tumble into it if seized by one of his erratic convul-
sions. These have been infrequent of late, as he has become more and more
adapted to the ways of the camp, but perhaps he is regressing. He has been
inert since seeing the corpse of Bain.

Water Music flips her bannock, near misses, and pushes it back into the
pan with a twig end. She does not want to look at the boy, for knowing he
wants her to look. His feet scuff the packed sand, alive with unexpressed
craving. She thinks of her husband, his red waistcoat, his urgent need to
dance when he heard pipe or fiddle music, his drumming feet. The boy's feet
make such sounds.

And the boy begins his dance macbre. Going stiff, walking erect, he is
immediately the incarnation of Bain – arrogant, inflexible and repressed. In
this persona, he loads and cocks a gun, lifts a tent flap. Leering, commanding, he grabs someone invisible within, and by the action of his hand groping breasts, shows the person to be a woman whom he pushes down, ripping
the clothes from her lower body, poking with the gun, threatening.

The boy stops his performance. Only an instant. Consciously breaking his illusion, yet making it more cruel by showing he is just a boy. Leering at Reid, he plunges back into his horrible pantomime, acting out in too private detail the rape of Water Music by Bain, the fervour of her struggle to resist, her groping for a knife, any weapon, Bain slapping her hand away, again pointing his gun, pushing her down, dropping his trousers with his free hand, the boy then climbing on top of the unseen but in his chimera present and prone Water Music, miming Bain's thrusting pelvis, his grunts and cries without guile, in the perfection of their animal intensity, even to rolling his eyes back as he, he who is Bain, reaches his climax and subsides, but keeps his hand tight on his gun.

Water Music sniffs the air. She has watched this presentation immobile, her bannock set over the fire. The bread is burning. She upturns the pan onto a flat rock she's dragged beside her. The crust is singed to black.

'We can still eat it,' she says, turning to Reid, playing her ability to remain calm after the boy's performance against Reid's horror until she sees the suffering on Reid's face.

'The boy acts well. With my people this is much honoured. He would be a medicine man. Now you know everything about me Reid. I am a woman, what is your word, violated...raped. I am too a murderer.'

'And you know everything about me. I am woman, not man.'

'I had forgotten that. It is funny. You were a very good man. I did not guess.'

'An odd compliment. Why did you not tell the Captain about Bain?'

'With my people, if a man tries that to a woman, she cries out and someone stops it or she fights him off. We have the same weapons, men and women. Bain had his gun. To much for me. The foreigner's power. I had great shame I could not kill him,but we were so close to the fort. I was afraid the Captain would send me back with him to be judged in your foreigner's law. I have seen the results of this. They make a high platform of planks then put a rope around your neck, drop you, and you choke. Like a snared rabbit. So I waited. The time came sooner than I thought.'

'Was it hard to kill him?'

'I followed him when he went to piss. He took no gun. It was dark. He dropped his trousers down. His legs were caught by them. I jumped from behind, and held him with my knees a small time, to feel him shake, then passed my knife.'

Water Music extends her arm out around an imaginary throat, knife in hand, then draws it quickly across, the same movement Reid has seen for cutting a sheep's throat, the struggling beast held between its executioner's legs.

'But there were only his tracks in the sand.'

'I swept mine away with a branch. He noticed,' she says, pointing at the boy, 'but you did not.'

The boy points at the cooling bannock. Water Music cuts it, picking up the biggest piece, and throws it across the fire to him. He smiles, a gentle grin, his face calm. She hands another piece to Reid.

'We have a more serious problem Reid. We are running out of food.'

'My name is Joanna. Call me that.'

'Call me Neeshta. It means cousin.'

>–·+›·–O–·‹+·–<

*R*aped. At gunpoint. Such a proud woman, she endured what every woman must fear the most. Yet she did not go to Captain Masse directly. I could not understand why but I am so habituated to her presence I forgot that all the time she was a stranger in the foreigner's camp. She did not expect justice from him or from his world, and in that she may have been right.

Something else in her reaction. What is it? She did not go to her husband Caan, which is what I would have thought she would do. Yet, upon contemplating this reaction, I see the nature of it. She saw no relation between her rape and he. Meaning that she was not his, she was herself. And, ultimately, she rectified the affair herself. This gives me strength. What depth of character and what powerful anger.

And yet, though she held herself after this horrible act so separate from Caan, her husband – she loved him, lived with him and respected him. This is the domestic relation I had presented to me as a girl, my mother and father separate, and I came to despise it. In spite of being disguised as a man, I am very interested in them, and my every urge would be to seek a man I with whom I could be complicit, the opposite of the relation I saw demonstrated daily by my parents. Perhaps the origins of this desire lie just in my great loneliness. Perhaps there are ways to live with a man that I do not know of?

The boy has suffered greatly being witness to the crime, thus witness to Water Music's loss of dignity. I will put the last few days out of mind. For all intents and purposes, the expedition is over. The expedition records were lost with Captain Masse and Guzman. I assume my contract and mandate as photographer is still valid, if circumstances require it.

*O*ur problem now is survival. We must get out, by way of this river, to the coast. I still have all my plates and will attempt to preserve them as long as they do not hinder us. If we are forced to walk, I will bury the plates in their sealed boxes where they may be found. There is little else to do. Nothing can be changed. We are all who we are and have done what we have done. The water now is crystal clear, the bottom smooth and sandy. Quitting the verdant back slope of the mountains, we pass through an inhospitable, rock strewn plateau sterile as a desert. I find bits of the preceding boat and their cargo each day, including some of my equipment, where it has settled out in a back eddy. The river has flattened. Night comes, and we sleep in the boat anchored in waist deep water, afraid of the wolves we hear howling along the shore. There is just room for three to sleep in the skiff's bottom, me in the middle, Water Music in the stern and the boy in the bow. The stars shine above. Water Music tells stories at night and giggles. Some nights I awake to hear her singing, and I think the boy sings along quietly.

I dress as a woman again, and this may be the reason I think of men these nights. Lying with one. The boy is not yet a man but his body has grown healthy and erect. Water Music, my 'neeshta', has lain with her man Caan, and though she jokes of refusing him at times I think she was well satisfied. I desire to touch a man's abdomen. I wish to slide my hands across his stomach at the same time I inhale the smell of his skin. I would do such right here in the bottom of the skiff if I had a man to do it with. Our blankets are warm, and the night sky is beautiful with stars. What more could a maiden ask.

For such I am, and I have no desire to marry. Neeshta tells me she was not married to Caan, though at the fort she was registered as his 'country wife'. He had several but she won out over the others and of that she is proud.

There must be ways I could have a man and not be married. This would not make me a whore like the professional women in the settlements, and I mean no disrespect. Of the men we had with us, all gone now, I preferred the company of Guzman, though I did not find him attractive, and I do not want to be intimate with a man of such experience. I would like a man of my own innocence, for intimacy must be a form of discovery – like our ill fated expedition a journey to an unknown place. I would like a man with a flat stomach, thin, but muscled about the shoulders. Of hair and eye and skin he could be any hue, though I would like said skin to be fine of touch. I would let him kiss me, and I would kiss him back. Silly small talk would not be necessary with me, but some intelligence or sensibility would. The Captain had that. A manly quality. A cock amongst the chickens for all his bluster.

>⊷⦿⊶<

[Captain Aaron Masse] Day 213

The river below distant as the ground from a barn roof peak. It will never rise. Little food left. Last two nights, an almost invisible black chigger hatched from the river. Woke with the warmer patches of exposed skin, wrists, behind ears, ankles, bit and blood-covered. Terrible itching that day.

Another fly also, in the heat of forenoon. Type of deer fly. Alights, takes one mighty chunk of skin, & flies off leaving bleeding wound. What I must look like, filthy & bitten. Am I the former leader of an expedition, which case my appearance means little, or still its commander, if said expedition still exists, for I know not the fate of those remaining, as they know not mine. If I retain my post & rank, I am a sorry sight. Could I face my men...& women...thus.

Thinking of Reid, wondering, praying she is still alive, I fathom the nature of her predicament dressed as a man, for I've just thought of how important my uniform was to me. Military men are uniformed from their first moments as a soldier & are trained to respond, thoughtless as animals, to the emblems upon hat, shoulder & sleeve that establish rank. I still recollect the day my officer's uniform was delivered from the tailor. Its arrival meant more to me than my scoring first in class or my impending marriage. I put it on, slowly, and stood before the mirror in the afternoon, adjusting it & admiring myself. A strutting peacock when I think of it. This enthusiasm never left me. One of my wife's few humorous exchanges with me was that I was the only man she knew who never complained of the time it took his wife to dress for a ball, because I took longer.

The Aaron Masse who left his marital bed, looked in upon his sleeping daughter before dressing, was not the same man who, some time later, brushed & uniformed, took his sergeant's salute. I doubt, if one of my dutiful captains passed me now, he would recognise me looking as I do. But if I was sitting on a street of the Capital, would he know me, or just think of me as another indigent? Did my fellow officers & soldiers in my command fathom me at all, or just the uniform with its head & hands sticking out? Probably the latter. Reid discovered this fact. She knew her trousers, with her shirt & boots, were more than half the battle of her identity. Her voice she managed altogether well, thus completing the illusion. She also kept to a profession that would allow its practitioner a certain artistic delicacy. Very clever in all, her disguise.

What of me? To what extent was I disguised in my uniform. In truth, how much did I hide within it? I must confess I felt better uniformed than in plainclothes at home. My uniform allowed no question of who I was, & each time I gained rank, I felt better in it. Towards the end of my domestic life, for I must assume it is over, I felt no contentment at home. I remember too, when accepting this assignment, being disappointed that all the members of the expedition would not be soldiers & in uniform. That is why I engaged Bain I reckon. To be honest, & there is now no reason not to be, I found command out of uniform difficult, & the lack of immediate obedience, the constant negotiation a strain, though it made me a wiser man.

><+>-0-<+><

*T*he water even shallower, the bottom near, and the current so slow we seem to be on a long lake and must drag the boat over shallows, sinking up to our knees in the sucking bottom, backs bent, and yet we still find lost objects from the other two boats glinting in the sand. The surveyor Guzman's sextant. I tried to manipulate it, but it is useless without a chronometer and tables. I estimate we are closer now to the western ocean than we are to the fort, our last contact.

We are out of food and flour, and hungry. Neeshta has us foraging. The boy is the best for roots and berries. She sets snares of fine brass wire that was used to bind one of Guzman's instruments we found in the river. I make camp and start the fire with a double convex lens. I've tried fishing, but have neither cane nor silk nor fly needed for the techniques my father made me familiar with, so am unsuccessful. My companions have detected paths along

the river bank. Neeshta also found signs of cutting and trapping. As always, the land is everywhere inhabited. The shore is almost treeless, just stunted trunks high as my head.

Fish feel the skiff slide over top them, its shadow deep and large as a cloud. Wary only of a hunting heron or raised spear's thin silhouette, they rest easy behind their chosen rocks and in the bottom's hollows and some, the yellow perches, glide up under the boat's flat bottom to take positions at the shadow's edge, where they are hidden, but their minnow prey will be lit by the penetrating sunlight. In this way they accompany the skiff, an escort unknown to its occupants, except the boy, who has seen the fish dart out many times and is quiet enough in his movements not to frighten them yet too ignorant of the techniques of fishing to catch them. The skiff slips over the three-sided trumpet shape of a woven willow fish weir, held on the bottom by flat rocks, bell end turned upstream. The boy, watching the fish, sees it, knows it has been fabricated by human hand, knows it is not one of the items of wreckage of the other boat, and even understands that the fish in the narrow, boxed end of the weir are trapped, and will be eaten.

A series of thuds drum through the skiff's bottom planks above the fish, pushing pressure pulses through the water. The perch have felt these before, so maintain position. Four women's legs, two white, two brown, pierce the river's surface above, punching down fluttering bubble beams and squirting clouds of silt as their foot soles drag bottom. All but the hungriest, youngest perch retreat, streaking away to shaded undercut banks or beneath sloping rocks. Some, in their blind fright, swim into the constricting corridors of the fish weirs, several set on the bottom now, and realise their entrapment in the narrow ends too late. The skiff, finally, is held fast. The clouds of silt clear to reveal four feet firmly planted on the bottom, legs showing to kneecaps. No longer drifting with the boat and current, the fish remaining under the boat turn upstream, finning, to stay in its shadow.

They do not see the other legs approach out of the shoreline murk, slowly, to with a stone's throw of the boat. Brown legs. Sturdy, muscled ones in front, a few sets swelling towards women's hips. Thinner one's behind – adolescents – mixed with bruised, varicosed veined pairs submerged just to the knee. At the taper of every calf is a heavy silver anklet.

Schools of minnow, also silver, are driven into the deeper water by the advancing wall of legs, and from their boat shadow, the perch snatch at them, sometimes getting one straightaway, sometimes forced to chase, down along the bottom, around stones and reed roots, kicking up silt tendrils.

>─┤─‹♦›─○─‹♦›─┤─<

*W*e are safe here, this was evident from the start. They seem neither hostile nor pacific, merely inquisitive in a guarded manner. The men carry the children as much as the women and neither sex sport weapons, though every person is adorned with splendid silver ornaments, bracelets, anklets, and even waist girdles, all finely worked with strange designs in which I can see the shapes of plants, animals and fishes. Why they have no rafts or canoes I do not know, fisher folk living as they do along the strand. Water Music knows not the language yet is responding to them. Some lingua franca, signs and simple words, used for trading and travel in the whole region. The boy too reacts. He has much relaxed since his theatrical disclosure of Neeshta's violation. He listens, thinks, and forms sounds to himself. I can see his lips moving. In any event, we have been given a house. Plain victuals, maize cakes, a barley broth and fish, are placed near the door each day. Neeshta is taken away mid-morning. She tells me that she participates in a sort of language lesson interrogation in the house of an old woman. The houses around us strike me as temporary, yet these people must have been here since time began. I do not know what lies beyond our hut, which abuts the strand, as we were instructed, in no uncertain terms, by having our path blocked, that we could not go beyond the immediate environs. For all restrictions, and the incapacity to converse, we are glad of the company and freed from the dire urgency of gathering food. Our first day, a delegation arrived with pieces of the other skiff and bits of expedition equipment which has preceded us including my chemistry book. These were shown to us but not left in our possession. By Neeshta's sign language, we communicated that the artifacts had a relation to us, and that we belonged in the same group as the equipment's owners. Neeshta re-enacted their demise in a very artistic manner, assisted by the boy. I was almost overcome with the pain of grief, and went to sleep suffering the most piteous regrets, especially since, in the possession of one elaborately attired man, I saw near all the sixty medallions we had nailed to the logs, the entirety of our very signal to our western comrades. The weather is late summer, hot and dry.

>─┤─‹♦›─○─‹♦›─┤─<

[Captain Aaron Masse]

God be praised, a miracle has passed. I awoke this morning to find green plants growing within spitting distance, in every crevasse & crack & depression. Over the years, soil must have collected in these tiny places, & the winter winds brought seeds & laid them there that could collect the smallest amount of airborne soil and seeds. They are watered by the river mist & morning dew. My first temptation was to grab the tiny plants and eat them. I will wait yet, till they are as large as can be & start to wither from starvation of their roots, then I will pick them one by one & savour them. I contemplate an attempt to climb out, the rock being very much fissured above me. Difficult for a one-armed man.

◦━┼━◦━━◦━━◦━┼━◦

Another delegation appeared this morning, all but one costumed like most of the people we see, in a knee-length loin cloth made of some rough material like jute and a doublet of an undyed, finer cloth like linen into which multicolored effigies of birds and fish had been worked around the shoulders. For the first time, it was I who was invited out, though I detected some force behind the request, and could see it might also have been an order. The leader, or assistant to the grand inquisitor as I was to find out, bore much more elaborate raiment than I had seen. His hat, a kind of toupe with intricate designs stitched around its base, was of such delicate material the finest felt fedora could not have stood it better. His knee length robe, of waterfowl feathers woven in luminescent horizontal bands, was of such fabulous construction I could not at all divine the technique. It seemed to weigh less than the air.

I was led away from the strand, somewhat uphill, deep into the village, which I now estimate at near a thousand inhabitants. All the houses are similar to ours, with what appears to be a permanent, mortarless stone foundation raising to waist height finished off by a wall of horizontal logs that have the appearance of driftwood topped by a peaked roof of thatched reed. The sometimes full length, sometimes short and butted horizontal logs are not trimmed at the corners – I imagine these people have no saws – so protrude, various widths and distances, and are used as such. I saw a basket of what looked like turnips, a hand loom, a skinned rodent, and an infant in a sort of vertical cradle, all suspended from these convenient appendages. The streets, average width of my outstretched arms, have no particular survey, their surface being hard pounded sand and clay. Waste water and sewage seems to run down trenches cut alongside the houses towards the river, and every so often there is a garbage heap, which must be cleared away periodically, for they are of such small size they can only represent a season's accumulation.

Our troupe, still led by the man in the magnificent cape, halted in front of an edifice of different architecture – long, thrice the length of the largest house, with walls a high vertical palisade, again untrimmed. There was a verbal exchange that had a formal tone, and I was beckoned in by the man. The others remained, but I could see Neeshta and the boy slowly working their way through the crowd towards me. Inside the walls, the roof, twice the height of our own hut, was suspended by crossbeams but I could see from its loose construction it was for shade only. All in all a type of council house or courtroom. And in front of me, the council, cross legged on woven mats in a horseshoe arc, dressed in variations on the theme established by the man who had preceded me except for a woman at the centre of the semicircle who's robe was full length, again of feathers, but without design, the whole garment being radiant, shimmering green neck feathers of a duck we saw often on the river but Neeshta was never able to trap.

There was a mat like the others in front of me, slightly to one side in the room, and this queenly personage motioned me to sit. I heard a shuffling behind, and glanced, and saw Neeshta and the boy taking positions on a mat right at the back of the hall. No doubt, I thought, to translate...which is her profession. I could see that Neeshta bowed to the woman and the council, so I did likewise though it came off more as a schoolgirl curtsy.

With all seated, several of the people in the horseshoe, about a dozen, made a short speech, which was not translated. I nodded my head after each. The woman in the long cape then talked for some minutes, making rather large, encompassing gestures, pointing to me, Neeshta, and herself. When she finished, there was a silence, and Neeshta's voice came next. I did not turn, remained instead looking at the woman, as I assumed I was hearing her words, though second hand, in my own language.

First, I was welcomed to the village. Next, condolences where expressed for the lost members of our party, followed by an odd compliment. Our hosting tribe, or clan, had heard of the white man and his ways. They had been told that the foreigners built settlements with walls around in which just men lived, no women and children lived, and went on pilgrimages and hunting parties in, again, groups of only men. This was very sad, that the white tribe had so few women, and that the men had to travel and live alone and so they were happy to see that our hunting party had not only women and children in it, but also a woman with child, for this was a sign of good fortune and a successful hunt if a child was born during the journey. They commended us for this superior way of travelling. They were happy the foreigners were learning the ways of the land.

At this point, the woman in front of me gave a slow, regal swing of her palms upward. The boy and Neeshta came beside me, lay down their mat and took a position beside me, placing Neeshta in the middle. Again the regal personage spoke, addressing us three, but nodding to various of the men and women around her, and again Neeshta translated.

More compliments were extended, for the fine construction of our boat and our skill at navigating it. The woodworkers of the village would like to know how it was made. They also extended their hospitality and invitation to stay at least until the child was born for they wished the good luck of this event, and the women, having been told that the child's father was a foreigner, assumed the child would be too and so wanted to see it born to find out if foreigners, such as I, were born light skinned or had been simply faded by the sunlight, which seems to be what they've been told about us.

It transpired that the action of light interested them greatly. Their God was light; the stronger God sunlight, a lesser God moonlight, many small Gods, like angels, of the star's light, then the God of firelight, who though not as powerful was the most loved. If foreigners were made pale by the sun's light, then the magicians of the tribe wanted to see it, for light magic was the highest magic.

Neeshta talked for the first time, replying to the translation she had given. She motioned towards me. There was a long series of exchanges. I could see that the language was a problem. The boy spoke too, and I could see, in his unerring mimicry, that he was describing me using a camera. Neeshta broke in at this point, telling me that she had told the lady in front of us, that I was a worker with light magic and that the discussion centred around this, but the woman wanted to hold private meeting with her council before replying to me.

All talk ceased. The grande dame spoke, extending her hands towards me, palm up. She told me I was no longer a guest, but a friend of the village. I was safe there, and could go where ever I pleased now, but in a few days I would be called back to the council. They had things to discuss, for summer would soon end, and the harvest days begin. As I left the meeting, I realised that I had not been a woman in a public circumstance for nigh three years. What travails. What a relief to be suddenly done with my disguise, the relief of pressure an animal must feel when shucking a too small skin.

[Captain Aaron Masse]

Eating the plants had little effect. I would estimate the total amount at the equivalent of a plate full, though I have not a plate. My fingers & toes grow more insensible. My eyes, especially at night, see poorly. I will not die here, though I feel no coward's shame if I did & gave up the fight. I have looked deep inside my heart, & I have done my best. I tried climbing out three days in a row, but it is an impossible task for a one-armed man. With two hands I could do it, many of the fissures allowing entry of my hand to the third knuckle joint.

Whether God desires that we accept or fight against death I know not. Surely there comes a moment when we must cease the preoccupations of this life & begin to prepare our souls for the next one. It is my hope that Heaven is an equitable place, & that all who reside there, save God & the various angels, share equal status though my understanding of hell is that the punishments are various, suited to the condemned's earthly crimes.

I am truly thankful God saw to let me have a copy of his divine word here. What fortunate chance I stuck it in the oilcloth pouch with my journals that morning. His hand guided mine. There is so much on every page. I draw my spirit's sustenance from them. The passion on each page lights a fire within me, throwing off the chill of these oppressive rocks that will be my unclosed tomb.

There is a comfort in knowing death lies inevitable ahead. It is like walking the cut trail, the surveyed line. The mind can set the chores of navigation aside, & focus on direct scrutiny of what abides nearby.

Of my sins I register the following. All the sins of boyhood, from stealing apples to peeking through a widow's uncurtained window. As a young man, I cheated on an exam, visited a brothel, made love to a colonel's wife. I have killed men, & ordered the killing of more. I have burnt & sacked the homes of many others, forcing them to flee their native soil. All this in war. I have been vain about my position & my command. I am proud. I have not been a proper father to my daughter nor husband to my wife. I have divorced, yet in fact I think there is a greater sin hidden there. I have not spent the time to fathom women's character. Had I, knowing what I know now, I would not have married the woman I did. I have begun to understand the jests some of my more mature fellow officers made about me. Though seeing myself as a rustic struggling amongst the well-bred, I think I was to them a self-important fuddy-duddy.

I've seen in Reid what a woman can be, that man & woman can share a life. I saw this too with Water Music & Caan. I did not love my own good wife. Did not know how to. I can say that now.

Reid. I love her. I do not even know her first name. J. Reid. Jane? Janice? Jennifer?

My ancestor visits me nightly now & brings his comrades from Heaven's home for dead soldiers. Their uniforms are splendid in their variety. On the cliff facing me, like the most practised theatre troupe, they act out ancient battles. Afterwards, they gather round, the victorious general presiding, & we debate strategy & tactics, the great changes that would have been had these battles been lost instead of won.

Temperature of the river & air dropping. Morn, the air colder, a thick fog rises, condensing. Nights a trial, damp & chill. I yearn for a plate of hot, fat marbled meat. Roused from a nightmare of violence, myself sitting at a council table with many other cavalry officers, the clatter of sabres & jangle of spurs as we sat down. After I presented my tactical solution for the battle plan, a fellow officer jeered me. I jumped across the table at him, pummelling him with my fists, pounding his jaw, crushing his nose to a bloody pulp & then awoke, surprised at myself, my fists still clenched. It was not before a long time I remembered my amputated limb, which I held clenched tight as my remaining hand, & in my rapture believed quite real. Looked down, through the air still thick with fog, could even see it in the force of my expectation it to be there, But it was not.

Having seen many soldiers, officers & men, lose the facility for rational thought in the duress of battle & slip into delusion, I recognise that they never possess any sensibility of their demented state. A man seldom has the luck to know himself this way. But I have just seen it. Some time ago I suffered a delusion, the renewal of my amputated limb. It was in every way real for me & I was awake. I now know that limb is not there, for I have regretted its absence every day. Having one arm has trapped me here. If I had two, I would have solid chance to make good a climb out.

Does the return of my limb represent hope. Is the body, slowly attacked & worn down by the vicissitudes of life, reconstituted to perfection in death? Has God given me this brief glance of what awaits me to ease my pain & speed my passage? Will I die soon? I have never had the courage to think that thought, yet it has always been evident there was no hope. Who could rescue me? How?

Winter nears. I could never survive it. I feel no shame for slipping into my delusion the morn. It refreshed my spirit, like the plants refreshed my body some time ago. I felt no pain, no doubts.

I have decisions to make, but before that, there are many fresh pages in my journal, & I have two envelopes. I will write letters of farewell, dividing them into official; those to the geographical society, the cabinet & the rail road company, & unofficial; those to my sister, my wife and my daughter.

>–·+›·—O·‹+·—<

'Do you plan to stay?' Water Music translates. She is near enough one interior wall of the large palisade meeting hall she can place her back against it, and easily watch the room's only other occupants; Joanna Reid, sitting on a mat its centre, and the stately woman in the green feather robe, opposite and facing her.

Reid looks over to Water Music, who nods. She faces the robed woman, much more intimidating alone then at the head of her council and bows to her. The woman nods back, and speaks again.

'How long?'

'I have given no thought to the future,' Reid replies after a long silence, turning to point East.

'My home is back that way, but it is closer to my people to continue that way.' She points West.

'And, I have the boy to take care of, and my cousin will soon have a baby. I must stay with her.'

'Winter begins soon, you cannot travel through the mountains if you want to go West.'

'Then I say I will stay the winter, if I may?'

'Two women, soon two children. No husband. Do you want a husband? Your cousin tells me you are probably still a maiden. This is a disadvantage but some men here are interested. There are more men in this village than women. A short time husband is possible. We could arrange for you to see them?' is the next translated question.

Her eyes bright with repressed laughter, Water Music watches Reid, head bowed, listen to this last statement. Reid looks up finally and blushes when she sees Water Music's teasing, openly lewd grin. Reid opens her mouth twice, words almost form, but none are spoken. Water Music replies at last.

'Here is what I will tell the council woman Reid my cousin. You are still a maid.'

'Why did you have to tell her that, it is so embarrassing, it is so private, and how did you know anyway.'

'Cousin, we must not argue in front of this woman. What I told her is simple women's talk. What I will tell her now is that you do not want a husband...unless of course you do?'

'Of course I don't. You are being horrible to me.'

Water Music chuckles. 'I will say that in your tribe it is not unusual to have no husband. They have women like that here also.'

'What kind of women...prostitutes like in the settlement?'

'No, a few women who have been raped in warfare but mostly women who help other women with child birth and who make medicines. What you call doctors in your world, but these women do magic also.'

'I see, I'm sorry for making such an erroneous judgement.'

'Erroneous...what is that?'

'Nothing, please continue.'

'First I must talk with the council woman. Be...without movement...what is that word?'

'Be patient.'

'Yes.'

Water Music stands, carefully erect, and makes a long presentation to the council woman. Her sentences are short, and she makes distinct hand signs, often pointing at Reid. The council woman listens, her face flat and without expression. When she says anything, it is only a few words, and has the tone of a question. Water Music concludes her speech with an elaboration of the mimed demonstration of Reid's photography the boy had made. During this mute dramatisation, the woman leans forward, and does not speak, at last understanding what Water Music is trying to explain. Reid jumps up. With gestures clarified by many nights of playing charades, she steps into her own role as photographer in Water Music's theatrical. Water Music becomes her assistant – the boy – and turning to the still seated woman, continues to explain what is being acted out. At the end, the ephemeral photograph developed in mime and in her hand, Reid seems suddenly disappointed that it does not truly exist, and sits down with a look of great fatigue. Water Music returns to her place along the wall. The council woman regards them both, takes a dried leaf from within her cape, chews a piece of it, and speaks. Water Music translates.

'You are welcome here Joanna. You will take the place as husband of my child to be born and the boy. You must help gather food for us, and protect us if there is war,' Water Music said, then laughed. 'I will have to teach you to hunt and fight dear husband. But I must be serious. Do you understand your...promises. Is there a better word?'

'Obligations. Yes I understand.'

'If you are able to show to them that your tool for making pictures with light works, you will be tested, and if you pass, admitted into the rank of magicians. Women of this rank do not have to take a man, but their magic must be pure. If the magic is impure, they will be cast out or killed. The punishment will be decided by the council. Do you understand?'

'Yes.'

'If you do not want to enter the rank of magician, you may work as a household slave. Harvest is coming. Which do you prefer?'

'To be tested as a magician.'

'Prepare yourself.'

'Wait, I have one request, that all the equipment the villagers have found in the river be given to me.'

><+>+O+<+>+<

*H*ow ironic. Within weeks of reverting to my female status, I have a male role – that of Water Music's husband – thrust upon me. I questioned her about this, and though she would not stop laughing, she replied that in this tribe, whoever is taking care of a woman with child is called a husband, be they male or female. I imagine the equivalent use of the word for us lies in the idea of animal husbandry, which implies guardianship, care and nursing, but does not imply that a man be assigned the task.

What did my man's clothing and work mean to me? Certainly the photographer's work is neither male nor female. Nor trousers, for on the frontier, horsewomen wear them, and there are men in tribes on other continents that wear various sarongs and lungis. But for me, each morning, attiring myself in my male raiment, a transformation took place. While in the settlement I allowed myself to be a woman when alone at night. The act of pulling on trousers was also my moment of transition into masculinity. At night, the trousers would come off, and I was again, woman, daughter.

On the trail, the situation was different. Except for an occasional early morning river bath, I remained night and day a man, for circumstances, and the men, are much harder in the wild, and the possibility of confrontation always there. The disgusting male habit of never bathing served me well thus, for there was no pressure to disrobe in company, and my overpowering bodily reek convinced even me of my virility. Day and night impersonation is much more burdensome. Many times I thought I would go mad with it, or never remember who I had been. The officer's bathhouse at the fort was a godsend. What joy to find a door that could be bolted from inside. And now, I am whomever I want to be. Who have I become is the question? Yet I will not ponder it, for the examination of my competence as a magician awaits me, and I must prepare. Luck is with me, for amongst the found objects returned to me, I found the instruction manual for photographers. The first portion, the history of the science including alchemical references, is intact. The second part, techniques and formulas, which seems to have fallen victim to a leak in its oilcloth wrapping, is almost entirely legible.

The book will serve another purpose. In the same way Water Music has instructed me how to hunt, I now possess a book that will allow me to instruct the boy in how to read.

>─┼─◆>─O─◆┼─<

J. Reid, apparatus and material inventory:

1 measure Plain Collodion

1/2 Bottle saturated Hypo

Large supply human urine

Crushed limestone

Vial nitric acid

Horn silver

Focusing glass

Half plate Gutta Percha tray

88 exposed plates in oilcloth

Animal and bird droppings

Silver grains

Vial sulphuric acid

River bank grape wine vinegar

Rabbit skin scraped transparent

Compound (12 deg F7) in brass tube Aperture stops F4 to F56

>─┼─◆>─O─◆┼─<

The old man sits alone in the council house. In front of him, its lid propped open, is Reid's case of exposed plates. This day, he will preside over the interview of Joanna Reid and the discussion which will follow. His face is without expression, and his thoughts calm and ordered.

'I did not wear my robes of office, for today I seek not respect, but to satisfy my curiosity. This pale woman has been well spoken of, and I have seen the metal and transparent clay objects that floated down the river which belong to her. The metal is unlike our own silver metal, dug from the hills and smelted. It is golden, and very hard, and they have formed it in curious shapes, tubes and brackets that are joined to bits of wood with spiraled rivets. The clay objects are also harder than our own pottery, but what is fantastic about them is their transparency, as clear as water in the highest streams that flow on rock. All the objects are of very fine workmanship, but have no designs upon them to show the magicians clan and totem.

'She has told us that she will show the results of magic she has done previously, that she cannot do actual magic without much preparation, certainly not before the night of the full moon, which is the night of the apprentice's initiation. She must be judged today. She has shown most of the objects, which are interesting, and also demonstrated that the round transparent piece of pottery can make things large and close, so it is possible to see the eyes on the head of a bug, and that it can also gather the sun to a tiny point which is hot enough to start a fire. This is magic, of a useful kind, but not truly high magic. It is enough however, but she has another thing she wants to show us, that came in a very well made box, wrapped in a greased black hide which was large and square and skinned from no animal imaginable.'

The old man reaches into the case of negative plates, and, with great care, slides one out of its wrapping and holds it up to the light like he has seen Reid do.

'These flat objects are as thin as pan bread, and stiff as pieces of slate split from the mountains. Again, they are perfect rectangles. This woman's people like very much rectangles and squares with perfect corners. They are very good at making them in all kinds of ways. This must be a magic shape for them. When she takes one of the flat plates and holds it up so we may see, she handles it with great care and respect, so it must be a magic object, and, from the way she knows exactly its weight and attributes, she has no trouble convincing me it is part of her own magic. The light shines through it in places, perfectly, much better than the thinnest scraped and oiled rabbit skin. In other places, the light does not shine through, and in many places, the light is blocked incompletely, like the light is blocked when smoke dirties a new tent or a new elk hide roof.

'She invited each of us near to see it, and before I went, many of my associates looked at it closely for a long time. When I went, I did not understand at first what I was to see. She looked at my eyes, and tilted the plate a little at a time so the light caught it at an angle, like a reflection in a bowl of water.

Then I understood. Sometimes the flat object was transparent, but at the right angle, it became a picture. Not the kind of picture drawn from a dream or a vision. A kind of exact picture, like looking at something but if it was frozen and taken down and put on the flat plate then in the box and kept. I could see people, drawn very small and exactly. People not of our tribe, but the tribe of our distant neighbours, and others pictures of her own tribe, dressed in the way of their warrior clan, with round things that attach their clothing at the front, like hers, and one with a long knife at his side who is a clan chief like me, as this has been told to me by travellers. I could also see trees, and count the leaves. The tree we cut in the hills to use as roof beams. All this very small, and perfectly made, like many of her things.

'I can see no important use for such a drawing, it does not have a magical source or inspiration. If it is what they tell us it is, a perfect picture of what was, made permanent, like the perfect picture a hand makes when it is pressed into soft clay and the clay fired, it might be a good way of keeping family records – who was married to whom, and who their children married. But we have women who do this. Remembering well is very good training for the mind. With this tool of the foreign woman's, the mind would have no work. It would become lazy. And we would have nothing to talk about in the time after the harvest when the weather is cold and we sit around our fires.

'There was one thing that she had that seemed useful. The little sticks with the red and blue head that burst into flame when dragged on a rock. This is a useful thing. Very good for hunting trips.'

<hr />

[Captain Aaron Masse] Day 213

I heard distant gunfire, single discharges of a large calibre, but too piercing to be cannon – perhaps shotguns, like the rebels used desperately in their last days, the country born men bringing them from home to defend their farms.

Two or three guns being fired intermittently, swabbed, loaded, fired again. Their barrels will get heated I thought. Wounds from these guns are the most horrible. At close range then punch a fist sized hole if the shot is taken in the body. They can remove a head entirely, or sever a limb. At greater distances, to twenty-five paces, they leave a mass of perforations, each containing an contagious round shot. These men die many days later, of infections and fever.

But perhaps the shots were duck hunters, on a marsh, bent

low in blinds made of plaited reeds, or dug into potholes in stubble fields. Is it that time of day? Would the ducks be winging in? It is the time of migration? Have they eaten well all summer and are fat of flesh. Is there a dog with them to retrieve the carcasses? Will they fill mattresses with the feathers, & quilts with the breast down?

Then the music of an organ in a country church. I saw its player at her double keyboard, head erect to see the preacher, hands thrown across the keys, legs pumping at the pedals, rapid when there are many notes, more slowly for the simpler parts.

The congregation rose. Coal smoke from the leaky stove behind the struggling organist cast a thin fog in the room. Its heat did not reach those in the farthest corners, they hunched in overcoats & shawls, & it was too great for those nearby, whose odours fill the tiny chapel. Camphor from dark suits & dresses long stored in attic trunks. Harsh perfumes hastily purchased in town. Cow & horse manure on boots uncleaned since doing the morning chores.

The reedy music faded. Six of the tallest men disengaged from their place in the pews & stepped towards the front. Shuffles & murmurs. Creaking floorboards. Winter feeble light filters in the tall, thin windows, each corner decorated with a frosty bracket.

A boy grown to adult height, his breath in clouds, his jacket pulled tight, tended a low fire an arms length wide & longer than he is tall. The fire's bed a black rectangle on the white & recent snowfall. The headstones in the graveyard black rectangles too, upright. The boys boot prints a crescent near the fire, trod down to the fall's dried grass, & a straight line to a horse & dray tied to a tree close by, the horse covered with a worn canvas tarpaulin doubled over twice across its back.

Last night, my ancestor's history lesson came to its conclusion. I was visited by the first soldier, a warrior from long ago, some time after our origination, but before the great conflagration sent down by God to burn away our sins, as written in the Good Book. This soldier's spare frame surprised me, for I had envisioned such men as stoutly made. His clothing was simple, the day warm. He stood in front of a his house, low, daubed clay, his family behind him, & waved his arm to his ripening fields, the plant stalks bent, heavy with the crop.

I was reminded of so many of my fellow countrymen, the frontiersmen turned farmer, proud of his homestead. Simple men, peaceful to the core, devoted to the pleasures of field & home fire, yet drawn, with their sons, into the bloody war of independence, & on the battlefield, like a ripe field unharvested, they fell to the ground & rotted, never bearing their labour's fruit.

In my dreams I unite with Reid. She came upon me suddenly like a summer storm. Her lips, breast, stomach, thighs against mine, unclad. I ravaged her, & she the same, a grand impact shaking the place we were abed. A place more a manger, deep in hay, & afterwards I could smell the sweat, the animal musk of us, the damp hay, hear light rain on the roof above & dripping into the yard outside. There we stayed, rolling deeper & deeper into our grassy berth, till night neared, for it was day when we began. She was magnificent in her agile beauty. Twilight gave me great pain, for I could no longer see her. She begged off, saying she must return. I do not know where. I asked her when next I'd see her & she said never.

I was overcome with a great tiredness. It is great labour just to make this journal entry. My missing forearm throbs so. My chest is tight.

The air along the ridge's east face so still the passage of living things provokes its sole disturbance. A hunting owl swirls the summit's atmosphere, a foraging badger prompts a fetid ground draught, and the four apprentices, two men and two women by the outlines of their bodies, one of these women Joanna Reid by her greater height and lean stride, sculpt a path of temperate eddies along the up slope. The moon has not risen yet the cold clear air suspends its own starlight luminance. Smoke columns from fires in the village, far off in the valley behind them, can be seen, silver on black. It is the first night of the season the fires have been lit, and all signs, birds fluffing their feathers, rings around the setting sun, the urgent scuttle of rodents, speak of an inaugural frost.

Silent, bent forward now as the slope increases, the four have been given their instructions in a deliberate and secretive way, each provided with the details of one fourth the voyage they are making, and an exact explanation of the place where their respective stage begins and ends. The journey to the site of their initiation is also the first test of their characters. Its first stage was entrusted to the women – the shortest outline of the shadowed group – who now marches last in the single file. She was given an engraved silver disc to carry, one just fitting in her palm, it bestowed the eve of her final instruction.

With her guiding, they left the village, found a path by its slightest traces, and attained the slope of the foothills. A man now leads – black hair, lean. He took over at a turn marked by a pyramid of white stones, the disc being passed to him. He conducts them to the ridge's hog back crest, where he stops, having been told that his duties conclude when he can see to both the East and West. He turns to Joanna Reid, takes her hand, presses the disc into it, and assumes a place at the back of the line. She turns North.

The narrow peak's atmosphere is chilled, has a weightless motion, and slips between their clothing and their skin, now damp with perspiration from the last, steep ascent. They shiver from its touch. Joanna leads them directly along the ridge's narrowing spine. To her left, the village can no longer be seen, its valley a murky void. To her right, the far mountain chain rises, darker black against the blue black sky. The mountains Joanna passed through one lunar cycle past. She can see a notch where the river passed, and tries to locate a trace of its meandering, but cannot. The starlight provides definition only in silhouettes. In front of her, a cliff, many times her height, rises vertical, like the fine prow of a large and graceful ship, which hull's sides face near perfectly East and West.

There is a smell, of spiced fruitwood smoke, and the air's texture is no longer constant, being marbled with veins of warmer savour. Joanna reaches the prow's apex, split from the earth's crust millennium before, slightly weathered with this times passing, but still angular, its geometry inclining down and away from her, as if the ship is down by its stern. Here she finds a cave mouth requiring she bend for entry, and a notched ledge of waist height. She turns, as her guide did before her, slips the silver disc into the hand of the man behind her, goes to the back of the line and reaching over her head, grasps the collar of her smock, and pulls it off, and then her shirt, in the same manner. The others do the same, each now shivering, folding each item of clothing and setting it on the ledge until their are four square bundles there, and four bodies, one ivory, two golden, one chestnut, standing at the mouth of the cave.

Bending at the waist, they enter, Joanna Reid second, without hesitation. They walk, as instructed nights before, arms outstretched in the complete blackness, fingers trailing the cave sides. Its ceiling rises and after a few mindful steps they may walk upright. Their skin feels the heat of a fire. Its glow reaches them as they turn, and they can see, before they see the fire, the cave expanding like a snail's shell into a smooth walled cavern, the fire to one end. They place themselves before it, two pairs shoulder to shoulder, facing the others, warming themselves, on places marked with a square package, its surface the soft texture of fine white bird feathers.

The warmth changes each candidate's posture. They stand more erect, each body and face slowly flushing with the heat, the men's thighs glowing, the women's breasts radiant. The wall opposite the fire shines even brighter. The geologic act that formed the limestone cave left it flat and this plane surface has been ground back to the unoxidised, ivory stone.

The fire steams and pops. Some liquid falls upon it from above. Another inundation, more generous, and the flames fizz out. By its last glow, the initiates bend and pick up the packages at their feet, and unfolding them, find capes of the finest down. As total blackness descends again, they slip the cloaks over their shoulders, and pull the fronts together. One of the men, he who was first to guide, gasps. Projected on the wall between them, the image of a full and silver moon, the size of the disc they have carried, glows.

>─┼─◆>─•─O─•─<◆─┼─<

I trusted Neeshta's admonition, and refused to feel fear. Three naked bodies around the fire with me and mine made four. Novices are always initiated in these quadruples, it was explained. The pair of women represent rising sun and setting sun, their name for the directions I call East and West, the male couple are winter wind and summer wind, my North and South.

It being a cold night, and we being high enough for frost, our unclad bodies were glad of the fire. I felt no discomfort of the cold. Sworn to silence, with little to look at but the cave walls and each other, which modesty precluded, I fell to contemplating my own body as it warmed, and with much enjoyment, found it of great beauty. I have gained some weight here, being less active, and my form has grown more womanly. Looking down at my breasts I found their rendering, from throat to apex, a slope of perfect curves and their termination the most exquisite double circles, the outer one making a ruddy transition from the pure white of my skin to the inner circlet, round and conscious of itself as a fingertip, tawny by comparison, easily the darkest spot on my entire body.

My neck I could not see, but know it from the mirror. My torso narrows in almost straight lines, my back must be here very much a triangle to my waist which has not thickened at all, and thence to my flat abdomen. My hips have as yet no great width, and taper directly to my thighs, though I can feel, hands set on my posterior, a spherical accumulation there, which is not unappealing. Descending from this round relief, my legs reach long and straight to well arched feet neither small or large, which well balance me upon the ground. All and all a pleasing spectacle, to my eye. My mother always assured me I was a superb specimen, only requiring that two vertical finger widths be cut from my waist and added to my neck for me to attain perfection. This slim physique, of which I am justly proud, has helped me greatly with my masquerade, in fact, its willowy boyishness may have been what set me off on my adventures. I remember well my own delight when I slipped on the kitchen boy's trousers stolen from the wash bin, and his shirt, and realised I could get away with the ruse I had so long dreamed of, and formulated in my mind. I cannot imagine the more generously endowed girls of my college dormitory, vast of hip and bosom, being able to accomplish my disguise. How picayune are the things that effect great changes in our lives. I wonder if this is true for the larger events, wars and empires. Have they been started or ended by a simple kiss, an upset stomach, or a deformed toe? A good question to pose Captain Masse, were he with me. I yearn for his company this day, a sentiment I am surprised to encounter.

There was a beauty to the exposition of the moonrise, but I guessed its trick immediately. At the end of the cave opposite us they had filled a reflecting pool. One magician, seeing the moon rise outside, signalled another to inundate the fire from above. There must have been a chimney hole for the cave was perfectly ventilated of the fire's smoke. He or she simply poured in buckets of water, that had a peculiar spice or mineral in it. When total darkness ensued, the other simply took away a cover from another horizontal shaft going into the cave and perfectly aligned with the moonrise. The moon shone in, its reflection bounced off the pool, and shone onto the polished wall for all of us to see. I stuck my hand out, and it left its shadow, which proves my analysis. I'm sure no one noticed. Exceedingly clever nevertheless. Luckily they have not discovered the camera obscura. I still have an advantage.

The world, when we left the cavern cloaked in our new robes, was of awesome magnificence. The season's first frost had settled all around. The village and its valley lay below us, sparkling in the moonlight, as if a troupe of fairies had dusted it with powdered diamonds. Nearing home, the stalks of the grass under our feet crackled, and the plants in the fields beside us drooped, dead. Harvest will begin.

Went through the alphabet with the boy this morning, but he being more fascinated by the engravings than the print in my photographic manual, I took up our remaining lens and explained, I think, the relationship between the diagrams and the way light is bent by the lens to form an inverted image. He remained sitting with the book all afternoon.

>─┤◆>─◦─<◆┤─<

[Aaron Masse] Day 231

I ceased to be a man today. As the starvation kills me, the body withdraws its privileges. My senses dim, the light in my loins goes out. The sexual urge no longer pulsed there. I could be with no woman now, father no children.

Yet still I think of Reid, as an angel or a priest would think of her & these thoughts glow with the golden radiance of their purity. It seems that actual death occurs by the smallest amounts. My legs are going numb from the soles of my feet up. At this point I have no sensation to about mid-calf, it creeping higher two finger widths each day.

A question arises? At what point, if I was rescued, & given normal food & medical care, would I still die? The writing of my thoughts no longer preserves me. I will cease it. There lies still about the square of oilcloth I do not use to cover me. I will wrap the journal in this, & unbraid the piece of rope I have into twine. It will bind the package. This thought gives me relief − to no longer write, but only dream thence. My name is Captain Aaron Masse. I have passed by my reckoning near a hundred days on a ledge below the third great rapids of the river we have named Clear, for its unclouded waters. I have lived on short rations cast up with me, & some plants hereabout this entire time, & they have run out. I regret giving up my limb for my country. If I had it still, I would not be here, but alive. I question if the sacrifice merited the purpose. I was a warrior, a lover of war. The opportunity to love in other ways was nigh my grasp then fled but I have at least declared this. I ask God's forgiveness for my sins, & place my soul in our saviour's benevolent embrace.

>─┤◆>─◦─<◆┤─<

The boy shifts on his sleeping mat. He feels the frost coming through the stone wall where his forearm touches it and hears the twigs snapping on a tree outside. Faint heat from the waning fire warms his face, and he turns his body so he may absorb as much of it as possible. He pulls his sleeping robe over his head. He knows this time of the morning, the coldest time when the earth is most still. He remembers laying like this against the stone wall in the settlement after the bearded man had captured them and brought them in. That day he was on the outside, with his sister, and the fire was on the inside, and he understood none of the sounds people made.

His sister is gone, he reflects, but now he does understand the sounds that people make, and is learning to make them, and he feels better and the hollow inside his heart does not seem so large and cavernous. This learning began to happen with Water Music, first with her singing then with what she said. Here in this place, he is also beginning to understand what the people say, and also some of what Joanna says, for that is her name as told by Water Music though he has never spoken it to her. He is also beginning to remember. Tattered images and sounds of a place where he once lived flit in through his mind. He feels these things may be important, but they are in disorder and make no sense. The things he does with Joanna and the picture making box, and the things he learns from Water Music and the foods he eats in this village make sense to him. It is easier to think of them then feel the hollow of his absent sister or try to gather the memories into focus so that is what he would rather do. Today, the people will start to cut the plants. They have talked of it. He will go out into the fields and learn to do this, like he learned setting up the picture making box, rowing the boat, and now how to understand what is in the book.

He hears Joanna's voice, the voice she uses when she is looking for him to help her. He is happy, it means she will be coming to cut plants too. But after he is up, she takes him to a room prepared like many of the rooms they have worked in. The picture making box things are there, though not all of them, and some are broken or bent or dirty. They set out the remaining bottles and trays. What she is doing is different from before, though she blocks the windows and mixes liquids in the dark. He brings her water, and sets out the flat pieces of rabbit hide which she has cut into rectangles. In the dark again, working by touch as they have many times, she pours the liquids over the pieces. They wait a long time in the dark. The boy sings a song he has learned, of which he is very proud. Joanna laughs, a bubbling sound that feels good. He repeats the song and she sings with him on a higher note.

After a long time, when they can touch the rabbit skins and they are dry, she does something which he cannot see and they take the thick double covers off the doorway. The light floods in and for a moment he is blinded. When his eyes see again, he sees that Joanna has laid something on every rectangle of rabbit skin but one. There is a leaf, a piece of string and a corner piece of one of the pictures she made before that broke while they were travelling. One rabbit skin is completely covered with a black oilcloth, and one has nothing on it. All the skins face the sunlight coming in the door.

Again they wait, but now he can go out so he returns to his lodge and finds a piece of yesterday's pan bread to eat. He brings another piece back for Joanna. People walk back and forth in the village but none of them stand around the hut where Joanna is working which is what they usually do if she is making something or repairing something. This is because it is the magician's hut and entry is forbidden. Even the boy feels a little afraid of the place but he senses Joanna feels no fear so his own fear goes away. After she finishes chewing her chunk of bread, she pours out some other liquids, which have terrible smells and bits of something floating in them, which he has never seen. The liquids she uses are always clean as spring water. She asks him to take the pieces of string and others things from the rectangles. When he looks at them, he is disappointed to see they have turned black, and he is afraid he has made a mistake, but Joanna sees them and says nothing. He lifts the leaf off first. Underneath, there is a white leaf, colour of the rabbit skin. The same when he plucks up the piece of string. He hands them to her. She puts one in each of the stinking liquids, then hands it back to him and he sets it to drain. Slowly, all the rectangles turn solid black, the one covered by the leaf taking longest. He thinks that this is what is supposed to happen, but when he looks at Joanna her face is very sad.

>─◆─○─◆─<

*E*xtremely vexed with the failure of my experiments. It has been imparted to me that my magic has been judged as adequate, but not visionary. They see it as a record keeping technique, thus my submission of work as an apprentice to be allowed into the master magician's guild, shall take the form of a portrait of the extended royal family, for want of a better definition. Some dozen souls. I have managed to formulate emulsions, for there is horn silver hereabouts. The historical section of the text book is a revelation. Again the eerie sensation of going back in time. I am experimenting here with an apparatus that resembles in many ways that used by the men who made the first photographs, and my problems are the same as those of the early masters. I have reached back into the past, and joined the alchemists. Animal droppings, urine and vinegar are my stock of chemicals. My greatest problem, the problem of the first creators of the photograph, is to fix the exposed work. I lack Hyposulphite in sufficient quantity, and must find a substitute.

My other problem is my lack of camera, but I believe we have solved that. Again I revert to the techniques of the ancients. I am truly travelling back in time. I have pierced a hole in the wall of the magicians hut, where it faces away from the noon sun and on a courtyard. I will sit my subjects here. Using the good clay hereabouts, I have set the condensing lens, my largest and with the greatest light gathering capacity, into the wall. Opaque hides cover the hut's window and door, thus converting it into a camera obscura. Focus is a simple matter. The boy holds up the camera ground glass I still possess and moves it back and forth as I stand behind it. When the image is sharp, we mark the spot, and there we place a panel we have made from the flat boards of the skiff's seats. It is held vertical by tripods of willow trunks. A scraped hide is attached to it. The image forms quite well on this. I even went so far as to invite the chief of the magicians guild to see it. He was impressed, I trust, but like the others, awaits an actual photograph. Water Music, now adept at the language, has described one in good detail to him. She is very much with child. We expect the new born soon. The weather is increasingly cold.

In spite of my deficient experiments, my initiation by the magicians sect, through which I was transported into their mysteries, gives me great comfort. My status as apprentice allows me freedom to wander too, and these excursions buoy my spirit. To seek relief from my travails, I've taken to walking the downs beyond the village, and discovered a extraordinary thing on an afternoon when the frost stood hard all day. Fascinated by my discovery, I found myself far from the village near sunset. Since it was again a full moon, I did not hasten to return, but continued my explorations.

The river does not flow to the sea, as I, and Captain Masse, indeed all of us, had assumed. This explains so much, the lack of canoes in the village, for there is nowhere to go, and the temporary features of the houses, for they must be deeply flooded each spring since a half day walk beyond the village, the river channel is plugged, and a vast fen begins. With the cold, I could walk upon its crust of fallen, frozen reeds. They go on, endless, as far and wide as I could walk and as far as I could see. The whole river is absorbed within this infinite slough. The river does not re-form beyond it for all that I can surmise. I am certain – I reached the farthest point in my exploration towards sunset – that the bog under my feet was growing drier, having absorbed the river waters entirely. It also seemed that the land ahead of me rose somewhat, meaning that the marsh may be a gigantic basin, which intercepts the river waters and lets them evaporate or sink into the ground.

My new knowledge makes this place more strange. In my mind it was always a way point, with the possibility of continuing, either forward or back a definite one. But it seems we reside in a monstrous cul-de-sac. The end of the world. I related this to Water Music, but got no response.

The boy can now pronounce his vowel upon seeing the letter.

[Aaron Masse] Day 236

A struggle to write even one sentence. Last night, death visited me in my dreams, inviting me to that other place. I had the choice, & refused, but tonight that may not be the case. Being a practical man, used to establishing order no matter the circumstance, I must tally this unreckoned account in my soul. My wife has passed her judgement of me, totalling the ledger of our marriage at zero. My daughter is a quantity affixed to the measure of that union. She alone can figure its final count. I have made my peace with God, who does not allot value.

For Reid, & the fullness of sentiment she has stirred in me, I must constitute my own ledgers. The currency is stirrings of the spirit. How does one tabulate a heart's awakening. By the force of its pounding within the breast, by the drying of the mouth or palsy of the love nervous hand.

Am I to measure my manliness by all the things I did not do, did not even express or know how to, me the most unpractised of lovers now facing the grandest tabulation of life's score? And I do not fear it. As a man, I awoke each morning thinking only of my first cup of coffee. That in hand I began my day, took it as it came, regretting never a minute or the accumulation of those minutes into days weeks, months, years. Loosing my arm taught me not to fear the decline of the body. From youth, we ascend to our prime, then descend, ever mortal, towards our earthly demise. I do not fear death. It is the final episode, & we are lucky to be allowed to know it, for we are ignorant of our birth.

I would say that I am new man from knowing Reid. And what is that? I am the same parts, reassembled, thus the total has not changed? I am now more than the sum of my parts, being improved by the vigorous waters that flooded me, like a field of bottomland enriched by a savage spring rivers leaving fruitful new soil. Have I had new portions added that were never there before, the sum thus being now greater? Am I entirely renewed?

Each thought is more clear, each breath more sweet, each heartbeat stronger from knowing her & imagine if we had had our chance & were united. Who would I be now, what great things could have been accomplished. I can only guess. She seemed to me a ever flowing fountain.

So in the end, I have no tally. I know not from whence to take my figures, & what column to set them in. There can be no total. My sentiments have no limit, like the sky has no top, & certain parts of the ocean I have heard, has no bottom. The arithmetic I was taught makes no allowance for what could have been, what never was.

> ⟶•⟶O⟵•⟵

Staccato breath betraying his considerable effort, Captain Masse lifts the rectangular package that holds the expedition daybook, his journal and letters. Its black oilcloth wrapping is tight bound with twine made of unplaited rope. The package, a red rag tied to its top, is fastened to three chunks of the boat's broken hull.

He suspends it over the ledge, his hand pressed flat against it, fingers spread on one side and against its other side the sallow stump of his forearm. He pulls himself closer to the edge on his elbows, the effort draining off what colour still persists in the patches of skin on his face that can be seen below his matted hair and around his eyes and above his dense and snarled beard. He closes his eyes and forces himself to breathe deeply, each intake of air sibilant, wavering. The water is far below and far off. He knows he must sling the package so it can reach the water closest to him, a pulsing back current full of twigs and leaves orange, red and yellow. He hefts the packet, considering its weight. Eyes still shut, he judges his strength, then looks down.

Contracting his arms, he makes his toss, thrusting out. The package tumbles, smacking the smooth, sloped side of the canyon and he closes his eyes again with the pain of his effort and possible miscalculation. But the package gathers speed on the spray slick granite, rocketing down slope, glancing off a concave outcrop of harder stone, and flips into a steep ravine that drops into the river with a splash that he does not see or hear.

> ⟶•⟶O⟵•⟵

ailure. Complete, utter, total failure! Regressing farther back in time when my last exposure miscarried, I did what was common in the days of the camera obscura, I simple traced the outline of my subject on my piece of parchment, and cut out the silhouetted profile. This was quite a common thing fifty years ago, and I remember seeing several in my grandmother's foyer.

Returning home, Water Music reminded me that I must gather firewood, for we have run out. I trod the impassable bog, searching. It snowed. I tried to take a short cut through a low place and broke through the ice crust. I almost drowned. When I came back to the village wet and mud soaked, I was asked how I got that way, and upon relating where I'd got to, was told that no-one has ever been beyond the bog. They are afraid of it, another reason they have no canoes. Each spring, the tribe moves to high ground. The flood is so great everything is washed over the bog and disappears. Water Music says if my experiments have finished, it is now time for me to learn to hunt, to snare rabbits and trap birds. The boy has caught a bird. She showed me how to take off the skin while the game is still hot. She is much heavier, and spends her time near the village. She will go out with me a few more times, then I will hunt alone. The boy will hunt on his own, for he catches things with his hands. Our days grow short. We must be approaching the winter solstice.

I set my snares at night, where Water Music instructed, as far as I could walk from the village into the marsh, along the faint paths of rabbits, a world of miniature turnpikes that only requires one bend down to see it. The iron wire is stiff and inefficient. I will use the good brass wire that binds my tripod legs next time. My first snared hare, I cut its breast open and peeled back the skin as I had seen my father do. The hide was thick and tough. It seems so supple when alive, but we forget that it is what shoes are made of, I could hardly drive the point of the knife through it. Mid day was a flash of heat, as happens here, and the hot blood on my skin dried instantly, and even as I pulled the guts from the body, blowflies landed on the slimy skin and squeezed out their tubes of white eggs into the pools of drying blood, this soon to be the nursery for the new born infant flies. Such powerful stuff blood. My arms itch where it has dried upon them. It is a chemical of great force, like developing pyro. It serves us well in life and must soon begin to decay the body when we are dead. It is no wonder that the first medical science was embalming, the draining of the blood to preserve the body.

The old man convenes the meeting in the council lodge, the same place Joanna Reid had been presented to the council. He explains to the men and women sitting around him why it is a meeting of not just the magicians, but those who the priests are magicians also. The problem is that the woman stranger has no magic, other than the magic of her round, transparent pottery that makes things large and can use the sun to make fire. The magic of her picture box is interesting, to look at a picture upside down, but he reminds everyone that they already do something similar with the moonrise in the magic cave.

He reminds the assembly that many days have passed, from full moon to half, and she has not made a picture. There has been much embarrassment. The priests who invited the chiefess and her family were embarrassed, and the chief was embarrassed. The problem, explains the old man, is that we cannot exclude her from the magician's society because she has some magics and she has been initiated. We cannot kill her because she is our guest, and it is forbidden to murder a guest. She is also the husband-to-be of the woman who is with child. It is forbidden to touch a husband of a woman with a child.

This is a dilemma, he continues, but one priest has told us an interesting thing. In the place where our woman guest comes from, they have another way of punishment. The priest heard this from the people who travel through the mountains with salt and fish. In that place they judge the person who has done a bad thing like we do, according to the laws and what is forbidden. Then they set a length of time, for worse things long, for small things short. They put the person in a small room for this length of time. They bring them food, and certain visitors are allowed, but they may not leave until the time is up. When the time is up, the embarrassment is erased.

We, the magicians, have discussed this a long time, the old man continues. What I have asked all of you is this, if a person is from another tribe with its own laws, should they be punished by those laws, or by the laws of where they are, our laws. What you have answered is that it is better to use her own tribe's laws, because our laws allow us to do nothing, and something must be done. The chiefess desires it. Many of the magicians desire it.

The old man pulls himself erect in his sitting position. He looks into the face of every man and woman gathered around him in the council lodge, then speaks, slowly, each word pronounced with great prudence.

Our decision, which I now declare, is to take her to the place of the magicians in the mountains. There are many caves in the rock there, easy to close with stones. We will place her in one and block the door. We will not let the woman she came with visit her, only the boy will be able to go. The other woman will soon have a child. The boy is young and strong and he also may bring her food. There are secret entrances. If he helps her get out, they will both be put there, we will tell him that. People say he is a good boy. What we have decided to do is unfortunate but required.

⊰⊱⊱⊱⊙⊰⊰⊰⊰

If I understand the situation correctly, I have been arrested, by my magician colleagues, male and female, all disguised by dark hoods that came down to their shoulders. The boy sat up as they entered our shanty, which we have divided with woven willow walls. He stared wide-eyed. Water Music talked with the leader, but made no attempt to stop them, after he uttered a few brusque words. The gravity of the situation seemed to paralyse her to the spot. Her belly has grown huge, the weight of it, supported on her thin legs, spread her feet out flat, and fused them to the hut's earthen floor. She spoke with some of the others. Her explanation to me was I had broken the law, for my magic had not worked. Though there was no danger, I was to be exiled, until the disrespect of my actions was cleansed, then brought back to the village as a slave. The night was cold. I was allowed a double set of moccasins. My arms were gently bound and I was led away.

We retraced the path of our initiation night. As we gained altitude, light snow began to fall and with the moon the briefest sliver, I could just see that we passed beyond the cave of reflections to a group of caves of much the same structure further up the slope, walking in line as the narrow path permitted, a handful of shrouded figures ahead of me, a handful behind.

I felt at no moment any fear. Indeed, at first I was convinced that the I had been accepted into the secret society and was being taken for the final rites of admission. Water Music's distress gave me cause to worry, but the stolid determination of my escorts did not allow any debate. The silence of our long march too did not trouble me, for I have developed no facility with the language, and spend a great deal of time in these people's company speechless.

Here I sit, a prisoner in her stone walled cell, the portal of its fourth wall built up before my very eyes by the combined efforts of my attendants, each rock needing six or seven to move it, and impossible for me. I have head-sized hole to look out. It gives on to a side passage. There is nothing to see. A day's food was handed to me through this. The seepage from a small spring runs in a rivulet across the back of the cave. I have only to dip my mouth into it to drink. There are sleeping robes, and a fire was lit when we arrived, the smoke escaping through some high passage which I cannot see. There is firewood here, I have but to keep the blaze lit. As a gesture of friendliness, they have even provided me with a crude chair. My construction of a chair for myself in the village brought much comment and laughter.

I am tired, from the trek's exertions and the shock to my mind of the event. Yet I will sleep, for in spite of my surroundings, I endure no dread.

>─┼─◇>─○─<◇─┼─<

The boy does not sleep, and hears the bright footfall of men and woman re-entering the village upon the rind of new snow and recognises each by these sounds without moving from his sleeping pallet. Light has not come when the hooded figure, whom he knows to be the head magician by his asymmetrical gait – a slow drag of his injured left foot – comes to the hut door and calls him, and hands him a wrapped package. Smells of cooked meat and tubers issue from it, a slight heat from within warms his palms. With few and simple words, the head magician instructs him to proceed into the mountains with it, pull back a certain rock, deliver the food to Reid, replace the rock and return to the village. He is to do this at the same time every day.

The boy pulls extra clothing from a branch stub on the ridge pole. Water Music is asleep on the other side of the partition. He does not speak to her before setting off. His mind has become a somewhat ordered place now. His memories are no longer jumbled nonsense, but discreet things that he relates to certain times and places, and feelings of his own. What he feels now is one of his most cherished feelings. The feeling of responsibility, of a task before him which he can accomplish. This feeling represents entry into the world of other humans. It is different than the feeling he had when he was alone in the bush with his sister. There, the first feeling was always hunger, and sometimes thirst also. Most of what they did was in response to this. There was another feeling, fear, which came when they saw anyone who could catch or trap them. They had found themselves alone in the bush because they had been caught and taken away. They did not ever want this to happen again. They avoided people.

Now he felt the opposite. He was with people, amongst them, and he did not ever want to leave. He did not ever want to be alone. Not alone like he was now, solitary walker on the path into the foothills, but alone and having to do everything himself. In the village, he did certain things, and others did other things and he did not have to do those things. Life was easier and he was never afraid. Except for the fear, a new fear, fear of being left out. For this reason, he was being very careful to do exactly what the chief of the magicians had told him, this last instruction being to not help Joanna in any way.

Joanna had done something to make her be left out. The boy understood this. She was taken away, like he had been taken away with his sister. Now she was alone, like they had been. He understood this aloneness. Joanna was good to him, she helped him do the things that let him find a place amongst people, though she was not as shrewd as Water Music and she was never funny. He did not want her to be alone. This was something he knew well. He could help her with it, like she had helped him to eat with a fork, ride the horse, and set up the picture box.

That he could help people was something he had just discovered. It came along with the truth that in the village some people did one thing and others did another, some people knew some things and other people know other things. At first he had felt that he alone knew nothing and everybody else knew everything, but now he knew he knew things. He could speak with the people in the village and Joanna could not. He could find ground nuts and Water Music could not. He could set up the picture box and the magicians could not. He had been on the other side of the mountains and the other boys and girls in the village had not.

The boy edged along the hogback, conscious of the precipitous ridge sloping away on both sides, the sky vault's boundless height and the light of morning seeping through a cloud seam on the eastern horizon. The emergent sun warmed one side of his body. The other side was still wet with sweat from the climb. This was a bad thing. He could catch what the villagers called wind sickness. He dropped down to a cliff face, and warmed the whole of his body in the horizontal sunshine. The coldness along his side went away. The package of food still gave off a smell of cooked meat, but no heat now. The smell made him hungry but he must keep it for Joanna. Now there was no path, just the track of the coming and going of Joanna's captors. He could see her footstep occasionally, for though she wore moccasins like the others, her deeper heel imprint made a sharp outline amongst the other foot prints, which were all more indented at the toes.

The cave mouth was blocked like the magician had said, each boulder many times the boy's weight. Only at small spaces between the boulders could he see a stone or two that he could move. The sun shone directly on these dark stones, and they steamed and dripped water from the melted snow. The boy found the second cave entrance just beyond and went in. The back of the cave was almost perfectly flat, and a spring had been diverted to

run along it and into the next cave. The humidity from the flowing water created a shimmering coat of hoarfrost on the wall. Wherever the sunlight flooding the entrance touched the wall, the frost had begun to melt, leaving the
stone face wet and black. The small shaft described to him lay to one side,
and he pulled out the stone blocking it and found he could almost fit his
head in. His eyes adjusted to the cave's dim interior, lit only by what sunlight
slipped between the boulders blocking its entrance. He could not see Joanna.
He made a sound, a sound he had learned to make when they worked with
the picture box, a sound that got her attention but did not disturb her when
she was busy.

He heard the rustle of a sleeping robe. He made the sound again, and
thrust the package of food through the hole. Nothing happened, and he
stood, bent, his arm extended into the cave. Then, like a fish grabbing at a
bait, hands inside grabbed the package. He pulled his hand out of the hole
and stuck his face to it, and found himself looking, eye to eye, at Joanna. He
laughed. She laughed.

><+>•O•<+><

I had forgotten so many things about him in just those few hours, and
other things I has never seen. There is the spark of intelligence in his eyes.
How I have been blind, thinking him a congenital idiot, a savage. He is but
a poor boy, deprived of a large portion of his childhood, and sister and family too. He has got some of it back. From me, from Water Music, from the
people of the village who have taken us in.

How long I thought we were of two different species, him the savage, me
the civilised. How wrong I have been.

><+>•O•<+><

In the early morning quiet, a girl from the village, about the age of the boy,
oldest child of a fishing family, sets off alone to check the family traps, set in
the river at the mouth of long willow branch weir. This cold morning, the
water is warmer than the air. A febrile mist rises wherever there is current.
Scum ice has formed alone the river bank, where the water has no movement. Thin and sharp, it could slice through her high greased moccasins and
let the frigid water in. She pulls a dead, wrist-thick branch from the underbrush and smashes a path to the open running water offshore. Her feet stay

dry, but still, the cold water sucks the heat from her legs as she wades out to the trap, and soon they are numb. One foot slips on a smooth and round rock, and she falls forward. A tiny splash of water goes over her leggings, no more than her cupped palm could hold, but it slithers uncomfortably down her calf to settle in the arch of her foot, and by the time she has waded to the first trap, she is shivering. No fish in the first trap. No fish in the second trap. Something is caught on the exposed vertical poles at the last weir. It floats, yawing to and fro in the weak current, a black thing, trimmed with red brighter than the red plant dyes of her village.

First she checks the trap. Three fish, one very fat. She picks each out by the gills, the cold water sucking what heat remains from her hands. They soon feel like wooden clubs. She squeezes the fish, forcing its mouth open, then sticks the thumb of her other hand down its throat, and pushes the head back till she hears the spine snap. Her mother has taught her to do this. When she has killed all three fish and slipped them into the fish bag she has slung over her back, she wades the few more steps to the floating object, which is about the size of a nursing baby in its cradle. Against the current, these few steps are all she can do, for the cold and the wading have exhausted her. She recognises the black cloth covering the object as similar to the cloth covering the objects brought by the three people who arrived in the village by the thing that floated on the river. She smells the cloth, it has the same smell too, like burnt resin of the pine tree they find in the mountains. She is too tired to try to open it, for it is tightly bound up, and attached to three billets of wood. Too tired and cold to be even curious, she breaks off the wood, which is a good size for a fire, and slips the package in her bag on top of her fish and wades across the current towards the shore, carefully, one leg upstream, the other in its lee down stream, step by step, her anaesthetised toes feeling dumbly for secure foothold. She slips again on the snowy bank, striking her knee on a quartz splinter, then scrambles up, finds a path, and heads back to the village.

Her family will not let her bring the alien object into the hut. Who knows what magic it contains. The fisher girl follows her mother along the narrow path between the huts. She carries the oilcloth-wrapped package with respect for its strangeness and importance, maintaining obedient distance, exactly two steps, behind her mother, though her mother is the smaller of the two by a hand. When they reach the stranger's residence, the mother stops before its entrance. The boy is inside, reinstalling the hide door and adjusting the fit of its two leafs. She looks at her daughter, watching the boy, and sees interest in her glance, for she knows her daughter, and girls of her age.

She see's no reciprocal interest on the part of the boy, something she has learned to judge with worthwhile precision, and this surprises her, but these people are strangers, so who knows. She knows where Joanna Reid slept, and where her things are kept. She observed these details when she brought fish to Water Music. She motions her daughter to pass her, and go inside with the package, and place it with Reid's effects. The girl walks in, suddenly clumsy in the presence of the boy, tripping, regaining her grace, and sets the package on Reid's largest camera box. She waits awhile, her back to the boy, then turns to look at him, but does not move her feet. Her mother calls and she still does not move.

Her mother calls again, grit in her tone, and the girl backs away from the camera case and out of the hut. The boy, recognising the mother, not at all noticing the girl, his mind occupied by thoughts of the pain he saw on Joanna Reid's face – drops the hut's hide door. The oilcloth cover of the package has been loosened by the way the girl carried it, and the contents exposed. Seeing no harm in looking at it, he unfolds the wrapping, to find inside, still perfectly dry, an object he recognises as belonging to Captain Masse. An object like the one with the pictures of the camera inside that he saved from the fire, except this one has no pictures and its thin paper leafs are covered with long rows of blue squiggling lines. A blue much darker than the sky. The blues of a dove's feathers at the joint of wing and body. The boy closes the diary and sets it where Joanna will find it when she returns.

>−∣−◆〉−O−〈◆∣−≺

*M*yself and the boy are of a different ilk. He is fascinated by my civilised science, and has sought to understand it and may. I have been fascinated by the wildness of the frontier and have sought to fathom its mysteries and may yet do so. We meet, like our eyes met through that aperture in the cave wall. We saw and understood each other, and took each others measure. By his presence, and his actions, I assume he is to be my keeper. What will follow I know not.

>−∣−◆〉−O−〈◆∣−≺

The boy fetches food and firewood for Joanna each day, and this separates him from the rhythms of hunting, fuel gathering and food preparation in the village. Water Music, now much with child, speaks to him little. He falls into a contemplative trance on his long trips into the hills with the bundled food and wood. A few words aside, he cannot talk with Joanna, but he sits with her the hour. There are a few tallow lamps in niche along the walls, and signs of a fire on the floor, but he has no flame to light either. The cave is located in a place of spectacular beauty. The sunlight through the high thin air is sharp and hot, and he has found a niche near the cave entrance where he can benefit from it. When this seating place falls in shadow, the cold becomes too great, and he returns to the village. The time spent in the bright sun gives him great pleasure, for with the cold weather, the hut is battened tight by thick double hides over the doors, and scraped rodent skins over the window holes. The interior is dim, especially morning and evening, when no sun may shine down through the smoke hole in the roof.

Water Music tells him what has happened, that the musicians are angry that Joanna's magic was a lie. The boy replies that it is not a lie, they have both seen it and Water Music counters that the magicians must see it too. This is called proof. The boy asks when Joanna will be freed. Water Music says that she will be allowed to return if she can make her magic work, make a picture, or after a time long enough time to pay for her dishonesty, which length the council will decide.

The boy has all of Joanna's apparatus at his disposal, for no one else will touch the prisoner's cursed effects. He cleans the lenses and boxes and puts them in order, as Joanna has taught him. He wonders what she knows that he does not, that allows her to make pictures. He thinks about this a great deal, as he makes his daily pilgrimage to the cave, and especially as he lays awake the early morning, listening to Water Music shift on her sleeping pad, and get up once or twice to re-build the fire. He understands that sunlight lets him see and also makes things hot. He knows that the lens increases this effect, for things that are far away become closer and easier to see, though upside down, and the lens can concentrate light to a point of such intensity a fire can be started on dry timber. It is his conclusion that pictures are made by heat, a more elaborate version of what the lens does when it is used to burn a black line on a piece of weathered wood. The bottles of liquids that Joanna had before they were lost or broken when the canoe tipped must have been the magic that let whole pictures be made by the lens, not just thin black lines.

The boy wants desperately to communicate with Joanna, and somehow enter a world where they can share their secrets. He looks again at the package the fisher girl found. He unfolds the oil cloth wrapping and opens it again, leafing through the journal of Captain Masse and looking inside the envelope of letters which were the last things he wrote. The boy remembers the power and authority of Captain Masse, and thinks that perhaps some communication can be established to help Joanna. He wraps up the journal, and on his next trip to the caves with food for Joanna, he slips it into his victual sack, and passes it to her with the food.

>─┤◆>─○─◆┤─<

Captain Masse loved me. Deeply and passionately, with all his being. An adult man, not the boys of the village or my college days. For him I felt no love. Awe, at times fear or hate, but never love. Yet, I think that our feelings towards each other were, though contrary, equivalent in intensity and depth. I could have subjugated myself to him with love and respect, as if he was a second father. But one father is enough. The Captain was a man for me, no more or less than that.

We were privy to each others deepest secrets – the secret of my identity, which was his secret from me, as my reading his diaries is now my secret from him. He believes in a heaven, so I trust he finds himself there now, and knows I have read his diaries. I believe in no such thing, so for me he does not comprehend my knowledge of his every thought and how from the apportioned circumstance and events we shared, he has drawn desire for me. And what have I drawn from it towards him. Some profound transition. That part of him, so like my father, the bluster and intolerance, interests me not. Another part, the strength, the ability to carry life's burdens lightly, interests me a great deal. So I can learn from him, learn to extract from the elements of my father in me some of the substances I can use to concoct the formula of my own being.

As I watched Captain Masse drowning, no one who has not been oppressed can understand my sentiments. No one who has not suffered blows to mind or body can understand that absolute power of an oppressor. They cover the sky, they black out the sun, and the only access to light is by doing away with them. Thus I watched him die. And saw in representation my own father, and realised, at last was able to separate myself from him – his acts – to see our interaction as simply a morality play, each in their role. And see who he was and who he was not and who I was and who I was not.

What can be learned from knowing of a man's love? Little it seems, for I who learned to denote phenomena at school and at college. Yet it is a knowledge of something with far greater gravity than the knowing of a science, or beauty. It incites perturbation, like the full moon keeps one awake, or the dropping barometer before a storm makes the brain press against the skull. It is something from the world of sensations. The day will come when I discern more of this emotional universe.

>─┤◆>──O──<◆─┤─<

The boy's sleep is interrupted by Water Music's staccato breath. He's been told to listen for this. He goes to the hut's door and shouts to the family across the path, then returns to build up the fire. He takes a gourd of drinking water to Water Music which she gulps down. A woman slips into the hut, her footsteps inaudible, voice a raspy mutter that obtains a nod from Water Music. Another woman arrives, bent, hair in thin grey straggles. Another enters, round faced, silent.

He keeps the fire up as the cycle of Water Music's respiration grows shorter. The women neither send him away nor encourage him. Staying on his side of the hut, feeding the fire, he finds excuses to turn towards Water Music, and watch. The women sit or crouch around her. They have a bundle of old, soft hides, gourds of water, and have set two bowls of burning herbs. Late in the night Water Music's gasping reaches a crescendo, and the women chant with her, the oldest one now between Water Music's legs, crouched, looking up at the place on a women the boy has never seen, except on his sister, and which he knows is very different than he. He knows that this difference marks some essential division in the way people are made and live. He does not understand this one thing about Joanna, for she seems to have crossed over the division, or be capable of living on both sides of it. When he learns enough of her language to talk with her, this is the first question he will ask her.

The sounds from Water Music do not reach a climax. They stay at a penetrating intensity. He looks over to her. The expression of surprise and pain, her eyes almost shut, her lips pressed tight, has been supplanted. Now her eyes are wide ovals, the whites showing all around her black pupils, and she looks at the women around her, each in turn, her body shaking, her hands opening, then closing into fists. The boy sets another few pieces of wood on the fire. He has never seen Water Music show fear. He has seen this expression mostly on Bain's face. He knows this expression foretells danger or death and he is afraid. He stops looking at Water Music. For a long time, he feeds the fire, sitting so close he becomes sluggish with its heat, as she cries in a more and more desperate tone, and he drifts off into a trance of impotent resignation.

The women exchange a few words, something affirmed by the grey-haired one at Water Music's crotch, and bending over her, they incite her, her screams now a rasp, to greater and greater efforts, their incantation so thunderous the boy feels he will be blown from the hut. He looks again. Her eyes are squeezed tight, her face purple. Her body convulses, and the women chant encouragement. And finally there is a crescendo, as the woman in the middle bends to Water Music, reaching between her legs, talking, working with delicate movements, rocking to Water Music's urgent clamour and body motion, on and on, the boy detecting, somewhere within the cacophony, progress. There is movement at the centre of the huddle. The other women have taken some of the soft hides from a bundle, and scraps of moss from another. They pass these to the middle woman, and the boy cannot see what is done. Water Music growls, furious as a dangerous animal. The centre woman leans back slowly, and suddenly, in the firelight, for night has again come, the boy sees the pale glow of human flesh. The woman raises her hands, and in them there is a strange miniature, smeared in blood and slime, of a human being. The other women bow towards Water Music's stomach, working a cord that hangs from the glistening dwarf, who coughs once, and cries, then freed of the cord, is patted dry and wrapped, and placed upon her drumming chest. A woman holds a hand lamp close. The boy, standing close as he dares, sees that the tiny being is female, like his sister was.

The boy understands he is in the presence of a greater magic than he has ever seen. He wants to celebrate, wants the women to invite him over, or ask him to help, but in spite of the astonishing thing they have just accomplished the women are not happy. They mutter to each other, and work at cleansing Water Music. The woman in the middle takes up the remaining hide and moss. The bundle of it disappears between Water Music's legs at the same time as the women to each side reach under the fur bed covering, and leaning forward, begin to rhythmically massage her abdomen.

The boy wants to talk with Water Music, congratulate her. At the same time, he wants to run to Joanna. He can do neither. In the sudden silence, he begins to feel fear. Water Music's face has lost all colour, and the women work over her with an urgent complicity that the boy does not trust. He builds up the fire. One woman opens Water Music's tunic, exposing her distended breast, and places the child's mouth upon it. Another leaves, to return with another bundle of moss, which is warmed over the fire and for the first time all day, the boy is noticed, but nothing is said. The bundle of moss, like the other, disappears between Water Music's legs, though the boy can see that some of it is placed under her. The talk of the women comes and goes, few words of which he understands, as they toil over Water Music, now colourless as snow. They massage her abdomen, encourage the infant to suckle, dab at it with the moss and hides. Some of these are tossed towards the boy. They are soaked with blood. Water Music does not move, and her breathing cannot be heard. The women's movements and tone change, like they did just before the small person emerged, but the boy does not like the change. It has the quality of a retreat. He knows these types of sounds and motions. Joanna would make them when a photograph did not turn out. The boy wonders what will not turn out. He looks at the women, looks at Water Music. He does not know why, but he thinks of his sister after she had fallen from the tree and was laying on the ground not breathing.

>—!—◆>—O—<◆—!—<

*I*s photography light magic? Certainly there is a supernatural quality to the perfect reproduction obtained of some vista or visage. But is this magic? Magic involves above all, the miraculous intervention of the magician, with his or her charms, potions and incantations. I can envisage a day when a well adjusted machine could accomplish a photograph without human intervention. Yet, I am a photographer, this I know. Even in this dull place, my thoughts are preoccupied with it. Would I have been a painter of landscapes if industrial progress had not provided me with the camera? I think not. Painting appeals not to me. I enjoy the very apparatus of photography, its brass, glass and varnished wood. Opening the camera cases at the overlook of some desolate vista excites me. I feel I am the lone hunter, stalking and ambushing my prey, bringing it back to clean it and cook it.

So it is not the magical aspect that prevails over me, it is this latter quality. I stroll out upon the landscape, and I am not there simply the useless observer. I have a purpose, and this enriches my connection to that landscape, makes my observations of it sharp and informed. There is something virile about this proud stance. There are other things. Though many complain of the chemical reek, I enjoy it. The darkroom too, for if there is magic, that it where it occurs. When I return, I will continue my photographic work It is my vocation and my avocation. Would that I had a functioning apparatus in the village. Surely the images could be of great interest, and could supplement the near hundred negative plates I have kept. I must seek an exposition. I'm sure Captain Masse would have supported me, for he often spoke of his connections in the Capital.

>—!—◆>—O—<◆—!—<

Gasping, the boy attains the level of the caves. He realises he has forgotten the wood for Reid, but does not care. He is near bursting with what he has seen and heard, what he wants to express. Reid hears him enter, and her

217

roaming eyes are tight to the hole even as he enters. For the first time, he does not go close to her, but stays in the middle of the low ceilinged cave annex. He has looked through the camera enough to estimate the perimeters of what Reid is able to see. Staying within this frame line, he removes his jacket and stuffs it under his shirt, at the same time bulging his belly and assuming a waddling walk, so that he is, instantly, the pregnant Water Music. He reaches to the cave wall for support, mimicking the heaviness of the child within, and then the supporting arms of other women who enter the room to help her. He lies down, looking up at the faces of those who attend him, and begins to act, with groans that rise in volume and frequency along with clenching fists and pumping hips, the slowly mounting energy of the process of birth. Finally, with a growl and a massive tremor, he gives birth, and falls quiet.

This done, he rises, and becomes the midwives, taking up the baby, cutting the umbilical cord, washing and swaddling the child. Still the midwife, he turns directly to face Reid. His face is happy, he holds the child up to her, vocalising its cries, then places it on Water Music's breast. He then lies down, again Water Music, and delirious, receives the child. This part of his performance is less joyous. The depiction of Water Music shows her exhaustion and pain, which gradually increases. She gives up the child back to the midwife. The boy's final look at Reid is one of pain and fear. He is afraid for Water Music, and wants Reid to know and share his fear.

><+>•◦•<+>+<

*W*hat marvellous acting talent, a wonder to behold, and what joyful news, for I am certain Neeshta has given birth, though if it is a boy or a girl I do not know. Our hosts are remarkable in letting a boy observe a birth. At home, the women were secluded for weeks, and all we saw was the final, pink, squalling result. As a child I had no idea of what occurred, and any expression of curiosity on my part was quickly differed by stories of angels or storks making the delivery.

Now we are four. And as the old women declared, I am the husband; protector and provider of food and shelter. How poorly I accomplish my domestic responsibilities. How painfully much I would like to see the child and Neeshta. What am I doing here? I must secure my release. But how?

><+>•◦•<+>+<

Returning, the boy spends his first night alone in the hut, his first night alone, for even during his years abandoned in the forest, he had the warm body of his sister against his. Before that, he knows he was not alone, but the details of who he was with never assemble themselves in any explicit way. He knows he was a child, and played with other children, like the children in the village, and he knows he had a place to sleep and food to eat. Often, like tonight, faces from this time past appear to him, but he never sees them in the life around him. This is one thing he does not fathom at all, this lack of comprehension makes his body shake like it has not for a long time. He cannot sleep, rises and sets extra wood on the fire. Its flames bloom, tracing orange tendrils of light upon the smoothed clay walls and across Joanna's boxes stacked in the corner.

The boy understands that Water Music will never come back, like his sister. He now understands the word dead, and what it means. He understands that Water Music has given birth to a little girl, who lived in her stomach, and that this girl is alive. The women from the village used the word sister when they told him this. He has a sister again. He would like to see her, would like her to be in the hut with him. He felt better when he had a sister. The village women told him only a woman could take care of a baby and feed it, and only the women can deal with Water Music's body. He must get Joanna back into the hut. Then he will get his sister with him. Joanna too. It is better when she is here. He knows that Joanna will be allowed back if she makes a picture. They had almost made a picture together in the magician's hut. The problem is to make it stay.

The boy sits on the one remaining camera. He looks through the photography manual, the etchings of optics, lenses and mirrors, the printed pages of instructions, and they make his head hurt like the confusing memories from the past. Growing desperately lonely for Joanna, feeling only pain, he throws the book on the fire, which blazes up as it consumes the outer pages. He stares at the bright light, flickering blue and green with the chemicals in the ink of the engravings. His head hurts more, and he puts his hands to his temples. He realises something about the muddle of images in his head. He does not have to let them control him. He pushes the confusing memories that are making him afraid out of the way and thinks of all the times he did what Joanna showed him and did it well. The times she smiled at him and talked softly. He pictures his hands manipulating the equipment. He remembers the things that Joanna did. He is sure he can do them too. Pictures are made by putting a lens at one end of a dark box. The picture comes upside down at the other end. The light makes heat and the heat makes the picture if you put paper wet with waters from the bottles they used to have exactly where the lens makes the upside down picture.

There are no longer any waters in the bottles, but there is one place where he saw the heat of the sun make a picture shape. He goes to the wall of the hut. Hoar frost on its inside surface has been melted by the heat radiating from the fire. Where the shadows in the hut keep the wall dark, the hoarfrost still blooms, crystal lace brilliant as stars. The boy drags his finger slowly across the frosty web. If he moves it slowly enough, it melts the frost, and he can draw a dark, wet shape within its gleaming mat. He flips open the long, thick hides covering the door. The cold air boils in, misting, and his wet tracing freezes, quickly turning to solid, black crystal. He breathes wet breath on the wall, and the frost flashes white. He grabs the flaming book from the fire. Only the first and last cover pages have burnt. He smothers the flames with a rag, and sitting on Reid's trunk, flips through the pages far into the night.

In morning, at the first sounds, he goes to speak with the leader of the magician's society. He waits a long time for audience with the old man. He knows members of the society will spend the evening with Joanna. He talks. Others are sent for. By mid-afternoon, arrangements have been made for the elders to remain in the mountains, and be at Joanna's cave early next morning. The boy returns to his hut to sleep.

>⊹+⟨⟩⊷O⊷⟨⟩+⊰<

The cliffs the magicians use, though much lower down, all face east. They came up, from some events of their own, to get me. I do not understand what the ceremonies are exactly but am virtually certain that they are either to undo my induction process into their cult, to uninitiate me...or to wash away my sins, for want of a better phrase. To purify me. They took me, the big rocks blocking me in being moved, from my caves to various others of theirs, and always placed me in centre of the circle of men and women. When they look at me they seem sad for me, as if they wish my magic would come back and help me redeem myself. There is no hint of jealousy, or satisfaction at my predicament. Though they do not wear the masks in these ceremonies in the other caves, they blindfold me before taking me to the new location. Though I understand nothing of what goes on in the firelight, the chants and elaborate motions, I am fascinated, and draw comfort and strength from both the ritual and their companionship and now, again shut in my cave prison, regret their departure. The air is particularly cold.

>⊹+⟨⟩⊷O⊷⟨⟩+⊰<

The boy rises after midnight. He detaches the double set of hides covering the door. He takes the fur sleeping robes from all the beds. He removes the one lens remaining from its box, bigger than his fist, then sets it and the lens board in the centre of the softest length of fur. He places a bag of food beside it then pulls all the hides into a tight bundle, and ties it with a plaited rope left from the skiff. He searches through Reid's pack, his face, for the first time, tense with the preoccupied concentration of a thief. He finds an oilcloth bound packet, and opens it. Inside are several rows of phosphorus tipped matches. He selects a few, slips them into a fold in his cuff, and redoes the package. He picks up the still smouldering book. The night is clear, with little moonlight, but he knows the path well, and is soon on the long sloped trail leading to the ridge of caves. The clumsy bundle is difficult to carry. It bangs against his thigh no matter how he slings the rope across his shoulder, and he is soon tired and his muscles sore. He sits on a rock to rest his arms, and remembers how the village women carried loaded baskets in from the fields. He reties the rope so it loops around the bundle's ends, and sets the bundle on the rock.

Placing his back against it, he slips the rope loop over his forehead and stands. The rope cuts into his forehead, yet he is more comfortable, and the weight presses through his neck down his spine through his legs onto the soles of his feet to the ground in a balanced way. He takes a few steps. It is much easier to walk. He pulls a loose piece of fur from the bundle, folds it, and slips it under the rope to cushion his forehead. The walking is very good, and the forward slope of his body makes a perfect balance with the upward slope of the trail as he passes the lower caves the magician clan uses. He holds the book in one hand. His muscles warm with the climb. The moon sets. A coyote howls. Frost begins to dust the ground with a crystalline mantle, as he had expected, and by starlight he can see far across the lustrous plains. He is happy. He will be glad to see Joanna, and she will be glad to see him, he knows that because she smiles when he arrives.

>─┼─◆>─○─<◆┼─◅

*W*hat stale stink of my being permeates this archaic dwelling. The clever diversion of mountain spring provides me, at its upper end, with drinking and washing water, and at its lower, after tumbling over a ledge, with a primitive toilet. The filth of my ablutions and my excrements passes out of the cave directly, no doubt discharging some place below, along the ridge's cliff face. Yet, my stench accumulates, on the furs, on my clothing and my skin, on the walls of the cave itself, and I am weary of it. I am tired of this place, lonely for the boy and Neeshta's company, crave the sight of her newborn. Crave its smell, so unlike my own, the chaste perfume of an infant, the aroma of unfettered life. When will my sorrowful confinement cease, and I be freed.

><·+>·—O·<+·+·<

The boy approaches Joanna's cave on tip toe. His breaths are ragged with the effort with the climb, and it is not until he has slipped into the cave annex next to Reid's dwelling and sat down to rest himself that he can hear her own slow breathing. The annex is utterly dark within. Only its back wall, covered with a white veil of hoar frost, is visible as a less murky shade of black. The boy searches around the entrance, and by the faint celestial illumination there, rolls several boulders into the mouth of the annex, blocking it to the point where he can just crawl in over the stones he has set on the ground.

He rummages in his sleeve for the matches, striking one along the rock ceiling. Its sputtering gleam lights the cave with orange eruptions, and before it wanes, he sets the flame to a ropy wick stuck in a pool of congealed tallow lodged in a natural rock bowl near his shoulder. The low flame, maturing, quickly liquifies a pool of fat around it. The match consumes its phosphorous in one last outburst, leaving the cave lit by the tallow lamp's soft golden bloom. The rear wall gleams under its fragile shroud of hoar frost, each crystal of frozen vapour twinkling tiny points of blue, red and yellow when the boys moves his head even slightly.

He hears Reid move on her sleeping pallet and her breath quicken, then a gruff murmur. He knows these sounds of hers. She will soon wake. He unties his bundle, rolling out the furry hides full on the floor, placing the lens to one side and the food bag below the hole that communicates with the other cave. He slides the hides up over the entrance to the annex, closing it off, and dipping out liquified tallow from the lamp, he applies it like paste to each hide's edge before pressing it then against the cave wall and holding it there till the tallow congeals, so its cementing it to the stone. He continues round the outer lip of his hide door, sealing the edge tight to the wall. He hears the first muttering of the birds that signal morning will soon come. Before he glues the last corner of the hide fast, he sticks his head out the hole he crawled in. The sky has lost its bottomless obscurity, and before him, across the valley to the east, milky radiance burns a line where earth and sky meet.

He sets the remaining edge with the tallow glue, leaving only a palm full of oil in the lamp. By this waning light, he inserts the lens board at the place where the inside edges of the hides meet and overlap. The covered inside element of the lens faces the hoary back wall of the cave. The outside element, its cap removed, faces directly at the place where the sky now glows brightest, where the sun will rise. He fixes the lens in place with the remaining tallow. The lamp flame shrinks, near suffocation. The boy goes to the hole communicating into Reid's cave and taps its side with a rock. Sounds of her waking into consciousness.

He taps again. Her eyes appear, their pupils blue cast just discernible as lighter than his black ones. She smiles, and her eyes seem to have found their own light source. The boy says her name, and passes her the food bag. When her face returns, he moves his head from the hole, beckoning her to come as close as she can to him. He points at the structure he has made at the mouth of the cave. When he perceives she cannot see it in the faint lamp light, he strikes another match, and holds it close to the hides, the lens board and lens, and finally the frosted back wall of the annex.

He stands behind the lens fixed in the cave mouth, and eases the back lens cap from it carefully, for the tallow is not a strong glue. Faint light plays on his hand, light transmitted by the lens – an inverted, out of focus image of the predawn sky on the other side of the hide and stone barrier. He replaces the lens cap. Working his way meticulously around the hide and the lens board, he refastens or plugs with wet clay any light leaks, which are now apparent, the sky's radiance increasing in strength with every passing moment. He leaves one tiny aperture open, at his eye level, though he fabricates a clay plug for it. He stands at this spy hole, watching the sky, as Reid stands at her larger spy hole, watching him, watching the blurred shaft of light from the world beyond play over his face. An eager, exited face, that turns to her several times, as if imploring her patience. He sees she does not understand, but is happy when he hears her laugh.

⤛ ⟩ ⟩ ◦ ⟨ ⟨ ⤜

*T*he boy is delightful in his attempt to please, though I must assert that I am always glad to see him. Glad of the food, glad of the sight of his face...how it quaked when he first appeared and how calm it is now...and glad of his company. Glad of the company of my own kind, for he is my own kind, with Neeshta. We are a tiny clan us three now four though in my family it is bad luck to speak of a child till after seeing it, for fear of the mother's health.

He is a natural actor. Thus far his peerless recital has been the acting out of Neeshta's giving birth. He has no vanity the boy. And today he is attempting, I think, to give me comfort by setting up a make believe camera for me, or perhaps he understands in some simple minded way that I am here because my magic did not perform as hoped and he wants to leave me opportunity to make it do so. So strange he did it in the dark. He has everything right, I must admit. This in itself is proof of a sort of if not intelligence at least aptitude. I have seen, during my tour of the old world, peasants miming miracles or battles of long ago with a terrible lucidity yet I imagine no actual understanding of the true event. The boy has done thus, placing the correct apparatus in the appropriate relations yet with no understanding of the chemistry or physics of it. And we await the sunrise, because for some reason, pure chance most probably, he has pointed the lens directly where it will occur. It is a pity he has left the rear lens cap on, for it would delight him no end if some vague image formed on the far wall of the cave. That is possible, for the lens is set to give a sharp image at about the focal distance he has placed it. Where has he gone to?

⊱ ┤ ◈ ┄ O ┄ ◈ ├ ⊰

The moon has waxed past half, and neither the boy nor his entourage, which includes the master of the magician clan and the woman who heads the village council in their plumed dress of office, are inconvenienced by walking the mountain trail at night. The magician leads, setting an unwavering pace, his head thrust forward, his face inert with impatience. The others are almost festive, enjoying the cold, clear night, the low azure moon and the unusual hour. Their voices skip up and down the column, the joking and deliberating of village gossip. The magician will have none of this, he who seems afflicted by the responsibilities of his office, and in response to the low voiced banter, sets an even harder pace on the steeper slope leading to the ridge of caves.

All voices stop when the see the boy waiting in front of the ceremonial caves. Deep draughts of the thin air are drawn into heated lungs and they trek in silence to the summit of the ridge, the silent vales to each side – not even a coyote yelp – as expectant as empty bowls of unfired black clay, their bottoms invisible underneath the down moon's raking light except where one of the bowls shows a faint, widening, crooked crack, the frozen river, its fresh ice a long, intact looking glass reflecting starlight, moonlight and skylight.

Along the ridge that parallels the river, ascending to Reid's cave as night begins its dayward creep, they stride obedient behind the magician in single file until the path, along the crest, widens and the boy trips past the others to take the lead, rushing ahead to the entrance of annex beside Joanna Reid's rock shut keep where all has been prepared, the opaque hides set in place against the stone barrier, and just a large enough opening left to allow one person at a time to pass crouched, and enter.

➤─┼─◆➤─•O•─◄◆─┼─◄

Saints preserve us. They are all present, my judge, jury and hangman. The miraculous boy has done this. Such a canny lad, but to what end? Each of them resplendent in the vestments of office, this is indeed a serious matter. But for the master magician, I detect a spirit of levity, a willingness to enjoy. The sky lightens.

➤─┼─◆➤─•O•─◄◆─┼─◄

With a hide flap, boy seals off the annex from the within. He stands behind the lens and slips the lens cap from its back element. Radiant beams illuminating his cheek condense, until they are a sharp golden circle. The sun has risen, its keen rays passing directly through the aperture. He stands aside. The back wall of the cave seems to burst into amber flame, as the sunbeams, focused by the lens, penetrate the hoar frost's crystal mantle. For the time of several breaths, the icy lace is lit aglimmer by the inverted silhouette of the mountain range across the valley, a perfect picture on the cave wall of the sunrise sky. Then, the light's heat begins to melt the fragile frost crystals, and they sag and dissolve into the rock, wetting the basalt face a glistening black where the light shines, but leaving the perfect white web where it has not.

Reid, the boy, the entourage, make no sound, as the back wall of the cave slowly becomes as perfect an image, in wet black stone and ivory frost, as can be made of the sunrise far across the valley. All eyes regard the miracle. Dilated pupils, adapted to the dim cave, constrict, each pulsing iris closing as the lens-sharpened slash of sunlight bathes the lower half of the cave's back wall in golden brilliance. The frost crystals glisten, each a rainbow flickering one last time indigo rouge and violet before liquefying, sagging to the wall like countless tiny tears. And the transposed effigy of the mountain range is born again; perfect black above, chaste bright crystal below. Only the old magician, burdened by his responsibilities as judge, seems not to fall under the wondrous spectacle's trance, and furrowing his brow he turns away to lift a corner of the hide sealing the mouth of the annex and peer out across the valley and the actual mountain crests. He turns back and forth thus twice, considering the beam of light passing out the back of the lens onto the mirror, consequently to the wall, while the others stare, overwhelmed, at the glowing wall. The magician seems finally satisfied, and lets the corner of the hide drop back in place before walking to the wall's veneer of white crystals delicate as moth wings. Not a handspan from the silhouette's edge, where wet and dry, hot and cold, black and white meet, he too is reduced to immobility.

><+>+O+<+><

*H*e understands, he understood. And I did not. How wrong I have been, thinking him, in my vain benevolence, the cordial but proficient idiot, never realising that the fault lay in the connection between the brain and the lips, not in his intellect itself. He has digested all that I have shown him, all that he has observed, and brought to these assimilations and what materials lay at hand his own ingenious observations and conclusions. He has made the outer cave into a perfect camera obscura, of immense dimensions. And he has used the hoar frost as his emulsion, and the reintroduced cold as his fixative.

A true scientist. I would have never in a million years thought of what he has thought of. And he judged the temperature so perfectly. Any warmer and the frost would not have formed, any colder and the sunlight would not have had the power to dissolve it.

He has forced a jury trial and presented the case for the defence, knowing well that emotion can here play its part. He may just get me out of this. This is what may carry my case, for, all and all, what the boy did was a magnificent and beautiful thing. Who could not be moved by it. And if I consider the other aspects, more scientific, what he has done fulfils my promises made when I committed to becoming a member of the magicians clan. Photo – graphy has occured, the making of a drawing with light. That drawing, via the lens has been produced without manual intervention. Step one. Said rendering, albeit inverted, and no more than an accurate silhouette in frost white and basalt black, has been fixed, by the cold if he repeats his process, onto the cave wall, where it could be left all winter. Step two. If the criteria are too rigorously applied, and the image must last forever, I am lost, but if it must only endure sufficiently to be exhibited and contemplated, I think I may be

all right. My fate is in the lap of the various gods collected here today, theirs and mine. Will that it not be too hot, nor too cold or too humid, or dry?

> — ⦁ ⟩ ⦁ ⟶ ⬦ ⟵ ⦁ ⟨ ⦁ —

It is the boy who moves first. He slips the lens board from its tallow attachments, and lays it on a piece of fur. He then tips open the hides blocking the door, letting in no light, only cold night air, faintly opaque with condensing vapour. The frigid vapours roll in, and before the magician's eyes, the alive wetness hardens to ebony ice as the freezing draught stops the melting process and renders permanent the magnificent silhouette, its top half a frosty white duplicate of the mountain crests opposite and its bottom a glistening black reproduction of the now brilliant sky.

The old magician touches the hardened surface with his palm. He motions to the head of the village council. She places one finger tip to it, and nods, and smiles and the others smile too, murmuring, like morning doves at first light.

> — ⦁ ⟩ ⦁ ⟶ ⬦ ⟵ ⦁ ⟨ ⦁ —

*H*e has done it. I am free. Even the old man, so heavily burdened by his office, smiled. We walk in single file, descending to our village. The decision was reached after little deliberation as I waited, for the first time shivering with the cold, sitting, my hands upon my thighs, thinking no thoughts, only hoping, asking for if not a miracle at least a little good luck. In truth I petitioned God, something I have never done. If that is what praying is, then that is what I did, for my eyes rose to the sky by instinct although I never begged. Pity Captain Masse is not here to consult about the specifics of prayer. He was fond of praying and apparently proud of being fond of such an inconsequential activity. Would he have been proud of me? Why do I think of him at this joyous moment of my liberation. That dour, pious man, so unappealing and yet in my thoughts recurrently.

> — ⦁ ⟩ ⦁ ⟶ ⬦ ⟵ ⦁ ⟨ ⦁ —

The boy is happy, leading the column's descent to the village. Pack of rolled up hides across his back, he's given the lens on its lens board to Joanna Reid, but when he enters the village no eyes follow him, all look to Reid, in the middle of the procession, pale, smiling, the lens and lens board in her hand. Seeing he is not noticed the boy strides ahead, between the huts, thinking only of getting the hides he removed pinned back above the door so the place will cease to be open to the elements. In his preoccupation, he has begun to pull at the knots of the bundle, looking down, his feet turning between the huts on instinct until he recognises a slate slab set in the ground that marks the short alley of his own residence and he looks up. He sees the open door, a little snow drifted over the earthen sill, the dark uncovered doorway. The bleak, black aperture causes bitter liquid to rise into his gorge, almost to his lips. He chokes it down, resisting the sudden urge to vomit.

He has forgotten that Water Music is no longer there, is dead. He knows much more now, what friendship means, this learned from the affection Joanna awarded, from his own joy at seeing her set free and knowing she would come back to be with him. His mind slips into the mind of another for the first time. He realises, a sluggish clot of feeling that thins and clarifies into a thought, what Joanna will feel upon finding out Water Music will never be with them. The memories come; all the times he saw or heard them laughing and talking together, on the horses, in the boat or in the hut. He comprehends Joanna has these memories in her own mind, and while he is trying to find some way to go into her mind to stop her from feeling what she will soon feel she passes him, giving him a look, but accepting his immobility as the politeness due a lady, and walks into the hut, becoming suspicious even before entering when she sees the uncovered passage and the low drift of snow yet she maintains momentum, her feet crunch across it and the boy can see from her back's angle that she has gone to and is looking directly at Water Music's sleeping pallet.

>─┼─◆>─O─<◆─┼─◄

y view, of a world where I stood (or sat, like a queen) always at the top, has crumbled. I appreciate now Captain Masse's constant impatience with me, which so often seemed like disrespect. He saw my blindness to the world around me, one which he knew well, had long lived in and esteemed. If he were here now I would ask his pardon. Not only have I discovered that another intelligence, which I considered insignificant, was equal or better than mine, I have also been forced to understand, by this precocious boy, that intelligence has manifest forms, something which the Captain well knew, and tried to explain to me. How much I have not seen or let pass that I could have learned so much from since the very beginning of the expedition. What conceit my affected tolerance and open-mindedness, founded all along on my superior origins. The boy is my match. Water Music is my kinswoman, and how I suffer for her company. Where is she?

➤‐┼‐◀▸‐○‐◂▶‐┼‐◄

For a long time, both of them are still. The women magicians, and the head of the village council collect in front of the hut. When Joanna Reid turns, having put her lens and its board on her trunk, and walks outside, the women flow around her like a female river, reaching out and touching her, stroking her back, untangling her hair, but leading her away always from the hut towards the centre of the village, back past the boy, who still stands astride the entrance's stone lintel, one foot in the hut, one foot without.

➤‐┼‐◀▸‐○‐◂▶‐┼‐◄

hat tragedy floats on this wave of ecstasy. My Neeshta departed, slain by the very act of giving life. They preserved her body, and it will be set onto the ice to be taken away by the flooding river as are all of those deceased in winter. Her death mask showed the strain of her last hours, or was it days. The women had washed and dressed her in simple smock of tanned skins. The clothing she wore, given to me in a bundle, is dark with bloodstain.

I quitted their mortuary, seeking my own hut, and all that I would not allow myself to feel came nonetheless. I stopped, and turned towards the outer edge of the village to face a low bush, tears already spouting from my eyes, soaking my face, I felt my stomach heave, the bitter vomit surge up, and I spewed it upon the snow around my feet, and I saw too that the inside of my thighs was wetted, that I had lost control of that too, and a yellow stain of urine joined the sallow vomit, and spotted into it the bright red stains for my menses, which, absent all the time in the cave, had begun to flow.

I remained thus, discharging fluids from every orifice, till, purged, wet from cheek to foot, I noticed the rainbow pool I stood in, for its reek had begun to rise. I shuddered one last time, and realised the terrible prediction made of our fate by the medicine women at the fort. The curse she put upon us has come to pass, and I endure the terrible melancholy of the survivor. There is no joy in it. Me alive because, as she said, my light magic. Do I believe in such things? I resolved to put it out of my mind.

The child is a beauty, I was allowed to hold her, and I think, the words they used when speaking to me indicated they are all now the mother. She is with a nursemaid, a healthy female specimen, broad of bosom, who looks as if she could sustain a dozen children. Though I am no natural mother, the woman began my own instruction. Even not knowing the language, I have grown accustomed to the teaching methods of these people. They explain little, but repeat the action again and again, encouraging the student to duplicate it, and finally replace the hands of the instructor. In this way I learned how to replace the child's soiled napkin. Here these people are at a disadvantage, for they have no cotton and animal skins are not absorbent. A bundle of soft moss is laid into the centre of the diamond shaped hide, and this imbibes the infant's excrement. Only the moss is changed after each incident.

The babe one month old, if I understood the mimed explanation. After the child was born things did not go well for Neeshta. The midwife pointed to her own sexual parts then to the blood stains on the clothing that had been given to me. I understood this to mean there was haemorrhaging. I know that this can occur at a difficult first birth, for though my mother made no references to my own entry into the world, our cook, scolding me for being disrespectful as only a young girl can be of her mother, made me understand that my delivery, and I was the first and only child, had come close to killing my mother and she had never been the same since.

I cannot in any way conceive of facing such a thing myself. Again, I feel the urge to pray. And again I feel uninstructed. Did Neesta have a soul and if so where is it. Does she suffer or is she only dead? Would my prayers be of any benefit and where would I direct them?

I pray, on my knees, for her soul, which activity makes me feel much better. The mind floats up, away from the individual body, to join some kind of universal soul and in this huge place, all connections can be made, hope transmitted to those we care for. It would seem it is like writing letters, or more like this new invention, the telegraph, except that the net of linking wires extends to everyone, and the message can be passed directly.

>─┤─◆>─◦─<◆─┤─<

Joanna Reid unravels the fine brass wire that bound the ends of her tripod, straightened the coil by drawing it around the centre post in her hut, the boy pulling on one side her on the other, and bent it into loops the diameter of a dinner plate. These loose coils now hang from her belt as she strolls across the frozen swamp below the village, pushing aside the wall of cold-stiff reeds to follow the footprints of what animals are still active. The new snow is not a finger deep. She finds a brief clearing at a pond, where a hawk has killed a rabbit, the birds great wings clearing a snowless arena on the black ice as it struck. In the centre, bits of fur, drops of blood. Backtracking along the rabbit's trail, she sights compact mounds of brown faeces pellets. She bends and breaks one open with her knife point. Totally digested, impossible to say what the animal was eating. The trail of old and new paw prints intersects with other lilliput avenues at an arc formed by a willow shrub. Leaning over so as not to trod the path herself, she pulls an armlength of wire from her roll, and bending the bright filament back and forth rapidly, breaks it off. She twists a tiny eyelet at one end, and passes the other end through it, forming a noose that would just set over her hatless head. She pinches a few dry leaves from the branches, and draws the wire through them, to remove her smell. Without touching the ground, or the branches, she suspends the noose vertically on the path, in the arch, were it seems to form a filigree portal, large enough for the head of a rabbit, too small for its body. She twists the wire's bitter end around the knuckle of a high crotch, where it cannot slip free.

She backs away, satisfied. The next set is along a wall of brambles so dense a small dog could not crawl into it. Again, the animal turnpikes intersect – where the underbrush cleaves at a quartz bright outcrop of pink granite. She sets another snare, with a smaller loop and a longer link, which, finding no thick branches near, she twines and forces into a crack in the rock.

Reid sets three more traps, to the remembered guidelines set out by Water Music; loops of a size the animal's whiskers will fit through, at a height its head will be centred upon, any place where the animal may be moving fast, so the loop will pull tight around its throat, and preferably at a corner, where it will not see the trap. Touch not the path, and leave no smell upon the snare, always wiping the wire with a piece of earth or a leaf or branch before setting it.

Weary with the effort of creeping across the frozen swamp, she returns to the village. It has snowed more, covering her tracks. She founders, breaking through the ice concealing a spring, sinking to her thighs. Surprised by how quickly the day has faded, though walking rapidly to throw off the cold from her wetting and dry her trousers with body heat, she does not reach the entrance of her home till twilight. The low ceilinged hut is warm, the fire bright. The boy is there, poking at something he has cooked in a clay pot. She hangs what coils of wire remain on a high peg, and pulls off her frozen outer moccasins, putting them on the hard ground just outside the entrance. Reid takes off her coat, and realising she has used its usual peg for her snare wire, looks around for another hanging place. There is an empty peg in a shadowed corner. As she steps towards it, arm outstretched, coat in her hand, the boy looks up and both of them, though her body keeps moving and she sets the coat upon the knot peg, make eye contact at the moment they also realise that this was and has been till this instant Water Music's place, her side of the room, her effects hung there, and neither of them has violated its sanctity.

Reid staggers back to her side of the room as if pushed. She sits on her camera box, looking at the boy, who's hand is still upon his stirring stick. Her eyes bloom with firelit tears, and she shakes her head to dispel them, willing her backbone straight, her face impassive. Her arms stay at her sides, her palms pressed to the flat wood of the camera box. She does not move, and the boy does not move, but takes up his stirring stick again. Outside, in the dark village, there are few sounds. A crying child, laughter of a victorious youth, the pop and crack of a resinous log flaring.

>―<>―O―<>―<

They bring the child to me every day. She is sometimes left in my care for as long as she does not cry for the wet nurse's breast. The splendours of my senior college year excursion to the artistic wonders of the old world did never approach the magnificence of this soft-skinned infant. Words fall short of describing her beauty. I am embarrassed by the phrases that come to my mind; the creamy skin of a princess, the delicate fragrance of the sweetest wildflowers, the smile of an angel, the soulful eyes of the most melancholy opera tenor. Yet my heart does not break when they take her away from me. I am not the motherly type. The boy is good with her too, equal to my increasing skills by his natural compassion, and I think of the pain he must feel remembering his lost sister. We are a pair, the two of us, cooing and fondling the gurgling infant. I have begun, now that I finally respect his intelligence, to speak with him, naming objects, and attaching verbs to actions. He speaks well in some other tongue, Neeshta's, and holds his own with the locals. In my language he is clumsy, but a good study. I see some of the village girls are interested in him, especially the girl who belongs to the family that has set out the fish weirs, for he grows into a comely lad. But he seems to have no sexual instinct whatever, and is no more attracted to girls his own age than to the ugliest hag or a door post.

>―<>―O―<>―<

A mouse nibbles up through the translucent snow crust. The thin rind collapses into frosted remnants. The mouse shakes them from her fur and pokes her head up to the sun bright surface. Her eyes adjusting, she can see the bush of wild millet a short trip across the wind flattened surface. Seeds have fallen during the night and are scattered around the dry, dead plant. In the blue sky, no dangerous shape of hawk wings can be seen, and no shadow flits across the whitened ground, or perches on a rock outcrop.

There comes a sound. The prattle of steel tools on stone. The mouse waits. The sounds are from far away, and up the mountain side. The mouse risks putting her whole body onto the surface. No movement, and the sounds cease. She runs to the first scatter of seeds, gulps them down. Winter in the high valley is long and cold. As she eats in complete silence, dashing from seed to seed, the mountainside far away bulges and splits. A cloud of rock splashes into the sky. A handful of errant chunks burst from the cloud. They rise like tiny rockets, then stop, motionless at the peak of their arc. An intake of breath later, the wet cough of black powder exploding in granite thumps the mouse's ears. As the blast echoes across the valley, the rocks fall back towards earth. The stone rubble dribbles down a slope, and finally its sound, like the roll and drag of a snare drum, reaches her. A duck-sized rock clatters down the slope opposite. It splinters into fragments when it hits a sharp boulder.

Dazed by the dull noise and the spectacular display, the mouse does not see a thickset spectre disengage itself from the cliff face, falling, opening its wings with a whoosh hidden by the echoes of the explosion. The mouse does not trace these wings' shadow on the snow as they turn in her direction, and does not remark, as the shadow approaches her, that its edges are growing more and more distinct. The mouse only feels the hawk's hooked talons sink into its haunch, and the ground fall away as it is born up for one last look at the earth from a high perspective it could never have had in a normal life, before the hawk twists the mouse's body, snapping its spine.

>—⊹—◦—⊹—<

*S*artled from my interval with the babe by a hunting party who, by crude and swift gestures and great bluster made me understand that some morning's quick march to the west, into the next valley they have seen a party of some six or seven foreigners like me. From their description it may be a survey party but with so much rambunctious commotion, the leaders shouting, I cannot say. I must investigate, must see for myself.

>—⊹—◦—⊹—<

Joanna Reid opens her eyes. She sees nothing but imagines the stars outside, above the sod roof. North star at her front to cross the plateau. Over the ridge bed, North Star on her right to follow the parallel valley they saw yesterday. By then it will be light. Almost a full day's walk there and back.

She slips both feet from under the blankets onto the hut's earth floor, tip toes blind to the door, inhales, then blows a puffy cloud of condensing breath. She presses her tongue to the roof of her mouth, constricts her larynx, and inhales again, sharply, to clear her mucous filled nose and throat. She steps a few paces from the blanket door, spits into the roots of a low bush, and squatting, urinates facing east.

She does not blow alight the fire. Struggling into her frozen moccasins, her cold, stiff outer clothes, she pads soundlessly out of the village, retracing her return route of the day before. She climbs the ridges, strolling at a hard pace, her body warming, each step requiring individual effort in the cold, meagre air. The sky is light, but a coverlet of shadow envelopes her. As her feet find the best path, she sets a rhythm for her steps, and heads west up the scoured valley, North Star at her front.

The sun ascends behind. A peak in front flashes, then the whole mountain. Golden light envelopes the valley, washing over her, warming her back and calves, and she lengthens her stride as she turns down the valley at the place where the hunting party lay on their bellies to look down the valley. The smudged emboss of their bodies still dents the snowy ground. A steep descent, towards an old river bed. A dry, cold wind blows from the western end of the valley, carrying sparse, light snow. Her eyes, moving with the snowflakes, follow an invisible line from the peaks there, to the beginning of the river bed, to where she stands.

She drops into the rocky bed of a winter-dry arroyo, walking stiff-kneed, slow across the round stones, pigeon egg to fist sized, exposed by the valley's constant wind, mobile as greased balls under her boot soles. Half way up the valley, wood smoke rises from a camp fire and is quickly bent by the wind, and born to her nose. Pitch pine, resinous and inflammable. Coffee. Bacon. Burnt bannock. Afraid of being seen, she climbs up the other side of the combe, placing herself directly between the low sun and tiny grey figures of horses and men she can now discern on the white valley side. Getting closer, keeping to whatever brush and thicket the crest offers, sun still behind her, Reid sees that it is a surveyor's camp, recognising the layout of the high tripods and plane table. As she watches, an advance party of two men makes its way along the deep snow of the slope, walking on something she has never seen used, long, broad footpads…snowshoes. They do not founder, as she had in the swamp. One sets up a tall pole, with a red diamond on its top that faces the camp.

Reid understands that this team is more elaborate than her own, for another man advances with a packet of powder, tamps it into a fissure and sets a fuse to it. He lights it, the whole group retreats, and with an echoing report, the charge blasts out a wheelbarrow load of rock that the same man bends to pick through, slipping a few pieces into a bag at his waist. She realises too that they are in the process of surveying a line, obviously up from the far seacoast that was her original destination. It seems the competing company had guessed correctly. West to east was the way to travel. Though they have not penetrated to the plains yet, they soon would.

Closer now she creeps, close as she dare, for the rest of the promontory stands proud and offers no hiding place. She wishes she had a telescope. Still, she can see some details of their camp. There is no photographic apparatus and not tents enough to house anyone but the surveyors, thus no scouts accompany them. From a protruding tent pole a pennant, red, with the green letters GTR, snakes and snaps in the breeze. The men seem to carry no rifles, but a clutch of shaggy ponies, hooves encased in thick hide boots, is staked out along the trail they've made. Might they be supplied from the rear, by pony caravan? This expedition, though its purpose was the same as the one Captain Masse had led, is equipped in an entirely different way, and seems to be based on an another philosophy. Joanna Reid sees the wisdom in it. Rather than avoiding winter, being stopped by winter, this team is using it to advantage. The entire world is frozen solid, thus no problems crossing rivers, or bogs or swamps. The snow presents one consistent surface, if the proper equipment was used. With winter on, there would be no bears, no bugs, and little chance of attack. She shivered in her thin coat, and noticed that the tiny figures across and slightly above her were round with thick parkas, and their actions slow and confident, as if they were not worried at all by the chill, and the wind.

>─┼─◈─○─◈─┼─<

And so utterly frightened and perturbed became I, realising that this is the expedition set out by the Grand Trunk Railway Syndicate, and that it represents their victory. Once to the village, and geography will head them straight into it, they will fall upon the river, retrace our own trail, and reach the railhead. Our own efforts, useless. The deaths of Bain, Guzman, Caan and the Captain, utterly without purpose. All the survey work, the maps, though probably lost, done for no effect.

Reeling from these dreadful conclusions, needing too an excuse for being away, I did not return to the village but passed it and set out, though hungry and somewhat chilled, along my trap line. A fat rabbit in the second snare. My first captured prey. I skinned it, and as I hefted its winter lean body, proud I would now contribute to the food store of the village, I wondered how much flesh lay upon its bones, and how much I had eaten these past months, and what percentage of that total the rabbit represented. A minuscule portion, not one day's ration. How generous these people have been. I slit the rabbit open, and dissected its stomach. Lean fare, purple titbits of willow bark, desiccated buds, millet grains.

The third and fourth traps yielded nothing, the fifth another wan rabbit, thus bringing my total contribution to one day's food. One day for one day. For three days actually, since I had set them the day before. I approached the last trap, set at the entry into the wall of brambles, with interest. It was a busy portal, I had made the snare loop a bit bigger and perhaps something more substantial lay entrapped. I could hear a chattering skirr even as I approached, and what I though was a flapping wing. The snow around my set had been beaten clean in a circle large enough to sleep within. The wire, long and attached high, was pulled tight and its branch bent down. Horribly, what I found in my snare, tucked under a hummock at the end of the taut cable, enraged yellow eye following my every movement, was an alive hawk. Large, wingspan the height of the boy. It alternately cowered into the snow or raged at me, twisting its head up, opening its keen beak, thrashing the blooded white ground. I could not touch it, for fear, and for repulsion at its injury, one wing broken and almost detached, torn open by the fine filament which I had set.

I turned away, and looked to see how it could have happened. The evidence was there, on the undisturbed surface of the glen. A large rabbit had come running, parallel to the bramble wall. Possibly it saw the hawk, and bolting, had lunged for the safety of the thicket on broad back paws. These last deep prints were pressed a thumb width into the snow. The hawk must have been low, diving at high speed. Probably it knew this place well, and had caught many a rabbit there. For any animal running along the hedge had to slow or stop to make the turn. And any animal caught at the entrance portal could be killed and devoured at leisure and in safety within, for even hawks have enemies.

Pointing straight at the opening in the brambles, in two parallel lines about a pace apart, were triangular brushings on the snow. The diving hawk's wingtips as it braked just before the blow, perhaps realising its prey was too small to absorb the energy of its impact and that it had far too much speed, for at the greatest speed of its descent, it would strike the rabbit, and use the blow to both kill the rabbit, and arrest its own movement. A delicate calculation. Its speed upon arriving at the entrance to the hedge skimming the snow, had been such that the wire of the snare had ripped half way into its wing. It had miscalculated, or missed entirely.

I turned to the poor beast, fast waning from blood loss, pain and cold. I reached behind it with my mitted hand, to clasp the claws. A tiny rabbit was fixed tight within them. I extricated it. Frozen hard, I could not skin it there. That made three for the pot. I grasped the bird firmly by its legs, knowing that I was going to, had to kill it, for mercy if not for food. The violence of its exertions when I'd slipped off the snare took me by profound surprise. Showing no gratitude, it attempted a ferocious attack, beating me with its good wing, struggling to twist its head to rake me with its beak. I began to struggle with it, almost unequal as adversary, and it grew more violent, and knowing if it escaped I would have a desperate time to retake it, and knowing I had to kill it at any rate, but also in frustration and anger, I swung it up, and swung it down, smashing its head against the rock jutting from a snow bank near the portal. What little blood remained in its body trickled from its beak onto the snow. Its muscles gave an involuntary heave, and before I knew what I was doing, I was furiously ripping fistfuls of feathers from the hot skin, pulling at them, first the back, then the breast, until the blue prickly flesh of its body lay bare. I snapped the wings off, the broken one simply pulling away, and tied them to my belt. I cut open the belly with my knife, and pulled out the hot, bloody guts, reaching in to almost my elbow, glad of the warmth, wiping my arm and hands with a clot of leaves I tug from under the snow.

I would have to tell the people of the village, the leaders and chiefs and kings and queens, what the expedition I had seen meant. What it meant for me, and what it meant for them. The survey line being set out would cut neigh straight through the village. In less than a week. I could not play the optimist. I now knew who the dusky denizens scrabbling their existence on the periphery of the settlement around the fort were. Its original occupants. What awaited the people of my village? My hosts. Disease, debasement? There was little land about that could be cultivated. That saved them from the settlers' voracious plough. Was there silver, or gold in the hills? Would the railway to come be enough? How wide was its strip of influence? Only time would tell. Certainly, in return for their generous hospitality I can but tell them what I know. A warning? The danger of my own kind? Have I grown to disrespect all that sustained me? I have forgotten education, medicine, cultivation. I am confused, but will request a council nonetheless.

><+>+O+<+><

Despite her attempt at silence the boy heard Joanna leave in the middle of the night. He had long ago learned to detect the more evident noises of someone who was trying to move silently. This ability told him much about the night time world. When she did not return by daybreak, he felt fright he had never considered before. He was afraid of being alone. He now knew what alone meant, he had gone to Joanna alone on the cliffs, and been alone in the hut and he did not like it. He did not rise from his sleeping pallet. When she arrived, proud with her kill, he felt sick, and could only stagger to his feet and blow the fire alight. He followed her all the day, stupefied with a new sensation, the tangible attachment to community. Joanna treated him terribly, insisting he speak with the old men and women, forcing him to speak with her, or read her hand signs. Other times before, he would have run off, or smashed something from the force of conforming to so much discipline and concentration. This time, he let himself be caught in the net of interaction, gave himself over to it, and when evening came, his mind and body had amassed no tension, expressed no need to rage. He fell into a slumber and slept a dreamless sleep.

><+>+O+<+><

*F*ar into the night, the boy long asleep, I came to a clear resolution. I cannot stay here. Yet, I cannot bear to be parted from the boy. We've been through so much. Neither brother, father, or husband is he, but, I feel love for him. The babe too, but she is already becoming a child of this village. I have my answer for what I asked of the others, Guzman the lover of women, Bain the lover of rivers, Captain Masse the lover of war. Joanna Reid is the lover of these two children. Neither father nor mother, she is yet their steward and husbander. The people whom we are with are neither the boy's nor mine. The same for the babe, but she was born here. The people in the survey camp are mine. It will be better for both children if they are with someone's people. I will contact the mapping crew, before they stumble upon us. This is my decision, which I will communicate to the elders, but I have other decisions to make before contacting the surveyors.

I now see the purpose of my male disguise. Part of it was some desire to possess my father's power. That part has died. But part is the very real safety and access and mobility that trousers gave me. That last is probably still the greatest benefit. I cannot possibly return to social and financial subservience. I will go forth as a man, if only for the privilege and monetary return it offers me. Much as I love and will keep the children, my affections do not translate into being a nursemaid. Such women, no doubt competent, may be engaged at very low salaries. Certainly, in a well managed household, I can be a motherly father to them, as credulous as a fatherly mother.

I have an important task to accomplish first. Reading backwards through the historical appendix to my photography manual, I discovered that common table salt, sodium chloride, had been used as one of the original fixatives, though its use could result in a mottled print. I remembered the time I had fallen in the marsh, a wet spot over and underground spring. The water had a foul smell, and inadvertently tasting it when I fell, I found it brackish. Guzman told us that valleys in these mountains had once been the seafloor of a deep ocean. Perhaps the spring had percolated through ancient subterranean salt pans.

This morning I found the spring, approaching it with caution. Even on that cold day, its heat and saltiness created a dark wet oval on the otherwise frozen marsh. I tasted the water again, found it indeed to be extremely salty. There was also a reek of sulphur. I filled three of my largest bottles. With a scientist's rigour, I tested solutions from undiluted, to one in ten with water as a fixative, using squares from the remaining blank pages of the Captain's notebooks. The stronger solution, no doubt because of excess sulphur, cause most of the print to go black, but a more dilute one, about one in three, gave me a good result. I will leave it exposed to direct sunlight for a few days. If the tones remain, success on that front. Working again with my photographic apparatus gives me great pleasure. The boy too. While the tests dried, and he tended the fire in the dark hut, more languid than I have ever seen him, almost contemplative, I examined the Captain's package. I saw several sheets of paper in it, under his journal, interleaves between a series of letters. Thick rag paper or parchment. I set them aside, assuming the letters to be private, addressed as they were to his solicited, but I must have that paper. I know well my lamentable curiosity. I will not be able to resist the temptation to read the letters.

369 Memorial Avenue
Freetown

My Dear Wife Eliza:

I may still refer to you as wife I believe, but please know that I did receive the couriered letter from my sister, and though my knowledge of the law is slight, I concur with your desire for separation and you may declare a divorce by mutual consent. This letter, along with others, I have set in a waterproof packet and have every hope it will be found.

The man who left on this expedition would have been surprised at your leaving him, but the man who lies on this narrow ledge writing this letter understands, for he is a different man that the one you knew. Pity you will never meet him.

I send you my blessing, and implore you to take care of our daughter. Raise her on sound principles. You will be spared the expense of her education. I have left a letter to my solicitor ensuring all such expenditures will be taken care of. Other letters provide for you, as my marriage vows promised.

With the most profound regret for so many things.

Still your faithful husband,
Captain Aaron Masse

>─┼─◇─┼─○─┼─◇─┼─<

Rubin Goldwell, Barrister and Solicitor
333 Revolution Promenade

Attorney Goldwell,

You have maintained all files related to my financial and legal affairs since my arrival in the Capital. I entrust the execution of these final matters to you. The details, and reasons for this letter will reach you by other channels. Please consider this document my last will and testament, overriding that in your possession. I am of sound mind and body, though in desperate circumstance.

My estate, hitherto divided between my sister and my wife, I would like pledged in the following manner: My salary from the expedition, my army pension, and all funds in all my bank accounts to go to my wife, Eliza Masse; My house, which she has quitted, to go to my sister Vera Masse-Eikens, condition that the deed be written to her, with no provision it should pass to her husband. In the event of her death, it should pass to my wife Eliza Masse, or if my sister has a child, that child; The funds from the sale of my father's homestead, which had been made for sale by you before I left, be set in a fund managed in trust by yourself. This fund to go to my daughter Matilda Masse upon her reaching twenty one years, and previous to that, to be made available to her for travel as relates to her education, tuition for any professional studies, and books and lodging that may accompany such. I further request you give her your good council. Deduct your own fees equally from my estate and pensions. My deepest appreciation.

Captain Aaron John Masse (retired)

>—•—O—•—<

President
National Railway Company
1 Industrial Boulevard

Dear Mr. President,

This final dispatch will be brief. I am in a weakened condition. Word will have reached you of our failed expedition. The burden of default rests squarely on my shoulders. The men gave their best at all times. The route is feasible to a point where the grand canyon of the Rock River begins, about half way from your rail head to the sea. Beyond that I cannot comment. If God has brought the others through, Dunbar Bain will give you a full report. His boat contained many of the maps, geographic and astrological observations, which I had divided into two waterproof bundles.

I thank the board for the trust you bestowed in me, and express regret for my poor judgement which led to the termination of the endeavour and the death of at least two fine men.

Yours Sincerely,
Captain Aaron Masse (Retired)

>—•—O—•—<

National Geographic Society
Exhibition Square

The Chairman,

Word having reached you of the fate of our expedition, I will state that the activities requested and funded by the Society were carried out in the fullest. The photographer, one J. Reid, engaged at the rail head due to the abrupt withdrawal of William Eikens, did yeomen duty. I can attest to the quality of the material, as many test prints were made.

To my knowledge, this material survived a misfortune that led to the destruction of my own boat and the death of its occupants. God willing, it is in your hands at this moment. I cannot recommend more highly the photographer Reid, who possesses all the talents of empathy and exactness needed for the type of studies you plan to make across the frontier.

I regret events, but convey to you the immense pleasure the activities of the expedition gave me, and hope that the materials gathered have reached you and can form the foundation of an institute dedicated to recording and preserving the panoply of people and places encompassed by our nation's borders.

Aaron Masse

>—⟨◆⟩—○—⟨◆⟩—◄

Presiding Judge
Probation Board
Central District Court

The Court,

I inform you of the death, by accidental drowning, of one Carlo Guzman, a death witnessed by me, September third, 1858.

Mr. Guzman acquitted himself well while in my charge, performing beyond the call of duty. With luck, the results of his efforts will be preserved.

I extend my patronage for a submission of pardon, which is provided for in meritorious cases.

Your respectfully,
Captain Aaron Masse (retired)

Clayton Bailey

>─┤◆├─O─┤◆├─<

S ure enough, I read the letters in the Captain's packet until I could no longer. I felt very much the meddler, but I have a certain right to know him privately, given his sentiments. Could I have loved him? No, but he is a good man.

I found a quarto sheet of fine paper folded over each dispatch. Wetting and redrying them flat will cure any creases. These will serve for prints. For plates, the only solution will be to risk destruction of my own precious negatives. The photographers manual describes an elegant process. It seems that it is possible to pry the collodion and gelatin emulsion from its glass plate, roll it up on a stick, and use the plate again. I will hazard this with four of my priceless landscape plates, for I have discovered the reason behind my frantic efforts. I want to photograph and print all the members of this tribe, and write down the names of their ancestors. I will explain it – and this is the truth – that the people who are coming, if not at first then eventually and perhaps not even through any ill will, may destroy the tribe, but if the names and pictures are kept, their grandchildren will know who they were and what they looked like. I will make and leave them prints, that is why I limit my negatives to four. I have five sheets of paper, one for a test. Four large groupings, organised as they see fit. I'll use what precious real hypo remains for my negatives, and I will keep them, and make prints for myself in the capital. The camera will be easy to repair, I have found a tree which oozes an adhesive pitch. This will serve to mend it now, though it will fall apart the first hot day. It is I who make the last entry in our expedition log.

>─┤◆├─O─┤◆├─<

[Entry, J. Reid for Captain Aaron Masse deceased]
Day 333 approximate

Estimated position lowland termination of Rock River. Date 03\29

Expedition equipment still in good repair;

1\2 measure Plain Collodion	Half plate Gutta Percha tray
1\4 bottle hypo	2 bottles brackish water fixative
Bellows camera half plate	Focusing glass to fit
Compound (12 deg F7) in brass tube	Aperture stops F4 to F56
4 glass plates	1 bottle millet wine vinegar

Expedition members deceased;
Captain Aaron Masse – starvation and exposure
Carlo Guzman – drowned
Dunbar Bain – unknown circumstances
A. Caan (engaged at Fort) – presumed drowned
Water Music (engaged at Fort) – difficulties following childbirth

>─I─◆>─O─<◆>─I─<

I can be so entirely impractical. It was not only the boy who fell into a meditative state during my experiments. I have forgotten so much of my life as a man, being so comfortable here in this village. The constant worry of an assumed identity. The dearth of female friendship. The continual withholding of any delicate sentiment. There is such a negative side to the assumption of masculine entitlement. An unmitigated loneliness which I was able to endure, my freedom thrilled me so. But the man's world is a narrow one. They leave so much unexpressed. The Captain, a grown man, was more inexpert at expressing his love than a young girl. It would be impossible for me to continue to live as a man.

And to be truthful to my own deeper needs, I want a mate, the urge grows in me every day, as I also want the genuine pleasures of female company. And the children. Men live so distant from them, where is the enjoyment in that. All will be denied me if I continue my masquerade. I cannot, for the minute set foot out of here in male raiment, the die is cast.

How would I encounter, or be courted by, or love or live with a man if I was a man. I had vague imaginings of somehow, upon finding a man that interested me, making my sex and intentions known. Ridiculous. Who would be capable of crossing such a gap. I have grown too used to being man without, woman within. I feel the woman, but I forget that all who see me see the man, and feel the man. I've been forced to create a divided self and grown accustomed to it. An unhealthy circumstance. I would even be introduced to women as a prospective beau. What catastrophes of deception that would bring on.

And my profession. What would I do – appear suddenly one morning in skirts, laugh it off, and prepare for my first setting of the day. Impossible when one considers the practicalities, and more important, the reactions of individuals and society. Captain Masse arranged that our wages be deposited automatically. I saw the documents. I have read his journals. Throughout, officially, I am J. Reid, as I requested. Other than the boy, no witness to the gender of the expedition photographer exists. The Captain's private diary is another matter, but it is in my possession. Perhaps that is as it should be, given his amorous declarations. I could consider them as my keepsake, a young woman's first love letters. How romantic.

On my return, I would transfer only his expedition journals to his family. I have my photographs, and will submit them myself to the Society. I am the only remaining member of his lost expedition. It is all quite spectacular. There is no need for me to present myself as a man. I will go forth as a woman. The intrepid Joanna Reid, explorer, photographer, and the expedition's sole survivor. My reputation will be assured by my work. I will establish myself with those funds that are my wages, and my own savings I left in the settlement.

I will leave the girl here. She is not yet weaned, and I have not demonstrated any motherly talent. When the railroad is built, I can return, to do the need be. I will take the boy with me now, and adopt him as my son. It is he I surmise will suffer more the leaving behind of the babe. I can do nothing else. I will visit my family as their daughter. Perhaps I will find changes at home. Death? Illness? Perhaps all will be the same. If I find a sympathetic ear, I will tell my story, in stages. Perhaps I will be able to reveal all, and bring my new family into integration with my old. Or perhaps I will not be able to reveal anything. In that case, I will simply leave, as their daughter, leave like I've left before, and arrange my life.

I realise now I was a spoiled child. Sequestered. On my worst days, only my Grandmother could bargain with me. I would wake enraged at all I had not received, the attentions not paid to me the day before in the household and refuse to budge from my bed. My mother and the servants would give up on me. Calmly, Grandmother would enter my room, take my hand, and ask me to count my blessings, one at a time, on my fingers. I would rebut that there weren't any, but, always, be forced to admit to one, then another. The list would grow. I would end with a laugh, ready to face the day.

So, as my Grandmother would entreat, let me count my blessings. I have learned to love these children, one thought a simpleton but actually a healthy young man, one a babe. I have learned that someone loved me, deeply, and that men, though inept, are able to speak of love in a serious way. I have had a tremendous friend in Water Music. I have learned a great deal about the world and my place in it. More important, I have found ways to make that world one that accommodates me, and that the company of women, and their council, is an important attribute of what place I will make for myself. I have learned that life is part illusion, part fact, and that the fates are by and large capricious and without compassion, at times generous, at times cruel. Most important perhaps, I have learned that one cannot live life without faith, and that to have faith it is not necessary to believe in God, although, from reading Captain Masse's journals, believing in God makes it easier. Whether this ease is a good thing is a question I cannot yet answer, but thus far, I find I prefer faith without belief.

This is a grand list, the large things. There are many small things too. The boy. They'll ask me his name. What will I say? But I am tired, I must sleep, tomorrow will test my every ability to think for myself. I feel ready, but ill prepared. My Grandmother's second edict was to always say my prayers before my bed. I have acquired some skill at prayer. I will pray, as my act of faith, but to no God. I will pray for, if not a miracle, some luck in this earthly life.

Rummaging through Water Music's effects, a sorrowful endeavour, I found sufficient examples of women's attire. Some in the native fashion, supple hides and furs, some in the our fashion, wool and cotton. We are about the same size. There is no mirror but the clothes fit me well enough, albeit a trifle loosely at the bosom. The dark colour of my forearms is a stark contrast to the white of my thighs. I imagine my face is the same bronze hue. What will the survey party think when they see me. I must consider that. I can be of great use to them, as I know well the way back – for them the way forward. I will present myself as who I am, and the boy as my adopted son. We will step out the morrow. Better to encounter them before they reach the village. I do not want to sit and wait for them to arrive. I sat and waited till the Captain came along, and look where that got me.

How strange. My thoughts turn to Bain. Sadness, which I never imagined I would feel. Not really a man in spite of his tense posturing. No one who was a man could do what he did to Water Music. Talking always of rivers, and afraid when manoeuvring upon one. Died floating in one, his corpse laid to final rest beside one. Perhaps we reserve our greatest obsessions for what we fear the most...

➤—◆—◉—◆—◀

The sun, rising strong in a windless sky, quickly brings the light snow cover and ground under it to thaw. Melt water, first a trickle seeking everywhere the lowest point, forms rivulets, finds gullies, refills dry creek beds under their ice cover and gurgling, bubbles over the brim of winter low river banks. This taking place all through the river's basin, from high in the foothills to its wide floodplain.

The river warms, rising invisibly beneath its flat coat of frozen water. Invisibly, but in the village the old people hear the crackle of straining ice plates. They look up from sleeping pallets, or turn from fires towards the river, or stop as they walk along paths between the buildings to consider the low permanent foundations of heavy field stone and the temporary driftwood walls fixed on top, the reed-thatched roofs. They feel an ache in their bones and muscles, the ache of the labour it will require to rebuild the village after the flooding river has wiped the strand clean, leaving only the thickest, heaviest foundation stones in place.

This pang, in their backs and forearms, reminds them they have lived another year, that the cycle of the year is coming to its final stage – the destruction of their homes by the flood that will also cover the fields with new soil and make better the harvest. They realise they have become old, and they are becoming wise, that they now see life in its larger cycle, of both death and life, destruction and growth. They get up from their sleeping pallets, or turn back to their fires, or continue along their paths comforted by the thought of their own place in the cosmos, the smallness of their own efforts to build a home on the earth when compared to nature's power over it. Within their musing on the ruin that will come, another thought grows, of the wonderful sound and colour of the migrating birds, the fresh green of sprouting grass and budding plants.

The rising river, along its full length, shudders with the pressure of accumulating waters, splitting the ice sheet, a zigzag rent down its centre first no wider than a infant's finger, growing here and there, as the ice shifts with the relieved pressure, to the width of a young girl's waist finally becoming wide enough to swallow a man, a woman, a canoe, a tree.

A north-east wind commences to blow as Joanna Reid begins exposure tests using the primitive technique she has devised. She tosses a thick pine root on the fire so her chemicals will stay warm. By day's end the river is maybe two-thirds open – a grey, choppy surface – and Reid stops her experiments to draw aside the door-cover for some fresh air. Beyond the snow-sheathed shore, across the wrinkled slate water which fades to a sullen night in an array of tones stepped white to black like the density scale of her exposure test, she can hear thousands of arrived and arriving waterfowl. Invisible, but she knows, from their honking chatter, they are white of breast, grey in body and black-headed, their arrival signalling for her since childhood, spring.

–End–

Thank you: Francene Adelmen and Harriet O'Brien, patient readers both, without whose support and inspired council this manuscript would never have seen the light of day.

Werner Stegelmeyer, who first draped a dark cloth over my head in his 5th Avenue studio so I might focus the inverted image on his Linhof's ground glass. Penny Cousineau-Levine for encouraging my interest in portraiture. Howie White, who inspired me to write. Merrily Wiesbord, who encouraged me to write. Diane Schoemperlene, my writing teacher. Wayne Grady and Merilyn Simonds for their unflagging literary hospitality. Kathy Tweedy for appraising my fictive photographer's world. Doug Leonard for his experience of location and historical character. Darlene Birch for illuminating the art and craft of natural childbirth. Alanis Obomosowin for her songs and stories. Marielle Nitoslowska, woman behind the lens on many an expedition, and Tom McCaughy for a child's perception of home death in his native Ireland.

Free Book Club guides for The Expedition are available on-line at www.greatplains.mb.ca.

About the Author:

Originally from Marquette, Manitoba, Clayton Bailey has travelled the world as a photographer and filmographer. He has written for film and television, and his short fiction has appeared in Frontier: Custom & Archetype, IRON and The Indiana Review. His feature articles have appeared in the Manchester Guardian Weekly. He currently teaches 16mm film production at Université de Montréal.